Riverbend Justice

BOOK 2 IN THE RIVERBEND SAGAS

Henry McLaughlin

D1519470

ISBN: 1518860737
ISBN 13: 9781518860737
Library of Congress Control Number: 2015918450
CreateSpace Independent Publishing Platform
North Charleston, South Carolina

Dedication

To my wife, Linda
Thank you for your support and encouragement
and for joining with me on this writing journey.
And
To my Lord, Jesus Christ, who makes it all possible.

Acknowledgments

THIS IS ONR of the hardest pages to write because I know I will forget someone who contributed to the writing of this book. If I don't mention you by name, please forgive and know that you are engraved on my heart.

I have to thank my mentor, DiAnn Mills, for her constant challenges to not give up or settle for less than my best. I met Jerry B. Jenkins and Brandilyn Collins early in my writing career and they both saw some tiny spark of talent and gave me the encouragement to build the fire.

Through their workshops and books on the craft, James Scott Bell and Steven James have taught me about the craft of writing good stories, to explore new ways of bringing characters to life, of adding tension and suspense, and the freedom to break the rules for the sake of my story.

Finally, I must acknowledge my writing buddies who gave so much of themselves to help me become a better writer: Diane, Amelia, LaWanda, Rachelle, Teri, and Tina. You guys are awesome.

CHAPTER 1

Monday, June 17, 1878

HE SQUEEZED THE trigger. Opened his eyes. Had he said a prayer? Was it granted or rejected when the kidnapper, Maria, slumped to the ground, dead at his hand?

Why would God listen to the likes of me?

Michael Archer's eyes focused on the flickering campfire, the heat warming his face, but his mind was back in that valley with its lush grass, gurgling streams and stench of death.

At the edge of his consciousness, he knew others moved around the camp, knew two sat at the fire with him.

"What time you figure we'll get in tomorrow?" Jeremiah Turner, awkward in his sling, poured coffee into his tin cup. He blew across the surface before risking a tentative sip.

"Late morning, I expect." Bill Barkston scooped a spoonful of beans into his mouth. "Looking forward to seeing my wife and boy." He looked at the wagon holding eight shrouded forms downwind from the campfire. "Ain't looking forward to bringing sad news, though."

Jeremiah sat on his haunches. "Yeah. That part's never easy. Especially this much." He nodded across the fire. "How about you, Michael? You looking forward to seeing Rachel?"

Michael started as if woken from a dream. His untouched plate of beans and bacon sat beside him. A stick was in his hand, random drawings in the dirt at his feet. *Rachel?* "Yeah. I guess so." But would she want to see him? Once she knew what he'd done? He tossed the stick in the fire. "Excuse me."

He walked toward the trees where the horses were staked out.

The conversation behind him followed the still night air. Jeremiah's deep voice was soft and low. "He's sure carrying a burden. Too heavy for one man, but he won't share it with anyone."

"Reckon he will when he's ready. If it don't crush him first." Bill's spoon scraped the bottom of his tin plate.

Michael stepped into the shadows of the trees, grateful to be away from the prying questions, the watchful, accusing eyes. His horse, Buddy, whinnied softly. Michael stroked the animal's neck and buried his face in the mane. He waited.

The tears wouldn't come. That well dried up during the days of the journey back, getting the wagon from the way station, retrieving the bodies of Vernon Phelps and his posse group. The lump in his chest grew heavier, the grief and shame pressed against him, his spirit bending, yielding, ready to break.

A twig snapped. Michael froze. Maybe whoever it was wouldn't see him.

His friend, Old Thomas, would have seen. But Old Thomas wouldn't have snapped a twig. Once again, Michael saw him spread-eagled on the dirt, blood around the hole in his chest, dead eyes staring into the crisp blue sky of the foothills, spirit gone before his body hit the ground. The rifle shot echoed in Michael's brain.

The rifle shot he fired echoed, too. The one that only postponed Sam Carstairs' death—but didn't save him.

Tomorrow they would return to Riverbend, bringing grief and horror to so many people. So much waste. And he contributed to it.

Jeremiah's words from the cabin rose up, as they had so often on the return journey. The part of him he used to hurt people could be used to help people? Really?

He killed his father to protect his sister. He fought Mark to protect Rachel. He killed Maria Alden to save Sam, to buy a few precious minutes during which Michael reconciled Sam with his youngest son, Ben. Because that was the only choice he had? He could use it as a tool for good?

At times, he could embrace the idea as life saving. At other times, his mind barraged him with memories of men beaten, women mistreated; memories of stealing and cheating; of using this same tool for meeting his own needs no matter what it did to others. How could he change that? How could he control it?

He deluded himself if he thought he could allow the old Michael to roam free because it *helped people.*

Maybe Jeremiah's words were what the hired gun told himself when *he* was feeling the weight of the lives he took.

Caleb Davis spoke from behind him. "Must seem like Buddy's the only one you can talk to."

Michael faced the sheriff. "Yeah. He's always been a good listener." He stroked Buddy's flank. "Don't talk much, though. Which is a good thing sometimes."

"Yep." Caleb pushed his hat off his forehead. "You ain't talked to anybody much. You ready to ride into town tomorrow?"

"Not really. I've never been part of bringing this much grief to anybody, or being such a big part of making it happen."

"Your part tweren't no bigger than anyone else's."

Michael shook his head. "If I had shot sooner, I might have been able to wound her. If I had waited, we might have come up with a better plan."

Fists planted on his hips, Caleb said, "There was no more time. She knew she wasn't going to get away. She figured she'd at least take Sam with her. But you stopped her."

"And Sam died anyway."

Michael waited while Caleb paused, rubbing his chin. "Yes, he did. But not by your hand."

Michael combed Buddy's mane with his fingers, separating snarls, avoiding Caleb's gray-green eyes. After a moment, the sheriff shrugged and walked to the fire.

When Caleb was seated, Michael edged his way down the picket line to the packhorses, their packs on the ground nearby. He slid his hand into one of the bags, grasped the hard, smooth cylinder. He held the bottle up, and, in the faint glare of the fire and the pale moon, saw the liquid shimmer when he shook it.

He held it like an infant. *About a quarter full. No one would notice.* His fingers touched the cork, danced away as if lightning struck, returned and gripped it firmly.

CHAPTER 2

Tuesday, June 18

THE NEXT MORNING, time raced, carrying Michael toward a place he didn't want to go. He took a long pull from his canteen, swallowing large gulps. He rammed the cork home and draped the strap over his saddle horn. If only he could wash away the shame as easily as water washed away thirst or liquor washed away memories.

"Almost home." Bill Barkston rode next to him, his body moving in easy rhythm with his horse's gait. "It'll sure be good to get there."

"I suppose."

Almost home? Could Riverbend ever be home now? The town loomed a few miles ahead. He shuddered at the thought of re-entering the place, the community with its heart about to be ripped out. Eight townspeople killed. Dread swept over him, bending his back. How could he face Mrs. Phelps? Pastor Luke and Martha?

How could he face Rachel?

Her last words echoed hollow in his head. How could she want to get to know him better now?

He took up the reins. Buddy tensed underneath him, ready to respond. How easy it would be to turn and ride away, to put the killing and this town behind him. For where? The nearest town with a bottle of whiskey. Shouldn't be too far—two, three days maybe, if he hurried.

"You okay?" Bill's voice rumbled.

Michael snapped back to reality and looked at Bill. *Am I okay? No.* He searched the older man's eyes. *But you wouldn't understand. Nobody can.*

"Don't do it."

"Do what?" *Can the man read minds?*

Bill nodded in the direction of the mountains. "Ride off before we get to town."

"I wasn't going to ride off."

"You're givin' it serious consideration." Bill leaned back so his right hand rested on the cantle of his saddle, looking like the most relaxed cowboy in the world. "Seen it plenty in the war. Before a battle, could see the ones who were going to run. Their hands'd get all nervous. They'd lick their lips, search around, lookin' for an escape route. They weren't planning in their heads on running, weren't gonna do it on purpose. But, at the first shot, they was headin' the other way."

"You think I'm going to do that?"

"Yep. Your hands are tight on the reins. Old Buddy there is ready to jump. All he needs is a direction from you. And I don't think yer in a hurry to get to town."

Anger flared. Michael gripped the reins tighter. "You calling me a coward?"

Bill held up a hand. "Nope. Not after what I've seen on the trail. I think you're scared, and you don't want to face the people. Don't know why."

Bill sat upright, rested his hands on the saddle horn. "Look. There are people in Riverbend who like you. Miss Rachel, Pastor Luke and Miss Martha. Caleb. Me. We want to help you deal with whatever it is you're carrying. If you let us. All I'm asking is, give us a chance."

Michael nodded and eased his grip on the reins. Buddy relaxed.

'Sides, Riverbend was the nearest town with whiskey anyway.

CHAPTER 3

Tuesday, June 18

"THEY'RE BACK." THE shout carried into Rachel's workroom, a faint noise in the distance.

"They're back." Louder now, the words drawn out and modulated.

Rachel gasped, pins dropping from her mouth to the floor. *Michael.* She tossed her pincushion onto the worktable, gathered her skirt in her hands and bolted for the door.

"Rachel." Lupe Carstairs' voice pleaded behind her. "You can't leave me like this."

Rachel turned. Lupe stood in her underwear, the new skirt around her waist at odd angles and lengths from Rachel's interrupted fitting. Rachel's eyes darted around the room without really seeing anything. Her brain focused on only one thing. *Run to him. He's back.*

She grabbed a length of fabric draped over her chair and tossed it to Lupe. "Here. Use this as a shawl."

Rachel darted to the middle of the street and ran toward the approaching riders. Couldn't make out the individuals. Where was Michael? Why so few? Her heart lurched. *Where is he? Why can't I see him?* She lifted the hem of her dress to her knees and ran. The distance didn't seem to be closing. *Why can't I reach them?* Tears flooded her eyes.

She ran.

The riders shimmered in the waves of heat rising from the almost white dust of the street.

She ran.

She bounced off people who stepped into the street. She pushed others aside. It was like swimming against the current wearing a buffalo robe. *Can't go fast enough. Can't seem to get any closer.* She had to get through, had to see him, hold him, know he was alive, know he was real.

She recognized the riders now. Caleb and Bill Barkston in front, Malachi right behind, arm in a sling. Next to him a stranger with his arm also in a sling. No Michael.

Frank and Harold sat in the wagon seat. Sitting between them was a strange woman, blond, bedraggled, blank-faced. Martin rode alongside. Three men were tied to saddles on horses tethered to the rear of the wagon. She stopped. No Michael. *Where is he? No. He can't be dead. No. Why can't I see him? God, help me.*

Lupe caught up to her, dressed with shawl firmly in place, and slipped her arm around Rachel's shoulders. "That must be him, at the back."

Rachel followed the line of Lupe's pointing finger. Michael rode several yards behind the wagon, leading a string of horses. Head down, he seemed to shrink even further at the noise of the townspeople.

Rachel skittered around the edge of the crowd as the riders came to a stop. She reached Michael as he dismounted. He turned, and she leapt at him, arms around his neck, clasping him tight, muscles straining. *Never let him go. Never. Ever.* Her head on his chest, she heard his heart, and she wept.

⊷⊷⊶ ⊶⊷⊷

Michael held her. Her embrace comforted and confirmed. He wanted to curl up in her lap like a little boy. Her arms released the fatigue plaguing every muscle, every bone.

The closest he would ever know to home and family was in his arms. So close or was it now unobtainable? His hands felt filthy and slick with the blood of his father and Maria and Mark and all the others he'd ever fought and killed. Hands that now held her and touched her back. Hands that could kill her just like his father killed his mother.

Was Jeremiah right? Could he really control that monster, the old Michael? A voice in the back of his head rumbled deep and ominous, *No, you can't. The old Michael is the real Michael.*

Where were the tears that would cleanse him? Gone. Dried up on the altar of violence and death.

He slid her arms from around his neck and stood back. Holding her hands against his chest, he looked at her, her warm, beautiful smile, the light brown hair pulled into a tight bun, violet eyes brimming with tears and—what? Was that love? Love he didn't deserve.

She kissed him, a long, warm kiss. A kiss that bounced off the hard wall around his heart.

She pulled back. "I…I…I'm so glad you're safe."

"Rachel…" Words died, specks of dust that drifted from his mouth to float away on the breeze, to drift to the ground, to never be heard.

The rifle shot flashed again. Maria slid down the wall to sit, legs splayed, hands in her lap, her one eye seeming to stare in unbelief that she was dead. He squeezed his eyes shut, willing the image to go away. It did. To be replaced by his father lying across the porch steps, overalls soaked in blood.

How could she love him?

"I'm so glad you're back, safe and sound." Martha's arms were around Michael's neck before he realized she was there. She kissed his cheek.

"Welcome home." Luke shook his hand, a firm, long grip. Michael gazed into the pastor's dark brown eyes and sensed the genuine care flowing from them.

Home? After a month away, he was surprised at how much he remembered of the five days he spent there.

At the far end of the street, the white church glowed in the afternoon light. The clear blue sky and white clouds drew his eye to the steeple. A beacon of hope when he first saw it, now a finger of judgment.

Caleb's brick office squatted next to the clapboard town hall like a fierce bulldog ready to defend the community. Good men had died doing exactly that, and for what purpose?

Across the street, the elegant façade of the Riverbend Hotel was now a monument to Sam Carstairs' ambition and dreams. Dreams now enshrouded in a blanket and arranged like cordwood in the wagon.

Further down the street, next to the general store, a sign on a porch post swayed in the gentle breeze. *Rachel's Hope.* Her store, another step into her new life. A life he had wanted to share but one he would tarnish if he stayed.

The urge returned to jump on Buddy and ride off. He didn't belong here.

Rachel slipped her hand into his and intertwined their fingers. Her eyes seemed filled with affection and happiness. And his unworthiness sucked him down like quicksand.

Abigail took his other hand and squeezed. Daniel tugged on his pant leg and motioned for Michael to bend down. When he did, Daniel hugged his neck, and said, "Aunt Rachel and me prayed for you every day."

Michael's heart weighed heavy, and he fought back the tears, grieving for the future he'd lost.

->=◎ ◎=<-

"Mrs. Matthews?" Caleb said.

Martha faced Caleb. "Sheriff?"

"Is Mrs. Phelps in town?"

"No, she …" Martha gasped and grabbed Rachel's arm. "Not Vernon? Not Alexander?"

Caleb nodded, grief boiling. *Not now. Have to take care of other business.* He squished the pain back down. "I'll ride out to her place as soon as we're done here. Will you come with me, Pastor Luke?"

"Sure."

Caleb turned to Michael. "Michael…Nah, you best stay here."

Josh Carstairs came out of the bank and stood beside his wife. Caleb touched the brim of his hat. "Mrs. Carstairs. Josh." Thumbs hooked in his belt; Caleb scuffed the dirt with the toe of his boot. "I'm sorry, Josh. We couldn't save your father or your brother. They were too beat up by the time we freed them."

Josh's blues eyes bored into Caleb, hard and unreadable. Caleb saw the man's jaw twitch and lips quiver. Josh nodded, put his arm around Lupe's shoulders and pulled her close. Lupe wrapped her arm around her husband's waist and rested her head on his chest.

Caleb pushed his hat back. "What was Mark doing out there? Why'd he try a one-man rescue mission?"

"He didn't." Josh's voice was soft, difficult to hear. "That dressmaker stabbed him, and they took him from Doc's office."

Rachel Stone? Stabbed him?

"He attacked Rachel in her store, and she fought him off." Josh's shirt muffled Lupe's voice.

Caleb shook his head. *Better get the details from Pete.*

"Would you mind standing with me while I talk to the people?" They followed Caleb as he mounted the steps to the boardwalk fronting his office. Mayor Meriweather waited for him, hands fidgeting, sweat shining on his forehead. Pete O'Brien stepped up to Caleb and shook his hand.

Caleb looked over the crowd gathered before him. "Pastor Luke, will you please join me up here?"

Luke trotted to the boardwalk, and Caleb placed him between himself and the mayor. Josh and Lupe moved to stand between Caleb and Pete.

Caleb took off his hat. The breeze off the river felt refreshing as it tugged at his hair.

"Look how gray his hair is," a woman in the crowd whispered loud enough to be heard.

"Look how thin he is," whispered another.

Caleb turned his hat round and round in his hands.

"This is one of the saddest days in my life." Caleb took a deep breath to control the strain and creaks in his voice.

"Good men died. Too many good men. Men who were my friends as well as yours. Men who cared for this town and wanted to see it grow. Men who worked and fought hard to find Sam Carstairs and bring him home."

He turned to Josh. "Son, I'm sorry we couldn't bring your pa and your brother back alive. Every man on this posse was willing to die to save your father. Six men did. I don't know what else we coulda done."

Josh nodded. Lupe bit her lower lip.

"Mayor, I need you to send for the circuit judge, ask him to get here quick." He gestured to the men behind the wagon. "I don't want to keep those three in my jail any longer than I have to. Then, you'll need to use your undertaking skill to get our own men ready for burying."

The mayor turned to leave. Caleb held up his hand. "Don't go just yet."

Caleb gestured at the woman still seated in the wagon. "Mrs. Matthews, we found this woman with the kidnappers. She was also a prisoner. Can you and some of the church women help with her, find out who she is and where she's from so we can get her back to her people?"

Martha and Sally Barkston and Helen Walters stepped forward. "We'll take care of her, Sheriff," Martha said.

Caleb turned to Luke. "Pastor, please say a prayer over us right now."

Luke stepped forward and surveyed the crowd. "God, we come before you—a community with heavy hearts. We lift up the families and friends of those who died in service to this town. We ask for your comfort and peace to surround each family member and friend. We trust you, God, for the answers to the questions that plague us about this event. We trust you will reveal those answers as we are ready to receive them. Thank you for the healing you bring to the grief-stricken. We know you have a plan for good for Riverbend, and we trust we will grow into the full manifestation of that plan. In Jesus' name. Amen."

The townspeople clustered in small groups as the mayor left to send a telegraph to the circuit judge and Pete took charge of the prisoners. Josh and Lupe stood on the boardwalk receiving condolences.

Caleb's attention was drawn to the small group of women with the woman the posse'd found.

Helen Waters wrapped her arm around the shoulder of the shivering, glazed-eye woman. The stranger stiffened and drew away, as if the touch was electric.

"I'm not going to harm you. I want to help you," Helen said in the soft tones of a mother of six and grandmother of fourteen, comforting a frightened child.

The woman calmed and snuggled closer.

"Can you tell me your name?" Helen said.

The woman cocked her head left, then right, jaw working as if it hadn't been used in a long time. "Lil…Lil…." Tears coursed.

Helen stroked her arm. "Take your time. There's no rush. You're safe with us."

"Sa…safe?" Some of the glaze faded from her eyes.

Helen nodded. "Safe. No one will hurt you here."

"Lillian," the woman said, voice creaking like an unused gate. "Lillian Price."

"Pleased to meet you, Lillian," Helen said. "Where are you from?"

Lillian closed her eyes. After several moments, she looked at Helen. "El Paso."

Helen pulled her closer, stroked her hair. "Do you have family there?"

Lillian sobbed into Helen's shoulder. "Husband. Two little ones."

Arm around Lillian, Helen took the woman's hand, and guided her to the boardwalk. "You best come with me, darlin'. We'll send us one of those telegraphy things to your family. You can stay with me and the Mr. 'til your family comes for you."

Caleb smiled. Good people in this town.

The mayor waddled back up the street to the wagon with bodies.

Some of them anyway.

Caleb watched Malachi dismount and approach the wagon, instructing the men to treat Old Thomas with the utmost care.

"He will have a Christian burial." Malachi's voice was loud, his face inches from the mayor's, who stood at the back of the wagon directing the men to take the bodies to his undertaking office. The mayor, hands quivering, face pale, looked at Caleb.

Caleb shrugged his shoulders, spat in the street. "I expect he will. Don't you, Mr. Mayor?"

The mayor looked from Caleb to Malachi to Pete, who suddenly loomed over him. Taking a silk handkerchief from his breast pocket, he wiped his face. "Why, yes, of course he will."

CHAPTER 4

Tuesday, June 18

CALEB ADJUSTED HIS hat to keep the late afternoon sun out of his eyes. Leaves stirred on their branches in the light breeze meandering up the valley. Chirping insects and the steady clop of hooves filled the silence that had marked most of the ride.

The entrance to the Phelps ranch lay a half-mile ahead, coming too fast. His hands tightened on the reins at the thought of facing Esther and adding her grief to his own.

Luke and Martha rode in the pastor's buggy. Gratitude had washed over him when she'd offered to come. The burden would be lighter and she would be able to help Esther in ways he never could.

"Sheriff, is Michael all right?" Martha's east coast accent with a slight southern burr gave off calm warmth.

Caleb flicked a bug off his leg, not wanting to look into those bright blue eyes. "I don't know, Ma'am. Don't know him well enough to speculate."

"You've just spent a month with him. That's more time than any of the rest of us."

Caleb had heard Martha could be sharp with people. This was the first time he experienced it for himself.

Her next words were softer, slower. "He's different. It's like there's a wall there, and he's locked himself behind it. I could see it, and I'm sure Rachel felt it."

Caleb sighed. "He was different on the way back. Real quiet. Kept to himself. I didn't think much of it. Kind of expected it after he killed that woman."

Luke brought the buggy to a halt. "He what?"

The pastor's eyes were wide. Martha's mouth hung open, her hands grasping her husband's arm. Her nails dug into the fabric of her husband's suit jacket.

Telling the story hurt, but he did it. The guilt rose up, the questions of what he could have done better, done different, raced through his mind as he recounted the last moments of the search and the deadly outcome.

At the end, Luke and Martha looked at each other. Caleb could see the frown creasing Martha's forehead. Luke turned his head, staring up the road. "How can he live with that?"

She looked at Caleb. "And how can you live with it?"

"It's hard. Lots of what-ifs and shouldas and couldas. I'm hoping I can find some answers and peace in your church."

Now Luke stared at Caleb. "Our church?"

Caleb told about finding the bodies of Vernon, Alexander, and the others. "That night, Michael helped me find Jesus and told me to get involved in church."

Martha cast her eyes downward. "So much death. And what did it accomplish?"

Luke squeezed Martha's arm. "The only good was Caleb coming to Jesus."

She nodded, pulled a handkerchief from her sleeve, and dabbed at her eyes. "Let's get going. This day has been sad enough already."

"That wasn't the only good that came of it." Caleb turned in his saddle. "Michael did accomplish his mission. Before he died, Sam admitted he'd wronged Ben and asked for forgiveness." He bit back the words about Sam's ledger. That was between him and Joshua for now. It was up to Joshua if he wanted it to be public knowledge.

Luke slapped the reins against the horses. "Well, thank God for that."

They rode on. Out of the corner of his eye, Caleb noticed Martha, hands clasped in her lap, eyes closed, lips moving in silence. *Strong woman.*

->==@ @==<-

Michael leaned back in the tub until the steaming water lapped against his chin. As his muscles unknotted, his mind churned. Eyes closed, he willed his thoughts to still. Once again, Maria slammed into the cabin wall and slid like molasses behind Sam's suspended body, her blood trailing on the weathered gray boards. His eyes snapped open and his body lurched upright, sloshing water over the side, every muscle tight and cramped.

He stood and reached for the towel on the chair beside him. He dressed with unusual care and slowness, postponing as long as possible the meeting that waited. Rachel. What to say? How to explain?

He looked at his hands. Clean. The dirt and grime of weeks on the trail gone from under chipped and broken nails and from the creases in the skin. Under the surface, the blood still slithered on his palms, staining everything he touched. He rubbed them down his shirt expecting to leave red streaks.

The mirror showed him clean-shaven, a little thinner, face tanned except for the hat line across his forehead. His eyes gazed back at him, void of emotion. The eyes of someone who killed, someone who might—no—would do it again. The old Michael lurked behind those eyes, under the surface, someone not to be trusted, who couldn't be loved.

He knew Rachel waited for him, but still he paused, unable to take the first step. He looked around, seeking anything he could grasp, any detail he could use to delay his leaving.

He had to go.

Outside, he nodded to people who greeted him. He hesitated as he passed a saloon, gazing over the swinging doors at the bottles arrayed behind the bar. The amber liquids beckoned like old friends. Maybe one drink would help him, give him the courage to face what lay ahead. His palm rested against the door. One slight push and he'd be inside. Didn't it always help in the past? No, it didn't. He dropped his hand, surprised he didn't leave a red palm print.

He stepped onto the clean-swept boardwalk fronting Rachel's store. *Rachel's Hope.* Yellow letters on a pale blue background with white flowers and greenery twirled around the edges. So like her. The delicateness and beauty of the colors undergirded by the solid strength of the wood on which they rested.

Rachel's Hope.

How could he crush those hopes, mar that delicateness, smash the strength? He turned to leave.

→──◯ ◯──←

He should be here by now. Rachel stepped away from the dress she was hemming and walked through the curtains into the main shop. Deserted. Displays of fabric neatly in place, ready for a customer's perusal, sketches of her designs placed on the walls and on stands on the counter. She inhaled. The aromas of cotton and satin warmed by the sun gave her a sense of peace. A fragile peace at the moment. Where was he? Maybe he fell asleep. She smiled. He looked so exhausted earlier. Fatigued. Maybe that's why he seemed distant. *No need to fret. A nap will do him good.*

She glanced out the window. *There he is. Why is he walking away? The open sign is still out. The door's unlocked.* Her heart stopped and jumped into her throat. *What is going on?* She opened the door.

"Michael?" Did his shoulders droop at the sound of her voice?

He turned. His mouth smiled, but dark shutters seemed to cover his eyes. "Hello, Rachel." He stood a few feet away.

She wanted to jump into his arms, but he stood as welcoming as a fence post. "Where were you going? Why didn't you come in?"

He patted the pockets of his vest and pants. "I thought I forgot something at the hotel." He chuckled. "But now I can't remember what it was."

He stepped forward and embraced her. She wanted to be crushed in his arms, to be held so tight it hurt to breathe, to feel his heart beating against hers, his breath on her neck.

His arms seemed stiff and unsure, the grip loose.

She stood back and gazed up at him, her hands resting in his, the touch light. She gripped his hand and led him into the store.

He took off his hat and held it with both hands. "Still looks nice. The sketches are new."

"Annabelle gave me the idea. They're to help people...*visualize* is the word she used."

She sat in one of the chairs arranged around the tea set. "Sit. These chairs will hold you. They're stronger than they look."

He smiled that smile again, the one that barely moved his lips and stopped at his nose. Was it a smile or a grimace? He remained standing.

She clasped her hands to stop fidgeting. "How bad was it?"

His eyes met hers, a glimmer showing through the shutters. He dropped his gaze to the floor, and folded his arms, almost hugging himself. "Bad. Too many people died. Sam's dead. Mark too. It was such a waste."

"But you're okay?"

"I'm okay?" He extended his arms to the sides and examined himself up and down. "Yeah, I guess so."

Rachel bit her lower lip. She wanted to go to him, hold his face, will those eyes to unlock and let Michael out.

"Clerk at the hotel said Mark attacked you and you stabbed him."

She nodded. "Him and two of his friends broke in the back door."

Michael's fists clenched, his jaw pulsed. "Did he hurt you?"

"I stabbed him before he could really do anything." She paused and turned her head. The memory of Mark's hands ripping her dress, pawing at her, pinning her to the table flooded her mind. She'd stabbed him. Now, in her mind, his finger seemed to point from under his shroud, his dead eyes accusing. "And then he was kidnapped."

"Sounds like he deserved what he got. We all do in the end, I guess. Some people's ends just don't come quick enough and some come all too soon."

Rachel's head snapped up. "What do you mean?"

Michael looked out the window. He shrugged. "Nothing. It's the trail talking." He snugged his hat on his head. "I'm not much company right now. I'm so tired my bones feel like jelly. I need some sleep."

He kissed her hand, a light brush, a wisp of a feather. She hugged his neck and drank in the aroma of his soap-scented skin.

She stood in the doorway, watching him walk to the hotel, fingers at her lips.

->=◉ ◉=<-

"Rachel." Annabelle O'Brien's schoolteacher-getting-your-attention voice rattled in Rachel's head. She jumped, flustered, clattering the teacup and saucer she held in her hand. She placed the cup on the low table and smoothed her dress.

"I'm sorry. What were you saying?"

Annabelle smiled, her freckled cheeks dimpling. "You look like a calf lost out on the back forty. What's troubling you?"

Rachel studied her companion, her best friend after Martha. One of two people she could trust with any secret. She thought Michael would be a third. Now doubt clouded her mind.

"It's Michael. Something's not right. He's not who I expected to come back."

"Who were you expecting? Sir Lancelot with the Holy Grail?"

Rachel paused, licked her lips, her mouth suddenly dry. "Maybe I was." She sipped her now cold tea. She leaned forward, palms pressed together, eyes fixed on the tabletop. "I expected him to be as happy to see me as I was to see him. Earlier today, it felt like he couldn't wait to get away from me."

"Did he talk about what happened out there?"

Rachel shook her head. "No. Only that it was bad. He called it a waste." Her eyes met Annabelle's. "But he said it like it was all his fault."

Annabelle frowned. "That's odd. It's not like he was the only one out there."

"I know. Something happened on that posse. I don't know how to get him to tell me about it."

"Maybe you can't. Maybe it's something he has to work out for himself."

"I don't think he can. When he left he looked like he'd fought the biggest fight of his life and lost." Rachel clasped her hands together. "How can God's promise walk out of my life so soon after he walked into it?"

The vision from the ridge flashed, as real as the first time: *Michael is to be my husband.* Dare she share it with Annabelle? She hadn't shared it with anyone. Too precious. What if they didn't believe her, tried to talk her out of it?

It was real. She hugged it to her spirit as the likelihood of its manifestation faded with every step Michael took away from her.

"God's promise?" Annabelle cocked her head, her face quizzical.

"I think God wants Michael and me to be together, but it feels like Michael is walking away from it."

Chapter 5

Tuesday, June 18

Esther Phelps stood on the porch of the two-story log house that served as her home and the ranch's headquarters, talking to a cowboy. Caleb recognized him. Putnam. Been with Vernon twelve years. Mid-fifties, hard worker, loyal, but not too bright after a bullet sliced open the top of his head during the war.

Esther turned to watch them as Caleb reined his horse at the foot of the stairs. She seemed puzzled, but then her eyes met Caleb's and she looked at Martha and Luke. One hand went to her mouth, the other to her chest. She sagged against a wooden pillar and slowly slid down until she sat on the floor of the porch.

Putnam ran to her, hands reaching for her. He stopped and looked over his shoulder at Caleb, confusion clouding his face.

Martha leapt from the buggy before Luke brought it to a complete stop. She brushed past Putnam, and took Esther in her arms, cradling the older woman's head against her chest. After a few moments, Esther lifted her head and looked at Caleb.

"Both?"

He nodded.

"Where are they?"

"Meriweather's."

She straightened up but still held Martha's hands. "Man's a butcher. Got his fingers in too many things to do any of them proper. Putnam."

The man snapped to attention. Caleb thought he was going to salute.

"Yes, Ma'am?"

"Tell Barker to build two coffins. Get Willie and Bobcat and dig two graves up on the hill next to the barn, where my mom's buried. When you're finished, take the wagon and fetch Mr. Vernon and Alexander."

"Yes, Ma'am." He mounted his horse.

"And Putnam."

He turned. "Yes, Ma'am?"

"You make sure those graves are good and straight and deep."

"Yes, Ma'am. They'll be the best graves this side of Gettysburg."

Caleb stood like a schoolboy who forgot his memory verses as Luke and Martha helped Esther to a rocking chair on the porch. Martha went in the house and came back with a glass of water. Esther pushed it away. "Coffee."

"I'll get it." Caleb jumped at the opportunity for physical activity. In the kitchen, he found the mug Alexander hand-painted for his aunt when he was seven. Esther's favorite.

Esther took the mug in both hands. "Thank you, Dar…" She stopped. "He won't be bringing this to me anymore. He won't be tying his gray stallion to that hitching post at lunch time, climbing those steps, giving me his big hug, smelling of cows and horses and sweat." One tear trickled down her plump cheek.

She lifted her head and gazed toward the mountains. "We won't be sitting here of an evening after supper, drinking coffee, watching the sun set, listening to Alexander play hymns on his banjo and harmonica."

She sighed, closed her eyes and bowed her head. "Lord, thank you for the years we did have and how Vernon made us cherish them."

The hot poker of fresh grief and guilt stabbed Caleb's side. And envy, too, at the peace and strength she drew from God. He didn't have that when his wife died, only angry bitterness.

Esther looked at Caleb. "Tell me what happened."

Caleb did.

At the end, she nodded. "He loved you like a brother."

He chewed his lower lip, fighting back tears that pressed like water against a dam. "I know."

"So don't go blaming yourself. I know Vernon went to heaven praising God and doing what's right. The last thing he'd want is you feeling all sad about it. Just remember the good times you both had."

Caleb looked into her hazel eyes rimmed with tears, his own vision blurred. "I will."

She rose unsteadily and embraced him, long and hard.

She stepped back. From around the corner of the house, the sounds of men talking quietly and shovels thudding against the ground reached Caleb's ears. He saw Esther notice it too by the way she cocked her head toward the sound. Another tear ran down her cheek.

→⊨◎ ◎⊨←

Michael woke. Unrefreshed. Restless. Hungry. He splashed water on his face, rubbing the sleep from his eyes. Outside, dusk was on the edge of full night. He thought of lighting the lantern on the table, changed his mind. The dark cocooned him, kept reality away. He stood at the window as he dried his hands, the sounds of the town seeping through the narrow opening.

Horses plodding, wagons squeaking, conversations rumbling as men and women strode the boardwalks. Music. He opened the window wider. A piano played an upbeat tune from a saloon up the street. Aromas of food cooking, men smoking, the town shifting from day to night drifted into his room.

An hour later, Michael stood in the shadows across the street from Grandy's Saloon. Piano and banjo music mingled with the smoke, and multiple, indistinguishable conversations drifted over the batwing doors.

Michael licked his lips, hesitated, hand on a porch column. The steak and potatoes from the hotel lumped in his stomach. He looked up and down the street. No one noticed him, everyone wrapped in his or her own concerns. He pressed his hand against the pillar as if to hold himself back.

It's not going to help.

Nothing else has helped, either. At least it will deaden the pain.

Will it?

"Shut up. Both of you." He looked around. Nobody nearby. He shook his head. *Not only am I talking to myself, I'm arguing with myself.*

He pushed off the column, squared his shoulders and turned toward the hotel. A woman's laugh rose from the saloon, a tinkling like a crystal chandelier touched by a breeze. Michael stepped into the street.

The door swung inward at his light, hesitant touch. The scents of cigars, beer, cloying perfume, whiskey and sweat washed over him. He inhaled deeply, faint, blurred memories stirring. He skimmed the room like he used to every time he entered a saloon. Back then, he scanned for potential victims or trouble. Now, he sought for any face he knew. Nope. Didn't recognize anybody. *Good.*

The bar ran down the wall on his right, dark wood, brass boot rail and matching cuspidors. Bare wood tables, tops scarred and stained, and mismatched chairs filled most of the space. Cowboys and gamblers in suits shared the tables, cards splayed out in front of them. At others, men talked and laughed, women in low cut dresses with them. At the rear of the room, others crowded around the roulette and crap tables. Memories of many nights in such places sharpened.

A hand grabbed Michael's arm as he stepped further into the room.

"Ain't you one of the ones who was on the posse?" A slurred voice mumbled.

Michael stared at the man who held his arm. An older man, swaying, breath foul with alcohol and tobacco. He gently pried the man's fingers from his arm.

"Yes, I am."

The man slapped him on the back. "Let me buy you a drink. Least I can do for what you men did." The man turned toward the bar, staggered, grabbed the edge to keep himself from falling. The man's wallet protruded from the inside pocket of his vest. Michael's fingers tingled. Too easy sometimes.

"Rupert." The man gestured to the bartender. "Give this gent a glass of the best stuff in the house. On me." He jerked his thumb in Michael's direction. "He was on the posse."

Rupert stood several inches taller than Michael. A black leather patch covered one eye. A bushy mustache hid his upper lip. "You was on the posse?"

Michael nodded.

Rupert planted a glass in front of Michael, took a bottle from under the bar and poured the dark amber liquid. "My boss says anyone on the posse gets a drink on the house. Old Hezekiah here'll pay for your next one."

Michael picked up the glass and raised it toward Rupert in a gesture of thanks. He sipped. The liquid burned all the way to his stomach. He coughed. Waited. The burning changed to the warmth he remembered. The glow spread. He finished the drink in one gulp.

Another appeared. Disappeared. Michael placed a coin on the bar and pointed at his glass. Another appeared.

Sometime later, a fog lifted. Michael found himself at a table, a half-empty bottle in front of him, Hezekiah and another man across from him.

Someone next to him stroked the back of his hand. He looked down. Slender fingers. Painted nails. A woman? He turned his head. Yep. A woman. Black hair, red at the roots. Dark brown eyes. High cheekbones. Full mouth. Painted lips. Lots of makeup. She pressed her body against him.

She whispered in his ear. "Let's get out of here and go have some real fun." Her tongue flicked the outside of his ear. She rested her hand on his thigh.

He focused on her eyes. One set seemed to meet his. Three other sets drifted around in lazy circles. He couldn't decide which set to stare at.

"Can't. Gonna get married." *I am? News to me.*

She squeezed his thigh. "But not tonight, honey? Right?"

CHAPTER 6

Wednesday, June 19

MICHAEL WOKE UP and wished he hadn't. Pain encircled his head like someone pulling a belt tighter and tighter. Pressure pushed against his eyeballs. He opened his lids to get some relief.

He squeezed them shut again as blinding light sent shivers of pain into his head. The light strobed behind his eyelids, and pain pulsed through his skull with the rhythmic beat of a blacksmith banging on his anvil. The belt seemed like the only thing holding his head together. If only it wasn't snugged so tight.

He laid still, eyes closed. His mouth felt like it had yesterday's socks in it. He must still have a tongue, but he couldn't feel it. The acrid odors of vomit, alcohol and sweat assaulted his nostrils. He clutched his stomach, forcing down the heaving that rumbled. No way he could sit up and vomit over the side of whatever it was he lay on. Hard slats pressed through thin fabric into his back. Ahh. Yes. Pain in a different place. *Wonderful. Yep. Everything hurts. Even my toes. Where are my boots?*

Where am I?

He opened his eyes slowly. That's better. The light didn't attack this time. A ceiling of unpainted planks stretched above his head.

Well, I'm not in my hotel room. Stable maybe? Under the loft? What am I lying on? His fingers probed. Spikes of pain jarred as they touched a narrow piece of wood. *Yipe.* A splinter. He brought the offended finger to his mouth, tasted blood. His stomach roiled. Some kind of very narrow bed. And short. His feet dangled off the end, pins and needles dancing from his toes to his ankles.

Where am I?

He started to turn his head. The phantom belt buckle dug into his temple. *That's not going to work.* He shifted his eyes, trying to hold his head still. Blurry awareness of vertical lines extending out of sight in each direction. His brain spun like a roulette wheel. More dizziness, more shifting of whatever lived in his stomach.

He willed his eyes to focus. *Bars. That's what they are, bars. I'm in jail. Well, you've come full circle, Michael Archer. Back in jail. Zechariah will be proud.* He squinched his eyes.

The clang of metal against metal snapped him to a sitting position. He clamped his hands over his ears. *There's no belt around my head. Who or what squeezed it? What is that racket?* He tried to speak. His tongue wouldn't cooperate, couldn't move around the sock in his mouth.

"Come on, boyo. Time to rise and shine."

Recognition of the voice penetrated like sun through thick clouds. *I know that voice from somewhere, that brogue. Pete O'Brien. Why is he torturing me?*

The clanging stopped. Michael lowered his hands and squinted toward the voice.

"Glad to see you back among the living, laddie." Pete held out the cup and gestured with the coffee pot in his other hand. "I brought you some coffee."

Michael shook his head and held his stomach.

"You know, in the army, men would put a raw egg in the pot after having a night like you did. Claimed it helped get everything back to normal. I can do that for you, if you want."

Michael lay down, closed his eyes, and patted his stomach like he would a sick puppy.

"Suit yourself, then. Give a holler if you change your mind." Pete ran the cup along the bars as he left.

Michael winced as Pete slammed the door separating the cells from the office. *He enjoyed that too much.* He turned his head to the wall. The smell of brick a few inches away triggered memories of similar mornings, similar pain. Those mornings had come with the thought of the next drink. What would come this morning?

→⊷ ⊶←

Michael stirred. *How long was I asleep?* His stomach seemed calmer, although the churning rumbled like a train through a tunnel. His head throbbed a steady beat in his temples and behind his eyes. He lifted his lids to thin slits. The shadow of a barred window cast a tilted pattern on the brick wall. Mid-morning? His stomach rumbled again. Not nausea. Hunger.

The door to the office slammed into the wall. Michael winced and squeezed his eyes as fresh pain seared like a lightning bolt.

"He's right in here, in all his glory." Pete's loud voice stabbed. "You got a visitor, laddie. A man of the cloth. Ye wouldn't be wanting your last rites, would ye?" Pete laughed. "He's all yours, Reverend." Pete swung the cell door open.

It wasn't locked? I could have walked out of here any time I wanted? Except standing and walking were the last things on my mind. Had to get the room to stop spinning first.

"Thank you, Deputy." Luke's gentle voice soothed like a warm bath. "Michael?" The voice closer, though Michael hadn't heard him enter the cell.

"Reverend." The word croaked from his burning throat.

Luke Matthews' dark brown eyes, filled with concern, shamed him. He faced the wall.

"Do you want to talk?"

Michael shook his head. Turned back to Luke. "Nuthin' to say." His throat burned. His voice sounded like his mouth was full of sand. He wasn't even sure he made any sense.

"I'll wait. There's always something to say." Luke sat on the floor, his back against the bars. He opened his Bible.

Michael closed his eyes. *What is there to say?* An apology sounded hollow. Repentance rang false. Was this it? His future? To repeat his past? Maria flashed before him, finger pointing, her one eye accusing. His hands clenched, but there was no bottle to grab.

"Excuse me for interrupting, Reverend." Caleb's voice roused him.

He couldn't face the man.

"Michael."

"Sheriff."

"You're free to go. Hezekiah's not going to press charges."

"Who's Hezekiah? Press charges? About what?"

"You don't remember? You punched him last night. Knocked him on his bony butt."

Michael shook his head, confused. "Why would I do that?"

"He got upset when you wouldn't go off with Suzette. Cost him money."

"Who's Suzette?"

"Michael, what do you remember?" Luke stood next to Caleb, frowning.

Michael tried to think, but nothing happened. Thoughts bobbed like apples in water, moving just out of reach with each attempted grab. Recollections formed from the dizzying fog of his mind. Vague shapes. "I walked into the saloon. Rupert poured me a drink. Hezekiah bought me a drink. I bought me a drink. I woke up here. That's it."

Caleb sighed. "You missed a lot. According to Rupert, you bought a bottle and got friendly with Suzette, one of Hezekiah's girls. She wanted to, let's say, get more friendly. You kept saying you couldn't 'cause you're gonna get married. Hezekiah got mad because Suzette wasn't making him any money. Words were exchanged, and you punched him. Pete walked by, saw what was going on, and decided arresting you was the best way to get you out of there."

"I remember Rupert and Hezekiah. Don't remember Suzette. I do remember somebody licked my ear. I hope it wasn't Hezekiah." He paused. "Or Pete. Oh, Lord, what a fool." He turned his face to the wall. He heard Caleb and Luke breathing. *Why don't they leave? Can't they see the side show's over?*

Luke cleared his throat. "Want to talk about what made you want to do that?"

Michael kept his face to the wall. "No. Ain't none of your business."

"None of us, except maybe Caleb, know what you went through out there, but we can see it's tearing you up inside. We just want to help."

"I can handle it."

"Like you've handled it so far?" Caleb's sarcasm buzzed like a mosquito. "Not talking. Getting drunk."

"Turning your back on Rachel," Luke added. "She's been praying and waiting for you the whole time you were gone."

Michael clenched his fist. It felt good. Distracted him from the memory of the questioning hurt in Rachel's eyes when he last saw her. *Was it only yesterday? Seemed like a month.*

He flexed his fist. *Yeah, that feels good. Power. Who should I hit? If I could only hit myself hard enough to do some damage.* "She deserves better than me."

"She doesn't think so." Luke paused. "And I don't think God does either."

"Well, he made a mistake this time." He turned to face them. "Just leave me alone, will ya? I can handle it. Don't need your help."

"You're no better than a drunk." The harsh, bitter words from the one of the other cells made Michael turn.

Intense hate from Jack Alden's eyes seared him. Alden held the bars in a white-knuckled grip. "You killed my wife, and the first chance you get, you go celebrating by getting drunk? What kind of a man are you? I wish I could get my hands around your throat. You destroyed the only good thing in my life." Alden's face melted as grief made his eyes droop and mouth sag, the mustache accentuating his forlorn hopelessness. He opened his mouth as if to say more, closed it and rested his head against the bars.

Michael covered his face with his hands.

⇥⊙ ⊙⇤

Rachel shifted the basket to a more comfortable position. She made her way across the street to the jail, each step tentative as if the ground might dissolve under the weight of her foot.

Which Michael would be inside? The one from last night? Or worse? Luke's description of Michael's appearance and attitude flashed across her mind. *Oh, Father, let it be the Michael from before the posse left, the smiling Michael, the tender and protective Michael, the Michael you showed me in the vision.*

Pete O'Brien opened the door as she reached the boardwalk. "Good morning, Miss Rachel." He removed his derby, made a sweeping gesture with his arm, and bowed. "Welcome to the finest accommodations this side of the river."

She reached under the white towel covering her basket and took out a plate. "Here you go, Deputy. Annabelle thought you could use some dinner."

He sat at the desk, peeled back the cloth, and inhaled the aroma of the plate of chicken. "Me wife is an angel, she is. 'Tis an angel you are too for bringing it. Thank ye."

Her gaze fell on the door to the cells. "How's our boy?" *Do I really want to know? Do I really want a man who enjoys violence and alcohol? Had enough of that in the brothels.*

Pete nodded toward the cells. "Quiet as a Catholic in a Presbyterian church at Christmas. Ain't heard a peep out of him since Caleb and the Reverend left."

Rachel took a deep breath. *Come on, you can do this.* She walked into the cell section with a boldness she hoped disguised her fears.

Michael lay on his back, hands behind his head, eyes open.

"I brought you some dinner."

"Thanks. You can leave it there. I'll get it later." His flat, emotionless tone felt like a hard slap.

She gripped one of the bars, stifling the urge to shout, *Look at me.*

"Michael, I know you need some time to figure out what happened out there. I'd like to help." He didn't move. Her hand slid down the bar. "And even if you don't want my help, I'll be waiting."

"You may have to wait a long time."

She willed herself to be calm, to still the anger boiling under the surface. She took a deep breath and slowly released it. "I've waited over a month. Prayed. Dreaded each day with no news. I was almost raped. Probably helped get Mark killed. Yesterday, before I saw you, I was convinced you were one of the bodies in the wagon."

She pressed her head against the bars, enjoying the few seconds of coolness.

"Maybe I should have been." Michael's soft, defeated voice grazed her ear. He still looked at the ceiling. "Might be better for you."

"How—"

"Hey, Señorita. If he don't want you, you can come to us. We'll take good care of you." The thick Mexican accent from two cells down jolted her. Two of the prisoners brought in yesterday stood, watching. The one who spoke made a gesture she hadn't seen since her days with Red Mary.

"And we'll take your food, too." The other motioned her to come to them.

"*Cállate.*" The third man in the cell barked the word. The two Mexicans glared at him but backed off to sit on the floor under his stare.

Michael stood. Swayed. Grabbed the bars to the neighboring cell as he started to fall. She reached for him, but he was too far away. He clung to the bars, eyes closed, and shook his head.

"You say one more word, and I will kill you."

Rachel covered her mouth. He meant it. Under the drunken exterior, there was a hard, cold man, ready to kill. This Michael gripped the bars as if to pull them apart. His profile was dark, mottled. The anger seemed to boil under the surface, stretching the skin taut. Evil oozed from his eyes.

She froze. This couldn't be the man God meant for her.

How could she ever let him get close to her? How could she ever know what she might do or say to release this violence, this monster? How could she ever defend herself from the rage?

Still holding the bars, Michael looked over his shoulder. His hazel eyes bored into her, challenging.

She dashed through the doorway, and was on the boardwalk before she realized she had left him. Fingers clutched, she stared at the jail, heart tripping like Sunshine at a gallop.

I can't go back in there. Not now.

CHAPTER 7

Wednesday, June 19

THE CONGREGATION RUSTLED as people entered the pews and others made space for them. Luke Matthews looked at the papers resting next to his Bible.

He gasped. His heart galloped.

The pages were blank.

Where are my notes?

He turned the top page over. Nothing on the back.

He fought down the wave of panic.

I know I took the right sheets off my desk. The words were here a few minutes ago. What happened?

He took a deep breath, held it, and slowly released it.

He looked up. Martha met his gaze, her eyes pinched in a frown. He closed his eyes, tilted his head down, and opened his eyes. The words were there. His heart slowed to its normal rhythm. He wiped the cold sweat from his forehead with a handkerchief, folded it precisely into quarters and slipped it into his coat pocket.

Six identical coffins crowded the space between the pulpit and the first pew, three on each side of the central aisle. Vernon and Alexander were already in their graves on the ranch, taken there yesterday evening by the ranch hands.

Small wooden plaques identified each casket. Sam and Mark occupied the first two on the left. Old Thomas's was next to the aisle on the right. Luke faked a cough to cover his smile at Malachi's machinations to have Old Thomas's coffin prominently placed and Mayor Meriweather's consternation that a heathen should be included in a Christian burial service.

He studied the crowd as more people filled the pews. Cowboys and others not used to being in church stood in the back. Standees inched up the sidewalls as a slight breeze wafted through open windows, bringing intermittent coolness.

Meriweather and his wife sat in the first pew on the left with Joshua and Lupe Carstairs and the town council. Caleb and Malachi sat across the aisle with Martha, the children, and Mrs. Phelps. He was grateful Mrs. Phelps had come to the service to share the town's grief.

Rachel and Annabelle sat directly behind them, exchanging glances with Lupe. *That's a relationship I hadn't expected to develop.* Lupe seemed to have blossomed over the last month as she formed a bond with Rachel, Annabelle and Martha. Rachel also glanced over her shoulder, as if expecting someone.

Would Michael show up? *I don't know after this morning. Lord, I pray Michael's heart be softened so he can hear from you. I believe you want him here, want him as part of this community.*

He cleared his throat, ready to begin, when the door opened one more time. Michael and Jeremiah stood in the entrance, silhouetted by the light behind them. They walked up the aisle, Michael using the end of the pews as support, his gait that of an old man hobbling on an unsteady cane. Somehow, Jeremiah and Pete had managed to get Michael bathed, shaved and in clean clothes. The man's face looked whitewashed above the dark suit that hung on his frame. *Caleb wasn't the only one who lost weight.*

They stopped at the pew where Rachel and Annabelle sat. Michael kept his head down as he and Jeremiah sidled into the seat.

Rachel's face displayed a range of emotions he knew from the months she lived with them. Love, yes, in the smile. Fear, too, in the eyes opened a little wider than usual. And, in that chin, the determination she'd shown in planning her dress shop. Rachel was not going to let him walk away. From her or from God. He almost felt sorry for Michael.

Luke scanned the room. The flock God entrusted to him. Grief etched the faces of so many. Anger, also. Some, he knew, questioned how God could let this happen. *How do I help all of them?* Words rang in his heart. "Through Me. One by one, as I direct you." *Yes, Lord.*

"Open your Bibles to John eleven, verse twenty-five." Luke read aloud. "Jesus said unto her, I am the resurrection, and the life: he that believeth in me, though he were dead, yet shall he live: And whosoever liveth and believeth in me shall never die."

He closed the book, centered it on the pulpit, and glanced at his notes. He stepped to one side, left hand on the pulpit.

"These men are gone from us. Noble men. Men of honor. Men we can admire and seek to emulate. They gave their lives protecting our community, seeking justice. They're gone, and we will miss them.

"Sam and his drive to build Riverbend into a town of excellence and prosperity.

"Vernon and his heart to serve any neighbor or stranger, his example of Jesus.

"Alexander and his love of music, his love of his aunt and uncle, the one among us who never met a stranger."

He paused.

"Mark and his love of life and adventure that sought reining in.

"Shorty and his loyalty to the Carstairs family and his dream of Wyoming.

"Dave and his love for his family.

"Mitch and his concern for his customers, cutting them off if needed, and his dedication to helping the church grow."

Luke stepped from the platform and rested his hand on the casket of Old Thomas. Mayor Meriweather stirred as if to stand, restrained only by his wife's thick hand on his arm.

"Old Thomas, one of the most spiritual men I've ever known, a man who saw Jesus in ways none of us did, a man who loved his Creator."

Malachi's sobs shattered the reverent silence. Esther Phelps embraced him and held him.

Luke stepped in front of the pulpit, and spread his arms. "These men are gone from us, but we have hope they are all in a far better place. We have hope that they are in heaven with Jesus, and they are waiting for us. And they are cheering us on. They are part of that great cloud of witnesses described in Hebrews twelve.

"They are gone. Evil happens in this world. It's not from God. He is love and will never leave us nor forsake us. Evil is from the devil as he seeks to drive us apart from God and each other."

He clapped his hands. People jumped. "I will not let Satan drive me or any of us away from God. I will fight him with my last breath. He is the evil who caused this, and his evil was defeated. Yes, it was at great cost. But it was a great victory. Brave men like these who stepped forward stopped the devil's plans. Men like Caleb, Malachi, Bill Barkston, Frank and Howard. And two strangers who joined us to see justice done: Jeremiah Turner and Michael Archer.

"Noble men who answered God's call.

"Grief hurts. But with our grief we can also celebrate. We can celebrate that evil was defeated, and we can celebrate that those who died are waiting for us."

→►═● ●═◄←

Michael studied the whorls of the wood grain in the honey-colored pew before him. Dizzy, he closed his eyes. He opened them. Where to look? Not at Luke whose words washed over him and kept on going. Not at his own hands, tools of death. Not at the people.

Definitely not at the coffins, bitter memorials to what he had been a part of, to what he had done. Not at Rachel, who sat close to him, their shoulders touching. Seeing the hurt and accusation in her eyes would push him over the edge of this precipice he clung to.

He pinched the bridge of his nose and squeezed his eyes. Rachel leaned closer. Shame and guilt flared like dry wood thrown on a fire. He wanted to pull away, but Jeremiah blocked his escape. Michael prayed, but nothing came after *Oh, God*. He wanted to leave, but disrupting the service would bring more unwanted attention.

Rachel's hand squeezed his arm. Her violet eyes, gentle smile, smooth cheeks. *She cares for me. How? Why?* An image flickered. His arms around her, his lips on hers, their embrace so tight it hurt to breathe. The image shattered. He mouthed, "I'm sorry."

She frowned, a question in her eyes. "Later," she whispered, and turned back to Luke.

Michael stared at the wall behind the pastor, seeking flaws in the whitewash to avoid looking at the coffins. *Hang on. The service will be over soon. Then I can go back to Grandy's.*

⤖ ⬗⬖⬗ ⤙

Rachel's heart burned in prayer. *Lord, you told me to love this man, and I do. But how do I help him? He's slipping away, Lord. From me. From you.*

The spark of the Michael she first knew had shone for a brief moment when he said he was sorry. But it died, and he turned to look at who knows what, off by himself, locked away in a private world no one could enter, just like in the store last night.

Where's the Michael who left with the posse? And who's this cold, distant man in Michael's body?

Tension built, a spring ready to release pent-up energy in an explosion of anger and hurt. She wanted to run, to climb on Sunshine and take to the fields behind the town, to ride for the mountains, to scream. Luke's words droned, a mumble…the scissors plunged into Mark's chest. The horror of the rape attempt vanished in the satisfaction of seeing pain and surprise on his face. She wished she'd held onto the scissors to enjoy the triumph of plunging them again…

She shook her head. No. Stopping the attack was enough. Now he was dead. Guilt washed over her, a wave of nausea roiling her stomach. Did the scissors weaken him to the point he couldn't resist the kidnappers? Was she at least partly responsible? If she had let him have his way, he'd probably be alive today.

She squeezed the fingers of one hand, mashing the bones together like she did when her uncle started abusing her. A different pain than what he brought, one to block out what he did. *Did Mark deserve to die? No. No one, not even the kidnappers did. But I didn't deserve to be raped either. I defended myself. Mark died, but not by my hand.*

Since the vision, she dreamed of Michael's touch, his kiss. She imagined their life together, a home, children, the church, the town. And now he was back, sitting next to her. Their shoulders touched, but a wall like cold steel divided them, her dreams gossamer strands torn by the wind. *He's here in body, but will the rest of him, his essence, ever return?*

She bowed her head. *God, I don't believe you brought us together for us to drift apart. I know Satan is behind this. Lord, I'm not strong enough. I can't bring Michael back by myself. Fill me with your grace and mercy and power to love Michael and to help him any way I can.*

The rustle of the congregation as Luke closed the service brought Rachel to reality. She turned to Michael. "Will you come to the burials with me?"

He frowned, hesitant. After a pause that seemed endless, he nodded.

They walked out of church, side by side, not touching. Her heart ached to loop her arm through his, but he did not invite her.

CHAPTER 8

Wednesday, June 19

MICHAEL STARED AT the three holes in the ground, perfect rectangles of dark brown earth ready to swallow the coffins of Dave, Mitch, and Old Thomas. Three more coffins waited to be taken to the Carstairs ranch. The soft sobs and sniffles from the townspeople blended with Luke's subdued voice reciting scripture.

Rachel stood on his right, her hand on his arm. He dared not break contact with it. When Luke began the final prayer, Michael took off his hat with his left hand. Rachel's gentle pressure seemed to be the only thing holding him to reality.

Again, his emotions swirled, and his mind tried to clamp them down, to control them, to understand them. The old Michael seethed under the surface, feeding on the enjoyment of last night's alcohol and this morning's anger at the Mexicans. Yet guilt and shame encroached like a blizzard over the mountains. Alden's words and crumpled face burned.

I killed someone who was loved by others. Could there have been another way? He knew in his mind there wasn't, but his emotions kept asking, accusing.

He licked his lips, savoring the memory of last night's first few drinks, the warmth radiating from his stomach, the good feeling, the wiping away of the death, of Maria's accusing eye. *Numb is good. Drunk is better.*

After the coffins were lowered into the ground, Caleb and Malachi each tossed a handful of dirt on Old Thomas's. Caleb looked at Michael, a question on his face. Michael shook his head. He did not want to see the final sign his friend was gone. He clung to the memory of Old Thomas next to him on the trail, the quiet man who could make others laugh with a word or a look, who could find a trail on solid rock. The quiet man who became his friend as they shared their love of the Creator.

A thin, pregnant woman with wisps of auburn hair peeking from her bonnet picked up a handful of dirt and tossed it into Dave's grave. The dirt made a hollow sound as it hit the coffin. Michael grimaced as the woman's sad eyes looked directly at him. He swallowed. Her life forever altered, she looked at him with a tender vulnerability that cried for protection.

Not me, God. I can't do it.

A man approached, a stranger. He shook Michael's hand. "I want to thank you for all you did."

Michael nodded. When the man acted like he wanted to say more, Michael looked away. After a moment, the man walked away with a "Well, thank you again."

Rachel leaned close, her voice a whisper. "I can't imagine how hard it was for you out there, what you must have gone through. What you all went through."

He shook his head. "It was bad. Good people died, and we couldn't save Sam."

"But you reconciled Sam with Ben, right?"

The river swirled in the distance. He wished he were on a raft floating away.

He swallowed. "Yeah. Did that much." Something tickled the back of his mind. A promise. A new purpose. He dismissed it. Whatever it was would probably require he be sober.

--->==⊙ ⊙==<---

Michael rocked in Buddy's easy gait as the horse clopped behind the wagon carrying the coffins of Sam, Mark and Shorty. They passed under the log arch that marked the entrance to Sam's ranch, the Double Bar Ruth. The brand symbol hung from the apex, a capital R with a straight line above and below.

Not how he imagined his first visit to Ben's home. What would have been different if he had been able to meet Sam at his home instead of at a collapsing line shack surrounded by the stench of death? His hands wouldn't be stained with blood. *God, why did it have to be this way?*

They rode past the two-story house with its wide, covered porch and wings of rooms that shot off to the left and right. Which was Ben's? What did it look like now?

A tree shaded the approach to the porch, its branches stretching over the house. Did Ben climb that tree? Did Ben have any fun? Any days free from the torment of his brothers and the disdain of his father?

Joshua rode in a covered carriage, his back straight, Lupe close to his side. In a carriage behind them, Luke and Martha rode in front, Annabelle and Rachel in the rear. Pete matched his horse's pace to the carriage so that he stayed at his wife's side. Rachel glanced over her shoulder. Michael smiled. A smile he didn't feel, and made no move to pull up alongside.

Frank came up beside him. "Never thought I'd see a day like this again. So many funerals. It's like Richmond during the war."

Michael continued in silence.

"Know what you mean." Frank stayed next to him but didn't speak again.

They stopped at a small cemetery behind the barn. A short, wood fence enclosed seven or eight graves marked by weathered wooden crosses. Next to a fresh-dug grave, two shovels leaned in a pile of dirt.

Michael dismounted and helped Frank and two other cowboys lower Shorty's coffin into the ground. He removed his hat and held it in front of him while Luke said a prayer. After the prayer, Frank handed him one of the shovels. Michael looked at it, wishing it would vanish. It didn't.

He slid the blade into the dirt, picked up a small pile, and tossed it into the grave. It drummed on the coffin. Michael stared at the dirt on the plain wood. His grip tightened on the handle.

He drove the shovel into the pile of dirt, scooped a heaping pile into the grave. Did it again. And again. And again.

Each time, he drove the tool in with more force, the muscles in his back and arms flexing in the effort. He dropped the last shovelful onto the grave and drove the shovel into the dirt, sinking it to the top of the blade. His muscles burned. Sweat ran down his face, soaked his shirt. His breath came in heavy gasps. He wiped his brow with his sleeve, settled his hat on his head and walked away.

As the others moved a short distance to an area marked by a wrought iron fence, Michael trailed behind, keeping to the edge of the small group. Joshua and three ranch hands lowered Sam and Mark into the graves next to the headstone of Ruth Carstairs. *Ben should be here, too.*

Again, Luke said a short prayer. Afterwards, Joshua shook everyone's hand. He approached Michael last.

"Caleb told me what you did to save my father. Thanks." Joshua's dark eyes peered from sockets shrouded by heavy brows.

Michael accepted the handshake, surprised at the strength of Joshua's grip, and focused on the space over Joshua's right shoulder. "Didn't save him, though."

"I appreciate you trying." Joshua rubbed the back of his neck. "Listen." A pause. "Come see me in a couple of days, after things settle down."

Confusion rose in Michael. *Why would the last Carstairs want to see me? Every Carstairs I meet dies. I might not even be here in a couple of days.*

"Sure."

Joshua turned away as if seeking something, someone. He quickened his stride to catch up to his wife and slipped his arm around her waist. Lupe looked up at him, smile soft, hand on his chest.

Envy stabbed Michael, sharp, cold. Something he wanted. Something he didn't deserve. Rachel stood next to Lupe. So pretty—no—beautiful. His heart ached. A beauty beyond his reach.

Rachel looked at him. Smiled. He nodded, mounted Buddy and kicked the animal into a trot toward the ranch gate.

CHAPTER 9

June 19, 1878

RACHEL HUNG HER dress in the armoire in her room, arranging the folds of the skirt, wiping traces of dust from the hem. Once again, the vision flashed through her mind. Michael standing next to her. The voice saying this man was to be her husband. She huffed. Apparently, he didn't know that yet. He acted as if he wanted nothing to do with her.

She unpinned her hair, and shook her head until the hair tumbled to her shoulders. She picked up the brush from a small table in the corner and pulled it through her thick mane with long, smooth strokes.

Had she missed it? Had she missed what God told her? The vision was so clear, so real. She hadn't missed it. She knew in her heart this was God's plan for her.

How to show Michael? He had cared for her, had desired her before he left with the posse. Did he still? He sure didn't show it.

In her old life, she would have used any number of skills to stir him, draw him to her. Not now. Not ever. She'd burned and buried those skills on the stage from Denver almost nine months ago.

For the last week she had looked forward to her and Michael beginning new days together. *What now?*

A knock on the door.

Rachel took a moment to set her brush in its precise place on the table, and wrapped a shawl around her shoulders. Gone were the days she would answer the door in her underwear—or less. "Come in."

Martha entered. "I'm going to make some tea. Do you want to join me? Do you need something to eat?"

"I'm not hungry. Thanks."

Martha sat on the edge of the bed. "Want to talk?"

"Is it that obvious?"

"As obvious as the mayor's three chins."

Rachel sighed. "I'm confused about Michael. I thought he would be happier to see me. When he left, it was obvious he cared about me. Over the time he's been gone, I've grown to care about him too."

She paced her room from window to door, arms folded. *Do I tell her about the vision?* "I've never felt this way about a man before."

"Never?"

Rachel shook her head. "Never. I believe God wants us to be married."

Martha's eyes widened. Her eyebrows arched. "Married? That's a big step from 'I'd like to get to know you better.' Are you sure?"

"As sure as you are about Pastor Luke."

Martha folded her hands on her lap. "That's pretty sure."

Rachel hugged her elbows. "I expected Michael to act the same way when he got back. Instead, he acts like he doesn't even want to be around me."

"Maybe you need to be patient. Let God work on Michael like he worked on you."

Rachel put her hands on her hips. "Well, I sure wish the Lord'd hurry up."

Chapter 10

June 19, 1878

MICHAEL PLACED HIS knife and fork next to the half-eaten steak on the plate before him, took a sip of water. Grimaced. *Need something stronger. Grandy's.* He dropped a coin on the table, adjusted his hat on long, shaggy hair that needed a barber's attention, and walked out of the hotel dining room.

Several men gathered in the street before the sheriff's office. Pete O'Brien stood on the boardwalk, one hand resting on the butt of his pistol, the other hooked in his belt loop. Michael stopped, curious.

"We don't need to wait for no judge." One of the men in the street spoke. "We know they're guilty. Save the town the cost of a trial."

Murmurs of agreement rose from the crowd. Other men wandered over, joining those in the street. The murmurs grew louder.

"You men just be moving along now. Go home to yer wives and families. These men'll get what's coming to 'em. The law'll see to that, to be sure."

Michael repositioned his hat, pulled the brim lower over his eyes, and crossed the street. He stepped onto the boardwalk and stood next to the deputy.

"Evening, Deputy."

"Evening, laddie." Pete kept his eyes on the crowd.

"Having a meeting?"

Pete jerked his thumb at the crowd. "Just some boyos with more mouth than brains."

"Where's the sheriff?"

"Still out at the Carstairs place with Joshua."

"Good thing he trusts you to keep the peace."

One in the crowd spoke up, the same one Michael heard earlier. "Let us have 'em, Pete. We'll make sure they get all the justice they need."

"Excuse me, sir," Michael said. "I don't believe we've ever met."

"Jacob Bradshaw. I run the tannery."

"That would explain the odor." Tension rippled through Michael, the excitement of a confrontation shot energy through his veins, pulsing into his head. "I don't believe I saw you on the posse."

"I had to take care of my business." The man glared at Michael.

"I'm sure you did. But you know, so did Vernon Phelps and Mitch and the others who died out there. But it's good to see you can now bravely put your business aside to lynch three men. Very noble of you."

Bradshaw clenched his fists. Michael smiled, the familiar smile that meant the monster inside was about to come out, and Michael looked forward to releasing him.

"Who do you think you are, Mister?"

Michael glanced at Pete. The deputy's eyes seemed to search him as if wondering himself who this stranger was, and what had happened to the other Michael.

"Just a stranger passing through, trying to help. Excuse me for a minute."

Michael entered the sheriff's office and came out a moment later carrying two shotguns. He handed one to Pete. He took the other and stepped in front of Bradshaw.

"Here, laddie," Pete said. "Don't do anything rash. I can handle this bunch of louts."

"I'm sure you can, Deputy. But Mr. Bradshaw here has aroused my curiosity."

Michael stood a foot away from the man, feeding on the fear in Bradshaw's eyes.

"Six people died on that posse, sir. Six. Died trying to save Sam and Mark Carstairs." He jabbed the barrels of the shotgun into Bradshaw's stomach.

He named each man, punctuating his names with jabs. Bradshaw staggered back a step with each jab. The other men gave way, forming a loose semi-circle. Pete O'Brien said something, but Michael didn't hear it.

"Those men died because they believe in this town, because they believe in justice, because they believe the law stands for something." Old Thomas spread-eagled in the dirt swam before him. Michael held the barrels inches from Bradshaw's chest.

"Michael," Pete called, urgency shaking his voice.

Michael ignored him, locked his gaze on Bradshaw. The man's eyes darted from side to side, sweat ran down his face, his mouth worked, but no sounds came out. Foul breath mingled with the tannery stink on the man's clothes.

His voice calm, cold, Michael said, "I will not have you bring shame on those men or their families because of your perverted idea of justice." With great deliberation, Michael cocked the barrels.

He heard Pete leap from the boardwalk to the street.

"No, Michael. Don't."

Michael ignored him. He focused on Bradshaw.

"Now get out of here, and take this herd of cowards with you."

As the men left, Pete grabbed his shoulder and spun him around. "What were ye thinking, lad? Why didnya let me handle it?"

Michael shook his head as if coming out of a trance. "You weren't there. You didn't see Old Thomas or Vernon or the others."

He broke open the shotgun, showing the deputy two empty barrels.

He touched the brim of his hat and handed the weapon to Pete. "Have a nice evening, Deputy."

⇥ ⇤

Grandy's beckoned, lights drawing him, laughter floating in the smoke drifting over the batwing doors. He entered.

Rupert took a rifle from under the bar. The sound of a round being levered into the chamber brought frozen silence to the place.

He pointed the rifle in Michael's direction. "Out."

Michael spread his arms. "'Out? Why? I haven't done anything."

Rupert gestured with the weapon. "And this is to make sure you don't. The boss said to throw you out if you show up."

"It was a simple misunderstanding."

"Don't want no more misunderstandings. Take your business someplace else."

Frank from the posse staggered up beside him, draped his arm around Michael's shoulder. "C'mon, Reverend." His breath reeked of tobacco, beer and cheap whiskey. The kind Michael's father use to drink. "We'll find some place that'll be more 'preciative of our bus—" he belched—"ness. There's a great little Mexican cantina near the river."

Michael shrugged Frank's arm off. "You go ahead." He focused on Rupert. "I want to drink here."

Rupert raised the rifle. Patrons scattered.

Frank's finger wavered in the direction of the weapon. "See, I don—I don't think he wants yer money."

Michael opened his mouth to speak, but a large hand fell on his shoulder. Hard. He turned.

Pete. "I think ye best call it a night, laddie."

He pushed against Pete's hand. It didn't move.

"All I want is one drink." He cocked his fist.

Something hit him. On the jaw.

Wagon tongue? Anvil? Mule kick?

Darkness fell.

-->==◎ ◎==<--

He opened his eyes. Closed them. Pain radiated in a perfect circle from his jaw to the top of his head. Raised his lids halfway. Lying on something hard. Shifted his vision. Bars.

Oh, no. Not again.

Ran his tongue over his teeth. *Didn't even get a drink this time.*

"Hey look, Señor Jack." One of the Mexican prisoners spoke. "It's the one who shot your wife. Two nights in a row. Maybe tomorrow they put him in cell with us. You can fix him good. Me and Pablo, we will help."

"Shut up." Michael said. Pain lanced through his eye to a new place in his brain.

He lifted his head. Dropped it back down and slammed his eyes shut until his head stopped spinning. It took a long time.

Try it one more time. Keep head still. "Hello in the office." Voice weak. *Try again in a minute.*

The door creaked open. A tall, thin figure, half-silhouetted, a star on his vest catching the dim light from turned-down lamps in the cell area.

"Somebody say something?" Tremulous, nervous, high-pitched.

"Me. Who are you?"

The man cleared his throat. "Deputy Sanders. Henry Sanders. I'm really just an aux—"

"Where's Deputy O'Brien?"

"Went home. Left me in charge. Said I can let you go if you promise to behave and go right to the hotel. Otherwise, I'm to lock the door and let Sheriff Davis deal with you tomorrow."

Wonderful. He stared at the ceiling. Head hurt too much anyway. Drink probably wouldn't stay down. Odors closed in. Chamber pot. Who knew the last time the Mexicans and Jack Alden bathed. Hotel sounded good.

"All right, Deputy. I promise I'll behave and go right to the hotel."

"Door's open."

Michael stood, bracing himself against the wall, probing his jaw. Not broken but painful to the touch.

One of the Mexicans walked to his cell door. "Señor, send your pretty señorita with breakfast tomorrow. We still have something for her."

Michael spun. His body stopped. His head didn't. At least the inside seemed to spin and spin. He closed his eyes and clamped his hands to the sides of his head. "You won't get within ten feet of her. If you do, you won't live long enough to get a foot closer."

He staggered out before he finished what the mob had tried to start.

CHAPTER 11

Thursday, June 20, 1878

CALEB SMOOTHED THE sheet of paper on his desk. His new desk. One with drawers that actually worked. Charley Akins wouldn't tell him who paid for it, only said it was a gift from some appreciative townspeople.

He sighed at the irony of what he was about to write on this new piece of furniture, and dipped the pen into the inkbottle. The pen hovered over the paper. He scratched the date, the sound breaking the silence in the pre-dawn gloom of his office. He put the pen down and leaned back in his chair, staring at the paper. How to begin? Who to address it to? He cringed at the thought of writing the mayor's name, at acknowledging the man had any authority over him.

From behind the closed door to the cells, one of the prisoners emitted long, loud snores, like a cow calling its calf. Metal clanged against metal. "Cállate."

A curse in Spanish followed. Then the noise ceased.

Caleb crumpled the paper and threw it into the pot-bellied stove. It flared in the embers before dissolving into ash and disappearing into the other burnt remains. He poured coffee from the pot he'd started when he first came in. Hot. Strong. Burned his tongue.

Back at his desk, he stared out the dust-streaked window at the brightening day. Vernon's face wavered in front of him, strong, quiet, and confident. It slipped into the image of what the posse found on the trail. Then Caleb saw himself shoveling the first dirt into the grave. He squeezed his eyes and pinched the bridge of his nose. *Need air.*

He stepped onto the boardwalk. A few people moved on the street, and storeowners prepared to open their businesses. Despite the promise of a pleasant, sunny day, the town seemed shrouded by the same grief that weighed on him.

He leaned against the wall of his office; the brick cool through his shirt. Tried to pray. *Need more practice.*

Pete O'Brien loomed into view. "Morning, Sheriff."

Even Pete's morning cheeriness seemed tainted by the somber pall hanging over Riverbend.

"Pete." Caleb raised his cup in salute. "Saw your note."

"'Twas quite an evening, I don't mind telling ye. Thought Archer was going to do some serious harm. Either to Bradshaw or in Grandy's. Or both."

"You didn't arrest him, though?"

"Nay. Put him in a cell. Told Henry he could go if he promised to mind himself."

"He must've accepted your offer. He's not in a cell."

"Good. Maybe I knocked some sense into the lad."

"Maybe you did. Did you have breakfast?"

Pete rubbed his stomach. "Aye, that I did. Me beautiful bride fixed me a delicious meal of bacon, eggs and biscuits to start me day."

Caleb studied his deputy, his friend. "Married life seems to agree with you. Sorry I missed your wedding."

"Me, too. But I think Annabelle and I both knew we needed to do it in a hurry before I changed me mind."

Caleb tapped Pete's shoulder. "That was wise." He tossed the dregs of his coffee into the street and handed the cup to Pete. "I'm going to the hotel for breakfast." He jerked his thumb toward the office. "Those three are yours for now. I'll have the hotel send 'em some grub."

Caleb settled at a table in the middle of the half-filled dining room, nodding to others in the restaurant. They kept a respectful distance, hesitant, it seemed, to intrude on his grief. He wished someone would be bold enough to strike up a conversation—grief was lonely.

Michael stepped into the dining room. Their eyes locked for a moment, then Michael turned to leave and bumped into Jeremiah Turner. Caleb motioned for them both to join him. Jeremiah's enthusiasm pushed Michael ahead of him like wind propelling a tumbleweed.

Caleb nodded at Jeremiah's arm. "No sling."

Jeremiah flexed his fingers. "No. Too annoying. The arm's tender, but the pain's tolerable."

The bruise on Michael's jaw spread like a squashed plum from his chin up his jaw line toward his left ear.

"How you feeling, Michael?"

Michael touched his jaw, eyes riveted on the table. "Sore. I think he must have had a horse shoe in his fist."

"Not likely. That's just the way he hits. Actually, for Pete, that jaw looks like he held something back."

"That's nice to know." Michael grimaced as he sipped the coffee the waitress had brought. "I'll try to remember that."

Caleb turned his attention to Jeremiah. "What's next for you, Jeremiah?"

He shrugged. "I'm going to stay for the trial. After that, I'll head for home— Dallas—see what the next job might be."

"What about you, Michael?"

Michael took a piece of ham in his mouth, and seemed to work to find some way to comfortably chew. The best he managed was to tuck the meat in his right cheek, and even there he still winced. Caleb smiled to himself, and waited as Michael washed it down with coffee.

"Don't know. Haven't given it much thought. Maybe head back to Missouri. Maybe Denver or San Francisco."

Caleb paused, knife poised over his steak. "What'd ya think 'bout staying here in Riverbend? Could make a nice life for yourself here. Work with Pastor Luke. Court Miss Rachel."

Michael's head snapped up, eyes hard, nostrils flaring, voice cold. "I think Miss Rachel can probably do a lot better than me."

Jeremiah chuckled. "I don't know. She seemed very happy to see you the other day. Always had an eye out for you during the funerals."

"She doesn't know what happened out there."

Caleb turned his cup, eyed Michael. "I expect she does. I'm no expert on romance and such, but I think you owe her—and yourself—the chance for her to make that decision."

Michael pushed egg around his plate, put his fork and knife down and folded his arms on the table. "I expect I know which way she'll go. My leaving will just make it easier on her."

"Coward." Jeremiah's voice was soft but firm. He didn't sound like he was joking, but the last thing Caleb would call Michael was a coward.

Michael jerked his attention to Jeremiah, fist clenched on the table.

Jeremiah leaned back in his chair, one hand on the table, the other in his lap, calm as a man discussing his crops. "You're afraid. You're scared you can't control that monster you see inside yourself. You're scared Miss Rachel won't want anything to do with you if she knows it exists."

He pointed a finger at Michael. "She already knows it's there. You told me about your run-ins with Mark Carstairs when you first got to town, so she's seen that monster in action."

He wiped his mouth on a napkin and stood. "You have some decisions to make, Michael. One, how do you really feel about Miss Rachel? I think you care for her. A lot. If I'm right, you need to stay and see what happens with that."

He leaned over the table, holding Michael's gaze. "Two, you need to decide who's in control, you or the old Michael, the one you call a monster. We talked about this at the cabin. You can use what's inside you to help and protect or you can let it control you so you hurt people. Satan's trying to get you to think you can't control the old Michael, that the old Michael is the real you. Don't let him."

He straightened, tossed his napkin onto his plate. "It's up to you. Let Jesus help you."

He put his hand on Michael's shoulder. "There's a lot of good in you, Michael. Let God bring it out."

He nodded at Caleb, placed a coin on the table. "Morning, Sheriff."

Caleb studied Michael, who looked like he'd stepped on the wrong end of a rake. "Strong words."

Michael shook his head and, after a moment, focused on Caleb. "Uhh. Yeah. Strong words."

Michael walked along the river's edge, head down,

A couple of hours later, Michael walked along the river's edge, head down, aware the water flowed nearby. Sunlight dappled through leaves stirred by the northern breeze, rabbits skittered, and birds sang. Jeremiah's words burned like they'd been carved by a blacksmith's white-hot punch. He longed for Zechariah's strength and comfort.

He clasped his hands. "God, I need your help. What would you have me do? Am I that monster inside, or is it a tool? How do I control it?"

He waited. Nothing. Then a stirring. *Go see Pastor Luke.*

He dashed up the gentle slope to Main Street. Once there, he strode, a steady pace, just under a trot, not wanting to draw attention to himself by giving in to his heart's desire to run.

He passed Rachel's store on the other side of the street. She waited on a customer, back to the window. Hair pulled into a bun, blue dress highlighting her slim figure. Memories of her smile, her touch, joined with the desires swirling in his heart. He hesitated, wanting to cross the street.

No. Luke first.

Martha answered his knock. "Michael. Is everything all right? You looked flushed."

Michael took a deep breath and touched his jaw. "I'm fine, Ma'am. Just wondered if I could have a few minutes of Pastor Luke's time."

Luke stepped into the doorway to his office, Bible in hand, finger marking his place, pencil tucked behind his ear. He extended his arm toward his office. "Sure. Come on in."

Michael stepped into the room. Books and papers were spread over the table Luke used as a desk, a pair of boots askew on the floor near the armchair.

Luke turned his wife. "Martha, could you fix us some tea, please?"

Michael saw the tender love and support pass between them.

"Sure." They kissed, a brief touch of the lips. Envy stabbed.

The pastor gestured for him to sit in the armchair while Luke settled into the straight-backed chair he used at his desk. He used the pencil from behind his ear to mark his place in the Bible. He leaned back, one arm on the table, feet crossed at the ankle. "What can I do for you, Michael?"

Michael's thoughts flew out the window and his words with them. Deep breath. *Lord, help me.* He opened his mouth, and the words poured out. The killing of his father. The violence of his life before meeting Zechariah. The monster who pushed and strained to get out, to take over, to hurt people. His conversations with Jeremiah.

Martha brought in tea. Michael used the interruption to quell the pounding in his heart that threatened to break his ribs. After Martha left, Luke linked his hands together over the small paunch developing around his waist. "Jeremiah's right. You have to make the decision. You call it a monster. I think the Lord has given you a keen sense of justice, of protecting people. You have a clear idea of right and wrong, and you got that from God, not man. You can use this in God's service to bring protection and justice to His people." He sipped his tea. "The devil tries to use it to lead you to hurt people. God wants you to use it to help them."

"So, I'm demon-possessed, like in the Bible?"

Luke laughed. "No. I don't think so. But, like all of us, you're susceptible to the tricks of the devil." He leaned toward him. "But you know how to deal with it. You don't always make the right decision. None of us do. But you have the ability to be in control, if you want."

Michael hunched over, elbows on knees, head bowed. "I know." He cleared his throat. Spoke louder. "I know."

Luke prayed. "Lord God, I lift up Michael to you. I thank you that you give him all he needs to control the emotions and desires within him and to use them for your good and for your people. Amen."

"Amen." Michael sat up. "Thank you, Pastor."

Luke smiled. "You're welcome. There's a young lady in this town who, I think, has grown very fond of you. You need to talk with her."

"I will."

Luke's hands went to his ear and patted his pockets. He looked at the desk, scratching his head, his face a mask of bewilderment. Michael reached over and opened the Bible to the place Luke had marked with his pencil.

"Ahh." Luke picked up the pencil. "Thanks."

As he stepped into the hall, Martha approached from the kitchen, carrying a basket. "Michael, this is Rachel's dinner. Would you mind bringing it to her? I put enough in for the both of you."

Michael took the basket, remembering the last time he brought Rachel a meal unbidden.

Martha patted his arm. "It's all right. She's expecting it."

CHAPTER 12

Thursday, June 20, 1878

MICHAEL HESITATED AS he approached the door to *Rachel's Hope*. Would he take away some of that hope? The dinner basket pulled on his arm, a burden far beyond its actual weight. She said she wanted to get to know him. What if she changed her mind after she learned what he had done in his life? What if that was more than she needed or wanted to know?

The bell over the door announced his arrival. Rachel swept aside the curtain to her workroom with one hand, the other tucking loose strands of hair behind her ear. Her face broke into the warmest smile he had ever seen, eyes dancing. Her rapid steps, almost a skip, brought her before him.

"That's quite a bruise you've got there."

He fingered his jaw. "Deserved it, too."

"So I understand. Annabelle told me this morning."

"Guess I can't keep any secrets from you."

The teasing in the corners of her eyes faded. "I don't want you to."

He handed her the basket. "This is from Martha. She asked me to deliver it."

"Thank you." She placed the basket on the counter and looked inside. "There's enough for two in here."

He held up his hands. "Don't look at me. It was Martha's idea."

Rachel chuckled. "Ever the matchmaker."

Her hands rested on the sides of the basket as if she didn't know what to do with them.

His heart fluttered, the beat rapid, mouth dry, palms damp with sweat. He coughed and wiped his hands on his pants. "Rachel, I need to apologize. I've been meaner than an old goat since I got back to town. I haven't treated you right. Can you forgive me?"

She studied him, her violet eyes a miner's drill, probing, seeking the mother lode of his heart. *God, help me reveal it to her.*

She held her hands at her waist, fingers woven together. "I forgive you, Michael. I don't understand what happened, but I forgive you."

He ran his fingers along the edge of the counter, finding it hard to look into her eyes. Could he tell her? How could he not? Seeing her open and vulnerable reminded him of how much he cared for her, desired her. So tempting not to tell her, to bury it, to pretend.

No. No more pretending. No more secrets. No more lies.

But what if it means losing her? Then she'll be lost but she'll be free, not deceived.

"Do you want to know what happened?"

"Yes." No hesitation, no doubt. Confident.

Postpone it. Make plans to see her tonight. Tell her then.

Coward.

He walked to the door and flipped her open sign to closed, turned back to her. "Better sit down. This may take a while."

He followed her into her workroom, failing in his efforts to not notice the gentle sway of her walk. She hooked the curtain back, leaving the room open to the store. She folded the dress spread out on her worktable and placed it to one side.

Her slender fingers mesmerized him as she spread a cloth and then arranged the meal Martha prepared onto plates. He helped her fetch the teapot and cups from the store and enjoyed the brush of his hands against hers as they gathered the supplies.

"Lord," he prayed. "We thank you for this food." He paused. "I ask you to bless our time together. Help me to speak the words you want spoken. Open our hearts to hear each other and you."

She cut a piece of chicken and placed the bite in her mouth. Delicate movements that enthralled him. Her eyes met his, open, friendly, direct. "What do you want to tell me?"

He swallowed, stomach knotted. "I care for you, Rachel. More than I've ever cared for a woman. I want us to have a future together."

She smiled, a soft, hesitant smile that said something he couldn't decipher. "I'm listening."

He hesitated. *Lord, this is so hard.* "I need you to know who I am, my past, my secrets. If we do have a future, it will be because it's something you want even after hearing what I have to say."

She put her cutlery down, interlocked her fingers under her chin. "Go on."

"I killed my father when I was fourteen."

→⊨◉ ◉⊨←

Her mind went blank, and Michael's image blurred. She wanted to cover her ears. Instead, she rubbed her forehead, trying to erase the creases she knew must be there. *Killed his father?*

She remembered his reaction to Mark, the tension in his muscles, the strength to lift Mark off the boardwalk, the punch.

In the jail cell, she again saw the anger that flushed his face, clenched his jaw, his threat to the other prisoners. She realized he would have killed the Mexican if he could have reached him.

Lord, I hadn't planned on this. This is the man you want me to marry? I've been hit by men before, but none had a punch like Michael used on Mark. None displayed the anger I saw in that cell.

How could she be free if this man could injure or kill her? How could she be honest if she never knew what might fuel his anger and trigger the explosion? The explosion that could cause damage beyond recovery.

She looked at her hands in her lap, and saw the dream of her store teetering, her dream of a family and children fading, dissipating like smoke in the wind.

But the vision seemed so real. Was it just an illusion? A fantasy set off by loneliness, concern for the posse, a desire for love? Did Michael represent her idol of a man, or was he the real thing? The vision came to mind as it did every morning upon awakening and every evening when she lay down on her bed, as it did so often throughout the day. Her hope, the beacon of her future.

She forced her feet to stay put, told her body to be still.

"This is the man I have chosen to be your husband."

I know, but….

"I knew this was in him. I will protect you. I need you to help heal him."

How? I don't know how to help him. I don't know how to love him. I'm scared.

"I will be with you. I will show you."

→▰◼ ◼▰←

The fear in her eyes shot like arrows. Michael regretted his words as soon as fear clamped down on her. She seemed to curl into herself like a porcupine. The silence dragged. *How to pull the words back? Can't. This is it. My future in eight words. My future balanced on her reaction.*

He searched her face as she looked anywhere but at him. His mouth dried, sawdust coated his tongue. Any words withered like grass in a hot August sun.

She lifted her head. Her cheek twitched, her eyes narrow and guarded. She licked her lips. *Such sweet-looking lips.* He longed to feel them on his. *Won't happen now.*

"Tell me about it." Her voice soft, trembling. She swallowed and asked again, the tremble under control.

He told his story of growing up, more than he had ever told anyone, even Zechariah. The drunken beatings, there never being enough money, the hunger, the clothes that were sometimes all patches, the lustful rages inflicted on Ellie as she matured. The final day. His mother dead at his father's hand. The drunken attack on Ellie. The day he released the monster for the first time. The pitchfork. He didn't tell of the satisfaction he felt when the farm tool penetrated his father's leg, striking bone, blood spurting.

He told of running, of drifting through cities, stealing to feed and clothe himself, developing a taste for whiskey, learning to use others for his own gain, cheating and manipulating them. Of fighting and hurting people. At first it was for money. Later the violence provided its own satisfaction.

He told of meeting Zechariah, and Jesus, and of the monster always lurking under the surface, always looking to get out, the battle to keep it under control.

Throat dry, he poured more tea. She seemed to recoil when he reached across to pour hers. Her thank you was tentative. He sipped, studying her over the rim. She had the look of a rabbit seeking a quick escape from a lurking predator.

He put the cup down.

"On the posse, I thought I had it under control when I shot a horse instead of the man riding it, but then I wanted to smash my rifle butt into his face because of what they had done to Vernon and the others.

"At the cabin, I tried to shoot just to wound or to provide cover fire for Jeremiah. Then he got shot, and that woman threatened Sam with a knife, using him as a shield."

His voice cracked. "Jeremiah said I had to shoot her. Said I was the only one with a shot. I didn't want to. I was afraid I'd hit Sam. I could feel the monster hovering over me, urging me."

The scene replayed in his mind in slow motion. The rifle in his hands, cheek against the stock, eye squinting down the barrel, finger on the trigger. The woman's head a small dot over Sam's shoulder. He fired. She flew back against the wall of the cabin.

"I killed her."

He stopped. The words hung in the air like those huge hot air balloons he had seen somewhere in his past. Floating, drifting. Almost oppressive in their closeness.

Rachel stood, a quick movement, a rapid stride to the entry to the store. She turned, leaned against the frame, arms folded in front of her. "Did you enjoy it? Did it feel good to shoot her?"

Her eyes pierced him, seeking the truth.

"No. I didn't enjoy it. It felt horrible to take another life."

"Even someone who was going to kill someone else, who had killed people you knew and liked?"

"I prayed there was some other way to end it, to wound her, to negotiate. Anything. But there wasn't. She was going to cut Sam's throat, even knowing she would die anyway."

"Did you enjoy it when you punched Mark that first night?"

He thought. "No. I wanted him to leave you alone, but he wouldn't listen."

She smirked. "That was Mark."

She was silent, eyes closed, face frowning.

After a few moments, she moved to stand in front of him, cradled his face in her hands, guiding him to look at her. "You've beaten that monster, Michael.

You've controlled it. You just don't believe it. You call it a monster. It was at one time. Now it's something for you to use for justice, to protect God's people. Don't fear it anymore."

"How do you know?" *I want to believe you, believe there is a future for us.*

She sighed, released his face, hugged her elbows. "I can't explain it. I just know in my heart this monster you fear is defeated. The only way its evil can come back is if you let it. And God can help you not do that."

She stroked his cheek and returned to her side of the table. "Now eat your dinner. I've got to open this store soon."

→▸═◉ ◉═◂←

Rachel broke off a piece of biscuit, coated it with honey, and popped it in her mouth. *Thank you, God, for showing me the goodness in Michael, for showing me he won't hurt me, for showing me you will protect me. For showing me the vision was real, not a fantasy.*

She smiled at the man across from her. "Did anything else unusual happen on the trail?"

Michael seemed to ponder the question, his mind searching. "Caleb came to Jesus."

"That's all?"

"That's all I can think of. Why?"

"Just curious. You didn't experience anything different during your time in prayer?"

"Like what?"

"I don't know. I just think that sometimes in a situation like that, all that time on the trail, all the tension, some people might experience a closer connection with God."

"Oh, that. Yeah. Prayed a whole lot more. Felt his hand guiding us. It was good to be with Old Thomas." Tears welled. His voice choked when he spoke. "He was a good man, very close to the Creator as his people knew him. Old Thomas had insights that were so biblical you'd think he'd gone to seminary."

"I would've liked to have known him better."

Michael nodded.

Rachel bit back her irritation and the urge to ask if God had told him anything about her, about them. *Did God give him a vision too? Or, was he like most men, too dumb to see something from God?*

I need to know. I can't blurt out God wants us to be married if He hasn't told Michael. Now, what do I do?

CHAPTER 13

Friday, June 21, 1878

CALEB WATCHED THE prisoners eat, hand on his pistol. Part of him wanted one of them to try something, anything. Give him an excuse to shoot. Give him the satisfaction of avenging Vernon and Sam and Old Thomas and the others. He realized he didn't need them to do anything. He could shoot, and no one in town would doubt they'd attempted to escape. His fingers tightened on his weapon, drawing it part way out of its holster.

He squeezed his eyes tight, and released his grip. The weapon settled into its place. He thought of the letter on the table at home. Not much of a letter so far, a piece of paper with today's date. He'd started it before he came in, couldn't think of the right words, and left it.

The one called Jack looked up from his half-eaten food. "When does the judge get here?"

Caleb shrugged. "Don't rightly know. Could be today. Maybe tomorrow."

Jack nodded, looked at the floor. "That soon? Good."

"Good?"

"Yeah. I just want to get this over with."

"Even if it means hanging?"

Jack lifted his head. Sadness surrounded him like clouds around a mountaintop. "Maria's gone."

Caleb massaged the back of his neck. Can't figure this bunch out. What drove them? What was it about Maria that triggered the love he heard in Jack's voice?

"You didn't know her." Jack's words broke through his thoughts. "Before this, before her father got sick, before she found out how Carstairs had cheated and framed him."

Jack swallowed. "She loved her father. More than anything. More than me. Her mother died when she was six, and he raised her. She wanted to be like a son to him, so she learned to shoot, and go on cattle raids, and sell the cattle for a profit. Everything she did was for him because he couldn't do for himself. That time in prison wore him out."

"How long had you known her?"

"We were married five years."

The door to the street opened. A waiter from the hotel came in, a large wooden tray tucked under his arm.

"Meal time's up." Caleb barked the words. "Plates, forks and spoons on the floor next to the door. Stand against the back wall."

One of the Mexicans continued eating with slow movements, glaring at Caleb.

"*Ahora mismo.*" Caleb snapped the words like a bullwhip as he pulled his Colt from the holster and cocked it. He caressed the trigger. *Go ahead. Give me a reason.*

Stew tumbled down the man's chest as he dropped the spoon. He retrieved it from the floor and put it and the plate next to the cell door. He raised his hands and backed to the brick wall, eyes wide, never leaving the pistol.

Caleb nodded to the waiter. The man scurried under Caleb's hand and rattled the plates and utensils onto the tray. He duck-walked backward into the office proper before standing upright and almost running out the door.

Caleb closed the connecting door, returned to his desk and stared at the paper left there by the mayor that morning. The man wanted an accounting of every item used by the posse, right down to the number of bullets fired and pounds of flour used to make biscuits. He weighed the paper in his hand, eying the stove, toying with the idea of burning it and telling the mayor one of the prisoners ate it.

If Malachi was sober, he could do this standing on one leg. The man had a head for figures. Blindfolded, he could tell how many drinks were left in a whiskey bottle by hefting it in one hand.

Caleb pushed the paper to the corner of the desk and put his rock paperweight on it.

A shadow passed the window, and the door opened. A rail-thin man, short, with a shock of white hair spilling over the collar of his black coat walked in. The man beat the dust from his clothing with his black Stetson and extended his hand.

"Afternoon, Caleb. Got here as fast as I could."

"I appreciate that, Judge Howard."

The judge took the chair across the desk while Caleb poured coffee into a mug for him. Howard took a small flask from his inside pocket and added a generous dash to the coffee. "Roads are dry this time of year. Man works up a terrible thirst."

In the fifteen years Caleb had known Judge Howard, the roads were dry every time of year, and coffee always needed fortifying. But he was sober at trials, gave defendants a fair hearing, and sentenced the guilty according to the crime and circumstances. Couldn't ask for more than that.

"How many prisoners? What're the charges?"

"Three prisoners. Charged with the kidnap and murder of Sam Carstairs, Mark Carstairs, Vernon Phelps and five others."

"Vernon? Sam? I think with Mark it was only a matter of time before someone killed him. But still…." His voice trailed off. "Vernon. Sam. Good men in their own ways. Tough for the town to lose them both. What about Vernon's nephew?"

Caleb spoke around the rock of grief and anger in his throat. "Killed. The kidnappers ambushed them, and slashed their throats."

Howard held up his hand. "Save the rest for the trial. Mortimer Anderson going to defend them?"

"He's the only lawyer we've got."

"Well, I know he'll give them the best defense he can. You going to prosecute?"

"It's either me or the mayor."

Howard rolled his eyes. "It's you. By judicial decree. Can't give Anderson too many advantages." He winked at Caleb. "Or open the door to charges of judicial bias against the prosecution."

Howard sipped his coffee, trickled in a little more fortification. "Trial like this is going to attract a lot of people. Where can we hold it?"

"Pastor Luke said we can use the church. Should be big enough."

Howard chuckled. "Seems fitting that justice should be dispensed from the house of God." He opened the gold pocket watch he pulled from his vest. He closed it with a solid snick. "It's too late in the day to start the trial now." He gestured with his mug. "Need to fortify myself after the ride over here and clean off the trail dust. Let's say tomorrow morning at nine."

"That's fine. I'll get word to Anderson and the rest of the town."

"Think you'll have any problems getting a jury?"

"None at all. Plenty have already volunteered."

Howard stood, settled his hat on his head, and drained his coffee. "In the morning, Sheriff."

CHAPTER 14

Friday, June 21, 1878

THE STEAK SETTLED into Michael's mouth like butter on a hot biscuit, warm and smooth. Supper at the parsonage. Good food. Seasoned with Martha's love for her family. Good family.

Rachel sat across from him, delicate bites of food slipping between those full lips. A warm smile every time their eyes met. For the first time since the shooting, peace. A gossamer, fragile peace. One that could blow away on the slightest breeze. One he dare not contemplate for too long lest it melt like spring snow. With the peace, hope. For his future with Rachel.

Rachel hadn't rejected him, had helped him see with greater clarity what Jeremiah and Luke tried to tell him about the power within him. Not a monster, but a tool for good. His choice to control, to tame. Not a beast that could never be repressed. Use it for God? Could he?

The conversation drifted over and around him like the river running over rocks. Tinkling, bubbling. Laughter. Joy. Could he and Rachel have something like this someday? Would she want it too, with him? Would he be able to give it to her, to learn to love her as God wanted her loved? For the first time he was confident he could.

After supper, Luke tried to teach him the game of chess while Rachel and Abigail helped Martha clean up. The game mystified him; the nuances frustrated him, and Daniel's superior knowledge embarrassed him.

"It takes a while to get the hang of it," Luke said. "Once you're settled here, we'll have more time to practice."

Michael looked toward the kitchen. Settled here? Not without Rachel. "We'll see."

"It's a good town, Michael. I think you'd do well here."

"Some things will have to be taken care of first."

"What do you mean?"

Michael hesitated, stopped the words he really wanted to say. His gaze drifted toward the kitchen again. "I need to go back to Zechariah. Make sure he doesn't need me. Get his blessing."

Luke leaned back in his chair. "I understand. It's important to be released to come. I think God has a work for you in Riverbend, but it'll be good to get Zechariah's counsel. You know it'll be honest."

"And to the point. Bluntness is one of his most endearing qualities."

Luke snorted. "Years ago, I really wanted to teach in seminary, but I had several offers to pastor. Zechariah wagged that sausage of a finger in my face, froze me with those grey eyes, and said, 'You need to pastor, boy. The people need you. The seminary don't.' He was right. Hard work, but I've never looked back, never regretted it."

Michael chuckled. "He told me not to even think about being a pastor. 'Be a helper, a servant. You're not called to lead a congregation.' I know he's right. I can't handle people and sermons and church business like you do."

"And I couldn't do it without Martha."

The two ladies walked into the room trailed by Abigail. Martha scooped Daniel into her arms from Luke's knee. "Luke, help me put these two offspring to bed. It's your turn to tell the bedtime stories."

Confusion crossed Luke's face. "I thought I did it last night."

Michael caught the slight jerk of Martha's head toward Rachel. "You didn't finish the story."

Realization dawned. "Oh. Right. Come on, you two. Off to bed."

Daniel managed to drag the good nights out another five minutes before he stomped up the stairs.

Muffled voices seeped through the ceiling into the otherwise quiet room.

Michael appreciated Martha's orchestration to leave him alone with Rachel, but he felt like all power of speech had left his mouth. Thoughts formed, words took shape, yet his tongue sat there like a broken saddle cinch.

"Shall we sit outside on the porch and enjoy the night air?" Rachel's voice danced in his ears like a cardinal's song.

"I would enjoy that," he managed to squeak out. At least the tongue was working again, even if the words weren't brilliant.

She draped a shawl over her shoulders and sat next to him on the glider swing. Her hair was still in a bun, but he enjoyed how strands had worked their way loose and framed her face. "You look real pretty tonight."

She blushed.

He coughed, trying to clear the cotton wad from his throat. "Rachel, when I left with the posse, you said you wanted to get to know me better. I've been a fool since we returned, but I need to know if you still feel that way. If you don't, I understand. I know I've given you plenty of reason to question my…my worthiness, I guess. If the answer's 'No,' I won't bother you again."

Her eyes seemed to search his face as if she was seeking hidden treasure. She put her hand on his arm. "I do want to know you better, Michael. Our talk at dinner helped me understand a lot about you, about what you've been through. I need to know more."

She bit her lower lip, shifted her gaze to somewhere up the road. The breeze stirred her hair. He clasped his hands to keep from reaching for it, knowing he would want more. A whole lot. Something he had no right to take.

She squeezed his arm. "I think God has a purpose for you and me. Something I need to be sure you share and believe in. So I need to know more, and I will try to be patient while I wait for God to show it to both of us."

Chapter 15

Saturday, June 22, 1878

Michael maneuvered through the crowd outside the door of the church. Not even eight-thirty and the building was crammed, every available seat taken. People stood along the back wall and up the outside aisles. Open windows let a breeze enter, which helped relieve the heat of so many bodies and so much emotion. Michael wondered how many had set foot in the church for the first time today.

Deputy Henry Jordan motioned him forward and escorted him to a pew reserved for the members of the posse. Bill Barkston's hand dwarfed his, the grip firm. Bill's other hand gripped his upper arm. The circulation to his fingers dropped.

Harold and Frank nodded their greetings. Martin flashed a lopsided grin. Malachi slumped at the far end, face pale, sunken eyes fastened straight ahead, the aroma of whiskey still lingering despite a bath, shave and haircut. Michael suspected there was a flask hidden in the folds of the sling.

The first two rows of pews on the right side were empty, reserved for the jury. The prisoners sat in the first pew on the left, bookended by Pete O'Brien and another deputy Michael didn't recognize. The second pew on the left was empty. Henry Jordan stood by it to make sure it stayed that way.

In place of the pulpit, a table and chair for the judge had been set up. The witness seat was to the right of the table. In front of each bank of pews stood another table and chair. Caleb sat at the one at the right, drumming his fingers, checking his watch. A large man with a square block of a head covered by thick, black hair and a long beard sat at the table to the left, turned so he could talk to the prisoners, taking notes.

The murmuring crowd hushed, the silence moving like a wave from back to front. A short man with the whitest hair Michael had ever seen strode to the front with a swagger that preached authority far beyond his physical stature. He stepped onto the platform without breaking stride.

The man's deliberateness and seeming obliviousness to the crowd struck Michael. The behavior said, "I am in control here." He took a sheaf of papers, ink well, pen, and several pencils from the satchel he carried, organizing them on the desk. Next, he took a thick book and placed it on a corner.

The last thing he removed from what seemed to be a bottomless magician's bag was a round block of wood, which he placed on the table. After putting the bag under the table, he pulled a large Colt revolver from the holster hidden under his coat. Holding it by the barrel, he rapped the butt on the wood three times.

The silence became even more profound.

"I am Judge Hiram H. Howard, and this court is now in session." He didn't shout, but his voice seemed to carry to the people crammed at the rear doors.

"Are the prosecution and defense ready to proceed?" He glanced at Caleb and then at the other man. Both affirmed. "Good to see you again, Mortimer. How's the family?"

"Very well, Sir." Mortimer Anderson's voice was a mellow baritone that seemed capable of soothing the most troubled of legal waters.

Irritation niggled at the edges of Michael's mind as the process of selecting a jury entered its second hour. "Is he always this fussy about picking a jury?" he whispered.

"Yes." The gravel of Bill's whisper rattled in Michael's ear. "Above everything else, he's fair."

From the other side of Bill, Frank mumbled, "These guys weren't fair to Sam and Vernon."

The judge's pistol rapped on the wood block. "Quiet." He turned the pistol so he held it by the grip. "This instrument of justice keeps order in my court room two ways."

Fair? Michael thought of Judge Abraham Barrett, the one who sentenced him for picking pockets, who sentenced Ben to hang, who wouldn't hear Gideon's plea for more time to prove the young man's innocence. He thought of other judges he had faced over the years. Fairness seemed like some politician's fantasy to get votes. Michael closed his eyes in gratitude that, in Jesus, he found genuine fairness and more. Grace, mercy, forgiveness. And maybe a woman's love.

After Judge Howard swore in the jury, testimony began. It went fast. Caleb called two witnesses, Bill and Martin. The two were able to place all three of the prisoners with the kidnappers.

Michael respected Mortimer Anderson's attempts to provide a defense for his clients, even though the situation was hopeless. Michael found himself wishing he had known the lawyer prior to coming to Jesus. Might have saved him from some legal grief, gotten Michael acquitted on a few of his charges, even though he was usually guilty.

They were done by noon. The jury returned a guilty verdict within minutes. Shouts of approval rose until cut off by the rap of the judge's pistol banging on his wood block. The judge ordered them transported to the territorial prison for execution.

Murmurs reached Michael's ear. "Hanging's too good for them." "Thank the Lord, it's over."

A voice from the rear shouted, "Let's hang 'em now."

Bradshaw.

Michael stood and found the man standing against the back wall. Bradshaw seemed to shrink under Michael's gaze. Bill stood as well, muttering. "Fool. That's not what Vernon stood for, not what he would've wanted."

Michael found Esther Phelps a few rows behind him; eyes squinted closed as if trying to block out the man's words.

"Bring that man up here." The judge's voice rang to the rafters and bounced off the back wall. Michael and Bill walked him before the judge, Bradshaw wincing under the firmness of their grips.

"Deputy O'Brien, is this the man who tried to implement some vigilante justice the other night?"

"Yes, Judge, that he is."

Bradshaw pointed at Michael who stood to his left. "Judge, this man threatened to kill me."

Just what I need. My stupidity laid out before the whole town.

"Mr. Archer was acting as me special deputy," Said Pete. "The shotgun 'tweren't loaded, yer Honor." Pete's defense sounded feeble under the glare of the judge.

"I didn't know that." Bradshaw's voice rose to a reedy whine. "I thought he was going to blow a hole in my chest."

The judge frowned, glanced at Michael, back at Bradshaw. "You don't seem to know much, sir. Especially about justice." He rapped his pistol. "I find you in contempt of this court, and a few other things."

Bradshaw opened his mouth.

"Be quiet. You'll only make it worse if you try to speak."

The judge stroked his chin, eyes toward the ceiling. "I'm not going to add to the town's financial burden by sentencing you to time in jail." He focused on Bradshaw. "Instead, I fine you twenty-five dollars."

"I ain't got that kind of money, Judge."

"I can have Deputy O'Brien turn you upside down and shake it out of your pants right now."

Bradshaw paled, reached into his pocket and pulled out some coins, placed a twenty-dollar coin and a five-dollar coin on the judge's table. Howard nodded at Caleb, who picked up the money.

"I don't think you'll be requiring a receipt, will you, sir?" The judged smiled at Bradshaw.

"N…No, your honor."

"You're free to go." As Bradshaw left, the judge pointed at Michael and motioned him forward with his finger.

"You're Michael Archer." Not a question, a statement. His tone was low, two men having a quiet conversation after the trial.

"Yes, your honor."

"Under any other circumstances, I would have you arrested and charged with at least assault for what you did to Bradshaw the other night, special deputy or not. Sheriff Davis and Deputy O'Brien told me all about it." He paused, eyes holding Michael like a vise. "Because of what you did to save Sam Carstairs, you have some special favor in this town. Don't wear it out by being stupid."

Heat rose up Michael's neck and spread to his cheeks. "Yes, your Honor."

Judge Howard picked up his satchel and packed away the tools of his trade.

Michael hesitated to turn around, expecting to see everyone staring at him. When he did, only Rachel looked at him, her expression unreadable. He wished he could disappear through the floor.

⤙══ ◎═══⤚

The afternoon galloped away for Caleb. So much to do, and it needed to be done quickly. He arranged for the wagon to transport the prisoners, oversaw the installation of bolts to secure their chains. Who to send? Pete was the logical choice, but Caleb couldn't part with him, couldn't spare him for the five days it would take for the round trip. Besides, he was newly married. Just didn't seem fair. In the end, he assigned one of his other regular deputies and two of the auxiliaries to take the prisoners.

Dusk settled over the town as he finished arrangements for horses, food and other supplies.

He returned to his small home, turned up the lantern on the kitchen table. The single sheet of paper beckoned. He sat. Picked up the pencil, licked the point. Hesitated. Put the pencil down.

He stared out the window at the creeping darkness. Trial completed. Justice served. Why did it feel so hollow? The emptiness of the night echoed what was in his heart. Vernon gone. Alexander gone. Sam gone. The nightmare of leading men into battle to watch them die flashed through his mind. So much waste in that war. So little accomplished in each battle. This kidnapping seemed the same way. Criminals brought to justice but Sam and Mark and six other men died. He did his job. Why did he feel like such a failure?

Worn down. That's me. Spirit. Body definitely. Each day brought new aches and pains, each morning a little longer to get out of bed. Headaches started pounding earlier each evening. He massaged his temples. The dull ache continued.

Wanted whiskey. Where did that come from? Desire had never been so strong.

His stomach rumbled. Oh, yeah. Hadn't eaten since breakfast. He scanned the small kitchen. Nothing here. Didn't feel like cooking anyways.

He adjusted his hat and glanced at the paper on the table. It would still be there tomorrow. Maybe the words would come then.

-→▬◉ ◉▬◁-

Rachel's lips met his, soft, tender, sweet. The taste reminded Michael of fresh strawberries. Did she even eat strawberries? A lingering kiss fulfilling every promise he ever imagined. Her body pressed against him, her arms tight around him. They melded together, a perfect fit. The meadow by the river, soft breeze, the water like music. He lowered her to the cloth they had spread for their food, food still in the basket....

He sat up, heart pounding. His hotel room? Darkness outside. Lamp dim. A dream? He reached for it, wanting to pull it back, to make it his reality. It swished away, a vapor eluding his grasp, slipping through his fingers.

A dream. So real. So vivid. Would it ever be his reality? Or always a fantasy? Out of reach, his fingertips brushing it, each touch pushing it further away.

He lay back on the bed, arm over his eyes. The image returned, the kiss faint, fading. How could he win her? She wanted to know him better. The urge to rush rose up. How to make it happen now? And not push her away or threaten her independence?

Why does she have to be so complicated? *Why do I feel like a bumpkin, just in from the farm, seeing the big city for the first time?*

This was the first time. The first time he wanted to be with a woman for more than physical pleasure. A whole new world. A language he didn't speak, one he could never learn. Deaf, mute, and blind in Rachel's world. A world of beauty, tender as a buttercup, strong as a mountain, deep and complicated as a canyon.

Was she thinking of him right now? He imagined her with her hair down, brushing it for her, molding it into a shimmering cascade that fell to her shoulders. He stood behind her, studying her in the mirror as her eyes closed and she allowed him to tend to her in such a simple way. Would she ever be that vulnerable? Would she risk her independence for those moments of intimacy? Would she let him love her?

Chapter 16

Sunday, June 23, 1878

Turned sideways in their usual pew, Rachel fussed with Abigail's hair, trying to get a braid to come out to the young girl's satisfaction. Her anxious glances toward the door distracted her. Would he come? He seemed so distant after the trial. She'd waited for him, and they walked out together. As they strolled to *Rachel's Hope*, she tried to talk with him, but his answers were often no more than one word, his face creased in a frown, his attention somewhere else. She'd hinted at having dinner together, but he missed the clues. At the store, he held her hand. She took the initiative to kiss him on the cheek. Her old flirtation skills pushed to be released, but that was the old her, never to be used again.

She looked past the people entering, some of whom frowned when they saw her, disapproval evident. People still talked, still commented that someone like her had no place in the front pew. The hurt from the stares and jibes, from the leers and fumbling hands, stung. She tried to walk in forgiveness as Luke and Martha explained, but she wanted to lash back. Just once. Surely God would forgive her giving one smite?

Even now, her fingers clawed as Mrs. Bradshaw entered, nudged her husband and gestured at her. *If you only knew what I learned about fighting in the brothel.* Mr. Bradshaw made no attempt to disguise his smile. A leer from eyebrows to lips. *And I'd like to show you what I learned about putting men in their place if they came on too strong, squirming, doubled over in pain, hands covering vulnerable areas.*

"Ow! Aunt Rachel. That hurt." Abigail's cry brought Rachel back to church.

"I'm sorry, sweetheart. Didn't mean to tug so hard."

Martha walked up, holding Daniel's hand. "This boy picks the strangest times to need the outhouse. And if I don't stay with him, who knows what'll he get into."

Daniel plunged his finger up one nostril and examined what he found.

"See what I mean." Martha pulled a handkerchief from her sleeve and wiped the boy's finger.

"Momma, can you fix my hair?" Abigail turned her back to her mother. "Aunt Rachel keeps pulling it, not getting it right."

Martha peered at Rachel. "Can't get it right? Abigail's hair? I thought you could do it blindfolded."

"Too many distractions."

Martha scanned the congregation. "Is Michael here?"

"No. The other kind." Rachel gave a slight nod in the direction of the Bradshaws.

Martha snorted. "Don't know what she's fretting about. A woman would have to be blind and have no sense of smell to want to get near him."

Rachel covered Abigail's ears. "Martha."

Martha placed her hand over her lips. "There I go again."

"And this one's growing up very fast. She's going to pick up on these things very soon."

"I know. Pray for me to learn to control my mouth."

"Everyday, my love." Luke spoke from behind her. His eyes widened as he glanced at the doors. "Never thought I'd see this. Look who's…" His voice trailed off as he strode down the aisle.

Rachel turned. Joshua and Lupe Carstairs stood inside the door, faces confused, eyes searching. Rachel stood and waved. The couple walked forward as Luke greeted them and escorted them to the pew behind Rachel.

She gave Lupe a brief hug. "I'm so glad to see you here." She extended her hand. "Good morning, Joshua. Welcome to Riverbend Church."

He gave her hand a brief shake. "Thank you." He put his arm around his wife. "Lupe wanted to come."

Awe tinged Martha's voice. "Will wonders never cease?"

Rachel followed her gaze to the back of the church. Michael. Michael was here, standing between two men. After a moment, she realized one was the stranger, Jeremiah Turner. Another moment passed until it registered the other man was Caleb Davis. The sheriff? In church? For service?

Where was Luke? Standing next to Martha, eyes wide, and mouth open.

Martha giggled. "The Lord works in mysterious ways."

"His wonders to perform," Luke finished.

Rachel forced herself to breathe as the three men walked up the aisle. Where would Michael sit? With them? With her? Why was it important? Because it would tell her his intentions—or at least give her a hint. She waited as he seemed to dawdle like Daniel getting ready for bed.

She searched his face. He looked out the window, nodded at Pete and Annabelle when he passed their seat. Waved at Bill and Sally Barkston. Smiled at Pastor Luke. His eyes seemed to land on everyone.

Except her.

He picked up Daniel when the boy scurried to him.

Martha's hand on her arm. Comforting. Encouraging. Ready to console if he didn't sit with her?

They reached the pew where Joshua and Lupe sat. Michael stepped aside to allow Caleb to follow the stranger into the bench. He put Daniel down and stepped front of her. Close. Very close. She liked how close.

The green flecks in his hazel eyes seemed to dance. "Good morning, Rachel. May I join you?"

She nodded. Where did her tongue go? It seemed incapable of forming words or any intelligible sound. Best keep it still and her mouth closed.

Daniel tried to worm his way between her and Michael. Rachel picked him up and planted him on her other side, where Martha placed her hand on his shoulder. Rachel noted the tightened grip as Daniel squirmed before settling down, seeming to accept somebody had a stronger claim on Michael.

Did she have a strong claim? Yes, according to the vision God gave her. When would Michael realize it? Did God plan to tell him? When? Was she supposed to? That didn't seem right.

All right, Lord, I need your help here. Show me what to do. I don't want to mess this up.

Nothing. Of course. She sighed. Michael's reaction told her she sighed louder than she intended. She smiled at the quizzical look on his face and turned her attention to the pulpit where Luke waited to start service.

She fought the urge to lean against him. Such boldness did not belong in church. That would really set the tongues wagging. His closeness and its promise of more to come comforted her. She daydreamed of future intimacy. The cloud of being vulnerable to a man crowded the edge of her mind. She pushed it back. *Trust the Father for protection. Trust Michael to respect me.*

At the end of service, Martha placed a hand on Michael's arm, reaching for Rachel's hand with the other. "Michael, will you join us for dinner today?"

Did discomfort or uncertainty flick across his face? He looked past her to the pew where Caleb and the stranger sat. Some communication happened. No words were spoken but doubt left.

His eyes were on her as he answered. "Yes, Miss Martha, it would be a pleasure to join you." His eyes seemed to caress her face. "And your family."

Rachael restrained herself, and allowed a small smile.

"Great." Martha's hand squeezed hers. "Come to the parsonage about an hour after service."

Rachel wanted to hug him, kiss him goodbye, at least on the cheek. *Need to wait. Let God deal with him. But how do I tell him I've changed?*

Michael followed the congregation out the doors, receiving handshakes and pats on the back for what he did on the posse. Uncomfortableness crept up his spine, muscles knotting. He held his arms close to his sides to keep from pushing people away. He chewed his lower lip to bite back the urge to shout, "I am not a hero. Don't make me one. I killed a woman, and Sam died anyway."

Ben was the only person to benefit as he was finally reconciled with his father. But could he enjoy it in heaven? Sam died before he could receive Jesus, receive His salvation. The image of Sam as the rich man in hell, begging for water, and Ben as the beggar Lazarus standing with Abraham in Paradise etched in his mind, the two unable to touch, Ben unable to help.

Jeremiah and Caleb stood at the bottom of the steps to the church.

"She is a beautiful woman." Jeremiah's voice had a hint of awe. "No wonder you're smitten."

Michael glanced back up the now empty stairs. "Yeah, but I don't know what to do. Don't want to push too hard and drive her away."

Caleb snorted. "You young'uns today. Too many fancy ideas about love. When I met my Annie, we knew right off we was to be married. Just took us awhile to convince her folks. If you love the girl, tell her. Tell her you want to marry her."

Michael scratched the back of his neck. "I don't think that will work with Rachel. She's been through a lot. Dead set against any man controlling her, telling her what to do."

They walked in silence, covering the distance from the church to the first buildings of the town in quick strides. Their boots hit the boardwalk in unison, like an army marching in formation.

Michael missed Zechariah. The one man he could talk to. One who would listen; help him make decisions, not send solutions. A friend, mentor. A father. One who was as comfortable in Michael's silences as he was in Michael's words.

Without Zechariah's anchor, Michael felt adrift, a raft floating downriver without rudder or oar, unable to avoid dangers and snags, unable to follow a true course.

When they reached Caleb's office, Michael excused himself and headed for the river. He sought a quiet spot, a place to talk with God. He needed guidance like never before.

The river welcomed him, its waters calm, slight ripples showing its life and movement. The breeze stirred the leaves, a soft rustling against each other. A cardinal chirped. Michael found it, saw its mate flutter to a nearby branch. He wanted to be that male cardinal for Rachel. The watcher. The guardian. The protector.

How to do that and not squash her? From what he'd seen, she would rebel against it, against him.

He wandered a short distance along the riverbank before finding a tree close to the water's edge. The bank was cut away, a dry place a foot or so above the surface. He took off his boots, rolled up his pants, let his feet dangle in the water while he leaned against the tree.

Lord. He stopped, mind blank, the urge to pray for himself stifled. He closed his eyes, waiting. Rachel's face came to mind. He tried again. *Lord, I pray for Rachel, for her happiness, for her peace. I pray for her complete healing from the scars of her past life, that they no longer torment her or cause her to doubt and not trust. I pray you bring a man into her life who will love her, respect her, honor her, cherish her. Not use her. Not control her.*

He swallowed against the lump in his throat, raised his feet out of the water and rested his head on his knees. *Lord God. I put my needs, my desires aside. Yes, I care for Rachel. More than I've ever cared for anyone. Lord, if I'm not the one you want for her, I will step aside. Not my will, not my desire. But yours. I believe you have a man for Rachel. The right man. The best man. Bring him into her life. Soon.*

He leaned his head against the tree, wiped his eyes. The cardinal and its mate flitted to a tree to his right, settling on two of the lower branches. The male cocked his head at Michael and sang a few notes loud, clear.

And Michael knew. A blanket of warmth and comfort and peace settled around him.

Then a voice in his heart. *I have brought that man into her life. But you must finish your assignment first.*

CHAPTER 17

Sunday, June 23, 1878

ASSIGNMENT? WHAT ASSIGNMENT? I fulfilled my promise to Ben. What else is there? Michael's mind spun like a roulette wheel, the ball clattering but never landing in a slot. The wheel slowed, an image emerged. He was back at the kidnappers' cabin, bending over Sam to hear the man's labored whisper. "Clear Ben's name."

Cold clinched Michael's brain. *Clear Ben's name? That's my assignment? Gideon and I tried and couldn't do it. It's impossible.*

Whoever killed the horse trader was too clever or too lucky. All the evidence pointed to Ben. Michael believed in Ben's innocence. Gideon did as well. But their beliefs carried no weight with the judge. They'd searched for clues. They'd questioned witnesses. They'd argued with the judge. What could they do they hadn't already done?

Impossible echoed in his mind. God had given him an impossible task.

I will help you. The voice rang in his spirit, a deep, chest-rumbling vibration like cathedral bells he'd heard in big cities.

Well, at least you know I'll need help. I don't even know where to start.

You won't be alone.

That's good to know. Alone, I'd mess it up something awful.

Rachel. Clearing Ben's name would mean leaving her again, leaving without knowing where he stood with her. What would she think of him, running off again on a mission that seemed even more impossible than the first one? Was he meant to have a relationship with her, or was it just a fantasy because she was so beautiful?

I will take care of her while you obey me.

Michael rested his head on his forearms, sucking deep breaths to slow the blood pounding in his veins. God's promise rang in his heart, but his mind reeled at the prospect of leaving Rachel for a task he wasn't qualified for, and didn't know how to do.

At least he knew where to begin. Tramlaw. But much sooner than he planned. His plan was to stay here until Rachel got to know him enough to where she could decide if they had a future together. Now, he'd leave with that still unresolved.

Sadness slowed his moves as he slid on his boots and walked back to town. At Main Street, he hesitated. To his left, the hotel. A place to brood and question. And to feel sorry for himself. To his right, the parsonage, and Rachel. The woman he loved and desired, the focal point of his future.

He turned right.

-->==◎ ◎==<--

Daniel greeted him at the gate, the puppy at his heels. Michael squatted and received the boy's hug, the arms around his neck reminding him of Ellie. The dog yapped and jumped, licked his face. The only dog they'd had as children was a mean, old, brown mongrel that mirrored their father's personality. It snapped and bit at him and Ellie, and his father laughed and urged the beast on. His father shot the dog when it attacked their milk cow, and cried afterwards while he got drunk. Michael shoved the memory back in the hole where he hid his childhood.

Rachel appeared on the porch. No sound of the door or footsteps. No words of greeting. One moment the porch was empty. The next she was there. His heart lurched. Her light brown dress with its pattern of yellow and blue flowers could have been painted on. Her bare toes peeked out from under the hem. Her brown hair flowed to her shoulders, gentle curls cascading around her face. Her lips parted in a smile, warm, inviting, happy to see him.

He hoped.

He stepped on the porch, only dimly aware of Daniel holding his hand and the puppy tugging at the bottom of his pants.

"You're early for dinner." Her violet eyes roamed his face, the eyes that were the last thing he saw when he closed his own at night. The eyes he imagined lying next to him when he woke in the morning, inviting him to linger before beginning the day.

"I need to talk to you." He wished he could pull the abrupt words from the air as she stepped back, concern crinkling her eyes and mouth, the face he would never want to hurt. "I apologize. That didn't come out right. I didn't intend to frighten you."

"I've never heard you speak like that." She paused. "At least sober, anyway. You didn't frighten me, but I was ready to pop you one if I needed to."

"I've no doubt of that." He cleared his throat. "Can we start over?"

"I think you should." She had the teasing tone he'd grown to treasure, but he heard the strong independent streak. He could never intimidate her, even if he wanted to.

He bowed at the waist. "Miss Rachel Stone, would you have a few moments you could spare so we might discuss some matters?"

She extended her hand, fingers pointing down. He took it, skimmed his lips on the back. "Why, Mr. Archer, I do believe my schedule allows for a brief moment in which we might converse." She gave schedule the English pronunciation he'd heard used in stage productions.

He continued holding her hand, the burden on his soul lifting in her lighthearted presence.

He gestured toward the front gate. "Shall we stroll?"

She took a step forward, stopped, looked down. "No shoes. How forgetful. I'll be right back." She skipped back into the house, Daniel and the puppy following.

Michael stayed on the porch, wanting to prolong the moment, the touch of her hand under his lips, the smile and hints of laughter, the aroma of lilacs on her skin.

He faced the sun, letting its warmth suffuse him. A beautiful day and a beautiful woman to share it with.

Clouded by the news he had to tell her.

After a few minutes, she was back, shoes on, hair pulled back and tucked under a bonnet, shawl around her shoulders. Outside the gate, she slipped her arm around his and guided him away from the town. "Let's go this way. There's a place I want to show you."

He followed her lead, enjoying her company, postponing what he wanted to say so as to not ruin their time together. Waiting for the right moment.

They talked of the morning's service and the surprise of seeing Caleb and Joshua. Lupe had been attending the last couple of weeks, but Joshua's attendance was unexpected, as he always seemed to have his father's attitude about God.

Rachel grew silent.

"Is everything all right?" he asked.

She sighed. "I was just thinking about seeing the Bradshaws this morning. She gave me a look that was pure poison. He leered at me like the customers in Denver. I think the mayor was going to as well until I smiled and offered to shake his hand."

She tightened her grip on his arm. "Sometimes I get so tired of the looks and the leers and snide remarks, I just want to punch some of those holier-than-thou women in the nose and kick their husbands in the...never mind. You know what I mean."

He covered her hand with his. "I do. That has to be hard. I know when I started to work with Zechariah, some of the congregation and townspeople didn't like it. They thought I'd be better as the town drunk. I can't imagine what it's been like for you."

"It's been harder than I thought, but Martha and Annabelle and Mrs. Phelps have been with me since I got here." She laughed, a dry, sardonic laugh. "And most of the men keep their distance now after they heard about Mark and the scissors."

"Time. They need more time to get to know you."

"I think you're right. In the last couple of weeks, I've had three women order dresses who, a few weeks ago, looked at me as if I was something that needed to be cleaned off the streets with a shovel."

"Maybe, after Mark, they're realizing you're not the threat to their marriages they thought you were."

"Could be."

She pointed to a trail that ran off the road. "Let's go in here."

The trail was narrow, the undergrowth low. She led the way, holding his hand in a loose grip. After about thirty yards, she ducked under a tree limb and stepped into a small clearing surrounded by pines. Fallen needles cushioned the thick carpet of soft grass. Branches swayed in the breeze softened the air and dappled the sunshine, their sweet, pungent aroma drifting on the wind.

Silence. Like a church. Reverent. Welcoming.

She stood a few feet away, hands at her sides. "I found this searching for Daniel one day. This is his place to track Indians. It's one of my places to be alone with God, to think, to pray."

"I can see why." He clenched his fists, nails digging into his palms, as desire welled up. Desire he had to control.

She took a step forward. He stepped back. Confusion shrouded her face, clouded her eyes.

"I'm sorry," he stuttered. "You're so beautiful standing there, glowing in the sun. I wanted—want—to do things I shouldn't."

She took her lower lip between her teeth, eyes downcast, hands clasped at her waist. "I'm sorry."

"Rachel." His tone was sharper then he intended. He didn't care. "You have nothing to be sorry for. It's me who should apologize to you for letting my desires almost get the best of me."

He wanted to step closer but dared not. He swallowed. "I think I love you."

"Think?" Her face was calm, no teasing.

He nodded. "I've never felt about a woman the way I feel about you." He put his hands in his pockets, kicked at a tuff of grass. "It's more than the physical desire. I want to be with you, to share a life with you. When I think of life without you, it's an empty black hole, like the night sky when the clouds hide the stars. Cold and raw like rain in January."

He shrugged. "I don't know what else to call it but love."

Her arms were around his neck. He embraced her, lifting her off the ground, holding her.

She broke away, took a step back, and wiped her cheeks. "I'm very happy to hear you say that." Her voice quavered. "I'm not very good at this, but I know I love you, too." She held up a hand. "And that's as new for me as it is for you. So we're going to have to figure this out together."

He took her hand, kissed the palm. "Yes, we are."

"But I don't think this is all you wanted to talk to me about."

"No." Once again, the power of speech deserted him. Her eyes didn't help; neither did her lips being so close. "I have to leave again."

"Oh." Her head dropped, eyes lowered, the word almost indecipherable.

He waited.

Her face pale, she hugged her arms close to herself. "Why?"

"At the end, just before he died, Sam said something to me, something I've ignored until today. Sam told me, 'Clear Ben's name.' I was praying at the river before I came to see you. I heard the Lord say my assignment wasn't finished, I had to do what Sam asked. Has God ever spoken to you real clear and direct?"

The vision played out before her.

"Yes." Dare she tell him? What would it change? He would still leave. Would he return? The vision said he would. How else could he be her husband?

"That's what this feels like, Rachel. I don't know how I'm going to do it, but I feel like I have to try."

She walked a few steps away, turned. "When are you leaving?"

->=◉ ◉=<-

The lantern cast a dim light on the kitchen table, his hands, the paper and pencil in the light, his face shadowed. Caleb studied the blank sheet as if willing the words to appear without his having to write them. He sipped from the small glass of whiskey and unpinned the badge from his vest. He weighed it in his hands, fingering each of the five points. He put it on the table, poured another drink.

Annie's absence, and now Vernon's, filled the room with smothering loneliness. It hurt to breathe. He stepped onto the small front porch and listened to the silence of the town on a Sunday night. If it could only be like this all the time. He snorted. Then it would be boring.

Back inside, he stood at the table, the paper lying there, beckoning, accusing.

Vernon's and Alexander's graves appeared before him, images imposing themselves on his table. No more Sunday afternoon fishing trips to the river. No more sharing a meal with Vernon and Esther and Alexander. And Putnam who waited on them, always serving the man he honored.

He chewed his cheek, touched the badge again. Sat down and began to write. Slowly at first. Then the words flowed, pouring out. Three pages later, the pencil stopped. He stabbed the last period. He tucked the folded sheets into an envelope and sealed it. The blank front teased him. With Vernon gone, who to give it to? Names of townspeople and distant friends scrolled through his mind. Grunting at the name that rose up, he scrawled Pastor Luke on the outside.

He pulled a clean sheet of paper closer, sharpened the pencil with his knife, wrote two sentences, signed his name and folded the paper in half.

He drained his glass, lay on his bed and slipped into a deep, dreamless sleep.

CHAPTER 18

Monday, June 24, 1878

MICHAEL CONTEMPLATED THE platter of steak and eggs before him, appetite shrinking by the second.

"If you're not going to eat that, I will." Jeremiah towered over him.

"I might just let you. I was starved when I walked in here. Now, I don't think I can eat a bite."

"Look at it like life. One bite at a time." Jeremiah sat and ordered the same breakfast for himself.

Michael forked a piece of steak into his mouth. Warm, tender juices oozed at each chew. The meal was no longer in danger of being left uneaten.

Michael swallowed. "When are you leaving for Dallas?"

"Day after tomorrow. Taking the stage to Culverton then pick up the train to Saint Louis."

"Looks like we'll be traveling together a good part of the way."

Jeremiah's knife and fork hovered over his just-delivered meal. "I thought you'd be staying on here, courting Miss Rachel while you figured out what to do next."

Michael shrugged. "That's what I thought until yesterday when it felt like God was telling me to go back and clear Ben's name."

"I kinda wondered about that. You haven't said a word about it since the cabin."

"I was hoping I wouldn't have to deal with it. But God wouldn't let go of it. Now it feels like I can't go on with anything else until I take care of this."

They waited in silence as the waitress refilled their coffees.

"Have you told Rachel you're leaving?"

Michael nodded around a mouthful of food.

"How'd she take it?"

Michael replayed his conversation in the grove on Sunday with Rachel. "Very quiet. Didn't really say much of anything after I told her."

Jeremiah pushed some egg onto his fork, hefted it before speaking. "Ever done anything like this—finding a murderer—before?"

Michael leaned forward, crossed his arms on the table. "Not really. Tried to help Gideon Parsons before they hung Ben. Didn't get anywhere. Right now, I don't have a clue how to do it."

Jeremiah's eyes could burn wood. "If you're right, if Ben Carstairs is innocent, there's still a killer out there. Most killers I've met don't want to get caught and will kill again to prevent it. Are you sure you're up to this? Do you want Rachel to live in fear of a letter saying you're dead?"

"No to both. But I feel like I have to. It's something God wants." He paused. "And I owe it to Ben to try. I do believe he was innocent, and I need to prove it. I owe it to Sam, too."

Jeremiah nodded. "Can you use some company?"

"You mean you? Don't you have other work waiting?"

"Not at the moment. That I know of." He planted his elbow on the table, chin in hand. "Look, I've been through this kind of thing. You haven't. I know Gideon Parsons by reputation, and he's a good man, but he's only one man. I think you could you use another pair of hands. If nothing else, I can watch your back, make sure you get back to Rachel, alive, well, and ready to marry her."

Marry her? Yes. More than anything. A life with her flowed before him, the two of them together. Would the dream ever become a reality?

--->======== ========<---

"Ow." Florence Meriweather yelped as Rachel's pin pricked her waist.

"Sorry, Mrs. Meriweather," Rachel said. "My finger slipped."

"Just make sure it doesn't happen again, young lady. I'm not your personal pin cushion." She lifted the fabric. "Am I bleeding?"

"No, Ma'am. It was an accident. It won't happen again." Rachel bit her tongue. Have to go in pretty far to hit blood. She repented immediately. Martha was having a bad influence on her. At least she didn't make her comments out loud. Yet.

Rachel was grateful that, this time, the mayor's wife chose a color and pattern more attuned to her pale skin and large proportions. Maybe Rachel's advice over the last few weeks was having an effect. As annoying and demanding as Florence Meriweather could be, she was a valuable customer. She was in every week for a new dress or alterations on an old one, usually to be let out. If Rachel kept her satisfied, her gossipy mouth would be sure to bring in more business.

Fitting finished, Rachel helped Mrs. Meriweather change back into her dress. The mayor's wife waggled her sausage-like finger at Rachel. "Now, young lady, I need this dress by the end of the week. I want to wear it to church on Sunday. Can you do that, or do I have to look for someone else?"

Who else is there? Rachel held her hands at her waist, squeezing the fingers. *Maybe Calvin at the livery stable. He's used to working on the canvas covers for the Conestoga and Studebaker wagons.* She tightened her grip.

She smiled. "It'll be ready. In fact, why don't you come in Friday afternoon? That way, if there's anything you don't like, I can fix it and give it to you on Saturday."

Mrs. Meriweather sniffed. "Well, I guess that will have to do."

Rachel escorted her to the door and, after she left, held back on the urge to slam it, and instead closed it with great care. She leaned her back against the door, arms folded, head down. "God forgive me for my unkind thoughts. Thanks for helping me keep my mouth shut."

She returned to her workroom, spread the fabric on her table, picked up her scissors and started to transform the yards of cloth into a dress, plans forming to make the clothing as pleasant to look at as it would be comfortable to wear.

The bell over the door sounded, a sweet musical tone.

"It's only me." Martha's voice carried into the workroom. "Brought you some dinner."

"Is it that time already?" Rachel greeted her friend. "You're alone?"

Martha laughed. "Yes. Luke took Daniel with him to visit some families. God does answer prayer."

The two settled in for their meal. Rachel served fresh tea as Martha arranged their sandwiches on the worktable, now cleared of Mrs. Meriweather's dress in-the-making.

"How's Florence Meriweather?"

"How did you know?"

Martha nodded at the mound of fabric. "Well, if that's not for her, you've gone into sail making, and we're too far from the ocean for that to be profitable."

Rachel gaped. "The way your mouth works sometimes, it's a wonder they still let Luke pastor in this town."

"You're right. I must embarrass him something awful." Martha lifted her head, smile bright again. "But I'm getting better. Now I usually only say things to you or him, not when anybody else is around. Besides, don't tell me you don't think the same things. You're just better at controlling your mouth."

"Maybe. I almost squeezed my fingers numb so I wouldn't say anything to Mrs. Meriweather."

"What happened between you and Michael yesterday? You didn't say a word after dinner."

Heaviness that had lifted during the morning returned. Dread of the future filled her. "Michael's leaving." The words sounded so final once they left her mouth.

Martha choked on a bite of food. "Why?"

Rachel toyed with the edge of the cloth covering the table. The same piece of cloth she used when Michael brought dinner on Thursday. Everything she touched today reminded her of him in some way.

In his arms yesterday, she felt complete and whole for the first time. What had been missing in her life clicked into place, brought by God. Now he was leaving.

Rachel swallowed. No more tears. Cried them all last night. "God's given him another assignment. To clear Ben Carstairs' name."

"Is he sure he heard from God?"

Rachel nodded. "I believe he did. He said Sam asked him to do it just before he died."

"A dying wish and a command from God. He must feel like he doesn't have any choice."

"He said he wanted to do it, needed to do it."

Martha covered Rachel's hand with her own. "How do you feel about it?"

"He told me he loves me." Rachel held Martha's gaze. "And I told him I love him. I'm scared. What if he doesn't come back? What if someone kills him?"

"He won't be alone, though. Won't that sheriff back there help him?"

"The men on the posse weren't alone, and six of them died." Her words sounded hard and bitter. She rubbed her forehead with her fingertips.

"God will protect him," Martha said.

"Like he protected Vernon and Alexander and the others?" The acid of bitterness rose in her throat. *Like he protected me from my uncle?* She pushed the anger down. How could she blame God? Her life changed because he sent Martha and Luke. "I'm sorry. I didn't mean to blame God. I want to trust Him to protect Michael but it's hard. Too hard right now."

Chapter 19

Monday, June 24, 1878

CALEB PATTED HIS chest. His letter still sat in the inside pocket of his vest. A sigh of relief was followed by an unpleasant surge of anxiety, his hands tingled, his head felt light enough to float off his shoulders. *No turning back now.*

The room took up a third of the ground floor of the town hall. Six rows of pew-like benches faced five small tables and chairs. Twenty or so townspeople scattered among the benches. About the usual number for a routine town council meeting. No big issues pending tonight.

That anyone knew about.

Caleb stood in his usual spot at the door. Later, when the meeting was called to order, he'd move to the front of the room in case people got unruly. It'd be nice if the mayor would get unruly one night. Just one night.

At that moment, Malcolm Meriweather walked in, nodded at Caleb, and hastened down the center aisle, shaking hands with the attendees. Charley Barnes, the carpenter, ambled in, shook Caleb's hand with a firm, calloused grip. Calvin Atkins, the livery owner, arrived next, followed by the last two members, George Brown from the bank and Herman Gunther of the hotel restaurant.

The four were good men, selected by Sam, who made sure they ran unopposed. Sam did the same for the mayor, although many had doubts about his abilities as well as his ethics. But he'd pleased Sam, ran the political side of town the way Sam wanted. Not for the first time, Caleb wondered what would happen now that the Mayor had lost Sam's protection. The next election should be interesting. Even someone like Malachi, drunk or sober, would be better. *Maybe*

Bill Barkston and I should sound the scout out about running. Have to catch him after he's had a few.

Meriweather gaveled the meeting to order. The next thirty minutes dragged like August in Texas as the council dealt with routine business and reports. Caleb resisted the desire to tell them to hurry up.

"That finishes our business for tonight," the mayor said. "But I understand Sheriff Davis has asked for a few minutes of our time." Meriweather opened his pocket watch, studied it like treasure map, and snapped it shut. "Go ahead, Sheriff."

Caleb cleared his throat, mouth dry, tongue like an unwashed kerchief. He took the letter from his vest, opened it and stood in front of the mayor. "Mr. Mayor." He coughed. Charley Barnes handed him the glass of water from his table. Caleb drained it, wiped his mouth with his shirtsleeve. "Mr. Mayor, Councilmen, I hereby tender my resignation as sheriff of Riverbend and I recommend Pete O'Brien be appointed in my place."

He handed the letter to the mayor who let it fall to the table as if it were on fire.

Silence. Then murmurs bubbled from the people behind him. He heard several scuffle to leave. He smiled. First, they'd go to the saloons, and within fifteen minutes, the news would be all over town. *Nothing like the whiskey telegraph.*

"Why, Caleb? Why now?" George Brown's voice silenced the room.

"Because I'm done. I'm tired. Eight members of this community died." He sighed. "I'm old, George. Too old for this."

Charley Barnes' voice cracked. "It's not your fault those men died. You did everything you could."

Caleb shrugged. "Maybe." The feeling he could have done more hovered like a vulture waiting for an animal to die. "Maybe not. I've been a lawman since before the war. It's time for me to step aside before I make any more mistakes."

Calvin Atkins seldom spoke at the meetings. He did now in a voice that rasped like sand blown against a window. "You're making one now, Caleb. A big one."

"I don't think so."

"Caleb, what happens if we don't accept your resignation?" Charley asked.

Caleb couldn't quite look him in the eye. "I'll leave anyway."

Mayor Meriweather cleared his throat. Caleb caught the gleam in the man's eyes, like the smile of a gambler with a royal flush. "Well, Sheriff Davis, I for one appreciate all the years of excellent service and dedication you've given to the town of Riverbend, as do all the citizens. You've protected us and helped create an environment for the town to grow."

And you can say all that with a straight face.

"However," the mayor continued. "I think it would be appropriate if you stayed on until your replacement is found and hired."

Gunther's German accent echoed in the room. "And vhat is wrong vith Pete O'Brien? He vill make an excellent sheriff."

Meriweather stroked his chin. "Maybe in a few years, after he's had some more experience."

"Ach. He's been deputy five years already." Gunther waved his arms. "He has no need of more experience."

"I tend to agree with Herman," George Brown said. "I think Pete is a solid recommendation. What do you have against it, Mayor?"

Meriweather cleared his throat, fiddled with Caleb's letter. "Like I said, I think he needs more experience. I mean, after all, he is…Well, he's…you know, he's Irish. You know what quick tempers they have and how violent they can be."

Caleb thought his last act as sheriff would be to punch the Mayor in the nose. Probably get acquitted of any assault charges too. *I may run against you myself, you pompous….*

Charley Barnes slammed his hand on his table. "Mr. Mayor, with all due respect, it's my understanding the Irish only attack the British who are actually in Ireland. I think you're safe. I move we accept Caleb's resignation and appoint Pete O'Brien as our new sheriff."

Meriweather flustered with his hands. "Wait. You're out of order. You can't—"

"Second." Gunther's voice drowned out the Mayor's.

Barnes raised his hand. "All in favor." Brown, Gunther and Atkins raised their hands in agreement.

Barnes looked at Caleb. "The motion carries. Pete O'Brien will assume his new duties tomorrow morning. Caleb, will you brief him?"

"Yes, sir. Thank you."

Meriweather sputtered. "This is out of order. You…you can't do this."

"Shut up, Malcolm." George Brown stood and led the other council members to gather around Caleb.

CHAPTER 20

Tuesday, June 25, 1878

TWO AND A half months ago, Michael sat at this table in the parsonage for the first time.

Two and a half months ago, Rachel Stone walked into his life and took his heart.

Two and a half months ago, his life changed. Forever. In ways he never imagined.

Now Rachel sat next to him, and in less than twenty-four hours, he would walk away.

He pushed the thought away, determined to enjoy this last night with her, to savor every moment as he savored each bite of the roasted chicken Martha had prepared. When Rachel's arm brushed his, his heart leapt, and his mind raced with thoughts of them together, married, alone. He forced himself to focus on the present, and the others at the table.

Pastor Luke sat to his left, at the head of the table. Martha sat on the other side of Luke with Daniel, and then Abigail next to her. Pete O'Brien sat opposite Luke with Annabelle to his left. Rachel, between he and Annabelle, completed the group, as she completed everything in his life now.

"'Twas a complete surprise to me, it was, Ma'am." Pete answered Martha's question. "Caleb walks up to me this morning, takes me badge off, and pins his on, and says I'm now the Sheriff of Riverbend. Coulda knocked me over with a puff of wind."

"Town will sure seem different without him walking the streets." Luke said. "Did Caleb say what he was going to do now?"

Pete shrugged. "Said he was going fishing, he was. Wouldn't say much beyond that."

Martha said, "How does it feel, being married to the sheriff, Annabelle?"

Annabelle took Pete's hand in both of hers, gazed at her husband. "I'm very proud of him. He's earned it." She turned to Martha. "And I'm scared out of my wits. Going to have to step up my prayers to keep my husband protected."

"We'll be with you." Rachel's voice was soft as if her words included something only she was aware of.

Pete turned to Michael. "Are ye sure ye need to leave us tomorrow, Michael? Can we not persuade you stay a little longer?"

Michael fiddled with his knife and sipped his coffee. How to answer? He didn't want to leave. Rachel's presence next to him reinforced that. He wanted to stay. Forever. "I think the sooner I leave, the sooner I can get back."

Rachel's touch on the back of his hand was light as a summer breeze.

"Well, I wish ye luck, laddie. And be careful, mind ye. We want you back among us."

After dinner, he and Rachel worked in the kitchen, finishing the cleanup while Luke and Martha put the children to bed. Pete and Annabelle had said their goodbyes and headed to their home. Once again, Michael envied them, tempered by the hope that perhaps, one day soon, he and Rachel would be sharing a bed, a home, a life.

He studied her now as she washed the dishes, focused on her task. He held out his hand for a cleaned plate, ready to dry it and put it in its place.

"You don't have to do this, you know. It's woman's work. You can sit at the table. Just knowing you're there will keep me company."

"I want to help. And besides, the table's too far away." He kissed her cheek.

She rested her hands on the edge of the sink, gazed out the window. Her profile mesmerized him, firm chin, slight upturn of her nose, full lips, rounded cheeks that dimpled when she smiled. Her violet eyes, brimming with tears, found his.

"I hate that you have to go. I want you to stay. I still want to know more about you."

He folded the towel, laid it on the work surface next to the sink. "I don't want to go, either. But it's like a hunting dog with a scent. I can't let it go. I have to finish it."

"I know. Can't you wait a few more weeks?"

He took her hands. "Yes, I can. And then we'll be in the same position—only it will be harder to leave then than it is now. Leaving now is already hard enough. In a few more weeks, I'll be even more in love with you. They'd have to use dynamite to get me out of town."

She nodded. "You remember when you first got here?"

"Yeah. You didn't want anything to do with me."

"But something happened. You touched my heart. For the first time, I thought maybe you were a man different from the others. When you left with the posse, I really did want to get to know you better, wanted to see if it was possible to trust, to risk my heart, my freedom."

He touched her cheek. "The whole time on the trail, your words 'I want to get to know you better' kept me going. For the first time in my life, there was something I wanted to come back to, something good and decent."

She smirked. "You're one of the few men in this town who see me as good and decent. Most of the others see me as good for only one thing, and it isn't making dresses or washing dishes."

He wanted to crush her to him. "Still feels like a long road, doesn't it? Well, I'm here to walk it with you. We'll show them."

She bit her lower lip. "Thank you."

The silence between them was broken by the sounds of laughter from upstairs. She stared at the ceiling, her face dreamlike. "Someday," she whispered.

He took her in his arms, not the crushing embrace of desire, but the soft embrace of tenderness and understanding. He kissed the top of her head, enjoying the scent of lilacs.

"Someday," he whispered.

Chapter 21

Wednesday, June 26, 1878

RACHEL LAY ON her bed wishing the sun would not rise, and the day would not come. The same wish she had years ago, when her aunt abandoned her to her uncle's abuse.

But the sun always rose, and the day arrived, and today was no different. Her uncle was out of her life now, the life he sold her into was gone, and her new life spread before her like a limitless prairie. But she didn't want this day to begin. She wanted to postpone it and postpone it and postpone it.

Michael would leave today, and she wasn't ready. She would never be ready. She touched her lips, remembering their good-bye kiss last night, full of love and passion and promise. She squeezed her fingers.

She chose her dress with care, the blue Michael seemed to like, the one she knew brought out the violet of her eyes. Brushed her hair before pulling it into a tight bun. She knew she wasn't being this fastidious for fashion sense. Anything to postpone the day, to delay his departure.

She thought of the makeup she wore in her old life. Applying some now would certainly slow time.

Is there a way I can make him miss the stage? I'll run away, and he'll come looking for me. Or I'll tell him wolves took Daniel to the mountains.

Even if he fell for any of those ploys, he'd only catch the next stage, and be angry with her for tricking him. Not a good way to begin a relationship she wanted to last a lifetime.

She ate breakfast in a fog, aware of Martha, Luke and the children in some muted world on the edge of hers.

In the store, she focused on Florence Meriweather's dress, made three errors and four times had to redo simple work she usually could do with her eyes closed.

No customers came in. Just herself and a mountain of fabric to meld into something wearable.

At exactly noon, Michael walked in, the bell over the door announcing his presence and how little time was left. She sighed, put her work aside and snugged her bonnet over her head as she walked out of her workroom.

She embraced him, heart trembling, and kissed him.

"Ready for dinner?"

She scanned her store, eyes coming to rest on him. "No. It only means you're that much closer to leaving." She took his arm. "Let's go. Maybe I'll think of a way to keep you tied up in my work room until it's too late to catch the stage."

He covered her hand with his. "Don't tempt me. I might help you cinch the knots."

Outside, the hotel seemed a hundred miles away—yet, it felt like they covered the distance in two steps.

Too fast. Everything's moving too fast.

The dining room held so many memories. Her first real job. Hard work and satisfying as well because it was demanding yet not degrading. The Gunthers' love for each other, for cooking, for their customers gave her hope for a better life. They took a risk in hiring her, and only asked that she do her best and let Mr. Gunther handle the difficult customers, the gropers, and the gossipers.

She looked at the chair Mark tried to pull her into the day Michael arrived. A stranger came to her rescue, and now he was in her heart, and he was leaving.

"Can you do something to make me hate you?"

Michael's spoon of stew stopped halfway to his mouth, which hung like a doctor's broken shingle, his eyes wide—warm, kind, hazel with their green flecks.

"Excuse me?" he said.

"If you do something to make me hate you, I won't miss you so much when you leave."

"Oh. I don't know if I can do that on command. I might have been able to do it naturally but if I have to think about it, I'll mess it up. Can't you just decide to hate me?"

"I tried. Doesn't work. Tried when we first met and you showed you were interested in me. Didn't work then. Not working now."

He gestured toward his bowl of stew. "I could dump this on your head, but you look much too beautiful in that dress."

She sighed. Her heart thumped like it wanted to leap out of her chest.

"Rachel, I'm going to be back as soon as I can. I think with Gideon's and Jeremiah's help, we should be able to find out who did the killing sooner than if I did it on my own."

She nodded, unable to trust herself to speak. Movement outside caught her attention. "Oh, no. It's too soon. I'm not ready."

The stage rumbled by, horses at a trot, harnesses jangling, the coach bouncing on its springs as the driver braked the wheels and sawed on the reins. It disappeared from view.

Their eyes met. *He doesn't want to leave. He wants to stay. I have to let him go. I have to let him finish what God's given him to do. I have to trust God to bring him back.* She squeezed her fingers until the knuckles sent bolts of pain. *It's hard, so hard.*

They walked to the stage depot, not touching, the few inches between them the beginning of a wall of protection until he returned.

Michael's bag squatted on the boardwalk next to two others. Jeremiah Turner and Caleb stood with Sheriff O'Brien. *How odd that sounds.* Annabelle held her husband's arm. She smiled at the other two, glanced at her husband with pride, but Rachel saw the lines of worry at the corners of her eyes. Married to a man who put his life at risk every day. How difficult to face each morning knowing it could be their last together.

Her heart rose to her throat. *This could be my last day with Michael.* She clutched his arm as if to hold him back, to keep him rooted next to her.

Martha and Luke stood to one side, Abigail and Daniel with them. Joshua and Lupe joined them. A horse approached at a trot from behind. Bill Barkston came into view, easing his mount to a stop in front of the depot. The pine tree of a man dismounted with the grace of a dancer.

He approached Michael, hand extended. "Take care of yourself, Michael." He put his arm around Rachel, his calloused hand heavy on her shoulder. "We'll help look after Rachel until you get back."

Michael smiled. "I appreciate that, Bill." He took Rachel's hand and drew her closer to him. "From what I've seen, Rachel will do just fine taking care of herself, but I'm sure she'll let you know if she needs your help."

She smiled. "Thank you, Bill. It's good to know you and Jeffrey will be around." Her heart surged. Michael respected her, her need to be independent, to be her own woman.

Joshua approached, touched the brim of his hat. "Miss Rachel." Lupe's eyes lit in a smile when Rachel glanced at her. Joshua turned to Michael, and offered him an envelope. "Mr. Archer, here's a hundred dollars. I'd appreciate it if you could see your way clear to bring Ben's body back with you. I want to have him here with Ma and Pa." He hesitated. "And Mark."

Confusion flickered across Michael's face. "I'll sure be glad to do it, but you don't have to pay me."

Joshua thrust the envelope closer. "Use it for expenses. Doubt the railroad will do it for nothing or the cemetery, either."

Michael slid the envelope into his bag. While he squatted, Daniel hugged him. Michael stood, the boy in his arms. "You're going to take good care of Buddy while I'm gone?"

"Yes, sir, Mr. Michael."

"Feed him, water him, brush him, exercise him every day?"

Daniel nodded so emphatically, Rachel thought his head might bob off his shoulders.

"Good boy. I'm counting on you."

Daniel trotted back to his father.

Michael faced Caleb, shook his hand. "Thanks for coming to see us off."

Caleb handed Michael's bag to the driver, then Jeremiah's. He picked up the third bag placed it in the boot next to the others and adjusted his hat. "Actually, I'm going with you, if you don't mind an old coot tagging along."

Michael was speechless, eyes clearly happy at the news. "Don't mind at all, but what about helping Pete settle in?"

Caleb waved his hand at Pete. "He don't need any help. Knows the job better than I do. I'd just be in his way. Besides, I haven't seen Gideon since the war."

It was time.

Her heart sank.

The lump in her throat made it hard to breathe, impossible to talk. Michael's fingers were under her chin, gentle, tentative. His touch, his eyes made her feel like a fragile rose. She wanted to memorize every green fleck, every feature of his face.

"I love you, Rachel Stone."

She nodded.

Their lips met. Soft, tender, warm. *Don't ever let it end. Make it last forever.*

It ended.

He kissed the tip of her nose. "I'll be back."

She clung to him and let the tears flow. She took a step back, touched his face.

"Michael Archer, if you don't come back, I will hate you."

CHAPTER 22

Tuesday, July 2, 1878

MICHAEL SAT UP straighter and tugged at his vest as the train slowed. Across from him, Caleb slumped against the wall of the coach, eyes closed, snoring. Jeremiah sat next to him, rocking with the rhythm of the train, Bible open in his lap.

Familiar country. Home for several years, the Ozarks on his left folded one upon the other until the treed slopes faded from green to soft blue in the high mists. To his right, prairie spread through Indian Territory to the Rockies.

Almost four months since he'd left for Riverbend. He rested his chin in his hand as the farmlands yielded their neat rows to the shanties that edged the town, the storage buildings, the train maintenance sheds. Since he left, the area had cycled from planting to growing, and soon preparing to harvest, the cadence of its seasons marching on, secure in its symmetry.

Four months. And he'd found a love he never expected, still wasn't sure he deserved. Fulfilled his promise to Ben. And killed. Again. But to protect and save.

Jeremiah nudged Caleb. "Wake up, old timer. We're there."

Caleb jumped, rubbed his eyes, and stretched his arms over his head. "Must be the stimulatin' company keeps me awake."

Michael smiled at how the three of them had deepened the friendship begun on the posse. Friends bonded by shared dangers from the past and a shared mission for the future. *This must be what soldiers feel for each other.*

The train wheezed to a stop. Michael and Jeremiah stood along with the rest of the passengers in the half-filled car. Caleb remained seated, gazing out the window.

Jeremiah poked Caleb's foot with the toe of his boot. "Aren't you coming?"

"Town ain't going anywheres. Figure I'll wait 'til this crowd leaves. Some of them don't smell too good."

"Kind of old to be getting picky about who you associate with."

"Ain't all that picky. Still with you two. And watch who you're calling old." Caleb stood and pulled his bag from the overhead rack. "I can still teach you a thing or two."

"Like how to fall asleep on anything that moves?"

"Sleep when you can. Work when you have to," Caleb muttered as he stepped past Jeremiah into the aisle.

"Nice to travel with a philosopher," Jeremiah said.

Michael followed the other two off the train.

Bright summer sunshine, bouncing off dust floating in the air, bathed the platform in a yellow glow. The air smelled different from Riverbend. More moist, rich in the soil of farms. Lazy, too. The kind of air that made him want to grab a fishing pole and park under a tree for the afternoon. Plenty of time for that later. Business first.

When his feet hit the platform, an embrace engulfed him like a blanket on a cold winter night. Deborah Taylor's arms reached around his neck and pulled his head down so she could plant a kiss on his cheek. "Thank God, you're home. And in one piece."

He kissed her cheek and held her at arm's length. "I missed you, Miss Deborah." Hair mostly gray with streaks of the original brown. Gray eyes with permanent smile crinkles. Round face. Dimpled chin.

"Welcome back, son." Zechariah Taylor stood at Michael's height but seemed much taller with his broad shoulders and straight posture. A voice able to reach the farthest person at an open-air meeting. Michael recalled it bouncing and echoing off the church walls as Zechariah pounded his fist on the pulpit to make a point. He would look like a biblical figure if he let his gray and black hair and beard grow longer. Somehow, the thought of Zechariah in one of those long flowing robes didn't fit. Nope. Zechariah was definitely a black suit, white shirt preacher. His coal black eyes held Michael in their own embrace.

"It's good to be back, sir."

He introduced Caleb and Jeremiah.

Deborah patted Caleb's arm. "An old friend of yours really wanted to be here, Mr. Davis. But…well, he said to tell you he's a little under the weather, and he'll see you later."

"Under the weather? Is he all right?" Michael said.

Zechariah harrumphed. "She means the fool is nursing a bullet wound. In his leg. Some drunk shot him when Gideon arrested him. Don't know how he expected 'under the weather' to keep it from you."

No. Not Gideon. Blackness crept to the edge of Michael's heart. If Zechariah was his father, Gideon was his uncle. The curmudgeon whose tender side was never far away. The man who lived the values of justice and mercy. The man who, with Zechariah, would not let him sink into his old self.

"How bad is he hurt?" Anxiety tinged Michael's voice.

Zechariah waved his hand. "Doc says it isn't bad. Bullet went through the calf. Didn't hit bone. But Gideon's old and takes longer to heal. We'll stop at his place on the way to the parsonage."

⇥◉ ◉⇤

Caleb's hand rested on the gate to Gideon's yard. *Gideon's old? Slow to heal? He's two years younger than me. Looks like I made the right decision after all.*

Gideon's house sat back from the street, small, light blue with white trim, one story with a covered porch. Curtained windows flanked the brown door. A three-foot high picket fence extended across the front and down the sides past the house. Similar houses flanked it. Caleb admired it from the front gate. Gideon's roots were here. He wouldn't have put this much work into it other-wise. Caleb's house met his needs but gave the impression it wasn't permanent, didn't tie him down, left him free to leave if the spirit moved him. Yet he stayed in Riverbend.

He knocked on the door. Gideon's garrulous voice rumbled. "Come in. It's open."

Gideon sat in a rocking chair, dressed in a faded blue robe, bandaged leg propped on a small stool. Wisps of gray hair stood at odd angles, and jowls dangled from his squarish face, its usual ruddiness replaced by a gray pallor. Gideon's brown eyes, eyes that always saw farther and sharper than Caleb's, burned bright and clear from under bushy brows.

"Caleb Davis." Gideon struggled to stand and winced as he put weight on his wounded leg. The two shook hands.

"Was glad to hear you were comin' but the telegram didn't say why. What brings you to Tramlaw?" Gideon eased back into the chair and used his hands to lift his leg onto the stool.

"The train." Caleb enjoyed the look of confusion then consternation sliding across his friend's face. "I came with Michael."

"What did you do about Riverbend?"

"Gave it up. Turned it over to my deputy. Can I fix some coffee?"

"I fixed some earlier. Should still be warm." Gideon jerked his thumb over his shoulder toward the kitchen area of the large open room.

"I figured you had. That's why I offered. Need to get some decent coffee into you. Yours'll melt an anvil. Mine has great healing powers."

"Maybe for snake bite."

Caleb busied himself making fresh coffee. When it was ready, he found Gideon's sugar stash and sweetened his friend's cup. He handed Gideon the drink and sat across from him on a small couch. "Got yourself a nice place here. Might almost think you had a woman takin' care of you."

"Not likely. Ain't had one my whole life. Ain't gonna start now. Too much work to break 'em in." He sipped his coffee. "So, why'd you give up Riverbend?"

Caleb blew across his cup, and cradled it in his hands. "Too old. Too many mistakes. Had a kidnapping. Lost six on the posse and the two men that was kidnapped. Town needs somebody younger. My deputy's a good man."

Caleb looked down to avoid Gideon's eyes.

"Eight men. Tough. Not like you to run away, though."

Caleb's head snapped up. "Ain't running. Just tired of it."

They drank their coffee, the silence a third person in the room. Two old friends lost in their own thoughts.

"So, how'd you get yourself shot?" Caleb said.

Gideon snorted. "Got sloppy. Thought I had this drunk under control. Took his pistol away. Turned out he had a Derringer tucked in his belt. First shot missed. Second shot went off as I hit him." He pointed at his leg. "Pesky little things, those Derringers."

"How's the drunk?"

"Sitting in his cell. Waiting for trial on attempted murder." Gideon shrugged. "Nursing a broken arm. Not quite sure how that happened. Maybe the Derringer had more kick than he imagined."

Caleb smiled.

"What are you gonna do now?"

Caleb shrugged. "Don't know. I'll see after we clear Ben's name."

Gideon whistled soft and low. "We tried that. Couldn't find anything. Don't see how things are going to be different this time."

"Don't know. Michael seems driven to do it. Says it's part of his assignment from God."

Gideon nodded, rubbed the stubble on his chin. "Figures. Michael's turned into a good man, considering where he was when I first met him. If he says God told him to do it, he'll stick it out until he's done. Or dead."

"Dead?"

"Michael's got that stubborn, get-it-done streak that don't know quit. Not a good mix with a killer who don't want to be caught. Be like two trains meetin' head on."

"If nothing else, I can cover his back."

Gideon raised his cup in a toast. "That you can." He sipped. "So Michael did connect with Ben's father?"

"Oh, yeah." Caleb gave him the details of the search for the kidnappers and Michael's role.

"Didn't know he was that good a shot."

"Neither did he. Found out later he shot with his eyes closed."

Gideon chuckled. "Good thing the hand of God was on him."

"Amen to that."

Gideon looked sharply at him. Caleb smiled and shrugged as a blush crept up his face.

CHAPTER 23

Wednesday, July 3, 1878

LIZZIE BARNES' TINY waist presented more of a challenge than Rachel anticipated. She rubbed her eyes and pinched the bridge of her nose, arched her back and rotated her shoulders. The knot of tension at the top of her neck eased, though a dull ache still lingered. She sighed and folded the garment. *Finish it first thing in the morning.* Maybe Annabelle could give her a massage. She'd stop by on the way home.

Rachel turned off the lantern suspended over her worktable, and stepped into the store, sliding the curtain closed behind her. Everything in order, she locked the door. Fatigue swept over her. Where did that come from? She stifled a yawn. No Annabelle tonight. Supper and bed. The cool night air brushed her cheek, refreshing her a little. Still so tired. She shook her head and stepped toward the parsonage.

With her next step, she wasn't in Riverbend anymore—

A place she'd never seen, a small city, railroad, shops, businesses, and churches. People. Some scurrying, others strolling, still others standing. They passed by as if not seeing her. She turned a slow circle. Behind her, a two-story brick building with a clock tower. Couldn't make out the time in the night. Sign over the double doors reflected in the ambient light of the street: Bank of Tramlaw.

Tramlaw. That's where Michael went. Why am I here? What's going on? Another vision? What this time?

Suddenly she was in the air, looking down on the main street. *This isn't right? Where's the peace that usually comes? What's that behind the bank?* Three men beating another man, fists pummeling, legs kicking. *Who is it? What do you want me to do, Lord?* The three men stepped back. One took out a pistol and fired at the bloodied man curled into a ball on the ground. Blood burst from where the bullet entered the shoulder. The three ran.

The man on the ground rolled onto his back. Eyes swollen closed, lips cut and bleeding, nose flattened. She peered into the dim shadows.

Michael.

Michael needs you. Go to him—

Her stomach lurched and fell to her ankles. Her head swam. Blackness.

Her forehead was damp, cold. Her eyelids danced like lightning bugs. Finally, they obeyed and stayed opened. A blur hovered above her, lifting whatever was wet and cold from her forehead. She closed her eyes and opened them. The blur took shape. Martha placed a cool, damp cloth on her forehead.

My room. How did I get here?

Michael.

She sat up. The cloth fell to her lap. The room spun, even with her eyes closed.

"Rachel." Annabelle's voice. "Are you all right?"

"Michael."

"He's in Tramlaw." Martha's soothing voice. "What happened? Pete found you passed out on the street and brought you here."

"Michael's in trouble."

Martha took hold of her arms. "How do you know?"

"Saw it." *Why won't my mouth work right?*

"But Caleb and Mr. Turner are with him," Annabelle said.

"Shot. Somebody shot him. Have to go to him," Rachel said.

Martha took on her parent voice. "You're not going anywhere until Doc sees you."

"Have to go now." Rachel swung her legs over the side of the bed.

"Don't you want to let him know you're coming?" Annabelle said.

Rachel stopped. *Send him a telegram? What if I'm wrong? What if this is all my imagination?* She didn't think so but doubt nagged. She nibbled her lower lip and squeezed her fingers.

"No. I don't want to worry him or distract him. Besides, it might already be too late." She looked from one friend to another. And never felt so alone. "I need to get to him as fast as I can."

CHAPTER 24

Friday, July 5, 1878

TRAMLAW'S MORNING RHYTHMS welcomed Michael. He exchanged greetings with several people as he and Caleb walked Main Street.

"You seem to have a lot of friends here." Caleb observed.

"Church folk mostly. Seems like half the town goes to Zechariah's church."

Caleb nodded. "Seems like they don't do much to celebrate Independence Day around here."

"Some wounds from the war are still raw. Folks just seem to try to get through the day with as little fuss as possible

A mustachioed man approached Michael in a hurried stride, black hair curling from under his cowboy hat. By his side walked a slim woman, brown hair tucked under a bonnet. The man extended his hand before he was close enough for Michael to grasp it. The woman's smile was that of someone greeting a favorite relative not seen in years.

"Michael, welcome home. It is so good to see you." The man pump-handled Michael's arm.

"Hello, Jed." Michael freed his hand, touched the brim of his hat as he nodded at the woman. "Barbara." He introduced them to Caleb.

Jed told Caleb the story of how Michael helped him to stop drinking and come to Jesus. He put his arm around Barbara. "Saved my marriage, you did." He patted Barbara's protruding stomach. "And now we're going to have a baby. Gonna name him Michael Jedediah after you."

Embarrassment crept up Michael's neck. "You don't have to do that."

"He wouldn't be coming into the world if it wasn't for you."

Caleb pushed his hat off his forehead. "And what if it's a girl?"

"Deborah Michaela." Barbara's answer was matter-of-fact, determined. "This child's going to be named after you, Michael Archer, even if I have to make up a name."

Jed leaned closer. "So, are you back to stay? No more trips? Right?"

Back to stay? What about Rachel? "Back for awhile, anyways. Then we'll see what the Lord has in mind."

Barbara studied him. "You've found a girl." Not a question. A statement of fact. "Congratulations. I hope she's everything you deserve. When are you getting married?"

Michael found his voice, although it stuttered. "Nothing's been settled yet."

She tapped her forefinger against his chest. "Well, settle it. And then bring her by here so we can all meet her. She has to be someone special to take your heart."

"That she is, Ma'am." Michael's voice became serious. "Very special indeed."

They walked on, Michael's feet on the streets of Tramlaw, his mind and heart in Riverbend. He and Rachel married. A house like Luke and Martha's. Flower garden in front. Children on a swing.

Caleb's elbow in his ribs brought him back to Tramlaw. "We're here."

The livery hulked over them, a large barn, doors open on both ends, sunlight showing rows of stalls, racks and pegs for tools and tack. The pungent, sweet smell of hay and horses mixed with the aroma of hot iron from the blacksmith's area. To one side, with the barn forming one wall, stood a small building, door in one corner of the front wall, two windows overlooking the street. A boardwalk but no overhanging roof to block the sun. A patina of dust clung to the dull, faded red paint of both structures.

A new sign was nailed to the small building spanning the area above the windows and door. Dark blue against a white background, framed by a simple dark blue border. *Horses Traded* read the upper line. *Winslow-Smythe Company* read the lower.

Michael pointed to the sign. "New owner or partner. The owner who was murdered was Donald Winslow."

"What was he like?"

"Older man. Seemed honest as horse traders go. Never heard where he purposely cheated anybody, but he was a tough negotiator. Heard where some folks thought he didn't pay as much for a horse as they thought he should. Others thought his prices too high."

"Sounds like pretty normal business. Somebody's always gonna be mad at you. We have to figure who was mad enough to kill him."

Caleb pushed open the door. The morning light didn't quite fill the room. Michael's eyes took a second to adjust. They stood in an open area with chairs scattered around, a couple of cuspidors, and a pot-bellied stove. A three-foot tall wooden railing separated the front from the rear area.

A swinging gate in the middle of the railing gave access to a desk with a throne-size leather chair behind and two hardback chairs in front. One wall was all shelves lined with ledgers. A large safe, door ajar, stood against the opposite wall.

A cloud of tobacco smoke added to the dimness of the room, and the air reeked from the cigar clamped in the mouth of the man in shirtsleeves behind the desk. He looked up from the ledger in front of him, put the cigar in a glass ashtray, and slid the pen into its holder on the inkstand.

He stood, smoothed his vest with one hand while he ran the other over his slicked-back hair. "How can I help you gents?"

He extended his hand. Michael shook it, and wished for a cloth to wipe off the pomade.

Caleb wiped his hand on his pants leg after shaking the man's hand. "Answer a few questions for us."

The man folded his arms. "And you are?"

Caleb gave their names. "We're representatives of Sheriff Parsons. We're helping him out. While he's laid up."

"I see." The man rubbed his chin. "In what matter? I'm not aware of any problems with the livery or the blacksmith, and there certainly haven't been any problems in my business."

Michael's fingers itched at the pomposity.

Caleb nodded. "We're following up on the murder of the previous owner…" He turned to Michael.

"Donald Winslow."

The man started to sit, changed his mind, picked up his cigar and puffed a large cloud of smoke. "I thought that was all settled. They hung some kid for it."

"We're just tying up some loose ends for the sheriff."

The man spread his arms. "I don't know anything about it."

"I understand. We just want to look at your ledgers from around the time of the murder."

"I'm afraid I can't let you see them."

"Why not?" Michael heard the irritation in Caleb's voice. It matched his own impatience with the man.

"They're private business records, and besides, I didn't own the business at the time of the murder so, technically, I don't have the authority to let you see them."

Michael's jaw tightened. *This wasn't going well.* "Who does?" He tried to keep his voice level and calm. He didn't think he succeeded when the man's eyes bulged.

"My partner. His widow. Emma Winslow."

"Partner?" Caleb spoke the word as if it were a foreign language he was trying to learn.

The man seemed to puff out his chest, stand a little taller. "Yes. She and I are partners. I thought it would be good for business if I kept the Winslow name, something familiar for people in these parts."

Caleb settled his hat on his head. "And where can we find the Widow Winslow?"

The man gave them the address. When they reached the office door, Caleb stopped. "And your name, sir?"

"Gordon Lucius Smythe."

They walked along Main Street toward the side street where Emma Winslow lived.

"What do you know about him?" Caleb stopped to let a lady pass into a dry goods store.

"Nothing. Never saw him before. Why?"

Caleb rubbed the back of his neck. "Seems familiar. Could be I've seen too many like him. Snake oil salesmen. Maybe Gideon knows more."

Jeremiah greeted them as they passed him coming out of the telegraph office.

Michael stopped. "Jeremiah, you've got contacts all over the place, right?"

"Not all over, but I can cover a good part of the country. Why?"

"Can you see if any of them ever heard of a Gordon Lucius Smythe?" Michael gave him a description.

Caleb added, "Slick kind of guy, maybe did some shady horse trading or land deals or something."

"I'll get started right now." Jeremiah walked back into the telegraph office.

Michael and Caleb resumed their trek to the Widow Winslow.

"Good thinking back there. Smythe got me so irritated, I didn't think to ask where he was from. See, another sign I'm slipping."

"Probably wouldn't have given us a straight answer."

->==◉ ◉==<-

Michael sent a quick prayer for favor as he and Caleb approached the Winslow home. Mansion more like it.

The Widow Winslow lived in a large two-story red brick home set well back from the street. A low wall of matching brick bordered the thoroughfare with spilt-rail fencing down the sides. Large oaks graced the sides of the circular drive, and a profusion of unfamiliar flowers dominated the middle, the aroma almost overwhelming in the still morning air.

He was grateful he'd put on his best suit. Not the kind of place you show up at dressed like a cowboy. Wonder what they'll think of Caleb.

After Caleb pounded on the door several times, a large black woman opened it, one eye peering around the edge.

"Who is it, Bessie?" A voice of southern honey came from somewhere inside and above.

"Don't rightly know, Missy. Just got the door open."

"Well, step back and let them in. I'm sure they don't mean us any harm."

"Yes, Ma'am."

The door opened onto an oak floor glistening with polish. A wide, cherry staircase curved up to the second level. A woman stood part way down, a low-cut blue dress sweeping behind her.

"You may leave us, Bessie. Make sure you get that ham done right for the dinner tonight. Don't dry it out like last time."

"Yes, Ma'am. No, Ma'am." The woman waddled off behind the stairs.

Michael had forgotten how beautiful Emma Winslow was. Mid-thirties, twenty years younger than her late husband. Tall, slender neck, round face, full mouth. Hair the color of cinnamon and auburn. Gray-blue eyes framed by long lashes and sculptured brows.

She sauntered down the stairs. "It's Mr. Archer, isn't it? Welcome back. And who's this distinguished gentleman?"

Michael introduced Caleb. She extended her hand, fingers and palm down. Caleb held it briefly and let it go. She looked puzzled. Michael swallowed his smile.

"Shall we go to the library?"

As they followed her, Caleb whispered. "What was that all about?"

"She expected you to kiss her hand."

"Oh."

In the library, Emma sat in an upholstered armchair turned so the sun highlighted her hair. Michael and Caleb sat in armchairs they spun away from a fireplace large enough to roast a side of beef. Books lined the wall in floor to ceiling cases. Michael had the impression none had ever been removed from its assigned rank.

"Would you care for some coffee? Or something a little stronger?" She gestured with practiced grace to a small table near the window on which stood crystal glasses and decanters of liquor. They both declined.

She arranged her hands in her lap and sighed deeply, straining the bonds of her dress.

"And what can I do to help you gentlemen?"

Caleb's voice was polite and soft as he explained their mission. "We'd like to see the business ledgers from around the time of your husband's murder. Mr. Smythe told us we would have to get your permission."

She put one hand to her chest and closed her eyes. When she opened them, she focused on some spot behind Michael and Caleb.

"Whatever for? That nasty piece of trash, Ben Carstairs, killed my husband and hung for it. It's all settled as far as I can see."

Michael cleared his throat. "You see, Mrs. Winslow, we want to make sure we got the right man."

"Got the right man?" She waved her hand dismissively. "Tosh. Of course, you got the right man. Sheriff Parsons found him standing over my husband with a gun in his hand. Judge Barrett made sure he got a fair trial. And a jury of twelve good men convicted him. I know you and Sheriff Parsons thought otherwise, Mr. Archer, but I'm convinced justice was done for my late husband."

She dabbed the corner of her eyes with a handkerchief she pulled from her sleeve.

Caleb leaned forward, elbows on his knees, spun his hat in his hands. "I understand, Mrs. Winslow. It won't take long at all for us just to glance at the ledgers. To make sure we didn't miss anything."

She stood as if shot from the chair. Her eyes glared. "Mr. Davis, Mr. Archer. The matter is settled. My husband's murder has been avenged. I am not going to open old wounds to satisfy some whim of yours. Your business here is finished. I would thank you to see yourselves out."

She turned and walked to the window

Chapter 25

Friday, July 5, 1878

"Come in," Gideon bellowed in response to Michael's knock.

"Sounds like he's in a foul mood." Michael pushed open the door.

"Never did like being forced to sit still." Caleb removed his hat as he stepped over the threshold.

Gideon's voice graveled, petulant and irritated. "Stop fussin' with me, woman. Just leave me be."

Deborah Taylor bent behind Gideon, adjusting pillows. "Shush, you old goat. Person trying to make you comfortable, and you act like a snapping turtle whose shell is too tight. Let people pamper you for a change."

"No. Pamperin' makes a body soft."

She poked at Gideon's stomach. "Looks like you been making yourself soft just fine."

Gideon sputtered. "Caleb, Michael. Save me from this woman tormenting an injured man."

Michael laughed. "Seems like an angel of mercy to me."

Caleb poked Gideon's foot. "You ain't fooling anybody. You know you like being spoilt, especially by such a pretty angel."

Deborah blushed, gathered her shawl. "There's soup on the stove. Michael, you make sure Gideon eats before he has any more of that swill he calls coffee."

"Yes, Miss Deborah."

"Swill?" Gideon's voice notched up. "How dare you call it swill?"

Caleb held his hat to his chest with both hands, a pleading look in his eyes. "He's right, Miss Deborah. You shouldn't call it swill. That's too good a name for it, and an insult to the hogs."

Deborah rolled her eyes. She opened the door and looked heavenward. "I leave them in your hands, Lord. A good smite wouldn't harm them any."

After the door closed and Deborah's steps left the porch, Gideon scanned the front windows. "Be just like her to peek in and see what I was up to."

He reached behind and pulled out the pillow she had fluffed and tossed it on the couch. "Coffee."

"How about some soup first?" Michael said.

Gideon glared. "You preacher types are all alike. Coffee."

Michael headed for the kitchen. "You must still make it with those extra-strong crotchety beans."

Gideon took a long slurp from the cup Michael handed him. "Ahh. Good coffee."

Caleb shook his head. "So what do you know about Gordon Lucius Smythe?"

Gideon took another sip and glanced at Michael. "You wouldn't know him. Didn't exactly travel in your circles." He rubbed his chin. Michael could envision Gideon's brain flipping through memories, selecting the right ones.

"Smythe came here about two years ago. Got hooked up with Winslow selling land up toward Springfield. When Winslow was killed, Smythe slid into the horse business real easy like. The business hardly missed a beat. He's done all right with it." Gideon focused on a spot out the window. He sighed. "I don't trust him, even when he's standing in front of me and I can see both his hands the whole time. Haven't caught him at anything, most likely cuz he's too slick." He met Caleb's eyes. "Maybe I'm getting too old for this, just like you."

Caleb sipped the coffee, grimaced and put it down. "I got me a mayor kind of like that. Our age ain't got nothing to do with it. Where'd Smythe come from?"

"Saint Louis. Did some riverboat trading, moving goods and such. Was supposed to have been a good gambler, too. Don't know much about before that."

Michael leaned back in his chair. "Maybe Jeremiah will find out more. What about Smythe and Mrs. Winslow? Anything there?"

Gideon shook his head. "Don't know for sure, but wouldn't be surprised. He's at her house several nights a week around supper time and for a few hours after."

"Maybe Bessie knows something," Michael said.

Gideon waved his hand. "Bessie won't talk to any white man or woman about what goes on in that house. The war may be over, and Lincoln signed that paper and all, but it don't mean things have changed much around here."

Caleb paced. "Records of the trial at the court house?"

Gideon shrugged. "Yeah. But what are they gonna tell you?"

Caleb rubbed the back of his neck. "Don't know 'til I look. Didn't get anywhere this morning. Got to do something. Maybe see if the witnesses have changed their stories any."

"Michael and I talked to all of them between the trial and the hanging. Didn't come up with anything."

Caleb nodded. "I know. Most likely a wild goose chase and a waste of time, but we've got to start somewhere."

In the kitchen, Michael poured bowls of soup and sliced the loaf of sourdough bread Deborah had left.

He imagined Rachel working in her back room on someone's dress. Maybe, soon, it would be her own wedding dress. She'd be standing with him before Zechariah.

His arm muscles twitched. They wanted to be around her, holding her. The taste and feel of her lips on his, soft and warm. Together by the river. He removed her bonnet and the pins from her hair. She shook her head and her hair fell to her shoulders, fluttering in the gentle breeze. Rachel in his arms.

Lord, help us find the murderer soon so I can return to her.

"Where's my soup?" Gideon's shout brought him back to reality.

Michael placed the bowls and bread on the table. Gideon shook off Caleb's attempt to help him out of his seat. He cringed in pain with each hobbled step until he settled himself at the table. As he lifted the meat and vegetable laden spoon from the bowl, Caleb cleared his throat. "Michael, will you bless the food?"

Gideon's spoon splattered into the bowl. "Not you too?"

"Shush. Let the man pray."

When Michael finished praying, Caleb told Gideon of the massacre of Vernon and the others and how Michael lead him to Jesus.

Gideon laughed, looked at Michael. "Yeah. He thinks he did the same with me, but I try to keep him guessing."

A shadow passed across the front window. "Jeremiah's coming to the door," Michael opened the door, then brought him a bowl of soup.

Jeremiah bowed his head, grabbed a slice of bread and dunked it in his soup.

"Sent a bunch of wires." Jeremiah slurped the dripping bread. "Probably won't hear anything until later today or tomorrow."

"Hope they turn up something." Michael drained his bowl.

"Why? Does he look good for it?" Jeremiah said.

Caleb shrugged. "Don't know. Right now everybody looks good for it. Not enough information. Just rehashing everything Michael and Gideon did."

CHAPTER 26

Friday, July 5, 1878

THE CLERK LOOKED from Michael to Caleb and back to Michael. His hands fluttered like a butterfly unsure of which flower to visit. He tugged at his black string tie, his face turning as white as his shirt.

"I...I...I don't know. This is highly unusual."

Caleb tapped the sheet of paper Michael had prepared and Gideon had signed. It lay on the counter between them like a dead mouse the clerk was afraid to touch. "This is a paper signed by Sheriff Parsons giving us permission to look at the records of the Ben Carstairs trial. You know Mr. Archer here, and I'm acting as Sheriff Parsons' representative. You do know the sheriff's been shot and can't get around too good?"

The clerk nodded.

Caleb pushed his hat off his forehead, rested his arms on the counter, and leaned close to the clerk. "All right, then. Why don't you just fetch those records? I'm sure Sheriff Parsons will be glad to know how cooperative the public servants of Tramlaw are."

Michael rested his hands on the counter. "It would help us make sure the real murderer was caught."

The clerk nodded again and scurried through a door at the back of the room.

Twenty minutes passed. Michael paced, glancing at the door the clerk had disappeared through. Caleb turned his back to the counter, rested his elbows on it and chewed on a toothpick.

Michael drummed his fingers on the counter. "Sure is taking a long time."

"Seems that way. Sometimes, these court houses ain't too well organized."

Ten minutes later, the clerk came back into the room. Empty handed. Sweat beaded on his forehead. Dust streaks splotched his sleeves and the front of his shirt. "Sirs, I don't know what happened. The records are missing."

Michael clenched his fists. Caleb grabbed the edge of the counter, knuckles white. The clerk backed away two steps, held up his hands. "I searched the whole room, moved every box and file. They're not there."

Michael kept his voice calm. "When was the last time you saw them?"

"Don't know. Haven't had much cause to go looking for them since the hanging."

Michael's head weighed with defeat. Caleb's gray eyes met his, brows knitted. "Can we take a look? Maybe we'll see something you missed."

"Sir, that's highly irregular. No one's allowed back there except me."

Michael's patience slipped away. He clenched his fist again to keep from reaching across the counter. "This is a highly irregular situation to begin with. Now, I suggest you let us back there. You can stay with us to make sure we don't do anything we're not supposed to."

Caleb shrugged, placed his hands flat on the counter. "Seems like a reasonable request to me. Sometimes another pair of eyes can be very helpful."

The clerk studied Caleb's hands—Caleb's thick, sinewy hands, with large knuckles. The clerk swallowed. "A…All right. But I'll have to stay with you the whole time."

Caleb lifted his hands, palms open. "I would prefer it if you did." He tapped Michael's arm with the back of his hand. "Come on, Michael. Let's go hunt for some lost treasure."

The room was cramped and dim. Two dusty windows cast elongated beams of muted light in the afternoon sunshine. Candles stubbed into holders were scattered throughout the room. Caleb lit an oil lantern hanging from the ceiling.

They moved up and down the aisles and soon learned the clerk's system for organizing the records was to stick them wherever they would fit. Michael's nose exploded repeatedly as clouds of dust rose whenever they moved a box or packet of papers.

After half an hour, Caleb handed the lantern to the clerk. Michael grabbed it. "I'm not done. I'm going to look one more time."

Michael scoured every shelf, opened every box. Nothing. Another forty-five minutes searching. Nothing.

Back in the main room, he sneezed four times as he and Caleb brushed dust from their clothes. Michael stepped to within a foot of the clerk, leaned even closer. The clerk batted his eyes, darted glances around the room as if seeking someplace to run.

"How could those records disappear?" Michael's jaw ached from the tension of his clenched teeth.

The clerk raised his shoulders to his ears, spreading his hands as if in surrender. "I don't know, Mr. Archer. Somebody must have snuck in and took them."

"That part's obvious. We'd like to know who."

"So would I. Judge Barrett will have my head when he finds out the records are missing."

Michael settled his hat on his head. "Let's go see him."

"Now?"

"Yes, now. Is there a problem with that?"

The clerk shook his head. "The only thing is, he's in court right now. Probably be there the rest of the day."

"Do you see that as a problem, Caleb?"

Caleb brushed more dust off his pants, suppressed a sneeze. "Nope. I think the man needs to know he's got problems in his court house."

"I agree." Michael took the clerk by the arm. "Let's go."

"You don't need me there, do you?"

Michael squeezed a little tighter. "Of course we do. We can't answer any questions the judge might have about how you run things."

The clerk's knees buckled, and color drained from his face. Caleb grabbed his other arm and helped Michael lift him up straight. "Don't go passing out on us. Won't look good before the judge."

Michael and Caleb marched the clerk through the large double doors into the nearly empty courtroom. Two men stood at the bench in conversation with the judge. Two other men sat at tables on either side of a central aisle. A clerk stood at the judge's side.

Judge Abraham Barrett looked up, hair black as midnight with, Michael always suspected, the help of shoeblack. Deep-set brown eyes like the beads used by doll makers peered from under cliffs of bushy brows. His long face, high cheek bones, lazy mouth that dipped to one side and white-washed pallor reminded Michael of a cadaver, except this one breathed, and talked—and sentenced Ben to hang.

The judge's eyebrows knitted into one. "What's the meaning of this?"

The clerk froze under the judge's glare. "Records are missing, your honor."

"Records? What records? What are you talking about?" The judge half rose from his chair. "You'd better have a good reason for disrupting a court proceeding."

Judge Barrett seemed to suddenly become aware of the presence of Michael and Caleb.

"Archer, are you back in town already? Still attacking windmills?" He turned to Caleb. "And who are you, sir? Do you always walk into courtrooms so disheveled?"

Caleb looked at his dust-streaked clothing. Michael was sure he looked the same, even to the dust smear on the cheek.

"Name's Caleb Davis. Assisting Sheriff Parsons while he's recovering."

The judge settled in his chair, folded his arms on his desk. "I thought the sheriff had deputies for that." He waved his hand and stared at the records clerk. "Never mind. What's the problem? And be quick about it."

The clerk sagged, and Michael braced him. The man's voice trembled. "The records of the Carstairs trial are missing. They're nowhere in the file room."

Barrett glared at Archer. "You still gnawing on that bone? Why were you looking for that record?"

Michael cleared his throat as his knees weakened. "Just wanted to make sure we didn't miss anything."

"We didn't," the judge said, eyes flaring. "Take my word for it. Of course, I told you that months ago, and you wouldn't listen."

He turned to the clerk again. "And by whose authority were you getting the records?"

"They had a letter signed by Sheriff Parsons."

"Another Don Quixote. I don't care who signs anything, you don't show any records to anybody without my permission. Is that clear?"

"Yes, your honor."

"All right. You and I will deal with the missing records later. All of you, out of my courtroom. Now."

Outside, Caleb lowered the brim of his hat against the sun bouncing off a store window. "You didn't tell me you had such a warm relationship with the judge. Might have done better if I'd had Malachi and a jug with me."

"Didn't seem too upset about missing records, did he?"

"Nope. Course coulda been because he wanted to get back to his proceedings real quick. Didn't want those lawyers to think he's the type to lose things."

"Could be. What's next?"

"Still need to talk with those witnesses. Still want to see those ledgers."

"Maybe Jeremiah turned up something."

"Maybe." Caleb checked the clock in the bank tower. "Going on five o'clock. Let's meet at Gideon's at six."

"See you then." Michael headed for the parsonage, head down, fists clenched. No closer to clearing Ben's name. Seemed even more distant now, with more roadblocks thrown in their way. Records missing. Other records barred to them. He shot a quick prayer heavenward.

Rachel's face came to mind, the memory of her never far away. Now, the image of her smile gave him peace, relaxed him. He saw her talking with customers, displaying fabric, getting to know what they really wanted, helping to meet that need or desire. The light in her eyes when she smiled glowed in him now.

She loved him. She said it. Her words sang sharp and clear like a cardinal calling its mate. He swallowed the lump in his throat. God brought a beautiful woman into his life when he wasn't even seeking one. A woman who could have any man she wanted; who said she didn't want any. Then said she loved him.

She'd listened to his story and still loved him. He'd listened to hers and wanted to wrap his arms around her, protect her, give her the freedom and independence she desired but also be the rock, the fortress she could turn to.

I need to get back to Riverbend. To Rachel.

CHAPTER 27

Friday, July 5, 1878

MICHAEL KICKED AT the door to Gideon's house, arms filled with two baskets of food Deborah gave him.

Jeremiah yanked the door open. "Is that food?"

Michael stepped in. "Well, it's good to see you, too, Jeremiah. Yes, it's food, Miss Deborah sent supper."

Jeremiah clasped his hands. "The Lord does answer prayer." He nodded over his shoulder. "These two were discussing who has the best stew recipe. We had Caleb's on the trail. I have a feeling Gideon's isn't much better."

"I heard that," Gideon boomed from near the stove.

Michael sniffed. "What's burning?"

Jeremiah glanced over his shoulder. "Not sure. I think Caleb's trying to cook some kind of meat. You got here just in time." He took one of the baskets from Michael and set it on the table. "Fried chicken and mashed potatoes. Miss Deborah has a place in heaven."

Michael took out two pies, a container of string beans and a loaf of sourdough bread. "We won't starve tonight."

"I'll make some coffee." Caleb offered.

Jeremiah held up his hand. "Please, let me. You gentlemen have done more than enough in the kitchen already."

Caleb looked at Gideon. "I think we've been insulted."

Gideon shrugged. "As long as I don't have to eat your cooking or drink your coffee, I'm fine with that." He hobbled to a chair, and stretched his wounded leg out before him.

They started to eat with the quickness of men on a mission but soon settled into savoring Deborah's culinary delights. Michael knew he could never cook like this. Could Rachel? As near as he could recall, any meals he'd eaten with her had been at the hotel. Or Martha had been involved. Did it matter? Not in the least. Love would get them through.

"Can Rachel cook?" Caleb's voice brought Michael back to the table.

"Don't know."

"Better find out real quick if you're fixin' to marry her," Caleb said. "Love won't fill an empty stomach for very long or soothe one hurt from bad cooking."

Michael grinned at the teasing in Caleb's eye. "Maybe I'll ask her to fix Sunday dinner for us when we get back to Riverbend."

Caleb held up his hand. "You go first. I'll come the following Sunday, if you're still with us."

After dinner, they sat with fresh coffee. Gideon stuffed a pipe with tobacco and struck a match, puffing until a pleasant aroma spread over the room. He pointed the stem at Michael. "Louis Reavey was asking about you."

Michael nodded. "I stopped in the store on my way to the parsonage earlier. He wanted to know if I was ready to come back to work. Told him I needed to take care of some other business first."

Gideon bobbed his head. "Like finding Winslow's killer."

Caleb toasted with his cup. "And getting married."

Heat crept up Michael's face. "If she'll have me."

Jeremiah pulled several sheets of paper from his coat pocket and smoothed them out on the table. "I heard from several contacts this afternoon. More should be getting back to me tomorrow."

He flipped through the papers. "Gordon Lucius Smythe is an interesting character, to say the least. During the war, he was suspected of stealing Union supplies and selling them to citizens or the Rebels. Before the war, he may have done some slave trading. One of my contacts reports that, for the right price, he would either help a runaway slave into the Underground Railroad, or tell the master where to find him. Sometimes both."

Gideon slurped his coffee. "Slaves couldn't pay him any money."

"No, but abolitionists or churches would." Jeremiah turned a couple of sheets over. "Before he came to Saint Louis, he was in a shipping business in Cincinnati. Shipments seemed to disappear unless the shipper purchased insurance."

Caleb held his hand up. "Let me guess. Smythe sold the insurance."

"Not directly, but he seems to have owned the company issuing it."

Caleb nodded. "And he stayed close enough to the law not to be charged with anything."

Jeremiah picked up one sheet. "That and made contributions to a law officer's fading eyesight when necessary."

Michael cleared his throat. "Is he capable of murder?"

"No record of any violence or killing, but I'm sure he associated with people who could murder if necessary. Nothing ever tied to him, though. In fact, he's never been charged with a crime."

Caleb's fist clenched. "But cheated and robbed people, and ruined lives just the same."

Jeremiah re-stacked the papers, folded them and slid them into his pocket. "Yep."

Gideon sighed. "All right. Here's my suggestion seein' as how I can't move around as quick as you fellers with two good legs. Michael and Caleb, you start talking to the witnesses. Jeremiah, you visit this Smythe fella. With the information you dug up, he might be more cooperative. Maybe you can talk to Mrs. Winslow, too. You're a little more polished than these two." He jerked his thumb at Caleb and Michael. "You might have more of that southern charm she likes."

Caleb snorted. "Yeah, Jeremiah, maybe you can sweet talk the ledgers out of her."

Jeremiah placed his hand over his heart, and spoke in an exaggerated drawl. "Gentlemen, I shall endeavor to maximize my natural charm and glowing personality to persuade the bereaved Widow Winslow to give us access to the information we so greatly desire."

Michael placed his chin in his hand. "Didn't seem all that bereaved to me."

->=◎ ◎=<-

Sleep wouldn't come. Michael rose from his bed, slipped into his pants and shirt and stepped out onto the porch of the parsonage. The town was quiet as the bank tower clock struck one in the distance. A low mist rising from the river smudged the shadows cast by the half-moon.

He sat on the top step, leaning against the post that supported the roof. Ben's hanging haunted him, from the boy's pleading eyes to the Celtic cross that now rested with Sam Carstairs to the gruesome sound of the rope snapping taut against Ben's weight. Michael let the tears flow. *He didn't have to die. He shouldn't have died.* He had to find the real killer. Not for Sam's sake, or even his own. For Ben's sake.

He bowed his head and prayed.

With his back against the post, eyes closed, he controlled his breathing to encourage sleep to come. He smiled at the thought of Rachel sleeping. He imagined her curled in her bed, hair splayed in a honey-brown rainbow, face soft, relaxed, lashes resting on her cheek. Did she snore? Her features so delicate, like porcelain, in the moonlight streaming through her window.

She's waiting for me. A miracle from God.

The door squeaked open and Zechariah stepped onto the porch.

"Didn't mean to disturb you," Michael whispered.

"You didn't." Zechariah sighed as he lowered himself into a chair. "Some nights, Deborah's snoring is enough to wake a bear from hibernation. This is one of them. Don't tell her I said so."

"Your secret's safe with me. I wouldn't say anything to put me on her bad side. I like her cooking too much."

"Nice to know where your loyalty lies."

Michael wanted to look away. Zechariah's gaze seemed to lift the cover to his heart.

"You've changed, Michael. That heavy cloud seems to be gone."

Michael picked a loose splinter from the floor of the porch. "Mostly. The Lord kind of showed me I don't really have a monster inside. Just a drive to protect people." He tossed the splinter into the night air, watched it spin to the ground. "Taking some getting used to, wish I didn't have to hurt—to kill— some to protect others."

"Sometimes you don't have a choice." Zechariah's voice sounded hundreds of miles away, lost in wistful melancholy.

"I know, but the guilt gets real strong."

"That's the devil trying to steer you the wrong way."

Michael shrugged.

"That's not the only change," Zechariah said. "Deborah saw it right off. Said she saw it as soon as you stepped off the train."

Michael felt his face scrunch into a frown as he looked at his mentor.

Zechariah chuckled. "She said you're smitten. Some girl's worked her way into your heart and won't let go."

"Can't hide much from Miss Deborah. Never could. Her name's Rachel, Rachel Stone. She's…she's a dressmaker in Riverbend. Lives with the Matthews."

"And?"

Michael shrugged. "And we care for each other. When this is over, I'll go back to see if we're really meant to be together."

"To hear Deborah tell it, you should have married her before you came back. Brought her with you."

Michael laughed. "It's a little more complicated than that."

Michael sensed Zechariah waiting, using the silence as an invitation to speak. "Rachel's a very strong woman," Michael said. "She came out of a lot of mistreatment and a bad life less than a year ago. She won't let any man control her again. It took a lot for her to admit she cared for me. She won't rush into this." Michael laughed. "I haven't exactly had a whole lot of experience like this with women, either. I'm feeling my way too."

Zechariah clamped his hand on Michael's shoulder. "You'll figure it out. You'll feel dumb as a mule while you're doing it but you'll get there."

CHAPTER 28

Saturday, July 6, 1878

"MAKES SATURDAY IN Riverbend look like a ghost town," Caleb remarked as he and Michael weaved through the jostling crowd of men in a variety of garb, hoop-skirted women and running children.

Michael nodded. "Tramlaw Saturdays always feel like holidays with all the planters and farmers swarming into town." He eyed the throng. With all the bumping and jostling, the crowd was a great place for picking pockets.

He smiled at the irony. Getting caught picking pockets was what led him to Zechariah and Jesus. And Ben. A cloud passed through his mind. And to Sam and killing Maria.

The cloud cleared. And to Rachel.

"Winslow was killed on a Saturday, right?" Caleb's statement snapped him back to the sultry summer Saturday morning in Tramlaw.

"I believe he was. Why?"

Caleb waved at the crowd. "Lots of people means lots of possible suspects. Instead of fishing in a pond, we're castin' nets in an ocean. Those ledgers sure would help."

Michael agreed, but he would settle for any useful information. He hoped the blacksmith Adam Jones would be more helpful than the three fruitless and frustrating interviews they had already conducted this morning.

At first glance, Adam looked as wide as he was tall. Further scrutiny revealed the well-muscled arms, shoulders and neck of a blacksmith. Sweat plastered Adam's red hair to his head as he stood at his anvil, bare armed, hammer ringing to shape and mold the piece of metal held by his tongs. His skin glistened under a coating of sweat.

Several men stood in a loose semi-circle around the smith. Farmers, from the sound of the conversations about crops, water, varmints, and taxes. Adam spoke little, pounded a few more blows and shoved the metal into a bucket of water. Hissing steam clouded his features for a moment. He examined the metal, a strap of some sort, nodded. He used his punch to poke holes in the strap, picked it up along with a few others.

"Here you go, Oliver." He handed the clanging bundle to one of the farmers. "These hinges should be just what you need."

"Much obliged, Adam." The farmer's face saddened. "Kin you put it on my account? I'll pay ya when I sell my crop."

Adam wiped his hands on his leather apron and took a notebook and pencil from his back pocket. "Sure. No problem." He jotted something in the notebook.

A grin broke across Adam's face as Michael and Caleb took Oliver's place. The smith shook Michael's hand in a grip that was amazingly gentle given the man's size and occupation.

"Michael, it's so good to have you back. We haven't had a good baseball game in this town since you left." He turned serious. "Did you get to see Ben's father?"

"Yeah." Michael wiped sweat from the back of his neck. "We were able to work things out."

"Can't tell that by lookin' at ya."

"His father died the day I met him." Michael shook off the memory. "I'll tell you about it sometime." He introduced Caleb. "Can you answer a few questions for us about the day Donald Winslow was killed?"

Adam shrugged, wiped his face and neck with a bandana. "Sure but I told everything I knew at the trial."

"I know. Ben's father asked me to try to clear Ben's name. Caleb and another friend are helping me."

Adam folded his arms across his chest. "What do you want to know?"

Caleb stuffed his hands in his back pockets, scuffed his boot along the ground. "Do you remember what day of the week it was?"

"It was a Saturday. I remember cuz I was so busy I coulda used two more arms and another anvil to keep up."

"Did you see or talk to Winslow much that day?" Caleb asked.

"A couple of times. He wanted me to shoe some horses for him."

"How'd he seem?" Caleb said.

"Fine. Didn't talk much. Customers kept me hopping."

"How about him?" Michael asked.

"I think he was pretty busy himself. I remember he had people in and out all day it seemed like."

"Anybody stand out?" Caleb seemed like he was discussing the weather, relaxed, unconcerned. Michael's stomach flip-flopped, anxious for some answer, some clue that would point to Ben's innocence.

Adam shook his head. "Like I said, I was kind of busy myself." He paused, rubbed his chin. "That banker fella came by two, maybe three times. Can smell that bath water he wears a mile away."

"Christopher Barrett?" Michael cringed at the name. The man whose pocket he'd been caught picking.

"Yeah, that's him."

"Anything else?" Caleb leaned against the anvil.

"Winslow was jumpier than usual. Told me he was waiting on an Army contract. Boasted it would bring in big money."

"You heard the shot?" Caleb said.

"Oh, yeah. I grabbed my shotgun from the office and went over to Winslow's. Got there the same time as Sheriff Parsons. He told me to wait outside. He came out a few minutes later with the Carstairs kid."

"Did you hear anything before the shot?" Caleb said.

"Like what?"

Caleb shrugged. "Arguing, maybe? Voices raised?"

Adam shook his head, gestured at the anvil. "I get to banging on that block of iron, I can't hear much of anything."

"Did you see Ben go in?" Michael asked.

"Nope. Too busy myself to notice everybody who went in or out. Remember the banker because he stinks to high heaven with that bath water."

Caleb seemed to run out of questions.

Michael shook Adam's hand. "Thanks for your time."

"Sure. There'll probably be a ball game tomorrow after church. You gonna play?"

"Maybe. Have to see this through first."

As they walked away, Caleb hesitated in front of the horse trader's office. "Sure is tempting to walk in on him, but we'll let Jeremiah work on him first."

Michael stopped short as a boy ran in front of him followed by a girl, her face flushed with anger, threatening the boy with bodily harm and eternal damnation. A memory of his sister, Ellie, chasing him across the fields after he slipped a frog down her back made him smile.

"What do you know about this banker feller?" Caleb said.

"Judge's brother. Runs the bank. And he's very sensitive about having his pockets picked."

"You tried to pick the pocket of the judge's brother? No wonder you got such a stiff sentence."

Michael shrugged. "I didn't he know they were related, and I didn't expect to get caught."

"Kinda explains why the judge doesn't hold you in the highest esteem."

Michael jammed his hands in his pockets. "That does appear to present a problem."

Gideon greeted them at the door to his house, crutch under his arm. "Well? What did you find out?"

Caleb pushed his hat back. "Think we might be able to come in and set a spell?"

Gideon opened the door wider and motioned them in with the crutch. "Come on. Come on."

"Careful with that thing," Caleb said. "Might break somebody's leg the way you swing it around."

Gideon swatted Caleb's butt with the piece of carved wood. "Or some other part of your body you've grown attached to."

Michael looked around the small room. "Where's Jeremiah?"

"Not back yet."

Caleb opened his watch. "He's been awhile."

Gideon stumped to the kitchen table. "Southern charm can be real slow sometimes. Can't pour it out all at once. Have to let it ooze. Tell me what you found out."

Caleb placed his hat on the table. "Michael, will you fix us some coffee please?"

Gideon slapped the table with the palm of his hand. "Don't keep me waiting."

"For a man who knows so much about Southern charm, you are seriously lacking. When I get my coffee, I'll talk. You know a true Southern gentleman would have already had it made with some fortifying spirits to go with it." Caleb winked at Michael.

"I'll fortify your spirit with this crutch if you don't start talking."

Caleb held up his hand. "Coffee first."

Michael expected Gideon's ears to spew steam and whistle like a train.

"You are the stubbornest man I ever did meet," Gideon said.

Caleb leaned back, stretched out his legs and closed his eyes.

Michael served the coffee. Gideon took a sip, licked his lips and pushed the cup towards Michael. "More sugar."

Michael sighed and added more to the cup. Gideon sipped again.

"Better," the sheriff said. "Now talk to me."

Caleb wrapped his hands around his cup, not drinking. "Not much to say. Didn't learn anything that put anybody else in that office to do the shooting. Nobody we talked to was in a position to see everyone who went in and out. They all remember it was a Saturday, and Winslow seemed to be real busy."

Gideon drained his cup and held it out to Michael for more. "We're missing something."

Michael refilled it, and returned to the table. "Will sure help to see those ledgers." He ran his finger around the edge of his cup. "Gideon, do you remember anything about Winslow hoping to get an Army contract? Adam Jones mentioned it, but I don't remember hearing anything about it at the time of the shooting or the trial."

Gideon shook his head. "Nope. Don't recall any mention of it. I'm pretty sure he bid every chance he got, but I don't think he ever got a contract."

Michael nodded.

Caleb sipped his coffee. "Tell me about this banker, Christopher Barrett."

Gideon rubbed his chin, eyes focused on the far wall. "Thinks very highly of himself. Don't know that many would agree with him, including the judge. Family is the richest in the county. Big plantation about five miles south of town. Christopher's always got big ideas, big plans. Don't ever seem to pan out."

Michael asked, "Could he be having money problems?"

"Doubt it. Family's got enough money to cover his schemes."

Michael's thoughts tumbled like rocks down a mountainside, except there was no bottom. The rocks kept tumbling and bouncing, sometimes ricocheting to places he'd never been. His heart told him Ben was innocent. His mind told him there was no way to prove it.

There had to be.

A knock rattled the door. Michael opened it, and Jeremiah entered, removed his hat and with a sweeping gesture of his arm, bowed at the waist. "Gentlemen, it is a pleasure to be among such fine, outstanding citizens of this fair city. I bring you tidings from the lovely Widow Winslow."

"I didn't know you had clothes that fancy," Caleb said.

Jeremiah examined himself as if he had never seen such a sight. Cream-colored suit and matching Stetson, pale yellow brocade vest and matching cravat, white shirt, gold watch chain, boots so polished they hurt the eyes and a black walking stick with a silver lion's head.

He sniffed, and spoke in a sophisticated drawl. "Sir, never underestimate the resources of sartorial splendor a Southern gentleman has at his disposal in order to assuage the troubled spirit of a grieving widow with the comforts and language of her class."

Gideon snorted. "Can you say that in plain English?"

Jeremiah dropped his hat on Gideon's head, placed his hand on the back of Michael's chair, and made a show of opening his watch. "Gentlemen, my partners in the pursuit of justice in this fair land, the beautiful widow Emma Winslow will allow us to look at the ledger of the day of her husband's murder at three o'clock this afternoon in her parlor."

Michael's heart soared. "How did you manage that?"

Jeremiah pointed a finger in the air and opened his mouth. After a moment, he looked at Michael. "I have no idea. I think I simply wore her down. And prayer may have softened her heart."

He accepted the coffee Michael poured for him, sniffed it. "Who made this?"

Caleb pointed at Michael. Jeremiah nodded. "Ah, good then." And sipped. "I appealed to the mother instinct in her, persuaded her that any mother would want to know beyond a shadow of a doubt that her son was indeed guilty. I also told her the sooner she let us see the ledger, the sooner we'd leave her alone."

"She didn't threaten you with the judge?" Gideon said.

"Oh, she did. She did indeed. But I responded with a higher authority."

"God?" Michael suggested.

"She may be a Christian but I think she views God as someone who must listen to her. No, I mentioned the governor is my cousin and has a particular interest in this case."

"He does?" Michael struggled to control the incredulousness in his voice.

Jeremiah shrugged. "Well, he will the next time I talk to him. I was exercising the gift of prophecy with Widow Winslow."

CHAPTER 29

Saturday, July 6, 1878

RACHEL SQUEEZED THE fingers of her right hand as the scenery outside the train picked up speed.

Is this train going to stop at every town between here and Saint Louis? Of course it is. That's the way of trains.

No matter what her heart wished, they were not going to go to Tramlaw non-stop just for her, a woman with a vision. They'd just put her down as a touched, overly excited female.

She tried to pray, but images of Michael, bloodied and shot, pushed the ability to string words together from her mind. Tears were her prayers, from her heart to God—pleading for Michael's protection. She imagined him lying on a bed, what could be seen of his body the same color as the sheet and bandages. Except for the blood. Bright, scarlet splotches and streaks. Eyes fired with pain, muscles tensed in agony. *Live, Michael. Live.*

"Excuse me, miss. I think we've met before."

She blinked the tears away and her vision cleared. A man, sandy hair streaked with gray. Well-worn suit straining over a paunch. Small eyes set in folds of skin. A stranger. He must have boarded the train at the last stop.

"I don't think so." Emotion choked her voice, softened it, weakened it.

He sat next to her, turned toward her, arm on the seat back behind her. "I know we have. Someone as beautiful as you is not easily forgotten."

"You're mistaken, sir. I've never seen you before." She tensed, started to rise.

His hand rested on her arm, holding her. "Yes, you have. Now where was it?" He snapped his fingers. "Eighteen months ago. Denver. Red Mary's."

His other arm encircled her shoulder. "Yes. It was quite an evening's entertainment you provided. Well worth the cost."

No one sat nearby. No one else in the car seemed to notice. Where was the conductor?

"This is such a serendipitous opportunity to renew our relationship." His grip tightened on her arm. "I think we should take advantage of accommodations at the next stop to celebrate."

She slipped her hand into the cloth bag she held on her lap. "Sir, the person you're referring to doesn't exist anymore." She moved the bag, drawing his attention to it. "In this bag, I am holding a Derringer. At this range, I can do serious damage to your heart, your stomach, or..." She glanced down his torso. "Other areas of your body. If you are not out of this car by the time I count to three, I will shoot you. Twice." She smiled. "I will try not to kill you, although you may wish I had."

The man's chin quivered as color drained from his face. "You wouldn't."

Rachel shrugged. "Sir, I am so tired of men like you thinking you can control me, make me do what you want. I will not hesitate to shoot to protect myself, and I might save some other girl from the likes of you in the future. Of course, you can sit here and see if I'm serious."

Sweat beaded his upper lip. His nostrils flared and he fiddled with the tie around his neck.

"One."

He stood as if one of Rachel's needles had risen through the bench to stab his backside. "You are one crazy woman. I just wanted to have some fun, and you threaten to kill me."

He swept his carpetbag from the overhead rack, throwing himself off balance. He grabbed a seat back to keep from falling and hurried to the connecting door. He turned to look back at her and bumped into the conductor who entered at that moment. His mouth moved, but no sound came out. He glanced at Rachel once more, and rushed onto the platform between the cars.

The conductor walked over to her. "Is everything all right, miss?" She relished the gentle concern in his eyes. Comfort instead of lust.

She nodded. "He thought I was somebody else. Everything's fine now. Thank you."

The conductor moved on. Rachel took several deep breaths, trying to slow her heart pounding against her ribs. After several minutes, the tremor in her arms subsided, her stomach unclenched, her knees stopped shaking.

She folded her hands over her bag. *Guess I'm going to have get a Derringer. Can't go around lying to folks.*

She closed her eyes. Her mind would not stop whirling through images of Michael, hurt and bleeding. Her fingers grew numb under her grip. Prayer started, then faded into a jumble.

The train slowed for the next stop. She stifled the urge to curse.

In a restaurant at the station, she choked down stringy stew and weak coffee. She hadn't eaten since breakfast the day before. She had no desire to eat, but her stomach told her she needed food. The meal rode like a rock.

As she re-boarded the train, the stranger did the same one car up. She nodded and held up her bag. He disappeared up the steps like a squirrel up a tree. The victory tasted bittersweet.

Three more days until she reached Tramlaw. Seemed like a lifetime. Time moved too slow. The train even slower.

Out the window, a hawk dove to the ground, picked up a rabbit in its talons. *Oh, to have wings like that, to fly, to soar, to be with Michael in a few hours.*

She opened her Bible to Saint Matthew's Gospel. "And said, for this cause shall a man leave father and mother, and shall cleave to his wife: and they twain shall be one flesh. Wherefore they are no more twain, but one flesh. What therefore God hath joined together, let not man put asunder."

The words burned into her mind, her heart. Her dream of God's plan for her and Michael in black and white. She sighed. *Please, Lord.* Her eyes drooped. She was in the valley of her vision again, Michael by her side. The voice, deep and strong, within and around her. "This is the man I have chosen to be your husband." More words now. "Trust me."

CHAPTER 30

Saturday, July 6, 1878

MICHAEL'S SHIRT COLLAR felt like it'd shrunk two sizes on the walk from Gideon's place to the Winslow…*mansion* was the only name he could call it. He covered his stomach with his other hand, certain its jumpiness was visible. To look as calm and collected as Jeremiah was as far away as the moon. The man exuded confidence like a politician giving a speech.

Jeremiah rapped on the door with the knob of his walking stick. It opened before he could put the tip of the stick on the paving stones of the front walk. Bessie bowed and held the door wide open. "Mizz Winslow is expectin' y'all. Please come this way."

Bessie escorted them through a set of double doors into the parlor. Michael stopped in the doorway. *How much money does this woman have?* The room was larger than Gideon's house. Fieldstone fireplaces filled each end of the room. Gleaming white wainscoting met green floral wallpaper that climbed to the ceiling. Portraits of serious-faced people mixed with paintings of hunting scenes and landscapes. Clusters of upholstered couches and chairs dotted the thick carpet like horses in a pasture.

Emma Winslow stood at one of the fireplaces, one hand on the mantle, the other holding a glass of reddish liquid. Her green dress was as intimately revealing as the blue she'd worn the first time they'd called on her. *Beautiful and knows it. Uses it.*

She faced them, a studied, purposeful turning of the head. Her smile stopped at her lips. She moved toward them, floating more than walking. She extended her hand to Jeremiah. "Why, Colonel Turner, it is so nice to see you again."

Michael swallowed his surprise as Jeremiah kissed the back of her hand. "The pleasure is all mine, Mrs. Winslow."

Her eyes flicked to Michael, a gaze one gave a dog traipsing mud on the furniture. She nodded. "Mr. Archer, so good to see you as well."

Michael bowed his head. "Thank you for making the time to meet with us again, Ma'am."

"Some refreshment?"

Jeremiah glanced at the glass in her hand. "A small sherry, perhaps."

She poured glasses for both of them and refilled her own.

Jeremiah sipped his. "Excellent sherry, Mrs. Winslow."

She tsked, put a hand on his arm. "Please, Colonel. Call me Emma."

Jeremiah chuckled. "Only if you call me Jeremiah."

Michael held his glass like it was a rattler. The pretensions grated his ears. *Enough with this folderol. Let's do what we came here to do.*

"Miss Emma, would now be a good time to look at the ledgers?" If Jeremiah was anxious about this meeting, he sure hid it well. Michael's knees knocked so much he expected his feet to dance out of his boots.

"Why, certainly, Colonel." She gestured toward a grouping of a couch and two armchairs around a low table. A squarish leather-bound book lay centered on the top, a piece of paper protruding from it. "Let's sit, and you can peruse the book for the day of my husband's ghastly murder." Her hand went to her throat and her voice quivered.

Jeremiah made a show of sitting on the couch so as not to crinkle his suit. Emma Winslow sat next to him, their arms brushing. Michael moved one of the armchairs close to Jeremiah's other side.

Jeremiah took a notebook and pencil from an inner pocket of his suit coat, flipped open the cover and, using the protruding paper as a guide, opened the ledger. He pointed at the date. Michael nodded. The date of the murder.

Michael studied where the pages met the binding. No obvious tears. No signs of pages being cut out. The column headings seemed simple enough: Date of sale, type of horse, stock number, sold to, bought from, and price.

Donald Winslow bought eighteen horses and sold twenty-three on the day he died. Some of the names were familiar to Michael. There were several he didn't recognize at all. He counted Christopher Barrett's name five times, all sales to Winslow.

Jeremiah wrote down each customer in a neat column in his notebook with a *B* for bought or *S* for sold by each name. Emma Winslow put her hand on Jeremiah's. "Such strong handwriting." She smiled and leaned forward. Michael turned the other way. He'd seen girls in saloons with more modesty.

Jeremiah moved his hand, leaving her to place hers in her lap. "Why, thank you, Miss Emma. The instructors at the Citadel made sure we could write clearly. All those maps and charts and reports, you know."

Michael held back a snort as she giggled and batted her eyes at Jeremiah. "I wouldn't know about such things. I'm so grateful you men can manage those affairs."

As subtle as a freight train.

After writing the last name, Jeremiah tapped his pencil against the paper as if thinking.

Michael flipped to the previous page of the ledger.

Emma Winslow cleared her throat. "Mr. Archer, I was quite clear with Colonel Turner. You could look at the ledger for the day of my husband's murder. That's all."

Crimson heat crept up Michael's neck. "Yes, Ma'am. I was just looking to see if this was a typical amount of business for him."

She stiffened. "Well, I wouldn't know. He never discussed his business with me in any depth. Said I didn't need to know about it. I do remember he always said Saturday was generally his busiest day."

She stood. He and Jeremiah followed suit. "If there isn't anything else, gentlemen, I do need to prepare for dinner guests."

Jeremiah slipped the notebook and pencil inside his jacket. "Miss Emma, I think we've accomplished all we can for now. Thank you again for allowing us to view the ledger. It was most helpful." He took her hand and kissed it. "Do enjoy your guests this evening."

"Thank you, Colonel." She let her hand linger in his. "Perhaps some evening you could join me for dinner."

"Perhaps."

Outside, Michael glanced over his shoulder. Emma Winslow stood at the window of the parlor. Michael had the distinct impression her eyes were on Jeremiah, not him.

"So what's with the Colonel bit?"

Jeremiah chuckled. "It's been my experience that Southern belles like Mrs. Winslow put a lot of stock in titles. And I *was* a colonel. I neglected to tell her it was under Sheridan in the Shenandoah. A minor detail I didn't want her to fret over."

"Let's hope Gideon recognizes some of those names. Like Caleb says, I still feel like we're fishing in the ocean."

→►═◉ ◉═◄←

Michael paced the narrow area of Gideon's parlor as the sheriff hunkered over the kitchen table, scanning the list of names, Jeremiah and Caleb on either side of him. An unfinished checker game sat at the other end of the table. The aroma of fresh coffee beckoned, but Michael's stomach lurched at the thought of adding any more coffee to it, no matter how good Jeremiah's tasted.

"Interesting." Gideon's soft-spoken comment stopped Michael in mid-stride.

"What's that?" Caleb's voice sounded sleepy. His eyes looked heavy.

"Never thought Christopher Barrett would deal directly in that much horseflesh."

Jeremiah handed Gideon a pencil. "Put a check next to his name. Might be worth looking at him a little closer."

"The judge's brother?" Caleb rubbed his eyes. "Seems unlikely."

Jeremiah sipped his coffee. "You're probably right, but we can look at him later if nothing else turns up."

"Here's one I don't know." Gideon jabbed at the paper with the pencil. "This Micah Grimmler. Never heard that name before."

Michael leaned over Gideon's shoulder. "Me neither. Looks like he was the last customer."

"Last one in the ledger, anyways." Gideon stood, gasped and grabbed the table. "Times I forget this blasted leg until I try to stand on it."

Caleb took the list from Gideon and scanned it. "If you don't know this Grimmler feller, he might have been visiting. Let's canvas the hotels and boarding houses. See if anybody knows him."

"Livery stables too," Michael said. "How about if we split up? Cover more ground that way." Michael took three sheets of paper, divided the boarding houses and hotels across the three and added Adam's livery stable to his. "There's a small livery at the east end of town, name of O'Malley's. I split these up geographically. Jeremiah, you have the west side. Caleb, the east. And I'll take the middle."

Gideon followed them to the door, hobbling on his crutch. "Meet back here at sundown."

Michael stopped at the open door and bowed his head. "Lord, guide our steps and our words. Help us to find this Micah Grimmler."

->==o o==<-

Two hours later, Michael walked out of a small boarding house near the railroad station. Frustration boiled. One hotel, six boarding houses. No one had ever heard of Micah Grimmler. *I'm chasing a ghost.*

He stopped on the boardwalk, used his bandana to wipe the sweat from his face and neck. As he re-tied it, he glanced at his reflection in a store window. He re-did it a second time, and studied a man across the street and a few stores behind him.

Why does he look familiar? Tall, heavyset, vest over a faded blue shirt, tan pants, boots. Left-handed gun, holster tied just above his knee. Empty right sleeve tucked into his coat pocket. Michael walked up the street, reviewing the man's features, trying to place him. He'd seen the stranger before. Today in fact, every time he came out of a hotel or boarding house, the man lurked nearby, within a few buildings.

Nah. I'm just imagining things.

At the next side street, Michael turned right. At the next street, he turned right again. As he did, he glanced back and noticed the man turn onto the street he'd just turned from. Michael trotted around the next corner and braced himself against the side of the building. He waited. He counted two minutes. Nothing. He peered around the corner. An empty street faced him.

He exhaled. *Spooked by shadows.* The dim sky fading to shades of gray reminded him sundown approached. One more stop before heading back to Gideon's.

His heart sank when he saw the door to the livery closed. *I missed him.*

Wait. Adam has a room at the back. A patch of lamplight spilling through a window guided Michael through the dimness along the side of the stable. He knocked on the door.

"Michael. What brings you back?" Adam held a frying pan. "I was fixin' to fry me some chicken. Want some?"

"Some other time, Adam. I'd really like to. I miss our chicken dinners. But I've got to get back to Gideon's."

"Sure. What do you need?"

"Does the name Micah Grimmler mean anything to you?"

Adam put the frying pan on the stove and rubbed his chin as he poured coffee for himself. Michael declined the coffee but accepted water from a wooden bucket. Cold and crisp, just from the well.

"Traveling salesman as I recall. Boards his horse when he's in town. Think he's involved in the murder?"

Michael shrugged and dipped the ladle into the water again. "Can't say. From the ledger, it looks like he might have been Winslow's last customer on the day he was shot."

Adam frowned, his brow like unevenly plowed rows. He took a notebook from one of several on a shelf above his bed and flipped through several pages.

"Here he is." He showed the page to Michael. The day of Winslow's murder. Adam scanned the page, his finger running across each entry. Michael could not decipher what passed for Adam's handwriting.

"The horse he came in on was pretty wore out. So he bought a new one from Winslow. Left his old one with me to rest and recover. I was to sell it when it was healthy again and use the money to pay any fees and keep any left over for profit." He flipped a few more pages. "Poor horse. Died about a week later."

"Did Grimmler say if his dealings with Winslow went all right? Did he say if there were any problems?"

Adam shrugged. "Can't say that he did. Don't remember a lot. Like I said earlier, Saturdays are real busy for me."

"Have you seen Grimmler since then?"

Adam closed the book, tapped it against the palm of his hand. "Can't say as I have. Which is unusual. He generally comes through here about once a month."

"Do you know where he stays when he's here?"

"Patterson's."

That was on Jeremiah's list. Maybe he learned something.

Michael shook Adam's hand. "Thanks for your help."

"My pleasure. See you at church tomorrow."

Michael touched the brim of his hat. "Looking forward to it."

"And baseball afterwards?"

Michael held up his hands. "Can't promise that. I'll be there if I can."

Full dark poised over the town as if held back by the pale streak of sky in the west, the remnant of the day's light holding on. Michael hurried his steps, anxious to hear what Jeremiah and Caleb had learned, pondering if what he'd learned about Micah Grimmler provided any useful information. He checked store windows for any sign of the stranger, but the fading daylight was too dim.

At Gideon's, the other three attacked steaks and mashed potatoes like men who hadn't eaten in three weeks. Michael's stomach rumbled.

Gideon sopped at the juice on his plate with a chunk of bread. "Miss Deborah said to tell you your dinner's waiting at the parsonage. But before you go, what did you find out?"

He relayed his conversation with Adam but decided not to tell about the stranger. Didn't seem as threatening now.

Jeremiah finished off his last bite of steak. "Agrees with what Mrs. Patterson told me. This Grimmler usually stays there two, maybe three, nights every month, but they haven't seen him since the murder."

Michael's mouth watered as Caleb popped another bite of steak into his mouth.

Gideon swirled his coffee cup. "All right. I think we've done all we can for one night. Everybody get a good night's sleep, and we'll meet up right after church." He cocked an eyebrow at Michael. "Unless some of us have a baseball game to get to."

Michael shook his head. "No, this is more important."

CHAPTER 31

Saturday, July 6, 1878

MICHAEL SETTLED INTO the rocker on Zechariah's porch. Deborah's dinner rested in his stomach like a head on a pillow. And apple pie waited. Hands resting on the Bible in his lap, he savored the warm night air stirring on the breeze off the river. He closed his eyes and Rachel came into view. Saturday night. He imagined her helping Martha with baths for Abigail and Daniel, laying out Sunday clothes. Heat rose into his face as he thought of her preparing her own bath.

He stole a quick glance through the window. Zechariah sat near the fire reading his Bible. Deborah sat on the couch, sewing a button on Zechariah's preaching jacket. Good. They didn't see him get red in the face over thoughts of Rachel.

He leaned back and dreamed of a time when he and Rachel would sit in their own parlor on a Saturday evening, at peace in each other's company. The rocker squeaked against the floor of the porch.

"Lord, let this assignment end soon. Guide us to Donald Winslow's murderer. Open our eyes and ears so we don't miss anything you want us to see or hear."

The hairs on the back of his head prickled. He opened his eyes but kept his head against the back of the chair. *What's out there?*

Head still, he scanned the area from left to right. Nothing. No movement. No sounds.

Must be imagining things.

No. Something or someone is out there. Where? Too many shadows.

Eyes scanning, ears seeking any noise, he counted five minutes. Still nothing.

That stranger on the street today has me jumpy. Seeing things that aren't there.

He opened the Bible but didn't look at it.

A skitter to his left. A black cat scurried from Zechariah's yard, chasing something Michael couldn't see.

He breathed a sigh of relief. *Relax.* Closed his eyes again, bringing Rachel back.

Another sound. Soft. Indistinct. *A boot on the ground? Another animal hunting in the shrubs near the porch?*

To his right, a shadow moved. Too big to be a cat or dog. *Did a horse get loose?* He strained to see across the street, to give a name to whatever was there, a name would make it real.

He spun his head to the left. The cat again, strutting this time, mouse dangling from its mouth.

He forced himself to grin.

A click. Like a gun being cocked. From across the street.

He squinted. Nothing.

A glint. Moonlight on metal.

A flame shot out as a hammer slammed into a bullet.

A chunk splintered off the back of the rocker. Glass broke behind him.

A voice. "Stay away from the Winslow murder, or the next one will be between your eyes."

Michael leapt off the porch, was halfway to the street, when he heard from behind him came a howl of pain, desperation and disbelief.

"Deborah. No." The sound tore from Zechariah's throat like a coyote's wail.

Michael careened into the parlor. Zechariah knelt by the couch, skin gray as granite, clutching Deborah to his chest.

Michael stepped closer, hesitant, bile rising in his throat. He peered over his mentor's shoulder, could only see part of Deborah's body. Blood seeped onto her dress, her face white, eyes closed.

He touched Zechariah. "Lay her down." He whispered. Hoping his words penetrated the man's pain. "Let me see her."

Michael cradled her head as the two of them stretched her out on the couch, her feet dangling off to the side. Blood on her chest. Near her heart. How near? Michael pressed his ear to her chest. A heartbeat. Slow. Weak. Blood continued to flow.

Grabbing a towel from the kitchen, Michael folded it, placed it over the wound, and placed Zechariah's hands on the cloth. "Press on it. Try to stop the bleeding. I'm going for the doctor."

He bolted out the door. A deputy jogged up the street, gun drawn.

"I heard a shot."

Michael skidded to a stop. "Miss Deborah's been shot. Didn't see who did it. I'm going for the doctor." He pointed his thumb at the parsonage. "Help Zechariah." He didn't wait to see what the man would do.

Two blocks over and one block south, Michael pounded on the door of Doctor MacKenzie's house. His breath came in gasps, his lungs burned.

When the doctor opened the door, Michael couldn't speak.

He gulped air, and pulled at the man's shirt. "Miss Deborah…Shot…Come."

MacKenzie turned inside but reappeared in seconds, shrugging on his coat, bag in his hand.

"Hurry." Michael tugged his arm. "It's her chest."

-→=◉ ◉=←-

Michael paced the hallway outside of Zechariah and Deborah's bedroom, head down, hands clasped behind his back. *What have I done?*

Through the slightly ajar door, Michael had a narrow view of Deborah on the bed, the doctor leaning over her, fingers on some sort of instrument protruding from her chest. "Come on. Come on."

The man sputtered an exasperated sigh.

Michael prayed. "Lord, save her. Help Doc find the bullet. Guide his hand. Save her, Lord. Please."

"Ah." The MacKenzie's arm moved with agonizing slowness as it pulled the instrument from the wound. The tool clattered into a bowl on the floor.

"She is blessed, Pastor," the doctor said. "The bullet hit a rib and deflected away from her heart. Lots of muscle damage and lots of blood loss. Maybe too much." He pressed a cloth against her chest. "We won't know for a few days."

Zechariah sat on the other side of his wife, holding her hand, stroking her face. "Do whatever you need to do, Mac. I can't lose her."

The anguish in the man's voice tore at Michael. *I've brought death to my dearest friends, to the closest thing I have to family.* The desire to run burned, to get away and take the danger he brought to others with him. "Is this your plan, God?"

"Michael, come in here." The authority in Zechariah's voice cracked like dry wood split with an axe.

Michael slipped through the door and stood at the end of the bed. His mentor's coal black eyes pinned him. "This is not your fault. You did not bring this on Deborah."

"That bullet was meant for me."

Zechariah gazed at his wife as if memorizing each feature. He stroked her hair. "I know." His voice choked on the words. "But the evil in this world knew shooting Deborah would hurt you more than if the bullet had hit you."

Michael stared at his boots, unable to bear the sight of Deborah on the bed. He wanted to sink through the floor. Zechariah was right. This did hurt more. He should be laying there, not this innocent servant who'd been like a mother to him.

An image—the last time he'd seen his mother, lying on the kitchen floor, breathing her last as blood seeped from his father's beating.

Now, another person he loved could die. Because of him.

Is this what he would bring to Rachel? Living without her would be hard enough. Being the cause of her death would be unbearable. His head reeled and his stomach lurched.

He ran from the room and into the front yard. On his hands and knees, he vomited. Dry, wracking heaves tremored through his body, cold clammy sweat covered his face. His throat burned as he sat on his heels.

A hand on his shoulder, a cup of water offered. "Drink this." Jeremiah's voice.

Where did he come from?

Michael gulped the water, slight relief for his throat. His stomach roiled, but the water stayed.

His friend squatted in front of him, concern in his voice. "You all right?"

Michael nodded, then shook his head. "She's dying. It should be me."

Jeremiah looked behind Michael. "You stay with him. I'm going to see if I can help inside."

One hand under his arm, the other pulling him by his hand. "Come on, Michael. Let's sit on the porch."

He followed Caleb's command as if in a trance, everything numb, body not responding to what he told it to do. Caleb guided him up the stairs and toward the rocking chair. The splintered wood screamed at him. He trembled. Balked at Caleb's urging and sat in a straight chair on the other side of the shattered window.

Caleb perched on the edge of the rocker, causing the splintered back to rock into the lamplight from the window. Michael looked down.

"What happened?"

The weathered floorboards of the porch held Michael's attention, their grain a convoluted map that led everywhere and nowhere. Like this search for Ben's killer.

"Somebody shot. Missed me. Hit Deborah."

"Did you see who?"

Michael shook his head. "Too dark. From across the street. Saw the barrel in the moonlight and the muzzle flash." He covered his face with his hand.

"Anything else?"

"Said leave the Winslow murder alone or the next shot would be between my eyes."

Caleb examined where the bullet nicked the chair. "Good shot if he was warning you. Close enough to scare supper out of you."

"How'd you find out?"

"Deputy went to Gideon's. Man still can't walk worth a nickel. Sent the deputy to the hotel for Jeremiah and me."

Michael clenched his shaking hands as he repressed the desire to find the nearest saloon. "It's my fault."

"How do you figure that?"

"If I hadn't come back to clear Ben's name, this wouldn't have happened."

Caleb leaned backed, pulled his lip with his thumb and forefinger. "Yep. And a murderer would be on the loose." He reached out and tapped Michael's knee. "This proves Ben was innocent."

"It also proves we're getting close." Jeremiah stepped onto the porch. "We've made somebody nervous. All we have to do is figure out who."

"How's Miss Deborah?" Michael's voice trembled.

"Sleeping. Zechariah and I prayed over her while the doc finished patching her up."

"She gonna make it?" Michael said. *Do I really want to know the answer?*

Jeremiah leaned against one of the posts supporting the porch roof, arms folded, and looked off in the night. "Right now it depends on how much she wants to live. Doc's done all he can. We have to make sure it doesn't get infected. We've prayed for God to heal her."

He turned to the others. "The fact she's alive now is a miracle. That bullet would have probably killed a man, never mind someone as small and frail as her."

Michael wanted to weep, couldn't. *Why, God? Help me understand.*

"Tell Jeremiah what you told me." Caleb's gentle voice urged him to speak.

After he heard Michael, Jeremiah said, "Like I said, we've got somebody's attention." Using his fingers to tick off names, he started listing the people they had talked to and what they had learned. "I pray we can find this Micah Grimmler soon."

Michael sat up straight. "I think I was followed today."

"And you didn't think to tell us?" Irritation laced Caleb's sarcasm.

"I wasn't sure. He was there, then he wasn't." He relayed his observations and his actions, described the man he saw.

"Left-handed gun?" Jeremiah stroked his chin. "Not too many around. Shouldn't be hard to spot. Let's ask Gideon to have his deputies be on the lookout."

Caleb snapped his fingers, pointed to the back of the rocker. "What about Conrad? Left-handed, and he's good enough to leave a warning shot that close."

"He is," Jeremiah said. "He's been up in Oregon for the last year. I don't see where he would have had time to get here. But I'll send some wires tomorrow. See if he's still there. Find out where he is if he's moved on."

Caleb stretched. "Don't know that we can do much more here. Let's turn in and start fresh in the morning."

Later, after Caleb and Jeremiah left, the street beckoned Michael to leave the porch. Aimless wandering took him near the railroad station where he found himself across the street from a saloon. The music, the lights, the smoke prom-ised escape. A drink. Maybe two. Probably more. A fight, fists pummeling some-one, his anger against the unknown gunman taken out on the first available man he could instigate into taking a swing.

"Tempting, ain't it?" Caleb's words startled him. He felt like he jumped a foot. His heart pounded.

"You followed me?"

Caleb shrugged. "Couldn't sleep. Saw you walk past. Decided to follow."

Michael focused on the saloon. Caleb nudged him with his elbow. "You know, if someone's gunning for you, yer sure making it easy for them. Parading through town. Not even paying attention to what's going on around you."

Michael stiffened, irritation building like water heating in a coffee pot. "Maybe it'd be better if I wasn't around, putting people in danger."

"That's about the dumbest thing I've heard you say. Get over feeling sorry for yerself."

Michael glared at him.

"Go ahead. Take a swing. I may have over thirty years on you, but I can still put you on the ground."

Age wouldn't make a difference. Caleb may be older, but he was strong, wiry, smart and able to put Michael on his butt. With one punch. That wouldn't help ease his mood. Only make him madder. He shrugged. "Zechariah always taught me to respect my elders."

"'Bout time you listened to other things he's told you." He grabbed Michael's arm. "People are depending on you."

He shook Caleb's hand off. "All I do is get them hurt."

Caleb spat. "I may not let you take the first swing. I may punch you myself, knock some of that self-pity out of you. I don't care about clearing Ben's name as much as I do about catching a murderer. We can't do that without you. Gideon's laid up. You know this town, these people. Something else you have is the pas-sion to do what Sam asked, to see Ben declared innocent."

He poked Michael's chest. "You want to do it as much for Ben and yourself as you do for Sam. Jeremiah and I are here because we actually like you and want to help, but you need to help us, and you can't do that if you run off to a saloon every time something lousy happens. And you can't catch whoever shot Miss Deborah if you're pickling your brain in cheap whiskey."

Michael wanted to look anywhere but into Caleb's eyes. He couldn't. He swallowed. "For a man who doesn't talk much, you sure give quite a speech."

Caleb shrugged. "You're too good a man to lose. I need to get you back to Riverbend alive. There's a beautiful woman waiting for you and a new life. I don't want you to miss it."

Michael looked at the saloon once more. The music was off-key, the lights dimmed by the cigar and cigarette smoke, the laughter false, fueled by cheap liquor, cheaper desires and false hopes. "Let's go."

When they reached Caleb's hotel, Caleb had him wait in the lobby. In a few minutes, he returned from his room and handed Michael a gun belt with a Colt snug in the holster.

"Until we catch this guy, wear this. And keep your eyes open."

CHAPTER 32

Sunday, July 7, 1878

MICHAEL SAT, ENTHRALLED, as Zechariah mesmerized the people crowded into every pew and the more who stood in the back and along the sidewalls. How could the man stand in that pulpit and preach when his wife lay next door, clinging to life? But he did. And he preached forgiveness and healing and on how harboring resentment hindered achieving all God wanted, each word an arrow into Michael's heart.

Forgiveness? For the man who may yet be responsible for Deborah's death? Forgiveness for those who framed Ben Carstairs for murder?

Impossible. Revenge and vengeance needed to be exacted.

"Revenge is mine saith the Lord." Zechariah all but whispered the words but they carried through the whole congregation. They hit Michael like a choir singing, resonating in his heart.

Not revenge. Not vengeance. Justice.

Zechariah's eyes drilled into him. An instrument of God to bring the killer and those helping him to justice.

Michael bowed his head. Caleb was right. Self-pity and guilt had no place. They paralyzed him, made him want to run away, run to the bottle and the old Michael. Sam had asked him to do this and, although Michael never answered him, this needed to be done. For Ben. And now, for Deborah.

Justice.

He looked to the pulpit. Zechariah's eyes bore into him once again as if he was the only one Zechariah preached to.

Justice.

Michael nodded.

CHAPTER 33

Monday, July 8, 1878

LEGS LIKE ANVILS, Michael stood at the foot of the stairs to Deborah and Zechariah's bedroom. Stairs like a sheer cliff. He climbed, the banister a life rope by which he pulled himself to the top.

Deborah lay on the bed, covers to her chin, asleep, chest rising and falling in slow rhythm, face white. Zechariah sat next to her, head resting on folded arms on the bed, snoring.

Mrs. Larkin, from the church, knitted in the rocker and smiled at Michael's appearance in the doorway. She rose and led him to the hall, their whispered conversation reminding Michael of a couple of bees near a honey pot.

"She's been like that all day." Mrs. Larkin was a thin reed of a woman, mother of thirteen living children. Many in the church referred to her as Major Larkin because of her ability to organize and direct people. Michael knew people used the name with affection and respect. Even her children called her Major more often than Mother.

"Doc was here a couple of hours ago, changed her bandage. Says she's doing better than he expected, and she might just make it."

"How's Zechariah?"

Mrs. Larkin shook her head. "Such a saint he is. He's been in that chair all day. Got him to eat some soup and drink some tea. He fell asleep right after doc left."

Michael moved to the end of the bed, heart heavy at the sight of his mentors suffering. Suffering from trouble he brought into their home. He prayed silently.

Downstairs, he replaced the window shattered by the bullet, thankful for a physical activity that required him to concentrate, distracting him from the couple upstairs. A footstep behind him, too heavy to be Mrs. Larkin.

"Thanks for replacing the window." Zechariah's voice, hoarse and strained, quivered. "Deborah seems to be a little better." A sigh. "She has to make it. God knows I can't do this work without her."

Zechariah ran his hand through his hair. "Join me for some coffee. Mrs. Larkin made a fresh pot."

They sat at the table, the atmosphere weighted by grief. Zechariah added sugar to his coffee. "Did you and the others make any more progress today?"

Michael toyed with the handle on his cup. His friend's eyes were swollen and red, with bags drooping. "Cleared up some things but not much progress. The gunslinger Caleb and Jeremiah suspected, Conrad, is still in Oregon. In fact, he's in prison. One of the neighbors heard the gunshot last night, looked out his window, and saw a man ride away. Left-handed gun." Michael sipped his coffee. "It's good information but it doesn't bring us any closer."

Zechariah's cup sat untouched in front of him. "Keep going to God. He'll help you sort it out."

Michael nodded. "Did you send a wire to Amelia?" Their daughter lived with her minister husband in Chicago.

"Don't know what to say."

"Let's work on it together, and I'll run it over to the telegraph office."

Zechariah nodded, shoulders still slumped. "How do you tell your precious child her mother's been shot?"

"God will give us the words."

They sat at Zechariah's desk, trying different phrasing, striving to keep the usual telegraphic terseness out of the message. They agreed on: *Your Mom's been hurt but is recovering. Will write with more details. Love, Pa.*

The final two words choked Michael, two words he'd longed to hear but never did.

Michael tucked the folded sheet of paper in his shirt pocket. "I'll get this sent right away." He picked up his hat and headed for the door.

"You forgot something." Zechariah pointed to the gun belt and holster hanging on the back of a chair.

Michael approached the weapon like it was a rattlesnake.

"It's for your protection." Zechariah's voice was soft.

"I know. Just doesn't feel right." He rubbed the leather, trailing his fingers over the loops of bullets. "Too easy to kill with it on."

"Less easy for someone to kill you. Make them think twice."

"Not if they're setting up an ambush."

"Wear it for me. And for that girl, Rachel, you told us about. She deserves that you be able to defend yourself so you can go back to her."

Michael fastened the belt around his waist, the weight uncomfortable. He touched the butt of the pistol and snatched his hand away.

"You do know how to use it?" The chuckle in Zechariah's voice warmed Michael.

"More comfortable with a rifle."

"Trust God to guide your aim."

CHAPTER 34

Monday, July 8, 1878

AFTER WAITING UNTIL the telegraph office closed without a response from Amelia, Michael returned to the parsonage. The rich aroma of beef filled his nostrils as he entered. *Deborah's up? That can only be her cooking.*

In the kitchen stood a woman who could be Mrs. Larkin's identical twin if Mrs. Larkin was twenty-five years younger. Becky Jo Larkin greeted Michael with a hug and a kiss on the cheek.

Fists on her hips, Becky Jo leaned toward him. "What's this I hear, Mr. Michael Archer, that you've gone and found another girl? I thought you was gonna wait for me." A smile creased her freckled face, but her blue eyes bore into him, serious, questioning.

Michael placed his hand over his heart. "I was going to wait, dear Miss Becky. Twenty years if I had to. But, our God had other ideas, and I couldn't go against him, could I?"

Becky Jo took Michael's hands. "If that's what God said, who am I to argue otherwise? I sure hope you heard from Him right." She dropped her chin and looked at him from under arched brows. "Besides, Edward Talbot, the cooper's son, asked Papa's permission to come courting, and Papa said yes."

"Which of your sisters does he want to court?"

Becky Jo punched his arm. "Sit down and eat your supper, Mr. Michael Archer, before I feed it to the hogs."

Mrs. Larkin joined them for the meal of beef, beans, and sourdough bread Becky Jo had brought. The moist, tender meat reminded Michael he needed to eat more often and had him wondering once again about Rachel's culinary talents.

Listening to Mrs. Larkin and Becky Jo talk about the farm, the other children, and Mr. Larkin showed why the mother was the Major. Becky Jo's responses proved she was at least a colonel. Michael smiled at the thought of what this family held for Edward Talbot. He prayed the young man would appreciate it.

During the conversation with her mother, the girl darted glances at Michael. When she served him another helping, her fingers brushed the back of his hand.

Michael brought a plate of food to Zechariah and sat with him while he forked food into his mouth, chewed and swallowed. Michael was sure the man didn't taste a bite. Deborah slept peacefully, except when an occasional frown cross her face and quickly faded.

"Wonder what she's thinking?" Zechariah's voice was reverential.

"Probably about giving one of us a piece of her mind."

Michael laid the holster on the floor, and sat in the rocker, enjoying the quiet broken only by the clock ticking in the hall. *Lord, heal her. Help us find the man who did this.*

Where Michael expected guilt, he felt anger. Something evil did this to her, and it had to be stopped. He thought of the pistol on the floor. He could use it to protect himself and others. The old Michael would have used it to threaten and steal. That Michael receded to a murky shadow, not the monster struggling to get out, to take control. The new Michael stood in control now, ready to defend, ready to bring to justice those who killed Donald Winslow, framed Ben Carstairs, hurt Miss Deborah.

Michael picked up Zechariah's empty plate. "I'll take this to the kitchen, then I'm going to Gideon's. See if we can figure anything out."

Zechariah nodded. Michael squeezed his mentor's shoulder.

"Michael."

Michael turned in the doorway. Zechariah nodded at his waist. Michael grinned, sheepish, picked up the holster from the floor and draped it over his shoulder. He prayed he would never reach the point where strapping on a gun became as second nature as putting on his boots.

In the kitchen, Becky Jo dried the last pan from the meal and hung it on its peg near the stove. She jumped when Michael stepped alongside her to slide Zechariah's plate into the soapy water in the sink.

One hand fluttered to her throat, the other rested on his chest. "Michael, you startled me. You was quiet as an Indian."

"I apologize, Becky Jo. I didn't realize you were concentrating so hard on your chores." He stepped back.

For the briefest of moments, it seemed like the girl was about to take a step with him to keep her hand on his shirt. After an awkward moment of her hand suspended in the air, her arm dropped to her side.

"'Tweren't nothin'." She brushed a wisp of hair of her forehead. "My mind was up on the moon. Didn't hear you come in."

"Thinking of the Talbot boy?"

Her cheeks turned pink and her freckles seemed darker. "No…wasn't thinking about him."

"You've got another beau?"

She twisted her hands and the briefest of scowls scudded across her face. "No, there ain't no other beau, Michael Archer." Her Colonel Becky Jo voice. "I got more important things to think about than boys."

"I'm sure you do what with helping your ma and pa and all the little ones." Michael settled his Stetson on his head. "Well, I best be going."

She rose on her toes and kissed his cheek. Her hands slid down his arms and brushed his hands. "When this is over, you're going to be staying in Tramlaw, right?"

He scratched the back of his neck. "Don't know for sure. I've got some people in Riverbend I need to see after this. After that, I'll see where the Lord wants me to go."

She brushed her lips against his cheek once again.

"You be careful, Michael. Folks around here need you."

At the front door, he turned back. Becky Jo stood in the kitchen doorway, hands at her waist, lower lip between her teeth.

CHAPTER 35

Monday, July 8, 1878

THE BREEZE STIRRED the humid night air and carried the croaking of frogs from the river. Crickets chirped nearby. As he walked, Michael listened for a sound that didn't belong. He turned onto Main Street glancing over his shoulder. The street to the parsonage lay empty in the light of the moon approaching full.

Several people strolled Main Street, comforting and troubling at the same time. Comforting to have them around. Troubling because they gave danger a place to hide. He scanned the passersby, alert for a left-handed gun, an eye that lingered on him too long, a person moving in the same direction and speed as him.

Three more blocks to Gideon's. He nodded at a passing deputy. Crossed the side street and walked in front of the bank. A poke in his back. He started to turn. The poke pressed. A gun barrel.

"Don't turn around. Turn right at the corner." The voice low, a hoarse whisper.

Michael complied. The gun still pressed. Michael filled his lungs.

The voice close to his ear, warm moist air on his cheek. "Don't try calling for help. You'll be dead before you hit the ground. In here." A large hand shoved him around the corner of the bank building into a narrow alley. On his left rose the blank back wall of a mercantile, closed for the night.

He stumbled over a rock. The gun in his back shoved him forward. "Don't try any tricks."

Now a few feet away from his assailant, Michael turned, drawing his pistol.

A lightning bolt shot up his arm, blinding light exploded in his brain. Someone had swung a piece of wood into his arm, snapping the bone. Through the pain, Michael heard his pistol land in the hard packed dirt and skitter away.

He started to scream. From behind, a hand shoved a cloth in his mouth, choking him.

A punch to his stomach doubled him over.

A punch to his back, over his kidneys, sent him to his knees.

He cradled his broken arm. From behind, someone yanked him to his feet and pinned his arms behind him.

A punch to his cheek, another to his nose.

He tried to curl into a ball. Couldn't. Whoever held his arms, kept him upright.

A kick landed in his stomach. Air rushed out.

Can't breathe.

Three men. The two in front disguised by bandanas up to their eyes. Right-handed guns.

Punches to his face, his eyes, his nose again. An uppercut to his jaw loosened teeth. Blood on his tongue. Filling his mouth. *Can't spit.*

Woozy. *Can't see. Let me sleep.*

Cold water in his face. Startling. Chilling.

The same voice. "We ain't done yet."

A punch to his stomach. "You don't listen, boy."

A fist to his face rocked his head. The man behind him yanked a handful his hair, exposing his neck.

Knuckles rammed into his throat.

The voice in his ear again. "Leave." A kick to his stomach. "It." Another punch to his kidneys. "Alone." A fist found his nose again.

They released him. He sagged to the ground, rolled on his side. They spread his legs. A booted foot slammed into the inside of his left knee. Pain. Sharp as a needle, hot as a smith's forge. Bright shafts of light stabbed his closed eyes. Pain he'd never felt before tore through him. *God, help me. Please.*

Two of them hauled him to his feet. His arm felt pulled from his shoulder. His knee yowled, buckled.

The voice in front of him now. The breath a foul, nauseating mix of whiskey, tobacco and bad food. "You understand?"

He nodded. Tried to open his eyes. Couldn't. Only a sliver of moonlight visible from his left eye.

"You're going to leave it alone, right?"

Leave it alone? Can't. Need to do it for Ben, Miss Deborah.

He shook his head.

A curse followed by others. A kick to his right knee.

They let him go. He slumped to the ground on his side, tried to bring his legs up to his chest, left leg wouldn't move.

"Stubborn preacher. Shoulda done this to begin with."

A pistol cocked. Michael tried to roll onto his back. The gun fired, the sound muffled in his head. New pain flamed in his right shoulder, blazing to his brain and then through his whole body. A scream couldn't get past the gag.

Darkness.

-->==◎ ◎==<--

"No." Rachel's own voice woke her and her hands flying to her chest. Around her, some passengers snored in tune with the hypnotic rhythms of the train. Others read newspapers or books. None seemed to notice her.

She could not slow the rapid beating of her heart. Under her fingers, it vibrated like that of the young bird she once held.

Visions of Michael beaten, shot, unconscious in a shadowy alley filled her mind.

Trapped on this train. Unable to reach him until tomorrow. Have to do something. What?

She closed her eyes and prayed, but the words slipped away as the image of Michael crowded everything out of her mind. His face, broken and bloody. Blood pooling under his shoulder. Arm at a strange angle.

She reached out and touched … nothing, her hand passing through his face when she tried to brush his cheek. She wanted to bathe his wounds, kiss those swollen eyes, the flattened nose.

Realization struck her. No one knew where he was. He would die. Her heart and mind screamed. She bit her lip to prevent crying out loud.

Lord, lead someone to him. Let him be found. Lord, he can't die. You promised me.

The window bounced her reflection back to her, sharpened by the outer darkness. Violet eyes wide. Lips trembling.

Lord, you promised.

>─══◉ ◉══◄-

Pounding. Loud booms rattling the door. Caleb snapped awake, pistol in hand, thumb on the hammer. Someone banging on his door.

"Sheriff Davis? Are you there? It's Deputy Snyder."

Something's happened to Gideon. Caleb snatched open the door. The deputy stared at the pistol, then at Caleb, and swallowed.

"There's trouble, Sheriff. Michael Archer's been shot. Sheriff Parsons sent me to fetch you and Mr. Turner. We've taken Michael to the preacher's house."

Too many words. Too fast. Michael's been shot?

The door across the hall opened. Jeremiah Turner, pistol in hand, stared at him. "What's all the ruckus?"

Caleb motioned both of them into his room. He stepped into his pants, knees balking. He nodded at Snyder. "From the beginning. Slow."

Snyder gulped air; his young face pale, eyes wide. "About a half hour ago, I heard a shot. One shot. But I couldn't tell exactly where. So me and another deputy, Billy Ray Andrews, started looking. I was checking near the bank and I heard a noise, like a moan. In the alley behind the bank, I found Michael." His voice shook. "He's beaten pretty bad. Bullet wound in his shoulder. I found Doc at the preacher's house, and he said bring Michael there. Then I went to Sheriff Parsons, and he told me to tell you and Mr. Turner what happened—that you'd know what to do."

"Let's hope his faith isn't misdirected," Caleb said. He turned to Jeremiah. "Let's start with Michael."

Jeremiah left to get dressed. Snyder returned to duty. Alone, Caleb stood at the window, fists clenched, eyes blind to the street. *Not again. Not another friend. This has to stop.* His hands encircled the neck of a featureless face, tightening, squeezing, crushing. Arm muscles trembled as he exerted more pressure. *No more.*

A knock on the door brought him back. Jeremiah entered, lips narrowed, eyes like a wolf stalking its prey.

They left the hotel and walked in silence. Their boots beat a rapid tattoo on the sidewalk. The few people they met cleared a path to let them pass, eyes averted.

Zechariah opened the door. Face pale, hands trembling. Wordlessly, he stepped aside and directed Caleb and Jeremiah into the parlor and followed.

Michael lay on the sofa, unconscious. Caleb fought down the wave of bile rising in his stomach. The doctor knelt on the floor, working on Michael's right shoulder, muttering curses as he pressed a cloth on the wound.

"Is he dying?" The words escaped Caleb's mouth before he realized it.

"Not if I can help it." The doctor spoke over his shoulder. "Come here and hold this cloth. Put pressure. Need to stop the bleeding."

Caleb moved into place. Zechariah stood behind the sofa, hand over his mouth, tears rolling down his cheeks.

Jeremiah moved to the other side of the doctor. "I'm another pair of hands if you need them."

The doctor arched an eyebrow at Jeremiah. "D'you ever set a bone?"

Jeremiah nodded.

"Help me set his arm. Hold his upper arm while I set this lower one. Hopefully, it's a clean break. Zechariah, make yourself useful. Get me some short boards to use as splints."

The preacher moved quickly, heading for the kitchen. Caleb heard a door slam.

The doctor took Michael's forearm, one hand near the wrist, his other hand about halfway to the elbow. Eyes closed, head cocked to one side, he manipulated the lower arm, tiny movements to the left and then the right. Muttered curses gave way to a quiet "There it is."

The doctor looked toward the kitchen. "Zechariah, I need those splints."

Zechariah came into the room, and handed the doctor two thin pieces of what looked like clapboard.

"Hold these in place while I wrap the arm."

Caleb closed his eyes as the doctor next sutured the front and back of Michael's shoulder, the sight of the skin being tugged and brought together by the horsehair had his stomach somersaulting.

The doctor bandaged Michael's shoulder and rigged a sling to nestle his arm. He knelt near Michael's head and moistened a cloth from a bottle in his medical bag. He worked on each cut, cleaning crusted blood, absorbing fresh blood as it seeped.

Standing, the doctor arched his back, hands at the base of his spine. He picked up a whiskey bottle from his bag and gulped, wiping his mouth on his sleeve before corking the bottle and returning it to his bag. "I know you're all good Christian men, otherwise I'd've offered you a nip."

A loud rap on the door. Gideon tromped in.

"Gideon, how did you get here?" Doc said. "I told you to stay off that leg." He threw up his arm. "How do you people expect to get well when you don't do what I tell ya?"

Gideon waved his hand at the doctor. "Be quiet, you snake oil peddler. Nobody bothers to tell me anything, so I have to come find out for myself."

"How did you get here, Gideon?" Zechariah's voice was low, concern surrounding every word.

Gideon jerked his thumb over his shoulder. "I had Snyder bring me over in a buggy."

He clomped to the couch, and gazed at Michael. A curse slipped from his lips. "I'd hate to see what he looked like before you cleaned him up. Is he gonna make it?"

The doctor sighed, wiped his face with his hands. "I don't know. I don't know how much damage there is on the inside. Lots of bruising on his stomach, back and chest. That bruise on his throat is nasty, and he's working hard to breathe. It's going to take a long time to recover from what's on the outside. Right now, I like Deborah's chances better than I do his."

Caleb's heart rose to his throat as he saw Gideon blink back tears. Zechariah stood erect and silent, eyes focused on Michael. Jeremiah turned his head.

"We…" Zechariah's coughed, cleared his throat. "We're not going to let either of them die. You gentlemen join me, please."

Caleb bowed his head with the others.

Zechariah began softly, almost tentative. "Lord, we pray for Michael and Deborah. Please heal their wounds, restore their bodies. We believe it is not yet their time to join you. We trust you, Lord."

"Zechariah, can we use your kitchen?" Gideon said.

Perplexion crossed the pastor's face. "Uhh…Sure. Do you need coffee or anything?"

Gideon shook his head. "Need to talk to my two friends here. Don't want to disturb Michael or get in Doc's way."

Caleb and Jeremiah followed Gideon. Gideon used the crutch to lever himself into a chair, leg extended before him. He rubbed his wounded calf. "Burns like the devil laid a hot poker on it."

"You're trying to do too much, old friend," Caleb said.

Gideon glared at him. "Ain't doing enough. Leaving it all up to you three." He nodded toward the living room. "Now look what happened. If he dies, I won't stop 'til I pull the lever to hang the killer myself."

Caleb knew Gideon shared his view about executions, the part of the job they both hated most. He'd been relieved when the judge ordered Jack Alden and the two Mexicans taken to the territorial prison to be hanged.

"My deputies are out on the streets asking everybody if they saw or heard anything." He sighed. "I'll be surprised if they get anywhere with it, but it's got to be done." He pinched the bridge of his nose. "Sure would like to find that left-handed gun."

"If we keep looking, he'll turn up," Jeremiah said. "Find him and he'll lead us to the one who hired him."

Caleb couldn't take his eyes from the back of the couch. "Maybe. If we can get him to talk. Your deputies know we need him alive?"

"Yep. Told 'em to shoot to wound if he draws on them."

Caleb crossed his arms. "He'll be fast. They shouldn't take him alone. Follow him until they can get help."

Gideon nodded. "I'll remind 'em."

Jeremiah leaned back in his chair, yawned. "Can you think of any other left-handed guns who could be in town?"

Gideon shook his head. "Everyone we've checked out is accounted for. I had Snyder send a message to the U.S. Marshal's for any leads, haven't heard back yet."

Caleb snapped his fingers. "What about the Rangers?"

"Texas Rangers?" Jeremiah said. "Good idea for an old timer. I'll send a wire first thing."

Jeremiah stretched his arms. "I'll wire Phil Addison at Wells Fargo too. He might have heard of some new names."

Gideon stood. "My office, tomorrow morning at eight, we'll see what we've found out."

"Your office? Are you sure you're up to it? We can meet at your house just as easy." Caleb said.

"My office. If I sit in that house one more day, I'll start shooting holes in the walls just to break the boredom."

The living room seemed deserted as the three headed for the door. The lantern burned low, and it took a moment for Caleb to spot the doctor in a side chair, legs outstretched, arms dangling over the sides, head back, snoring. Michael was as white as his bandages, breathing shallow, eyelids fluttering. He moaned softly.

Caleb studied the young man. How quickly he had grown into a trusted friend. He remembered the day when they found the four murdered posse members, including Vernon Phelps, Caleb's closest friend. Michael prayed over the temporary graves on the trail, and shared his wisdom as he talked with Caleb about death and God.

Caleb rubbed his eye. Michael helped him find Jesus when no one else had been able to, when Caleb had turned his back on God years earlier for letting his wife die. "I owe you a lot, Michael. Don't go until I pay you back in full, with interest."

Michael moaned, stirred, shivered. Caleb found two blankets folded on the back of the couch. He spread one over Michael, careful to avoid moving his arm.

He straightened up, found Gideon watching him. "The son you never had?"

Caleb looked at Michael again. "Yeah. I guess so. Never thought of it like that."

Gideon nodded. "He's the same for me. This is beyond justice. This is personal."

Caleb took the other blanket and draped it over the doctor who snorted, shook his head and resumed snoring.

At the door, Caleb looked back. "I better send a message to Riverbend tomorrow, have someone be with Rachel when they tell her."

CHAPTER 36

Tuesday, July 9, 1878

CALEB ENJOYED THE warm sunshine on his back and shoulders as he mounted the steps of the parsonage, fighting the sleepiness crowding his eyes. The disturbed sleep; late night, and frustrating morning made his head feel stuck in the middle of a bale of cotton. His brain couldn't put two thoughts together. His neck muscles cramped with tension that wouldn't let go.

Zechariah opened the door at his knock. Drooped shoulders, red eyes, lips a line in the gray pallor of his face, tremors in the hands. *How can this man even stand?*

Inside, the doctor had sliced the seam of Michael's pants. The swollen left knee was red, the mark of a boot heel standing out like a brand on a horse. The doctor pulled a cloth from a steaming pan of water on the floor, wrung it out and began to wrap the knee.

"Wait."

The doctor jumped, dropped the cloth, turned to Caleb, fatigued-fueled irritation in his voice. "What?"

Caleb patted his vest pockets. Empty. He scanned the room. "I need paper and pencil. Quick."

Zechariah shuffled to a writing table in the corner, removed paper and pencil from a drawer and brought them to Caleb. Caleb elbowed the doctor to one side and knelt by the couch. He sketched the imprint of the boot heel, focusing on each detail. His hand shook, whether from fatigue or excitement over the clue, he couldn't tell. He took a deep breath, flexed his fingers and resumed drawing.

He showed it to the doctor. "Does that look accurate?"

The doctor studied the drawing and the mark on Michael's knee. "Yeah. Very close. Is that going to help you?"

"If I can find the boot that matches it."

"Good. Can I finish my work now?"

Caleb stepped back from the couch. "How's he doing?"

"Good news is the knee's not broken. Hopefully, the warm cloths will bring the swelling down." He pursed his lips and arched his back, hands rubbing the base of his spine. "Bad news is he's feverish, his heartbeat is weak, slow. If his breathing doesn't improve, I'll have to a cut a hole in his throat so he can get air."

"Is he going to make it?"

MacKenzie rubbed his chin, met Caleb's gaze. "Don't know. Not hopeful. If he breathes better, and we can keep infection from the wounds, he might."

Someone descended the stairs. Becky Jo Larkin appeared, carrying a tray. "Reverend Taylor? Miss Deborah's awake and asking for you."

In an instant, it seemed like fifty years and one hundred pounds dropped off Zechariah. Becky Jo twisted to one side to avoid him as he bounded up the stairs two at time. The girl stopped behind the couch, her eyes tender. Caleb wondered, was there affection there?

The doctor chuckled. "I better get after him before he hurts himself or her." He picked up his bag and climbed the stairs like a man who hadn't slept in several days.

Caleb stared at Michael's grotesque face. *God, I'm kinda new at this praying stuff, but if you could see your way clear to keeping Michael alive, I'd appreciate it.*

Becky Jo's voice startled him. He thought he was the only one in the room. "Sheriff, I've got some vittles in the kitchen if'n yer hungry. Beans and ham, chicken soup, corn bread. Coffee."

Caleb smiled. Food would be good, coffee better. A few minutes later, he was at the kitchen table, a plate of corn bread and beans in front of him, coffee to the side. Becky Jo sat across the table from him with a cup of coffee and a smile that made her freckles dance.

"Sure does a woman good to see a man enjoy his food."

"It's delicious. You made this?"

"Uh-huh. The Major had me making biscuits by the time I was four. Said I needed to be useful 'cause I was the oldest, and she needed help takin' care of the young-uns." She gazed out the window. "And the young-uns just kept comin'."

"I'm curious. Do you know Michael well? I only met him a few months ago but he seems like a good man."

Caleb had never seen anyone dreamy-eyed until Becky Jo looked at him, blue eyes bright. "Michael's the one who kept our family together." She looked away, hesitant. "Y'see, my Pa used to have a problem with the liquor. Couldn't pay the bills, keep up with the farm work. Reverend Zech tried to talk with him, but Pa wouldn't listen. Then Michael started work- ing with the pastor—helping him in the jails and with some of the families. Michael worked in Reavey's Mercantile and met my Pa there, and then they got friendly over baseball, of all things. I don't understand it, but Pa goes every Sunday after church. He can't play since the war, but he sure does love to watch."

She sipped her coffee. "Anyway, one night Pa got crazy drunk, started bustin' up a saloon. Sheriff Parsons locked him up. Michael visited Pa, talked to him. Took him to the cemetery, showed him the graves of men who died because of drink, of the wives who died cuz their menfolk mistreated them, of the kids who died cuz there 'tweren't enough money. He took Pa to the state prison, showed him how some men ended up. That was three years ago. Pa hasn't touched liquor since."

Her gaze held Caleb. "Michael's been part of our family ever since. Has supper with us at least once a week. Helps with the harvestin'." Her eyes misted. "He's very special to me—I mean to us. To Pastor Zech and the church."

A tear slid down her cheek. She wiped at her eyes with her fingers and glanced at the living room. "He has to live."

Becky Jo's teasing of Michael on Sunday took on new meaning. Caleb won- dered if Michael knew this young woman was in love with him. On the trail, Michael clearly didn't have a girl in Tramlaw, thought he wasn't worthy of the women in the church and avoided the women who weren't in the church.

"Sheriff Davis, tell me about this woman he met in Riverbend."

Blood rushed to Caleb's face. He fiddled with his cup, seeking words. "She goes to church in Riverbend, a bit older than you. Owns a dressmaking shop. Sweet girl."

"Is she pretty?"

Calling Rachel Stone pretty would be like calling a mountain big. Caleb felt like a fish that had been hooked and tossed on the riverbank, flipping and flapping, but not able to get back to the water.

"Yes, she's pretty."

Becky Jo nodded, put her elbow on the table, chin in her palm. "Are they gonna git married?"

Caleb stifled a laugh, gulped his coffee to wash it down. "They've just met. I think they're still at the getting to know each other stage."

She took his plate to the sink. Eyes on the sudsy water, she said, "I think it's more than that. A woman can tell these things." She swiped her cheek with her forearm.

<hr />

Caleb flattened his sketch of the boot heel on Gideon's desk.

Gideon grunted. "Good work. It's good to see all those years of teachin' you weren't wasted."

"Looks like you could've used a little more work on finding Derringers," Caleb said.

Jeremiah tapped the paper. "Do you recognize it, Gideon?"

"Nah. Kind of fancy though. Must be new. Not too much wear on it."

Caleb's heart skipped a beat. "Probably custom-made. Anybody in town who can do this kind of work?"

Gideon rubbed his wounded leg. "There's a couple of boot makers who think they're kind of special. There's one, Hayden Chase, makes really fancy boots for the rich folk."

"Any of these rich folk have brands or emblems that look like this?" Jeremiah pointed to the paper.

Gideon frowned. "Two stars in a circle? None that I can think of."

Caleb slipped the paper into his vest pocket. "Think I'll visit this Hayden Chase. You want to come along, Jeremiah?"

"I'll check the telegraph office. We should get answers from Phil Addison and the Texas Rangers soon."

→══◉ ◉══←

Hayden Chase was a round man with a round face. Brown eyes bulged under thick sand colored hair that spilled over his forehead and ears. Pug nose and thick lips made him one of the strangest men Caleb had ever seen.

The man's long, slender fingers looked like they'd been taken from someone else and grafted onto Chase's pudgy wrists. They were stained a muddy brown from leather and oils. Chase's firm handshake revealed the callused hands of a workman.

Caleb surveyed the shop, brightly lit by the sun and lanterns hanging from the ceiling, boots displayed in glass cases and on shelves. Hats, belts, bandanas and other neckwear mingled with the primary product. A pair of boots displayed on the main counter would cost him three months' salary. Then he remembered he didn't have a salary anymore.

"How can I help you, Sheriff Davis? How's Sheriff Parsons doing?"

"The Sheriff's doing tolerable. Startin' to get around a little more." He showed Chase the drawing. "Have you ever seen a design like this?"

Chase blinked, cleared his throat, took the paper near the window and brought it close to his eyes. Caleb waited. After several moments, Chase handed it back. "Can't say that I have."

Caleb didn't lower his arm. "Really? I was led to believe you're the best boot maker in town. This is pretty fancy work. Take another look, maybe you can tell me which of your competitors could do something as detailed as this."

Chase looked at the paper in Caleb's hand. "Sorry, Sheriff. Can't help you. Never saw anything like it." He sniffed. "And I don't really know my competitors' work because they don't come close to what I do."

Caleb resisted the urge to punch Chase in his nose, even as he thought it might improve the man's appearance.

"Mind if I look at your receipts and design books?"

Chase stiffened, back straighter. "As a matter of fact, I do. I've already told you I don't recognize that drawing. I resent the implication that I'm lying."

Caleb shrugged. "If I'm implying anything, it's only that you might be forgetful. Man of your caliber must do a lot of work, can't expect you to remember every masterpiece you create."

A smile crept into Chase's eye. "It's nice to be appreciated, but my designs are secret. I can't let just anybody see them. Who knows where they might end up? I know my competitors would pay dearly to get their hands on my work."

Caleb wished he had Jeremiah's talents of persuasion, or even Pete O'Brien's gift of wearing people down by simply talking and talking until they gave in to shut him up.

"Now, if there's nothing else, Sheriff?" Chase gestured toward the door and touched Caleb's arm.

Caleb snatched his arm away. "In fact, there is. Deborah Taylor is fighting for her life from a gunshot wound. A good friend of mine, and of Sheriff Parsons, Michael Archer, was beaten and shot. He may die. Whoever owns this boot heel stomped my friend hard enough to leave this impression. The two are connected, and this boot heel belongs to someone who thinks nothing of killing people. Deborah Taylor and Michael Archer are good people. They represent the best of this town."

He held the drawing under Chase's nose. "This represents the worst. If either Miss Deborah or Michael dies, I will personally let everyone know you are part of the worst because you refused to help us find the owner of this boot. And if I can figure out a way to arrest you, I will. At the least, I will put a serious dent in your business."

Chase put up his hands, backpedaled. "You can't do that. It's slander."

Caleb smiled, enjoying the man's squirm, the sweat beading on his forehead. "It's only slander if it's not the truth. I will be telling people the truth." He paused, folded his arms, and leaned forward, bringing his face close to Chase's. "Now, may I see your receipts and design books?"

Chase paled and nodded. "This way."

Caleb stared at the stack of ledgers and notebooks Chase piled on a table in the backroom. *It'll take a month to go through these.* He drummed his fingers on the top of the pile, rubbed his chin. His sketch lay on the table next to the stack.

"Mr. Chase."

The boot maker turned a grayer shade of pale. Eyes darting, he rubbed his mouth with his fingers. "Sheriff?"

"I think you can save me a lot of time and yourself a whole lot of trouble if you just tell me who you made the boots for. I'd sure like to be able to tell Sheriff Parsons how cooperative the citizens of Tramlaw are."

Chase seemed to seek out a hole to dash through. Caleb kept his eyes riveted on him, no longer drawing any pleasure from the man's squirming.

"You're afraid of him, ain't ya'?"

Chase nodded.

"After what he did to Michael, I can see why. If you tell me which ledger to look in, then you can say I found it on my own, you didn't tell me his name."

Chase seemed to ponder Caleb's words as if they held the secret for turning lead into gold. He raised his hand and, finger shaking, pointed at the bottom ledger.

"You was hoping I'd give up before I got to that one."

Chase nodded.

Caleb moved the ledger to the top of the pile and opened it. Line upon line of entries greeted him. Customer names, measurements, prices, design names. Caleb sighed. It could still take all day to wade through this hen scratching. "Page number or date."

"Page three."

Caleb flipped to the page. More lines of almost indecipherable scribble. He squinted until he could distinguish some letters. He ran his finger down the column labeled "Designs." Halfway down the page he saw "Circled stars." He looked at Chase who nodded. Caleb slid his finger to the column of customer names. Jordan Dennison.

Caleb's finger froze under the name. Jordan Dennison. Reports said he died in a shootout in a little Mexican town south of San Diego. Six months ago. This ledger said he bought the expensive custom-made boots with the fancy heel one week ago.

Caleb searched his memory for a description of Jordan Dennison.

"Is this man a few inches taller than me? Stands almost six-and-a-half feet?"

Chase glanced over his shoulder into the store proper. Nodded.

"Wider than me?"

Another nod. Had the man swallowed his tongue?

"Two gun rig? Black handled Colts?"

Chase shook his head.

"No?" Could there be another Jordan Dennison?

The boot maker cleared his throat. "He's only got one arm."

"Which?"

"His left."

Dread crept up Caleb's back and clamped around his neck.

CHAPTER 37

Tuesday, July 9, 1878

AT LAST. RACHEL hoisted her bag from the shelf and made her way to the end of the car. Bright sunlight flooded the platform and thick, moist air crowded her lungs. A bath sounded enticing, but it would have to wait. First, she had to find Michael.

After securing directions from the telegraph attendant, she set off for the parsonage, hoping Reverend Taylor could put her in touch with Michael. In the fifteen minutes it took to walk there, Rachel's bag dragged like someone slipped an anvil into it. On the porch, she straightened her dress and poked stray hairs under her bonnet. She blotted the sweat from her face and neck before knocking.

Freckles spread like wildflowers across the nose and cheeks of the young woman who answered the door. Eyes of cornflower blue and a warm smile welcomed her.

Rachel's tongue seemed to lose its capacity to form words. She hadn't expected someone so young and pretty to be in a parsonage. Must be the housekeeper.

"Can I help you?"

It took a moment for Rachel to decipher the girl's rustic accent. It reminded her of some of the girls when they first arrived at the brothel in Denver before Red Mary refined their speech. "Is this Reverend Taylor's home?"

"Yes, it is."

"My name's Rachel Stone, from Riverbend. I'm looking for Michael Archer, and I'm hoping Reverend Taylor can tell me where he is."

The smile dimmed, and the blue eyes clouded. "Reverend Taylor's upstairs with his wife. She's feeling poorly." The girl hesitated, looked over her shoulder.

She sighed. "Michael's here, too. Y'all might as well come in, but I need to tell ya he's doin' a might poorly himself."

Rachel stepped into the sunlit parlor. Before any of the furnishings registered, her eyes shot to the form on the couch.

"The vision's true." The words came out in a gasped whisper.

Her bag fell to the floor. Her hands came to her mouth. She knelt beside him, brushed sweat-matted hair off his pale, sweaty forehead. She longed to take his face in her hands, to kiss him, but her tear-clouded eyes stopped her. She blinked, and groaned when Michael's face came into focus. Eyes swollen. Cheeks puffed, cut and bruised. Nose spread like a mushroom. Lips cracked. Where could she touch him and not aggravate his pain? Nowhere.

Above the blanket covering his chest, his bandaged shoulder and sling stabbed at her. His left leg was wrapped in cloth, and propped on a couple of pillows. His breath rasped. She placed her hand on his chest, the rhythm of his heart slow under her palm.

She sat on her heels, covered her face with her hands and let the tears flow.

A hand rested on her shoulder. It belonged to the girl who let her in. "Would you like to sit?"

The climb into the armchair felt like a slog through thigh-deep, hot desert sand.

"Let me fix ya a cup of the Major's chamomile tea. It'll strengthen ya." The girl left.

The room receded into a grayish mist as a cocoon formed around her and Michael, her world now. *Lord, You promised he would be my husband. He can't die. Can he? I don't understand.*

She knelt beside him again, needing to be close. She touched his hair, kissed his forehead, the fever hot on her lips. He moaned. Said something though his lips barely moved. Rachel found the bowl of water on the floor, wrung out the piece of fabric soaking in it, placed the cloth on his forehead. Another moan. Another word sound.

"Be careful." The girl's voice stung like a wasp. Doc M says he's hurt real bad."

Rachel bit her lip. "I will. Just trying to help."

"Here's yer tea. Why don't ya drink it while I tend to him?"

"I'll have it in a bit, thanks." Rachel couldn't take her eyes from him, yearning for some sign he knew she was there. "When did this happen?"

"Sometime last night."

The same time her vision revisited her. She swallowed. "It's true." She touched his cheek. "Michael, I'm sorry I couldn't get here sooner."

"What's true?" The girl knelt at the end of the sofa, her hands on either side of Michael's head.

Rachel's mind reeled. *How can I explain a vision to her when my mind can only think about Michael?*

"I had a dream that he was hurt."

A stair creaked, and a man stepped into the parlor. The girl stood and turned with a swirl of her dress.

"Reverend Taylor, we have a visitor. Rachel Stone come all the way from Riverbend. Said she had a dream about Michael getting hurt."

The reverend helped Rachel to her feet, held her hand in both of his. His tired eyes filled with compassion. "I'm so sorry we have to meet under these circumstances. I've heard a great deal about you." He nodded at Michael. "You must be a very special woman to get his attention."

A sharp intake of breath from Becky Jo. Rachel wondered about the frown creasing the girl's face.

The reverend continued, "I see you've met Becky Jo. She's been helping take care of your young man." The Reverend's voice commanded Rachel's attention. "We have a room we can fix up for you if you'd like to stay here. It's small, but I think it will be adequate."

I can be here, close to Michael. "But Reverend, your wife's doing poorly too. I can't impose on you at a time like this."

Reverend Taylor smiled, and, in those caring eyes, Rachel saw the grandfather she always imagined. Eyes that carried such pain but still reached out in love. She wanted to be a little girl and crawl into his lap, search his pockets for treats, feel his fingers tickle.

"It won't be any trouble at all. In fact, you can help out, take some of the load off Becky Jo and her mother."

"Ain't been no trouble, Reverend. Me and the Major can handle it." The girl's face clouded.

What am I missing here?

"Miss Stone, my Deborah would not let me hear the end of it unless I insist and keep insisting until you agree." Rachel wanted to laugh at the gleam in his eye. "So, for the sake of my own marital bliss, please say yes."

Rachel bowed her head, and swallowed the lump of gratitude in her throat. "All right, Reverend Taylor. Thank you for your kindness. I will try to be a help and not a hinder."

Becky Jo muttered something, but the Reverend didn't seem to notice so Rachel let it dance away on the breeze of the warm welcome and the opportunity to be close to Michael.

"And please call me Zechariah."

"I'll try."

"How's our patient doing, Becky Jo?" he asked.

"No change." Becky Jo spoke without inflection, her eyes focused somewhere over Rachel's shoulder.

"He did moan and try to say something when I put the cloth on his head." Tension rocked against Rachel as she spoke. Her eyes met Becky Jo's until the girl looked away.

"That's different." Zechariah examined Michael. "Becky Jo, will you please go let doc know Michael may be waking up."

"Yes, sir. I'll be right back." Becky Jo darted out the door.

Zechariah escorted Rachel to a room at the end of the upstairs hall. "This used to be our daughter, Amelia's, room. She lives in Chicago now with her husband."

Double bed with a flowered spread tucked under a sloped ceiling. Pale yellow wallpaper with blue wildflowers. Pine dresser and mirror with a pitcher and basin. A little alcove held hooks for hanging clothes. An east-facing window promised abundant sunshine to help start her day. A place cozy and warm—so unlike the rooms of her past crammed with the soil of men's lust. And so close to Michael.

"I can't thank you enough, Rev—I mean, Zechariah." Her heart wanted to say *Grandpa.*

Zechariah fumbled with his hands. He coughed. "Come on, let's get you something to eat and some tea."

More tea. I could really use some of Martha's coffee.

As they walked past a partially closed door, a tired voice called. "Who's with you, Zech?"

He held the door for Rachel to enter the room. "Deborah, this is Rachel Stone. She came all the way from Riverbend to see us."

Deborah's watery eyes held her, and Rachel felt as if they peeled back a layer of her person and peered into her soul. "You saw something was going to happen to him, didn't you."

How does she know? "Yes, Ma'am, I did."

"That's not the first vision you've had."

The call to pray for the posse, the vision of her and Michael in the valley, God's word they were to marry flashed in a swirl of memories.

"No, Ma'am."

"Reverend Taylor, Doc's here." Becky Jo's voice boomed from the foot of the stairs.

Zechariah kissed his wife on the forehead. "Michael may be waking up, dear."

As Rachel followed Zechariah from the room, she glanced back. Deborah smiled and winked at her.

Downstairs, Rachel saw a slender man with black hair leaning over Michael. The man turned at the sound of her and Zechariah entering the room. He pointed at Michael. "Miss, you heard him groan or moan?"

Rachel nodded, taken aback by the thin face, ice blue eyes and abrupt manner as the man pointed at Michael and then at her, like she had done something wrong.

"Anything else?" The man's impatience grated, like one of her old customers concerned he wouldn't get his money's worth.

"I think he tried to say something. It sounded like a word."

"Could you make it out?"

"No, sir."

The man removed his spectacles and tapped them on his hand. "I think I'm going to let him wake up. He'll be feeling a lot of pain, but I can give him some more laudanum if it gets too bad."

Awake. Yes, let him hear me, see me. I'll help him with the pain.

Zechariah stepped between her and the doctor. "Here I am forgetting my manners. Doc MacKenzie, this is Rachel Stone, a friend of Michael's from Riverbend."

The doctor nodded. "Somebody needs to be with him all the time. Like I said, he's going to be in a lot of pain, and he'll feel disoriented."

"I'll do it." Rachel and Becky Jo spoke together, their words tumbling over each other.

The doctor glanced from one to the other. "Let Miss Stone do it. Becky Jo, you know where my office is. She doesn't. You come running for me as soon as he starts to wake up."

Becky Jo hung her head. "Yes, sir."

MacKenzie adjusted his glasses. "Let me check on Miss Deborah while I'm here."

Rachel replaced the cloth on Michael's head, aware of Becky Jo's eyes stalking her.

Chapter 38

Tuesday, July 9, 1878

"JORDAN DENNISON." CALEB spoke the words as he entered Gideon's office. Gideon sat behind the desk, wounded leg propped on the pulled-out bottom drawer. Jeremiah sat across from him, with several telegraph messages spread out between them.

Confusion clouded Gideon's eyes. "What about him?"

Caleb poured a cup of coffee and sipped it. He spat into the cuspidor by the desk. "D'you throw an old boot in the pot? Jeremiah, can you fix us some decent coffee?"

"Enough about the coffee. What's this about Jordan Dennison?" The impatience in Gideon's voice humored Caleb. He took his time to place a chair near the desk, plant his feet on the drawer next to Gideon's leg, toss his hat onto a peg by the door.

"He's our left-handed gun," Caleb said.

"He's dead," Jeremiah set the pot on the stove and added wood to the fire. "Killed six months ago in Mexico. A border raid."

"I'd say the reports of his demise have been greatly exaggerated," Caleb said, "probably by himself. He bought a pair of custom made boots from Hayden Chase a week ago."

"Are you sure?" Gideon's brows formed a straight line across his forehead.

"Yep. Chase identified him from my description, and his name's in the ledger. Somewhere along the way, probably in Mexico, he lost his right arm."

Gideon ran his fingers through his hair. "I'm getting too old. There's no way he should be in my town and me miss him."

Caleb shrugged. "He must be laying low. Only coming out when he needs to."

"Question is, who hired him?" Jeremiah checked the coffee. "He wouldn't be this far east except for a lot of money."

The two looked at Gideon, who stared out the window. "Has to be one of the big families. But who? None of them are feuding."

"How about in town?" Jeremiah said. "Anybody trying to take over somebody's business? Any grudges?"

Gideon shook his head. "Nothin' that's reached my attention."

"Anybody come into a bunch of money? More than normal business would account for?" Caleb felt like they grasped at fish with their bare hands. Even if they touched something, it slithered away.

"Not that I know of."

Jeremiah poured coffee, and they brooded. For want of something to do, Caleb picked up a single sheet of paper from the desk. The list of names Jeremiah had obtained from the Winslow ledger. He scanned the list, seeking inspiration and ideas for his muddled brain. "Why would a banker sell five horses in one day? Is that normal?"

Jeremiah shrugged. "Maybe someone gave him the horses to pay down a loan."

Caleb tapped the desk with the edge of the paper.

"What are you thinking?" Gideon said.

"Not sure. Could be nothing."

"Out with it." Gideon barked, cheeks red.

"It just strikes me as odd, is all." Caleb paced. "I'd like to know how often he does it. Do we know how often he forecloses on a mortgage or calls in a loan?"

Gideon turned his palms upward. "I only get involved if there's an eviction. I'd say we've done two or three in the past year. People, especially the small farmers, are still struggling to rebuild after the war and the panic in seventy-three."

"And the bank holds the property."

"Yeah, until it's sold. What're you drivin' at?"

"I think I know," Jeremiah said. "You're wondering if the bank is forcing people to sell?"

"But why?" Gideon's exasperation was tangible. "The Barretts are the richest family around here. And the most respected and powerful. What would they have to gain?"

"I don't know." Caleb turned to Gideon. "Can you get us access to the deeds for the last year or so? I want to see who's buying land."

"Sure. I can set it up for first thing in the morning. But I don't think it's gonna get us anywhere."

"You may be right." Caleb kept his voice calm. "But it gives us something to work on until we can find this Micah Grimmler. Jeremiah, do you think you can use your Southern charm to get another look at those ledgers, see how much horse trading the banker's been doing?"

"I'll try but I may need a chaperon. The Widow Winslow is…let's just say she's not a shy person."

"But where does Jordan Dennison fit in with all this?" Gideon said.

"Persuasion." Caleb said.

⋯⊶⊷⋯

Rachel blinked as the parlor brightened. Becky Jo lit the oil lamp closest to the couch and adjusted the wick.

Rachel slipped to her knees next to Michael and brushed her fingertips along the furrow between his brows, wishing she could erase the frown. She wished she could brush away the bruises, the cuts, the swollen knee, the broken arm, the bullet wound. She prayed.

The frown deepened, and Michael squirmed before quieting again. Her heart flew on the eagle's wings of hope. More often throughout the afternoon, he'd shown signs of waking. A groan, a squirm, a frown. Once, his eyelids fluttered. She'd willed them to open but they didn't. How far would that swollen tissue spread? Would he even be able to see? Doctor MacKenzie suggested his vision might have suffered. He might even be blind.

She touched the one unbruised, uncut spot on his cheek. *I'd love you still.*

Michael would live. She knew, despite the doctor's continued prognosis that Michael's internal injuries were worse than the external and could kill him. She heard those words but did not accept them.

Michael would live. God had promised. She didn't know how God would make it happen, but she trusted Him to keep the promise of the vision.

She and Michael would marry.

A horrid, raspy, hoarse voice whispered in her ear, like the speaker had gargled gravel and washed it down with acid. *How can you marry a cripple? You deserve better. This is God's joke on you. Deliver you from the brothel and saddle you with half a man for the rest of your life.*

Rachel gasped and spun around. Becky Jo sat on the edge of the armchair nearest the couch, leaning forward, elbows on her knees, hands clasped, eyes on Michael.

"Did you hear anything?"

Becky Jo studied Rachel, like a cat stalking a mouse. "No, Ma'am. Didn't hear nothin' 'cept the Major working in the kitchen. What d'ya think you heard?"

"Not sure. It may have been just my imagination."

"I know what you mean." She waved her hand. "Sometimes my 'magination gives me a fright. Pa says it's cuz my head is always in the clouds."

Rachel smiled.

"Won't you have something to eat, Miss Stone? The Major's made a real good roast with taters and carrots. You ain't ate since early this afternoon." She glanced at the grandfather clock. "More than six hours ago."

Rachel's stomach rumbled as it had for the past hour. She brushed Michael's hair, fingers lingering.

"I kin keep an eye on Michael. I'll call you if anythin' changes."

Rachel's hand went to her stomach to still the rumblings. "Thanks. I think food would do me good." She stood and steadied herself on the arm of the couch as pins and needles shot from her feet to her thighs. Her other hand went to her forehead as the room spun.

Becky Jo tsked. "Comes from staying in one place too long. Body gets all scrunched and then can't straighten when you first move."

Rachel leaned over and kissed Michael's forehead. *Did he just smile? He felt my lips?* She waited. Whatever she saw faded, and Michael lay as before.

In the kitchen, Mrs. Larkin placed a platter of beef roast, potatoes and carrots in front of her along with a cup of tea. Rachel prayed a blessing over her food. As she ate, the Major sat at the other end of the table with her own cup of tea.

After several quick bites, Rachel slowed and savored the tender beef seasoned with the lightest touch of sage, the vegetables sweetened with butter. "This is delicious." She dabbed her lips with a napkin. "So why do they call you the Major?"

Mrs. Larkin sipped her tea. "After we had number six, I needed more help keeping the brood and all my chores organized. Mr. Larkin said I reminded him of his major in the army who had everything organized to the smallest detail. Every man in the command knew his job. I had the children doing chores as soon as they could walk. Becky Jo started cooking at four and watching the older young-uns at five. Couldn't run the place without her."

"Is that why she's called the Colonel?"

Mrs. Larkin laughed. "You've been talking to the Reverend." Melancholy slipped over her face. "Mr. Larkin and I are gonna miss her when she gets married."

"Has she got a beau?"

"One young man has asked to come calling. But Becky Jo's had her heart set on marrying Michael since she turned sixteen."

The food lumped in Rachel's stomach. "Oh."

Mrs. Larkin smiled. "Now, don't you fret none. We told her to treat you with nothin' but respect."

Rachel fumbled for words. "Does...does Michael know?"

"I doubt it. Men can be thick as a stump about these things."

"I'll respect her, too. Thank you for telling me. I'll be careful what I say around her."

"So, when are you and Michael getting hitched?"

Rachel kept her head down, and poked at the last carrot on her plate. *Can't tell her about the vision.* "Michael hasn't asked me yet."

"Oh, he will. As soon as he wakes up. We could see in the way he talked about you."

Zechariah walked in, his step lighter, the color of his face more ruddy. He carried empty plates and eating utensils. "Major, Deborah said to tell you the meal was delicious. You can see she ate the whole thing, and a good bit of mine."

"Good to see she's getting her appetite back. You'll see, she'll be up and about in no time."

"Rachel." Zechariah's soft, tentative voice beckoned her. "Would you mind visiting Deborah? She'd like to talk with you."

Rachel passed through the parlor on her way to the stairs. Becky Jo knelt where Rachel had been, mopping Michael's brow with a damp cloth, her other hand resting on his.

You can't take what God has promised me and I will fight you for him. The thought startled her. *Haven't wanted to fight another woman since I battled to get out of Red Mary's.* Other girls would want to fight for certain well-paying customers. Rachel never bothered; they were all lower than pond scum to her.

Upstairs, extra pillows propped Deborah into a semi-reclined position. Her hand felt like fine parchment.

"Thank you for visiting. I know it's hard to leave Michael, even for a few minutes."

"He's in good hands."

Deborah's laugh turned to a cough. Rachel helped her sip from a glass of water on a table next to the bed.

"You must mean Becky Jo. Be careful, or she'll try to steal him from you."

"She won't succeed."

Deborah's hazel eyes searched Rachel's face. "You're very sure about that. Very secure in what you say."

"Yes, I am."

"Why?"

Rachel bit her lower lip, and found herself returning Deborah's steady gaze. She told about the visions.

Deborah listened, stroking Rachel's hand. When Rachel finished, the older woman squeezed her hand, the slightest increase in pressure, hardly any force behind it. Deborah's weakness also showed in the droop of her mouth.

Rachel attempted to pull her hand loose. "I should let you rest."

Deborah wouldn't let go. Rachel knew she could slip her hand away, but she waited. This woman touched her heart, saw into her soul the way no one had.

Neither Martha nor Annabelle penetrated the way Deborah did. She could keep no secrets from this woman.

Deborah patted her hand. "You have something from God you don't understand. Neither do I, but I believe these visions are for a purpose which He will reveal to you over time."

Deborah's shoulders sagged, and her eyes drooped. Rachel started to rise. Deborah stopped her. "He has something special for you and Michael. I don't know what. But you must trust Him, no matter how hard it gets."

"I will." She choked on the words.

"Leave me now. I'm sleepy." She smiled. "Ask Zechariah to come up and read to me. Philippians, I think." She released Rachel's hand.

Rachel kissed the top of Deborah's head and let her fingers trace the vein on the back of the woman's hand before she turned and left the room.

Pain. Everywhere. Even his eyelids. Michael had woken in pain before. Most recently in Riverbend. Although that was a hangover. This was…different. Physical beyond anything his father ever did. Beyond anything from any barroom brawl.

And he remembered. The fists to his face, his stomach, his back. Air rushed from his lungs, leaving him unable to breathe. The boot to his knee. The board across his arm. The snap of the bone. As sharp as ice breaking in winter.

The bullet. Oh, the bullet. Burning as it passed into his shoulder. Searing as it chipped bone and tore through muscle. Ripping a scream from his throat as it exited, a scream he had no breath to express.

And he remembered why. Ben on the gallows. Sam at the cabin. Miss Deborah bleeding, face the color of death.

A killer loose and still trying to kill. Have to stop him.

He pushed to get up. Nothing moved.

And a voice. Her voice. Soft. Soothing.

Her hand on his, on his forehead, touching his face. Cool and dry. Gentle.

Her lips. Warm. Tender on his cheek.

Rachel.

Here? How?

Didn't matter. Had to see her. Hold her. Touch her.

He opened his eyes. Multi-colored stars swirled. A pattern of fireworks exploded. A canon in his head.

He closed his eyes.

Oblivion.

CHAPTER 39

Wednesday, July 10, 1878

CALEB AND JEREMIAH turned down the street to the Winslow mansion. Jeremiah brushed his sleeves. "I don't know if she's going to fall for the Southern gentleman act again."

"Just turn on your masculine charm."

Bessie answered their knock, her round, ebony face peering around the door, eyes wide. "Mizzy ain't dressed. She don't entertain no one afore eleven o'clock." She closed the door despite Jeremiah's protests.

Jeremiah gazed up at the three-story brick building. "We may have worn out our welcome."

"Maybe. Let's come back at eleven and see what happens."

Trees provided an oasis of shade along the quiet street in the breezeless morning sun. Jeremiah stopped to wipe his brow. "Don't know how these Southern gentlemen can stand these clothes. Feel as tight as a corset. Don't let a man breathe. Give me a pair of dungarees and a cotton shirt any day of the week."

The sound of a carriage brought their attention back to the Winslow place. A small, ornate buggy came out of the gate and trotted past them.

"Doesn't entertain before eleven? Seems Bessie lied to us." Caleb said.

"That would depend on what time the Widow Winslow started entertaining."

"Did you recognize the driver?"

"No."

"Well, it wasn't Smythe."

Jeremiah settled his hat on his head. "Maybe Gideon'll recognize our description."

Gideon sat at his desk, sorting through a stack of papers, as Caleb and Jeremiah entered. "This job's getting to be as much about pushing paper as it is arresting people. You two are back sooner than I expected."

Caleb dropped his hat on Gideon's desk. "Apparently the Widow Winslow doesn't entertain before eleven."

The clock behind Gideon's desk read nine-thirty. "Must be a strenuous life for her."

Caleb chuckled. "Must be. A man left her house right after we were told she wasn't dressed. Driving a Studebaker Phaeton, fancy trim. He looked to be just under six feet tall. Not fat, but definitely not slender. Silvery hair, fair complexion. One of them chin beards, don't remember what you call them."

"Goatee." Jeremiah leaned against the desk and picked up a stack of wanted posters.

"Christopher Barrett," Gideon said. "Owns the bank. Judge's brother."

"Is he married?" Caleb said.

Gideon nodded. "Twin boys. They live at the old plantation about ten miles out of town."

Caleb poured coffee. "Does he keep a place in town?"

"Yeah. He keeps some rooms over the bank. How'd you know?"

Caleb shrugged. "Guess mostly. Figured he wouldn't want to be too far away from his money." He paused. "Or other diversions."

"You think he's involved with Emma Winslow? I thought she was seeing that horse trader, Smythe."

Jeremiah chuckled. "From what I've seen, the Widow Winslow is not one to limit her options."

Gideon frowned. "Can't say I like that. Opens the door to all kinds of shenanigans."

"And trouble," Caleb said.

Two hours later, Caleb and Jeremiah knocked on Mrs. Winslow's door. It swung wide open.

"What can I do for you gentlemen?" One hand on her hip, the other on the door, Bessie smiled a gap-toothed grin.

Jeremiah's Southern drawl sounded like honey on a biscuit to Caleb. "We'd like just a few moments of Mrs. Winslow's precious time."

"She ain't home."

"Ain—Isn't home? When did she leave?" Jeremiah said.

"'Bout an hour ago."

"Didn't you tell her we stopped by to see her?" Jeremiah said.

"Yessir, I did, but she said she had important bidness to take care of."

"Did she say where?" Caleb asked.

"No sir, tain't none of my bidness. I just packed a couple of bags for her."

"Did she say when she'd be back?" Jeremiah said.

"No, sir."

Jeremiah rubbed the back of his neck. "What if you need to get in touch with her?"

"She tole me to go see Mr. Christopher at the bank if anything happened."

Caleb touched the brim of his hat. "Thank you, Miss Bessie. Please let Mrs. Winslow know we need to see her as soon as she returns."

"Yes, sir." Bessie stopped just short of slamming the door.

As they walked up the street, Caleb said. "Couple of bags? She could be away for a while."

Jeremiah laughed. "For Mrs. Winslow, a couple of bags might be what she'd take on an overnight trip."

"Let's go to the train station."

In the almost deserted depot, one woman waited while, next to her, a girl played with a doll. The ticket agent looked bored as he flipped through a newspaper. He stirred as Caleb and Jeremiah approached, slapped a fly on the counter, looked at his palm and wiped his hand on his vest.

Caleb leaned on the counter. "Any trains leave in the last hour?"

"Nope. First train of the day won't get here for at least another half hour."

"Do you know Emma Winslow?"

The agent frowned, took a step back. "What's that to you?"

Caleb looked down at his vest. *Oh, yeah. No badge. Need to have Gideon deputize us.* "We're helping Sheriff Parsons while he recovers from his wound. We need to talk with Mrs. Winslow about some horse-trading business."

The clerk smiled. "I heard about you two. Ain't you with Michael Archer? Did I hear he got shot?"

Caleb resisted the urge to reach through the narrow window and grab the agent by the shirt. "Mrs. Winslow?"

"She ain't been in here."

Caleb turned to go when Jeremiah leaned over. "What do you know about our friend getting shot?"

The agent's hands fumbled at some papers on the counter. "Just heard there was a shooting behind the bank, and it was that Michael Archer feller."

"How'd you hear?" Jeremiah asked.

"Just talk at the saloon."

"When?" Jeremiah leaned closer.

The agent raised his hands, palms out. "It was last night."

Outside, Caleb asked Jeremiah, "What'd'ya think?"

"By last night the whole town knew about the shooting."

"What about Mrs. Winslow?"

"Let's check the stage depot." Jeremiah strode off.

Within a few steps, Caleb caught up to him, matching his strides. "What's got you so riled?"

Jeremiah sighed. "We're not getting anywhere. Records disappear. People won't let us see ledgers. Miss Deborah and Michael get shot. Mrs. Winslow has business that takes her away. We've got Jordan Dennison lurking somewhere, working for someone, we don't know who. Right now, we only know two things. Ben Carstairs did not kill Donald Winslow. And, whoever did, is willing to kill again so we don't find him. Or her."

"You think Mrs. Winslow killed her own husband?"

"She's capable." Jeremiah paused. "Or, at least she's capable of getting someone to do it for her."

At the stage depot, they learned the next stage through town would be the following day. The agent there had not seen Mrs. Winslow.

Back at Gideon's office, Caleb folded his arms and tilted his hat over his eyes as Jeremiah told the sheriff about their morning.

Gideon nudged his foot. "Anything else? Or, are you turning into one of those old timers who falls asleep in the middle of a conversation?"

"Can still work you into the ground if I have to." Caleb wondered if his voice sounded as tired as his brain felt. Even his muscles were sore. The thought of stretching out on a bed for several hours enticed him. Not now. After this was over he could relax. "Give us badges. Tired of having to explain myself to everybody."

"Should've done it when you first got in. On your feet. Let me swear you in official. Of course, I don't have any money in the budget to pay you."

"Figured. That's all right. This is personal now anyway."

Caleb pinned the badge to his vest. Felt complete again. The last few days without a badge had been like walking with one boot too small. He touched the metal. Amazing how you could get attached to something that brought so much danger. And he thought of Pete O'Brien. Good man. Careful. More careful than Caleb had been at that age. *He'll do fine. Annabelle will help make sure of that.*

Jeremiah slipped the badge into his coat pocket. "I'll put this on after I change."

Gideon stood and slipped the crutch under his arm. "Let's go."

"Where to?" Caleb eyed his old friend.

"Town hall to see those deed records you're interested in. Then I'm going to Zechariah's to see how Michael's doing."

Rachel held Michael's left hand, caressing it, relishing the time alone with him. The Major and her daughter would be back from their errands later. Rachel hoped they'd take their time, let her be with Michael without Becky Jo's hovering.

She'd left Zechariah upstairs with Deborah, their eyes expressing how much they treasured each moment with one another, moments that were almost stolen from them.

No one was going to steal any of the moments God planned for her and Michael. Michael's hand in hers was the tangible reminder of the vision and the promise.

"Michael, wake up," she whispered. "I know it will hurt. I will be here. I'll help you handle it. I need you here; I need you to tell me you're back to stay. I need to tell you I love you."

His head turned side to side. His brow creased in deep furrows. He puffed a breath of air, made a sound.

She leaned closer, ear near his mouth. "What are you trying to say? I'm listening. Tell me."

His face relaxed as he sank into a deep sleep again.

Did he smile?

She sighed and bit back the tears that still wanted to fall. They welled up when she sat with him, and whenever she washed his wounds, cooled his forehead with a damp cloth, when she saw the bruises on his chest and stomach and back.

She started to rise to get fresh water.

Pressure around her fingers.

Did Michael do that or did she imagine it? She attempted to pull her hand away, more pressure from his grip stopped her. She wanted to hug him. Couldn't. Kiss him. Dared not touch those bruised and swollen lips.

She put her free hand to her mouth, kissed her fingers, and brushed them against his lips, a light touch. He squeezed again. Tears flow and she laughed. He knew she was there. He didn't want her to leave.

She suppressed the desire to shout, to jump, to sing and dance. She held his hand to her chest. Brought it to her lips. Held it against her cheek.

"Thank You, Lord."

He mouthed something. She leaned closer.

"What, Michael?"

His lips moved again. She brought her ear as close as she dared without touching him.

"Amen." Soft. Pushed out more than spoken. But he was here in body as well as soul.

With her free hand, she soaked the damp cloth and wrung it out, leaving some water in it. She held it over his lips and let moisture drip. His tongue darted out to catch more.

His face contorted, and he coughed. His chest heaved as he coughed again. She heard the fluid in his throat.

"No. You're not going to drown on me."

She turned his head to the side, pushing his groans and moans from her mind. Liquid dribbled out the side of his mouth onto the pillow. He coughed again, breathed easier. She bowed her head against his chest. "Thank You, Lord."

His lips moved. She leaned closer. A breath against her ear, a sound to penetrate her heart. "Love you."

Rachel brushed wetness from her cheek and lowered her head to his neck. The gentlest kiss she could do. So inadequate when she wanted to smother him against her. "I love you too."

She took his hand again. His response wasn't as strong as before, but still there. His hair, thick, matted with sweat and blood. Beard stubbled his wan face. "You need a bath, a shave and a haircut. I'll talk with doc about getting it done before Becky Jo takes it on herself."

The pang of jealousy surprised Rachel. *She has a crush on him, that's all.* Then she remembered the major telling her Becky Jo would turn twenty in December. *Five years younger than me. Michael's twenty-eight. Nope, that girl is serious.* "Lord, help Becky Jo to accept your plan for Michael and me. Help me to befriend her. Bring the right man into her life."

--->==◎ ◎==<---

The neatness of the clerk's office in the town hall impressed Caleb when he thought of the hodgepodge sprawl in Riverbend. A few feet inside the door, a counter ran the width of the room. Behind it, shelves lined three walls with volumes of record books marching in rank and file around the room.

The clerk who rose from a desk in the middle of the room struck Caleb as being as out of place as a gelding in a breeding corral. The man stood several inches over six feet and had the girth and width of a teamster. Then Caleb noticed the left sleeve pinned to the shoulder and the left leg ending in a wooden stump that echoed like a drum beat in the quiet room. The left side of his face bore the tight, pinched wrinkles of burn scars.

Gideon introduced them to Walter Fleming.

"Where?" Caleb said.

"Shiloh. Polk's artillery. Yankee shell hit our cannon just as we were about to fire. Blew us all to kingdom come." He wiggled his empty sleeve. "And back again."

Gideon cleared his throat. "Walter, we need to see the deeds recorded for the last six months."

The man managed to stack three of the volumes into the crook of his right arm and slide them onto the counter.

An hour later, Caleb closed his book with a loud slam. "No Christopher Barrett here."

Gideon and Jeremiah had finished before him. They reported the same result. Everything seemed in order.

"Another theory we can cross off." Gideon's lips twisted in a grimace, his eyes narrowed. "And still not any closer."

Fleming clomped to the counter. "Did you mention Mr. Barrett, the banker?"

Gideon nodded.

Fleming flipped open one of the books. "Mr. Barrett came in here several times with the owner of the property. Helped them register the deed."

"Is that unusual?" Gideon said.

"For him. He usually only comes when the bank's foreclosed and taken the deed."

Jeremiah tapped the pages. "Were any of these foreclosures that he then sold to a new buyer?"

Fleming fitted a pair of spectacles over his eyes, turning his head so his right hand could fix the frame over his left ear. He scanned the list of names, flipped back several pages, lower lip between his teeth. "No, these were all direct transfers from the old owners to the new."

An idea niggled at the edge of Caleb's mind, one he couldn't quite grasp. "Can you give us the names of any foreclosures the bank's done in the last six months?"

Caleb paced the public area while Fleming sat at his desk, flipping through pages, stopping occasionally to write some information on a sheet of paper. Jeremiah and Gideon leaned against the counter. A ticking clock, and Fleming's rustling papers and writing were the only sounds. The knot between Caleb's shoulders tightened like a tourniquet. He massaged his temples, but the dull ache persisted.

After several minutes, Fleming slid a piece of paper in front of Gideon. Caleb looked over his friend's shoulder at the precise handwriting. He asked Fleming, "Eleven names. Is that an unusual number for six months?"

Fleming shrugged. "Hard to say. Seems a little high. I'd have to go farther back to be sure. Folks are still struggling since the panic." His eyes narrowed, and he nodded at the list. "Don't know as Barrett's willing to work with folk when they're having hard times."

Gideon straightened up, wincing. "How do you mean?"

Fleming shifted his eyes to the window then back at Gideon. "My sister and her husband are breeding horses and couldn't make a full payment on their mortgage last month. He had them give him four of their horses. Two would have covered the payment."

Jeremiah whistled soft and low. Caleb remembered the trader's ledger entry. Barrett had sold five horses on the day of Donald Winslow's murder.

Outside the town hall, Caleb squinted in the noon sun as sweat beaded on his forehead. The humid air hung heavy in his lungs.

"All right," Caleb said. "We've got a banker who's not a knight in shining armor, but he's well connected and had some dealings with both Winslows. But I don't see where we're any closer to finding out who really killed Donald Winslow."

Gideon sighed. "Michael and I ran into the same thing. Nothing solid. No suspects. We ran out of ideas and places to look."

Jeremiah said, "Anybody take shots at you? Try to scare you off?"

Gideon shook his head.

"So what's different now?" Caleb said.

Jeremiah adjusted his hat. "All I can think of is we're making someone nervous."

"Why focus on getting rid of Michael? Why not us?" Caleb said.

Gideon sighed. "Maybe they think if they scare him off, we'll follow him."

Caleb fisted his hands. "Not now."

-->==◉ ◉==<--

Rachel snapped awake. How did she get in the high-backed armchair near the couch? She'd been kneeling on the floor, holding Michael's hand. The fog eddied in slow swirls: Zechariah helping her to her feet, guiding her to the chair, bringing her a cup of tea. The Major and Becky Jo coming in and rustling in the kitchen preparing dinner. Michael sleeping through it all.

Michael lay as still as before. The swelling around his eyes and knee seemed less. She prayed, "Lord, I thank you he will live. Let your healing power flow into him. Bring him all the way back, Lord."

"Amen." Becky Jo's voice startled her. The girl stood behind the couch, hands clasped, eyes riveted on Michael.

"Are you hungry?" the girl said.

Rachel shook her head. She wanted to kneel next to him, but the chair felt so comfortable, cocooning her. She wanted to tuck her legs under her and curl up beneath a blanket. Michael needed her. No. She needed Michael. She needed to see him, touch his hand, his face, nurse him, help him be well and whole. Love him.

Is this how you love? Give and give? Can I do that? I want to. Michael will have to be blessed with abundant patience while I learn how.

Now Becky Jo's eyes were on her. Rachel met her gaze, studied her. *Here's a first. I've never had to compete with another woman for a man. Until now.*

Rachel wanted Michael, had known it by the end of their first picnic, although she wouldn't admit it, especially to herself. The vision confirmed it for her.

Would Becky Jo fight for Michael?

A knock at the door. Becky Jo went to answer it. Rachel stood. Behind her, Zechariah tap-danced down the stairs, his steps as light as his spirit as Deborah improved. He carried an envelope.

Caleb introduced her to Gideon. The sheriff bowed his head. "It's a pleasure to finally meet you, Miss Stone." He glanced at Michael. "You've had quite an influence on our young man here."

"Thank you, Sheriff. It's good to have a face to go with the stories Michael told me." Her picture of Michael's world shifted as another piece of the puzzle of Michael Archer snicked into place. Michael's other mentor besides Zechariah. But mysteries still remained. Ellie was out there somewhere. Would they ever meet?

Gideon hobbled to the couch. He wiped his face with his hand. "How did he live through this? I've seen men stove up by a horse who looked better than this."

Zechariah stood next to Gideon. "He's strong in spirit and body. Doc MacKenzie's done his usual great work. But there's two things that have gotten him through." He nodded at Rachel. "One is love. And the other is, God isn't through with him yet."

Out of the corner of her eye, Rachel saw Becky Jo's face cloud over, and caught the quick glare the girl shot in her direction.

Gideon and Caleb agreed to mail Zechariah's letter for him.

"It's to Amelia, telling her about Deborah and not to fret," he said. Gideon received it as if it were ancient parchment.

"I'll make sure it gets handled right," Gideon said.

After the others left, the Major called Becky Jo into the kitchen. Zechariah checked on Deborah and returned downstairs.

"She's sleeping." He opened his Bible.

Rachel sat on the edge of the couch and applied a damp cloth to Michael's forehead. His fever was down, but there were still times he shivered, even in the warm room.

"You're an excellent nurse, Rachel," Zechariah said.

She smiled. "Only because it's Michael. Anybody else, I'd be flustered, dropping things, probably doing more harm than good."

"Maybe. Love can be a great motivator."

She stroked Michael's hair. "Yes, it can." She squeezed the words past the lump in her throat.

CHAPTER 40

Wednesday, July 10, 1878

UsING HIS SLEEVE, Caleb polished the badge pinned to his vest. "Think I'll put this to use."

"Where you goin'?" Gideon looked up from his paperwork.

"Visit our banker."

A frown creased Gideon's face. "Why?"

Caleb hitched his gun belt. "Because he keeps popping up. First on the day of the murder, he sells five horses. He's at the Widow Winslow's when she's not receiving visitors, and she's supposedly keeping company with someone else." He paused. "And I'm not too sure I like his banking practices. How much of the money from those horses do you think actually made it to the bank?"

"That's not much to tie him to the murder."

"I know. But until we find this Micah Grimmler, we don't have anything else."

Gideon nodded. "Scratch that itch if you have to. Just remember who he is. I know that don't mean anything to you, but it means a great deal to him. He'll think he can squash you like a bug if you irritate him."

Caleb put his hand over his heart. "Gideon, in all the years we've known each other, have you ever known me to irritate anyone?"

"Only on days that end in d—a—y."

Jeremiah adjusted his hat as he stood. "Want some company?"

"Sure. Maybe your Southern charm will smooth any feathers I ruffle."

Gideon shook his head.

Caleb held the door for Jeremiah to precede him. "By the way, Jeremiah, where are you from anyway?"

Jeremiah tugged the cuffs of his jacket. "Boston."

This place stinks of money. Caleb had never seen a bank like this. Tall, freshly cleaned front windows spilled sunlight onto the gleaming hardwood floor. Teller cages of dark wood and wrought iron bars stood like a three-eyed monster guarding the large safe behind them. Near the cages stood a man of medium build, muttonchops, handlebar mustache, two-gun rig on his waist and a shotgun cradled in his arms.

To the left, a three-foot-high railing separated the main area from a couple of desks and an office with a frosted window in the door. Painted on the glass were the words, *Christopher J. Barrett.* The line below read, *President.*

From one of the desks on the other side of the railing, a man stood and approached them. He tugged at his collar and squared his shoulders while his fingers did a dance on the carved gate.

"Can I help you gentlemen?" His voice squeaked like a teenager reaching manhood.

Caleb suppressed a smile. "We'd like to see Mr. Barrett."

"Do you have an appointment?"

Jeremiah's Southern charm oozed. "No, we don't, my good man. But we would sure appreciate it if you would ask Mr. Barrett if he could spare just a few moments of his time for us."

Caleb was surprised the Southern charm didn't leave a puddle on the floor.

The man cleared his throat. "What is this in regard to?"

Caleb felt Jeremiah's fingers tug on his shirt. Jeremiah pointed to his badge. "You see, we're helping Sheriff Parsons with some matters while he is still somewhat incapacitated. They're of rather a preliminary nature so the sheriff asked us not to share them with anyone except Mr. Barrett. I'm sure you understand."

"Wait one moment." The man knocked on the frosted window and stepped inside.

Caleb leaned toward Jeremiah. "You could charm a cougar from a tree. D'you ever think of running for office?"

Jeremiah's smile resembled a grimace. "Perish the thought. I can only maintain this for so long."

After several minutes, the clerk reappeared and gestured them forward. He sniffed as if a skunk passed by. "Gentlemen, Mr. Barrett can spare five minutes, so please be brief."

Jeremiah patted the man on the upper arm. "Thank you for persuading Mr. Barrett to give us even this much time from his busy schedule."

The man grinned and seemed to grow at least an inch. *I've seen peacocks with less pride.*

The only desk Caleb had ever seen larger than Christopher Barrett's belonged to the governor. *You could hold a church service on that thing.* The mahogany glowed with a deep luster.

Two chairs of black leather and mahogany fronted the desk. Two windows on the left-hand wall faced the street. Opaque shades diffused the sunlight to a warm glow that muted the shadows. Behind the desk, a credenza holding a cigar humidor and a silver tray with glasses and several decanters of liquor flanked a miniature replica of the safe in the main room.

A burgundy leather sofa stood against the right-hand wall. Above it were three portraits, one of Judge Barrett and a second of the banker. The third showed an older couple whom Caleb assumed to be the parents because of the family resemblance of the judge to the woman and Christopher to the man.

Barrett rose from his high-backed tufted chair like a prince greeting his court. One hand waved a thick cigar at them as he extended his other. *How many horses did that cigar cost?*

His hand was soft, his grip limp, only his fingers brushed theirs. *It's like shaking hands with a wet rope.*

Barrett sat, crossed his legs, and stroked his goatee.

Caleb pulled up one of the chairs and sat, enjoying the look of annoyance that flashed across Barrett's face, confirming the man had purposely not invited them to sit. Caleb sat back, crossed an ankle on his knee and placed his hat on the desk. He clasped his hands at his waist, as if ready to spend several hours in the banker's company. Jeremiah followed his example.

Barrett pulled his pocket watch from his vest and studied it. "What can I do for you gentlemen?" He closed the watch but held it in his hand.

Jeremiah spoke. "Thank you for seeing us, Mr. Barrett. We'll try not to take up too much of your time. As you know, Sheriff Parsons is not operating at full capacity because of a nasty wound suffered in the line of duty." He paused. "Such a brave man. So dedicated to the community. My colleague, Deputy Davis, and I are endeavoring to help him clear up some matters."

Barrett opened and closed his watch. "What kind of matters?"

"The murder of Donald Winslow." Caleb regretted his sharp tone as soon the words left his mouth.

Barrett puffed on his cigar, the smoke forming a wreath around his head. "Why? They found the murderer. Hung him. Justice was served. What needs to be cleared up?"

Jeremiah brushed a piece of lint from his pants. "Sheriff Parsons is concerned because, in the past few days, two people have been shot, almost killed. The attempts seem to be directly related to renewed inquiries into the murder."

"I heard about that. Tragic. Horrible to think such things could happen in Tramlaw. I did hear that Mrs. Taylor is recovering. What about Archer?" He said Michael's name as if it carried a disease.

Jeremiah lowered his eyes, pitched his voice low. "Mr. Archer is seriously injured. As of right now, his life hangs in a delicate balance. Doctor MacKenzie has done all he can. I'm sure the Taylors and he would appreciate your prayers."

Barrett waved his hand, cigar ash falling to the floor. "Of course. But what has all this to do with me?"

"You were one of Mr. Winslow's last customers the day he was shot. His records show you sold five horses to him."

"I may have. Donald and I did a good deal of business. This bank handled all his accounts. Still does, in fact. Well, his widow's actually, as well as the business under its new ownership. I do remember seeing him that day. A tragic day none of us will ever forget."

Caleb started to speak, but Jeremiah made a slight motion with his hand. Caleb relaxed and let Jeremiah continue.

"Do you remember anything unusual? Was Mr. Winslow concerned about anything?"

Barrett looked at the ceiling before shifting his gaze to Jeremiah. "Can't say that he was, not that I recall. Everything seemed normal."

Jeremiah nodded.

Barrett checked the time. Again. "Gentlemen. I've told you all I can about that day. And I do have pressing business." He came around the desk. "If you will excuse me."

"Of course." Jeremiah stood. Caleb followed.

Barrett had his hand on the doorknob.

Jeremiah kept his voice casual. "And how is Mrs. Winslow bearing up? It must have been quite a shock to her."

Barrett blinked. Twice. "She…She's doing all right now. It was difficult at the beginning. She'd just lost her husband and had no idea how to run a business."

"You were able to help her out?"

"Yes, I was able to use the resources of the bank to help her through the tragedy of her husband's death and the transition of the business."

"I'm sure she must have greatly appreciated your assistance."

Barrett smiled, although his eyes glared. "I believe she did. This bank is always willing to help our customers in their time of need, no matter how great or small." He opened the door. "Good day, gentlemen. Please give my regards to Sheriff Parsons and Mrs. Taylor and tell them I wish them both speedy recoveries."

Once outside, Caleb said, "So why'd you shut me up?"

"I suspected your tone was going to be…shall we say…surly."

"What makes you think that?"

"You were about to jiggle your foot right off your ankle."

Caleb snorted. "You got that right. He was gettin' on my nerves."

"I know. I wanted to keep him talking, hoping the more he spoke, the more likely he was to let something slip."

"D'ya think it worked?"

Jeremiah glanced at the bank over his shoulder. "Hard to tell, but I do think he knows more than he lets on."

"Yep. But how do we get it out of somebody as slick and arrogant as him?"

Jeremiah rubbed his chin. "I think we just keep pushing."

Caleb shook his head. "He's too polished."

"Sometimes that can work in our favor."

CHAPTER 41

Wednesday, July 10, 1878

DRYNESS GRATED MICHAEL'S throat like sand. *Need water. What's holding me down? Can't get it off.*

He pushed with his hands. Burning pain shot up his right arm into his shoulder. *Who's using a branding iron on me?*

He opened his eyes. Narrow slits of dim light. *Lamplight? Are the curtains drawn?* Disorientation circled. *Where am I? What time is it? What day? What happened?*

He blinked. Pain like a shard of glass entered his eye and lay trapped under the lid.

He inhaled. Hardly any air. His lungs ached. Nothing came through his nose. He opened his mouth. Chapped lips tore apart. Air stung tender skin like sleet in a winter gale.

Hot. Cold. Hot. Can't get warm. Need a blanket. Too hot.

The memory came back, one slowly turning page at a time. The gun in his back. The foul breath in his ear. Turned into the alley, tripped on a stone, reached for his gun.

Blinding pain as wood swung with the force of a blacksmith struck his arm, and the pistol skittered in a pirouette into the darkness. The fists and kicks came too often from behind, from in front. At least three men, one holding, two hitting.

Unconscious oblivion taken away by brackish water thrown in his face. More punches and kicks. Face. Stomach. Back. The words "Leave it alone." A stomp on his left knee like a mule against the wall of a stall. *Why did I say no?*

A gunshot. His shoulder exploded. Then the darkness. Sweet, painless darkness.

Painless no more. Darkness only when he closed his eyes. Pain when he opened them. Pain when he closed them.

He turned his head to see if he could.

Pain.

What didn't hurt?

He prayed for the painless darkness to return.

It didn't.

A voice whispered. Soft, gentle. Who's? Couldn't tell. Couldn't understand the words. Who stuffed his ears with corn silk?

Moisture on his lips. A damp cloth, a gentle touch. Shafts of pain followed. He turned his head away. More pain.

The voice again. Warm air on his ear. Whose voice? What did she say? How did he know the person was a she?

The darkness started to come as a warm rush up his legs. He welcomed it. It reached his chest and stopped. *No. Keep coming. Take me away from this.*

He waited. Breathing hurt. Pulling and pushing air through his throat brought spasms. His lungs cried for more. He gave them all he could, but it wasn't enough.

The whisper returned. His name. He knew that voice, so soft, so sweet. Ma? Ellie? No. Who? A name floated, the letters smudged and torn by the swirl of pain. A face shrouded by the mist crying for the darkness. Wait. Don't leave. He concentrated. The agony shattered his thoughts.

Desperation flooded his mind. *Who is it? Who's there? Why can't I form words?*

The voice again. "Michael? I'm here."

Who are you? Where's here?

What's that? What's wet on my cheek? The moisture trickled into a wound, stung. He inhaled sharply. Coughed. More pain like a smith pumping his forge hotter and hotter.

Don't take the darkness. Fight the darkness. A new voice, inside his head. *Who's talking to me now?* Keep the darkness away. It will kill you.

"Michael. It's me. Rachel."

Rachel. Her violet eyes and warm smile. Her long brown hair flowing in the breeze as she rode her horse. Her hand in his. Her lips soft on his cheek. Her words when he left with the posse. "Come back. I want to get to know you better." Rachel. *Why is she here? That's right. I'm in Tramlaw. Clear Ben's name.*

He forced a sound from his mouth. He wanted it to be her name. He hoped that's what came out.

More wet on his cheek, her face against his. Pain, but the pressure of her cheek, the warmth of her tears, overcame it. He welcomed the new sensation.

Rachel. Here in Tramlaw.

He moved his left arm. No new pain. He lifted it, found her arm, her shoulder, her hair, her neck.

He hugged. It hurt. He didn't care.

Rachel. His heart sang her name as his fingers found her hair.

An hour later, Doc MacKenzie squatted next to him, offering a spoonful of liquid.

"What's that?" His voice croaked, his throat still full of sand.

"Laudanum to help ease the pain, help you sleep."

Have to get up. Can't lie here. Have to find the killer. He pushed at the blanket with his good foot. Too tight. Couldn't budge it. Have to.

"Here," MacKenzie said. Hard glass touched his lips. *No. Have to move, to get up.* He shook his head. Wished he hadn't.

"Suit yourself," Doc said. "I'll leave the bottle in case you change your mind."

Rachel perched at the end of the couch, eyes red, face white, hands gripped in her lap. Her hair tangled to her shoulders. His vision cleared. Others were in the room. Zechariah in the armchair. Becky Jo behind the couch, hovering.

Rachel leaned toward him, violet eyes caressing. Rachel. *She's here. Not a dream.*

"Water," he said. Get this gravel from my throat.

The doctor held a glass to his mouth, and he drank, small sips.

Michael lifted his left hand. Rachel took it in both of hers. The pressure of her palms, the strokes of her fingers warmed him like a campfire. He wanted to speak, had to say something.

He squeezed her hand, weak and feeble. "I love you." He sounded like a frog.

She smiled and wiped her cheek. "I love you, too."

Somewhere, a sob bubbled and footsteps retreated to the kitchen. He turned his head. Becky Jo was gone.

CHAPTER 42

Friday, July 12, 1878

MORNING AIR BRUSHED Michael's face, cool and fresh, tugging his hair. Shadows on the porch held back the heat of the day. He rested his head on the back of the rocker. Good to be outside, to see blue sky, to have Rachel by him, holding his hand.

By late Thursday, the pains of Wednesday—a day of constant, at times excruciating, hurt—had receded into dull aches, constant reminders of the abuse his body had received. Light kept his eyes in a permanent squint. He had caught his reflection in the windowpane, raccoon mask smeared over a black and blue nose and puffed lips. He could go to any masquerade ball in New Orleans without having to wear a disguise.

Thursday afternoon he had stood. And he walked using Rachel's shoulder as a crutch. A small victory but one that strengthened and encouraged. He lived. He would recover. They had not defeated him. And he had a woman who said she loved him.

He turned to her now, the movement slow to keep the pain dull. She smiled.

"Did you say you loved me the other day?" His voice croaked, rough—like sand still coated his throat, rasping every time he breathed and spoke.

She squeezed his hand. He relished the warm pressure of her fingers, their tenderness. "Doc says not to talk, give your throat time to heal."

He shook his head, and wiggled the fingers of his right hand resting in the sling around his shoulder. "Can't write." He coughed.

Worry crossed her eyes and she reached for a glass of water on the table next to him, holding it to his lips as he sipped. She then picked up a small bowl and teaspoon. Filling the spoon with a syrupy liquid, she offered it to him. "Take some of this hoarhound syrup. Doc thinks it will help your throat."

He swallowed the dose, closed his eyes, and nodded thanks.

"Of course, I did have to double check the spelling to make sure what kind of hoar he was talking about."

Michael smiled as she took his hand again. "Answer." It didn't hurt as bad to talk. Maybe the syrup would do some good.

She frowned. "Answer? Oh, to the question you asked." She stroked the back of his hand, bit her lip.

Why does she hesitate? Did I hear wrong? Wish I could talk.

Her eyes met his, violet dark and inviting. He remembered the day they met at dinner at the parsonage in Riverbend. Those eyes enthralled him then with the mysteries they held, some she shared, some she held back. Like her feelings. When they first met, he suspected she liked him but wouldn't or couldn't build a relationship. Until he left with the posse to find Ben's father. Then she said she'd like to know him better.

The posse hadn't changed him in one respect. He still believed he was unworthy of hers, or any woman's, love. And she had given him hope that he wasn't, that she might indeed be that woman.

But now, she kept her silence. *What is she trying to tell me with her eyes? If only I could draw the words from her, make her feel secure, not threaten her like so many in her past, make her know she would always be free.*

She sighed. "To love a man, any man, means I have to give up something of myself. Something I vowed I would never let happen. No man was going to be able to hurt me ever again."

She tilted her head to one side, and smiled. "And then you came along. You touched me, touched my heart. And then you left. Twice. This second time was so much harder."

He waited, grateful his throat prevented him from speaking because he would probably only mess things up.

"Michael, I do love you."

He pulled her to him with his good arm, holding her awkwardly. "Wait."

He stood and tugged her up to stand with him. He embraced her. Still not enough with the sling and splints acting like a moat between them. He put his lips on hers, and ignored the pain, although the kiss felt as romantic as kissing Buddy, his horse.

"I can't wait for you to get better." She sat and clasped her hands. "Something happened to me a few days before you returned with the posse. I've only shared this with Miss Deborah because she somehow knew."

She paused, hesitant. "If you laugh, I will be tempted to break your other arm."

She inhaled deeply and the words rushed forth. "I was on the ridge at the end of town, watching for some sign of you and the others, praying. Suddenly, I wasn't there anymore. I was in a beautiful valley, one I had never seen before. Then you were there next to me, your arm around me, and we looked out over the bluest river you've ever seen, the thickest grass, trees reaching so high they almost blocked the sun, and the mountains were capped with snow."

She stopped, closed her eyes. "And this voice said, 'What God has put together, let no man put asunder.' And then it said, 'This is the man I have chosen to be your husband'."

A tear rolled down her cheek. He wiped it away with his fingertips, savored the wetness. He held her words close, etching them in his memory. *She does love me. We're supposed to get married.* Even if he could speak, he wouldn't know what to say. Even if he could kiss her without pain, it wouldn't be enough.

She loves me.

He took her hand, and smiled. For the first time, she seemed shy, head down, eyes looking at him under lowered brows.

"Thank you." Throat didn't hurt as much. "Guess I need to propose."

She laughed. "I guess you do if you want to make it official."

He pointed at the hoarhound syrup. She helped him slurp another dose. He waited, let it flow down his throat. He swallowed. That didn't hurt.

His left knee screamed as he tried to kneel before her. He stretched out the leg and put his weight on his right knee. Sweat popped out on his forehead. He didn't care. He wanted to do this right.

"Miss Rachel Stone." Would his voice ever be normal again? "Would you do me the honor of being my wife?"

Silence. Hands cradling his face, her eyes glowed warm and soft. A small smile creased her lips and crinkled her nose. He wanted to kiss that nose, those cheeks, those eyes, and those lips for a long, long time.

"Yes."

He closed his eyes and let her soft voice wash over him.

She kissed his cheek, and brushed his lips lightly. "Now, get back in that chair before you collapse."

Not even married yet, and she's ordering me around. She can order me around anytime she wants.

He settled back in the rocker, left knee sending fire to his brain. He leaned back, breathed deeply, filled his lungs for what felt like the first time in a week.

I'm going to get married. To Rachel Stone, a woman I don't deserve. Lord, help me be the best husband possible, to be the husband you want her to have.

No way his throat would let him say all that needed to be said. He realized he'd clenched his right fist with only minor discomfort. Soon he'd be back to normal. Impatience grabbed him. Not soon enough.

Rachel took his hand. Words weren't easy. He pressed her hand, letting his touch and his eyes express the love filling his heart, the joy her answer brought.

Becky Jo stepped onto the porch carrying a tray. "I made some sand—" Her eyes met Michael's then looked at his and Rachel's entwined hands. She snapped her wide-eyed gaze back to Michael, hurt and pain behind the tears. She put the tray on a small table next to Michael's chair. Hand to her mouth, she darted back into the parsonage.

"Oh, dear." Rachel's voice held a heavy weight Michael didn't understand.

He squeezed her hand. "What?"

Rachel shook her head. "Men can be so dense."

"What did I do?" He coughed again. The pain of talking made him want to remain mute.

Rachel patted his arm. "Nothing, my love. You had no way of knowing she's in love with you."

"What?" Raising his voice in surprise hurt like shards of glass being raked across his throat.

Now he couldn't speak. *Becky Jo's in love with me? She's only a kid.*

"Let me go talk to her." Rachel kissed the top of his head and entered the parsonage.

Michael rubbed his forehead, stunned. *Becky Jo's in love with me? How was I supposed to know? Lord, why did you make women so complicated?*

CHAPTER 43

Friday, July 12, 1878

CALEB STUDIED GORDON Lucius Smythe as the horse trader paced in front of Gideon's desk. Gideon leaned back in his chair, eying the man like he would a buzzing fly, waiting for it to land so he could swat it and sweep it out of his life.

"Mr. Smythe, please sit down." Gideon pointed to one of his chairs. "You're making me nervous."

Smythe sat on the edge of the hard-back chair. "It's just that it's not like her to go away and not tell me." He stood and paced. Gideon rolled his eyes. Jeremiah covered his mouth with his hand but couldn't hide the smile crinkling his eyes. Smythe didn't seem to notice.

Sitting across from Gideon, Caleb took out his pocketknife and cleaned his nails, softly whistling the "Battle Hymn of the Republic." Gideon glared at him. Caleb shrugged and grinned.

"Smythe." Caleb barked. The man stopped, mouth hanging open. Caleb pointed to the chair. "Sit down. Now. Your pacing so fast you're gonna step out of your britches the next time you turn around."

Caleb leaned against the front of Gideon's desk. "Now what makes you think Mrs. Winslow is in trouble?"

Smythe started to rise. Caleb put his finger on the man's chest. "Sit."

The trader sank back into his chair, wringing his hands. "Well, in all the time I've known her, she's never gone away overnight without telling me."

Gideon sighed. "She's a single woman of independent means. Why should she have to tell you anything about her activities?"

Smythe blushed. "We sort of have an arrangement."

"What kind of arrangement?" Gideon emphasized the last word.

"I'm planning on asking her to marry me."

"That would explain the late suppers almost every night," Gideon said.

Smythe flared at the sheriff. "What business is that of yours?"

"I'm the sheriff. Everything's my business until I decide it isn't."

"I don't see where that gives you any right to pry into people's private lives," Smythe whined.

Gideon shrugged. "Ain't nothin' in the town ordinances says I need your approval."

Smythe folded his arms. "Maybe we'll see what Judge Barrett has to say about that."

"Go ahead," Gideon said. "In the meantime, is there anything else about Mrs. Winslow's being away that means she's in trouble?"

"It's just that she's never done this before—left so quick and without a word. Bessie didn't know where she went. And, now, Bessie's gone, too."

Caleb thought there was a big difference between Bessie not knowing and Bessie not saying, a difference Smythe didn't seem to grasp. Probably because he thought with his heart and not his head.

Gideon stood. "Mr. Smythe, I thank you for bringing your concerns to my attention. We'll poke around and see what we can find."

Smythe glanced at Caleb, who nodded. The trader stood and shook Gideon's hand like it was a pump handle and he hadn't had water in three days. "Thank you, Sheriff Parsons. Thank you very much."

After the door closed, Jeremiah shifted from his place near the windows. "Think he knows about Christopher Barrett being a rival for the widow's affections."

Gideon snorted. "We don't even know that for sure."

Jeremiah rubbed the side of his nose. "Yes, we do. Christopher Barrett is courting the widow, probably since before Mr. Smythe arrived."

Gideon gaped. "You mean she's courtin' both of them?"

Jeremiah smiled. "I don't know that she's seriously courting either one. I think she likes having alternatives."

"And people wonder why I never got married." Gideon stood, took his hat from a peg by the door. He picked up the crutch. "Need to return this to Doc. But first, let's go visit the Widow Winslow's."

"How do we get in if Bessie's gone?" Jeremiah settled his hat on his head.

Gideon smiled. "We'll get the key from Christopher Barrett."

→─■○ ○■─←

Barrett leapt from his chair when Gideon walked into his office, Caleb and Jeremiah close behind. "What is the meaning of this? You can't just walk in here. I'm conducting confidential business."

Caleb surveyed the room. Judge Barrett sat in front of the desk. A glass of amber liquid stood in front of each of them, a pen and inkstand angled toward the banker's chair, an ornate oil lamp to one side. Otherwise, the desk was bare. Cigar smoke wreathed the two men like clouds covering a mountain.

Gideon's eyes flashed to the grandfather clock ticking in the corner. "Whiskey at eleven o'clock. Yeah, if I was a banker, that's something I'd want to keep confidential. Mornin', Judge Barrett. How are you this fine day?"

"Sheriff Parsons." The judge's lips were a thin line, his eyes narrowed, shoulders hunched.

"Well, what do you want, Parsons?" The banker's voice pitched high and brittle.

"The key to the Winslow place." Gideon sat in the chair next to the judge, picked up his whiskey glass, and sniffed it. "You have excellent taste, Barrett."

"What makes you think I have a key to Em—Mrs. Winslow's place?"

"You're her personal banker. It's your responsibility to protect her assets when she's out of town." Gideon let the words *personal* and *assets* hang in the air. "How can you protect her interests without havin' access to her property, 'specially now that her maid ain't around."

The banker folded his arms. "Why do you want it?"

"It's been brought to my attention that Mrs. Winslow's absence ain't part of her normal behavior. As sheriff, I need to check it out."

"Who told you?" Judge Barrett spoke.

"Ah, well now, you see that's what we in the sheriffin' business call confidential."

Barrett looked at his brother. The judge rolled his cigar between his fingers. "Give him the key, Christopher. Let him satisfy his curiosity."

Opening a drawer in his desk, the banker took out a key and dangled it from his fingers. "Maybe I should go with you. Make sure everything is all right."

Gideon snatched the key. "Ain't necessary. It's best if trained law officers handle it alone. We'll let you know if we find anythin' suspicious." He slipped the key into his vest pocket. "I regret that our pressin' business prevents us from joinin' you in enjoyin' what I'm sure is an excellent whiskey. But we sure do appreciate the offer. Perhaps another time."

In deference to Gideon's still gimpy leg, Jeremiah had secured a buggy. As they trotted to the Winslow mansion, Caleb observed, "You enjoyed that too much, my friend."

Gideon laughed. "Christopher is so in love with himself, I can't resist pokin' holes in him, deflate him a little bit. 'Sides drinking in the mornin' irritates the blazes out of me. That was not their first glass we walked in on."

"Would have been nice to know what they were talking about," Jeremiah guided the horse onto Mrs. Winslow's street.

"Yeah," Gideon replied. "Though it was probably just plantation business."

The Winslow house greeted them with a cold façade despite the sun bouncing off the white columns and woodwork. Wealth with a cold, calculating heart. Caleb doubted love or warmth found a place behind the richly curtained windows. Except maybe for Bessie, whose devotion to her mistress beamed with every attentive word and action on the widow's behalf.

The three stood in the two-story foyer, the wide staircase circling up to the second floor.

"Where do we begin?" The size of the place overwhelmed Caleb. For one person to have so much was beyond his comprehension. Mrs. Winslow's practiced sensuousness revealed she had little compunction about using any means to get what she wanted. Did it include murdering her husband?

"Let's start in the library. That's where she would keep business records. Maybe it'll have something about where she's gone."

A roll-top desk snuggled in an alcove, its pristine top glistening from repeated polishing. Caleb ran his finger where the desktop met the side of the hutch portion. "Bessie hasn't been gone long."

Gideon opened drawers. Caleb stepped back while Jeremiah examined the slots, cubbyholes and small drawers above the desktop. Letters from family and friends were in one drawer. In another, they found a stack of letters tied together with a ribbon, notes and plaintive pleas of love from Smythe. Bankbooks. Gideon whistled and showed them to Caleb. The lady was wealthier than Caleb imagined.

"She's sure not hurting for money," Jeremiah glanced at the totals. "That much money can make grief easy to handle."

"It's a pot of honey big enough to wake a hibernating bear." Gideon returned the books.

Something pressed into Caleb's back. Two barrels worth of shotgun.

"Awright, y'all jes stop what yer doin' and put yer hands up."

Gideon, hands raised, turned. "Samson, what do you think you're doing? Put that gun up before you hurt yourself."

The gun left the middle of Caleb's back. He made a gentle turn to keep the man behind him calm. He faced a short, skinny black man with snow-white hair, dressed in overalls and a checked shirt. Caleb put his hands on the barrel of the shotgun. "May I?" Samson released the gun. Caleb opened the breech, removed the shells and placed them in his vest pocket. He snapped the gun closed and handed it to Gideon.

Gideon gestured to a chair. "Sit down, Samson. Tell me what's going on here."

Samson looked as if the chair would swallow him in one gulp if he sat in it. He remained standing. "I don't know, Sheriff Parsons. Miss Winslow's went away. Now my Bessie's gone, too. I don't know where. I come by today to see if Bessie was back, and saw you three going in the front door. My eyesight's failin' so I didn't recognize you. Went and got my shotgun."

Gideon leaned against the desk. "When did Bessie leave?"

Samson rubbed his head and brought his hand down over his face. "Las night, right after supper. Said she had to go help Mrs. Winslow."

"Did she say where she was going?"

"No, Mr. Gideon. She just said she had to go and didn't know when she'd be back."

"How'd she leave?"

Samson frowned, his eyes wide. "She walked, like always, back here to Mrs. Winslow's. I'da gone with her but she said she didn't need no company, somebody was picking her up here." He rung his hands and his knees jiggled. "Bessie's all right, isn't she?"

Gideon placed his hand on Samson's shoulder. "As far as we know, both she and Mrs. Winslow are fine. We're going to look around the house some, see if we can find out where they went. You want to help us?"

Samson's voice quavered. "No, sir. This is only the second time I been in the house. I helped at the Christmas party Mrs. Winslow did, but I ain't never been anywheres but the kitchen until today."

"Why don't you wait outside until we're done?" He handed him the shotgun, and Caleb placed the shells in his palm.

"Yes, sir, Mr. Gideon." His smile covered half his face. "I'll wait by the front door."

An hour later, the three gathered in the foyer.

Gideon rubbed the back of his neck. "This was a waste of time. We didn't learn anything."

"Oh, I don't know about that, Gideon," Caleb said. "We learned she keeps a real neat desk."

"And," Jeremiah said. "More dresses than I've ever seen in one place."

Caleb snapped his fingers. "Where are the ledgers?"

"I noticed that, too," Gideon said. "Nowhere to be found. Odd."

"She either took them with her," Caleb rubbed his jaw. "But why? Or she gave them back to Smythe."

"Or Christopher Barrett has them," Jeremiah suggested.

"Nah," Gideon shook his head. "She guarded those books like some women guard their virginity. She's got them with her. But we can check with Smythe and Barrett to make sure."

CHAPTER 44

Friday, July 12, 1878

RACHEL TUCKED A blanket around Michael's legs as he dozed in the rocker. She stroked his cheek and kissed the top of his head. Heart in her throat, knees weak, she took a deep breath and walked into the house. The parlor was empty, quiet. From upstairs, came the sounds of Deborah and Zechariah singing "Amazing Grace." In the kitchen, the Major wound a wooden spoon round and round in a bowl filled with batter. At the sink, Becky Jo cleaned pots and pans, shoulders hunched, head down.

The Major gestured at Becky Jo. Rachel nodded. Mrs. Larkin bobbed her head. "Becky Jo, this needs to set awhile. I'm going to see if Pastor Taylor or Miss Deborah need anything."

Becky Jo nodded without turning.

Rachel stepped further into the room. "Becky Jo?" She kept her voice soft.

The girl jumped, soapsuds flying as her hands leapt out of the water. "You spooked me." Her tone accused Rachel of much more than that.

"Can we talk?"

Becky Jo exhaled loudly and shrugged her shoulders. "About what?"

"You and Michael and me."

Back still turned, the girl said, "Don't seem like there's much to say."

Rachel bit her lip while her mind sought for something, anything, to say—some words to bridge the distance, to help the girl understand.

"I know you love Michael."

"Didn't stop you from stealin' him first chance you had." The words jabbed like a sewing needle under her fingernail.

Rachel squeezed her fingers, tight. *Lord, help me here. Don't let me lose my temper and make matters worse.* She eyed the knife Becky Jo picked up and lowered into the water. *Maybe this wasn't such a good idea.*

"I didn't know you loved him when I fell in love with him."

Becky Jo scrubbed vigorously.

"Until this morning," Rachel continued. "I don't think Michael knew you're in love with him either."

A single laugh dripped with sarcasm. "It's not because I wasn't trying to show him."

Rachel wanted to move closer, to put her hand on the girl. She hesitated, stayed by the table, the edge pressing against her thigh. *Not yet. She's not ready to receive it. How do I know that?* "And he didn't realize it, did he?"

Wiping her nose on her sleeve, Becky Jo sniffed, and shook her head. "He was always helping Pastor Taylor or Sheriff Gideon or working at the mercantile. Never had time for me. Even when he came for supper, he'd rather wrestle with my brothers or play checkers with Pa. Even when I walked him to the door, he'd pet the dog rather than hold my arm." She laughed her single laugh again. "I even tried to understand baseball so I could talk to him about something I knew he liked."

"Sounds like you tried real hard." Rachel's heart ached for the girl and, in a way, envied her. Rachel had never experienced the feelings Becky Jo described. There'd never been a man she loved, she pursued. Until Michael.

Becky Jo looked over her shoulder. A tear glistened in the light from the window. "I tried as hard as I knew. But nothing worked. He treated me like I was a little girl, like I was his sister."

Ellie. "He may have seen you as the sister he left back in New England."

Becky Jo shrugged. "He treated all the women in the church like they was his sister. Sometimes, I don't think he has a romantic bone in his body."

Rachel smiled. *Oh, yes, he does.* Rachel pulled out a chair and sat. "I need to share something with you."

Becky Jo dried her hands on a towel. "What?"

Rachel pointed to another chair. "It'd be easier if you sit with me."

The girl shrugged, flopped into the seat, feet tucked around the legs of the chair.

Rachel told her about the vision, losing herself in reliving it.

Brows knit into a deep scowl, Becky Jo narrowed her eyes. "I don't believe you. I think you're just making it up to make me think God wants it this way. I prayed to God, too. Why'd He answer you like that and not me? It's just a lie."

The words beat against Rachel like hail on a tin roof. She squeezed her fingers, tighter than before, anger creeping through her shoulders and up her neck.

"I don't lie." She snapped the words. "I'm only trying to help you understand."

Becky Jo jumped to her feet, stepped toward Rachel. Rachel stood, keeping her chair between them.

"No, you aren't." Face red, Becky Jo's voice teetered on the edge of screaming. "You're trying to take Michael from me."

Rachel's anger seethed, like water roiling to a boil. "Becky Jo, you never had him." Rachel wanted to snatch the words and the cold, almost heartless, tone back.

Becky Jo's mouthed dropped open. She covered her face with her hands and ran out the back door, sobs trailing.

Rachel sank into the chair, hands limp in her lap. She let silent tears flow. *Oh, Lord. What have I done? Please forgive me.*

→──◑ ◐──←

Michael lazed like a cat in the afternoon sun. The aches and pains had lessened, and the puffiness in his face had shrunk over the past few days. Being out in the sun, with warm air wafting, his constricted muscles relaxed, and knots of tension eased. The power of prayer joined with Rachel's tender nursing brought healing. Even Doc MacKenzie marveled at Michael's progress.

And I'm loved by a beautiful woman.

The bristle his fingers found on his face sparked the urge for a bath and a shave.

The only cloud was Rachel's somber presence in the other chair. She sat now, hand on his, faced turned toward the street, eyes, he knew, not seeing as her mind recalled her encounter with Becky Jo.

Her profile was still as a sculpture carved from the finest marble. Delicate features of nose and chin and lips that blended into a strong woman, a woman who'd be by his side forever.

"Rachel." His voice was stronger now; his throat didn't burn with each word. "It's not your fault."

She grimaced, touched his cheek. "Yes, it is. I lost my temper. I wanted her to understand, but I did it in the worst way possible." She sighed. "I wish she'd come back so I can apologize, somehow make it up to her."

"Time will help her get over it."

"Only God can heal her hurt, but I don't know if she'll let him in after I told her about the vision."

Mrs. Larkin stepped out of the house. Rachel lowered her eyes.

"Has she come back?" Michael said.

Mrs. Larkin shook her head. "She'll be back soon, needs time to be alone. I figure she's down by the river, throwing rocks at a tree stump."

"I'm so sorry. I didn't mean to upset her." Rachel kept her eyes lowered.

Mrs. Larkin sighed. "Like I said, Miss Rachel, tain't yer fault. Me and Miss Deborah have both talked with her, even before Michael left. She wouldn't hear it then, so I'm not surprised she wouldn't hear it from you. 'Specially as she's convinced you're the one what stole him."

Michael's mind reeled. *Was I really so dense I didn't see what was happening?* "You know, if I'd been paying more attention before I left, I might've been able to say something to her, let her know I didn't feel that way."

Rachel and Mrs. Larkin exchanged glances, confirming Michael's suspicion that women communicated in a language men could never comprehend. *Marriage should prove very interesting.*

Caleb and Jeremiah climbed the steps to the porch. "How's the patient today?"

"Doing better," Michael said. "Got nice sunshine and a beautiful nurse."

Rachel lifted her head and smiled at him, a small smile that broke through the heaviness he knew weighed her heart.

"That's good to hear," Jeremiah said.

"Let me fetch you gents some coffee." Mrs. Larkin turned to enter the house.

"I'll help." Rachel kissed Michael on the cheek and followed the Major inside.

Jeremiah frowned. "Is Rachel all right?"

Michael couldn't hide his surprise. "What makes you say that?"

Jeremiah tapped the side of his nose. "A trained investigator like myself notices the subtle changes in a person's demeanor. She doesn't seem as happy as she usually does around you. Did you two have words?"

Michael laughed. "No, we didn't. She's just got something on her mind. Are you getting anywhere with finding Winslow's killer?"

Caleb leaned against the porch post and shrugged. "More questions. Fewer answers."

Guilt pinched Michael's spirit. "I'm sorry you both got caught up in this. It's my assignment."

Jeremiah hitched one leg onto the porch railing. "Remember, we asked to come along. It was our choice." He nodded at Michael's shoulder and sling. "You getting beat up just made it a little more personal."

Zechariah followed Mrs. Larkin and Rachel onto the porch. "Thought I smelled the Major's coffee."

Mrs. Larkin returned to the house while Rachel resumed her seat. Michael caught her eye and received a brighter smile and a nod.

A teen-aged boy ran up the front steps, a thin envelope scrunched in his hand. "Here you go, Reverend Taylor. This telegraph came in just a few minutes ago. They told me to bring it right over."

"Thank you, son," Zechariah said and handed him a coin.

As the boy dashed off, Zechariah gently lifted the flap and slid out the message. His eyes teared. "It's from Amelia," he said. "She's coming to help take care of Deborah. She'll be here on the sixteenth."

He folded the document and tucked it in the pocket of his vest. "I'll tell Deborah when she wakes up. She'll be happy to see her. Last saw her at Christmas. Just wish the visit was under better circumstances."

They drank in silence for a few moments.

"How's your investigation going?" Zechariah asked. "Any new suspects?"

Caleb balanced his cup on the porch rail. "Yeah, and with good reason, too. Jeremiah likes Mrs. Winslow because her dresses are too tight."

"He's got a point there," Zechariah said over the rim of his cup.

Jeremiah jerked his thumb at Caleb. "And he likes the banker because he's so pompous."

Caleb nodded. "And Gideon likes the judge because the man just plain irritates him."

Michael nodded. "Good reasons all, but not much evidence for court."

Caleb folded his arms. "And we've got this left-handed gun, Jordan Dennison, running around for no reason we can figure. And the mysterious Micah Grimmler, who no one has seen since the day of the murder."

"So we're nowhere?" Michael said.

"That about sums it up," Caleb said.

Rachel's soft voice was edged with determination. "Except someone shot Miss Deborah and left Michael for dead." She looked at Michael. "Why are you such a threat to whoever killed Winslow?"

CHAPTER 45

Monday, July 15, 1878

IN THE HOTEL restaurant, Caleb, chin in hand, watched as Gideon attacked his second platter of flapjacks and ham. "Where do you put all that food? You're going through flapjacks like Sherman through Georgia."

Gideon waggled his fork. Caleb flinched, expecting the piece of ham balanced on the tines to fly off and smack him in the eye. "I told you a long time ago, eat when you can, as much as you can, cuz, in this line of work, you never know when you'll git to eat agin. Ain't that right, Jeremiah?"

Jeremiah placed his knife and fork on the table, aligning them alongside his half-eaten plate of steak and eggs. He sipped his coffee and dabbed his mouth with his napkin. "There may be a small kernel of truth in that, but you seem to have raised it to a religious doctrine."

As Gideon opened his mouth to respond, Adam Jones slammed open the door and dashed to their table. "Sheriff, you've got to come quick."

"What is it, Adam?"

"It's Smythe, the horse trader. He's been shot."

Gideon's knife and fork clattered to the plate. "Adam, go fetch Doc MacKenzie." He scooped his hat off the back of his chair. "What'd I tell you about not knowin' when yer gonna eat again?"

They stopped at the door. "Jeremiah, you go to the parsonage in case they try something with Michael."

While Caleb walked with Gideon to the stable, Jeremiah ran up the street. Even though he'd abandoned the crutch, Gideon's limp seemed more pronounced as he hurried.

Gordon Lucius Smythe lay face down on the floor of his office, desk chair on its side, papers scattered on the floor. One round hole centered in his back, blood pooled under him. His eyes stared under his desk.

Caleb bent down. "Looks like the barrel was right against his back. The shirt's burned around the hole."

"I hate back shooters. Never give a man a chance to defend himself."

Caleb scanned the office. The back door stood open. Several footprints showed in the soft dirt. "Jordan Dennison was here."

Gideon snorted. "Figures. But I never heard him to be a back shooter." He looked down at the body. "I did hear he'd shoot unarmed men but never in the back."

Caleb examined some of the papers he picked up from the floor. "Receipts from yesterday it looks like."

"Any from our banker friend?"

Caleb riffled through the sheets. "Nope. Nothing else seems unusual."

The front door banged into the wall as Doc MacKenzie rushed in. He stopped just inside. "Too late?"

Gideon nodded.

"Got here as fast as I could." MacKenzie bent over the body. "Forty-five caliber looks like. He went quick, dead before he heard the shot."

Caleb and Gideon walked next door to the livery, where Adam Jones stoked the forge, building the heat. Gideon pushed his hat back. "Tell me what happened, Adam?"

"I came in like always, fired up the forge, lined up my first jobs. Everything seemed normal."

"Did you see or talk to Smythe?"

"No, Sheriff. But that ain't unusual. 'Bout the only time he talked to me was when he wanted a horse shod. He wasn't the friendly type, at least with me."

"How'd you know he was shot? Did you hear anything?"

"Walter Fleming came in and asked if I knew where Smythe was. Said the door was locked and he wasn't around. I knew that wasn't right. Smythe was always here at dawn. I found the back door open, saw him layin' there and ran for you."

On the way to Gideon's office, Caleb asked, "You trust the blacksmith?"

"Yeah. He's a good man. Town could use more people like him."

Gideon turned abruptly into the bank. "Let's see if Barrett's around. Make sure he's all right."

Barrett's clerk stood as Gideon stepped through the gate in the railing. "Can I help you, Sheriff Parsons?"

"No. I know where I'm going." Gideon shouldered the man aside.

Caleb brushed the man's sleeve and shrugged. "Forgive him. His breakfast was interrupted this morning."

The office was deserted. Two empty glasses and the liquor decanter stood on the desk. The aroma of stale cigar smoke stung Caleb's eyes.

Gideon turned on the clerk. "Where is he?"

The clerk gulped and backed up a step, eyes darting between Caleb and Gideon. "I don't know, Sheriff. He hasn't come in yet today."

"Isn't that unusual for him?" Gideon said. "Did he send any message?"

"It is highly strange. He's here before any of us every day. And he didn't send a message, either."

"Did you send anyone to the plantation to ask about him?"

The clerk batted his eyes as if Gideon asked him if he could fly. "No, Sheriff. Mr. Barrett left explicit instructions we are never to bother him when he's at the plantation."

"What about his rooms upstairs?" Caleb asked.

"Empty, sir. They look like he hasn't used them since Friday."

Gideon planted his hands on his hips. Frustration tightened his shoulders and deepened his scowl. His eyes all but disappeared under bushy eyebrows protruding like a ledge from a cliff.

Back in his office, Gideon dispatched a deputy to tell Adam Jones to prepare two horses. "We need to ride out to the plantation," he said to Caleb.

"What about Jeremiah?"

"I want him to stay with Michael. A deputy might get called away. Jeremiah will stay no matter what."

Michael sat on the sofa, head resting against the back. The scrape of the razor across his face cleansed more than he'd thought possible. Rachel's steady hand stroked with easy smoothness. No trace of the nervousness evident when he first asked her.

"Think of it as sewing fancy trim on a dress," he'd said. "I've seen how fussy and careful you are when you do that."

"The dress don't bleed when I do it wrong." She wiped her hands on her dress. "What if I cut too deep? Your blood will be all over Deborah's nice furniture."

He cocked his head. "You're worried about the sofa?"

"If I cut your neck, you'll probably be dead before I can do anything. I've seen a girl cut her customer with a razor. The blood doesn't just seep a little."

Before he could respond, two sharp knocks rattled the front door. The Major hustled in from the kitchen. "You two just sit," she said. "I'll see who it is."

Jeremiah seemed to explode into the room. "You're all right?" he said. "All of you?"

"What's going on?" Michael asked. "What's got you so riled?"

Jeremiah tossed his hat on a table near the sofa and adjusted the gun belt on his hip. "Smythe's been murdered."

The Major's hand covered her mouth. "The horse trader?"

Jeremiah nodded. "Shot either last night or early this morning. The smith found him."

Michael closed his eyes. *So much death. Would he ever know a time without it? How could he protect Rachel?* "Where are Gideon and Caleb?"

"They're investigating. Gideon sent me here to make sure all of you are all right."

Pushing with his good arm, Michael swung his legs off the sofa, biting the curse from his tongue as the left knee protested like a cat caught in a trap. Rachel's hand on his shoulder stopped him. "Where do you think you're going, mister?"

"I've got to help. I started this. I'm not just gonna sit here while people get killed because of me."

Rachel pushed harder and Michael sank back into the sofa, gasping in pain.

"Too soon, my young friend," Jeremiah said. "You'd be more of hindrance, hobbling around like a three-legged cow. Get your strength back."

"I almost lost you once, Michael Archer." Rachel eyes burned into him with the determination of an unbroken horse. "I am not going to risk that again. You stay right here until the doc says otherwise."

Michael started to speak then closed his mouth. He knew words would not change her mind. He'd have to work harder at getting better, at getting back to clearing Ben's name. *Lord, help me. I need one of your miracles. Heal me like Jesus healed in the Bible.*

He waited. Nothing. *At least he didn't say no.*

"It looks like we'll be both be here a while, Michael," Jeremiah said. "How about I introduce you to the finer points of chess."

Michael groaned. "Rather have a tooth pulled."

On any other day, the ride to the Barrett plantation would have been an enjoyable canter down roads where trees formed cool, green tunnels and sunlight dappled the ground. Caleb inhaled the sweet aromas of wild flowers along the side of the road. Almost enough to forget the stench of death that made the journey necessary.

Caleb's mind jerked when he saw the plantation house. He was back in the war, fighting in and around houses like this. Three stories, gleaming white, portico entrances, columns soaring to the roof. White gravel paved the drive from the road to the house.

But Caleb saw the manicured grounds littered with blue- and gray-clad bodies as smoke rose, cannons roared, deafening rebel yells and deafening screams filled the air. Eyes closed, he shook his head to banish the images. When he looked again, sunlight filled the air, flowers bloomed, and birds flitted and sang.

Mrs. Christopher Barrett met with them in the library. Two walls were lined with books from floor to ceiling. A fieldstone fireplace filled another wall. Above it, a large portrait of a stern, older man glared down on the room with patrician disdain. The fourth wall was French doors that opened onto a patio.

With her long brunette hair and green eyes, Mrs. Barrett may have been pretty once. Now, pale gauntness marred her face, as if illness or worry weighed, her eyes pinched, mouth thin. She clasped her hands at her waist. Her reedy voice washed away any of the charm her Southern accent once held.

"Why, Sheriff, my husband left here yesterday afternoon, right after dinner, to go to his rooms over the bank to prepare for this week's work." Her emphasis on the word *rooms* struck Caleb as perhaps having another meaning. Did she suspect her husband was philandering with Mrs. Winslow?

"I'm truly concerned," she continued. She brought her knuckles to her mouth. "Is it possible something may have happened to him? Could he be hurt somewhere?"

Gideon rotated his hat in his hands. "My friend and I didn't see any sign of an accident on our way out here, but we'll look again as we ride back to town. In the meantime, please let us know if you hear anything from your husband. It's vital that I talk to him."

⋗▬ ▬⋖

Michael stepped forward and shifted his weight to his left leg. The joint protested, sending a stab of pain up his thigh and into his spine. He waited, Rachel on his right, Jeremiah on his left, hands extended to catch him. The knee didn't buckle. It protested, but it supported him. "Stronger than this morning," he said.

He limped two laps around the parlor, each step more tolerable. He grinned. "Tomorrow, we'll walk around the block."

Rachel's eyes flashed warmth and amusement. "Better bring some camping gear. At your speed, it'll take a couple of days."

"As long as you're with me, I can handle it."

She stroked his back. "No overnights without a chaperone until we're married."

The Major appeared in the doorway from the kitchen, holding a tray with a platter of food. "I've got your supper here."

Michael waved toward the dining room. "I think I'd like to join all of you and see what it's like to eat at a table. Been eating on that couch too long."

The walk was long, slow, painful. Sweat ran down the side of his face as he managed short strides and shuffles to the dining room. Rachel's hand rested on his back, support and comfort radiating. Jeremiah hovered, ready to grab at the slightest falter. Michael sat, exhaled loudly, and gulped the glass of water next to his plate.

Zechariah said, "Hold everything. I'll be right back."

A few minutes later, he entered the dining room, carrying Deborah. He set her in the chair next to his, adjusted her shawl and kissed her hand as he took his seat.

Rachel rested her hand on Michael's arm. "How nice," she whispered.

He nodded, a lump in his throat. *Lord, help me love Rachel like that.*

Becky Jo placed bowls of potatoes and vegetables on the table and sat next to her mother. She darted a glance at Michael. He smiled. She lowered her eyes to her plate and spoke to no one, eating as if by rote.

Taking his wife's hand, Zechariah prayed a blessing over the food and protection over those gathered around the table.

"Becky Jo, this is delicious," Rachel said. "You'll have to give me the recipe for this peach cobbler."

Becky Jo shrugged. "Ain't nothing to it. Can of peaches and cobbler. You could probably steal it from Miss Deborah just as easy."

"Becky Jo." The Major's voice snapped. "There's no need for—"

The front door burst open at the same time the kitchen door slammed into the wall. Three men entered the dining room, pistols drawn, bandanas covering their lower faces, hats pulled low on their foreheads.

Jeremiah rose, reaching for his pistol. One of the gunmen swung his handgun. Left-handed, right sleeve pinned to the shoulder of his shirt. *Dennison.*

The *thunk* of metal striking human bone cracked Michael's ears. Jeremiah collapsed to the floor, unconscious.

Zechariah stood. "What is the meaning of this?" Another of the invaders swung his pistol against the side of the pastor's head. "Be quiet, old man."

Zechariah fell to his hands and knees, head hanging. Deborah moaned and fainted against Michael. He lowered her to the floor, bearing her fragile weight on his left arm.

When he straightened, his left knee buckled and he grabbed the table while stars exploded in his brain.

Rachel reached to help Zechariah. One of the gunmen twisted her arm and pushed her against the Major and Becky Jo. The third pointed his pistol at Michael, hammer cocked.

"What do you want, Dennison?" Michael spat the words.

The left-handed gunman grunted. "So you know who I am. Don't matter none. You don't take warnings very well, do you?"

Michael fixed on the man's eyes, said nothing.

Dennison pointed at Becky Jo. "Her."

The closest gunman put his arm around Becky Jo's neck and held his pistol against her head.

Dennison shoved the barrel of his gun under Michael's chin, pushing his head up. He cocked the hammer.

Rachel gasped. "No!" She stepped toward Michael.

The third gunman pointed his pistol in her face. "Don't move."

Dennison leaned closer, breath reeking of stale beer and onions, his voice a low rumble through the bandana. "You and your friends be on tomorrow's train outta here. If you're not, the girl dies." He paused. "After we've had some fun with her."

He forced Michael's head further back. "Shoulda stomped yer neck stead of your knee."

Dennison's eyes burned into Michael.

Becky Jo opened her mouth.

"Gag her," Dennison barked. "Don't need another female yakking her fool head off."

He turned back to Michael. "Tomorrow. We'll be watching."

"How do we know you'll let her go?"

"Trust me. I don't need a female slowing me down, and I want to be quit of this town as soon as I can. We'll let her go when our business is finished." He nodded toward the back door. "Let's go."

The men headed for the door, one holding Becky Jo around the waist and lifting her off the floor. Her arms and legs flailed in the air as he sidled out the door.

"Beck—" The Major stopped as Dennison aimed his pistol at her and cocked the hammer.

"Quiet, woman, or it'll be the last thing you say."

The Major clamped her mouth shut. Tears ran down her face as she surrendered to Rachel's embrace.

The outlaw followed his men out the door.

Michael forced his knee to bend, squeezing his eyes and biting his lip to cover the pain as he examined Deborah. She stirred and batted her eyes. "Zechariah?" She whispered.

Michael shimmied on his hands and knees to his mentor, fear gorging in his throat. A lump the size of a small egg bulged where the pistol butt had struck in front of his right ear.

Pain fought with white-hot anger as Michael knelt there. He pounded his fist against his thigh. He'd failed again. Failed to protect his friends, his family. His father flashed, drunk, fists smashing at Michael and his mother, hands grappling at Ellie. Then the pitchfork and the satisfaction of feeling it stab to thighbone. He'd been too late to save his mother. Tonight, he'd been too slow to save his friends.

"Michael." Rachel's voice sharp and clear. From a child's view, he looked across the table top at her. "This is not your fault."

Can she read my mind, too?

She helped the Major into a chair and came around to him. Using her arm and the table as supports, he stood, gasping as the knee protested every movement, every pressure.

"I'm going to find Gideon."

He grabbed her wrist. "My job."

She freed her hand. "You'll be too slow. You stay here. Take care of these people."

"Take my gun."

She picked up her bag. "Got my Derringer now. I'll get word to Doc, too."

She kissed him. He clung to her, left arm as tight as he could make it, useless right arm in its sling, keeping them apart. Her arms around his neck comforted. He wanted to stay this way forever.

She pulled away. "I'll hurry."

The door closed, and Michael sank into a chair. The Major cried softly into her arms folded on the table. Jeremiah moaned, stirring, hand reaching for the back of his head.

Deborah knelt next to her husband, stroking his hair, whispering his name over and over. Helplessness closed over Michael like a fist—a weak, useless fist. He stared at the remains of supper and tried to pray. Nothing.

Chapter 46

Tuesday, July 16, 1878

Michael stepped onto the platform, Rachel's arm looped around his, as the train huffed like an old buffalo. Zechariah, head swathed in a bandage, face pale, body sagging, sat on a bench with Deborah. Caleb and Jeremiah stood to one side, engrossed in a conversation with Gideon. Relief seeped into Michael's shoulders—the Major and Mr. Larkin weren't there. He'd brought enough heartache to their family.

Gideon ambled over, limp hardly noticeable. Rachel gave him a quick hug and kiss on the cheek. Gideon wrapped his arm around her shoulder, and jabbed Michael's chest. "You take good care of this girl, or you'll answer to me."

Michael nodded. "I will." He couldn't muster any comment to banter with Gideon's bittersweet words. "I'm sorry it ended this way."

"Don't fret," Gideon said. "We'll catch the killer. We've made him this nervous, he's going to make a mistake sooner or later."

Michael nodded.

On board the train, he and Rachel sat on one bench, his leg propped on a piece of luggage. Caleb and Jeremiah took the bench across the aisle. Michael brooded. He'd failed. To clear Ben's name, he needed to find the real killer. Stopped at every turn, no closer than when he began. Becky Jo kidnapped, Miss Deborah shot, Zechariah and Jeremiah knocked unconscious.

He'd brought death to his own family, and been unable to save Sam Carstairs, and now he placed more people in danger. People he cared about.

Rachel touched his arm.

He let himself sink into those violet eyes, into her and her love. "I hate running away like this, scared off like a jack rabbit." His teeth ground together as his jaw tightened.

She stroked his arm. "What else could you do? You know what they threatened to do to Becky Jo."

He nodded. "Still should have been able to do something."

She rested her head on his shoulder.

An hour out of Tramlaw, the train slowed for a curve. Jeremiah and Caleb stood and headed for the door, grabbing bench backs for balance.

"Where are you two going?" Michael said.

"Take care of some business." Caleb grabbed his shoulder. "You take care of Rachel. We'll be back soon."

Michael hauled himself to his feet. "You're getting off, ain't you?"

Jeremiah made a show of looking out the window. "Getting off? Here? There's nothing to get off for."

Michael grabbed Caleb's arm. "Where are you going?"

Caleb sighed and looked at Jeremiah, who shrugged. "We're going to go back and help Gideon," Caleb said. "He arranged for horses to be left for us around this curve."

"I'm coming too."

Caleb put his hand on Michael's chest. "No, you're not. You can hardly walk, and your shooting arm's in a sling."

"Besides," Jeremiah said, "Gideon only arranged for two horses."

Michael's neck tightened and his shoulders hunched. The nails of his hands dug into his palms. "This is my—"

Caleb held up his hand. "It's not just your assignment or mission or whatever. When we decided to come along, it became ours as much as yours." A hardness invaded Caleb's eyes. "Besides, there's something rotten in that town, and I'm going to help my friend get rid of it just like he would help me."

He pointed at the seat. "Now, I want you to sit down, enjoy the company of this beautiful woman, and heal up."

Caleb spun on his heel and followed Jeremiah to the door.

Michael stood as if struck by lightning. Rachel tugged his sleeve. He shook her off and hobbled to the door. Caleb and Jeremiah were gone, and the train picked up speed as it came round the other side of the curve.

Rachel touched his arm again. He turned and let her lead him back to their seat. "They could get Becky Jo killed. What if Dennison or whoever he's working for finds out they got off the train?"

The door opened. Michael turned, hoping to see Caleb and Jeremiah stroll through. They didn't. Two men walked in, strangers, wearing Caleb's and Jeremiah's shirts and hats. They took the same seats, nodded at Michael and Rachel.

Rachel suppressed a giggle behind her hand. "Guess those old lawmen still have a few tricks up their sleeves."

"They could've arranged a double for me." Michael cringed inwardly at the childish whine he heard in his voice.

Rachel turned his head with her hand. "Yes, they could have and you'd still have been injured and slowing them down, putting yourself and them in more danger. You do understand I don't want to lose you?"

He nodded. Farms and fields flashed by the window as Michael pondered her words. She was right, but that didn't make it any easier to take. His place was with Gideon and Caleb and Jeremiah. They should be working together.

Useless.

A one-armed, one-legged store clerk. He looked away and beat his fist against his thigh. He didn't do what he came here to do. His promise to Sam broken. Ben unavenged. "You're right, but it still doesn't make it any easier to sit here leaving them to finish my work."

She laced her fingers through his. "I know." She gazed into his eyes, searching. "Michael, you're one of the bravest men I know. You're a man I can feel safe with, protected. And I want to be with you for a long, long time."

She kissed him, long, soft, sweet.

->═◉ ◉═<-

An hour later, the car jolted and jounced as the train slowed for the next station. Michael braced himself as the locomotive wheezed and the brakes screeched. When the train halted, he opened his bag and removed the pistol Caleb had given him. He checked the chambers and slid the weapon into his sling, adjusting it a couple of times until it was in a comfortable position.

"What do you think you're doing?" Rachel's eyes were wide, her mouth grim, her tone like a mother with a mischievous child. "Michael Archer, what are you going to do with that pistol?"

He removed bullets from their loops on the holster belt. Some he put in his shirt pocket, others in his pants. "I'm going back."

"You're what?" Her hands were on his arm, grip tight. She tried to pry the gun belt from his hands. He shook her off. For the first time, he couldn't look into her eyes. He didn't want her to see his fear.

"I have to go back. I have to help. I started this mess. I have to finish it."

"Michael, you can't. You're not well enough." Hysteria edged her voice. She touched his right hand. "You can't even shoot."

"They won't know that."

"They will soon enough. And then what? You'll just be in the way. Someone else for Caleb and Gideon and Jeremiah to worry about instead of focusing on Becky Jo and Dennison and the killer."

How do I make you understand? "Rachel, I have to do this for Ben, for Sam."

She shook her head with such force she knocked her bonnet askew. She bit her lower lip. "You're going back there could be the distraction that gets your friends killed." Her eyes misted. "What if someone's watching the train and reports back that you got off or, even worse, follows? You could get yourself killed."

He wanted to smile. "According to your vision, that won't happen, because we're supposed to get married."

Her eyes narrowed and her nostrils flared. He prepared for the sting of a slap across his cheek. It didn't come. Instead, Rachel clasped the fingers of one hand with the other. Her chin jutted. "Not if you do something foolish."

He put his left hand on her arm, gave a gentle squeeze. "I'm not going to do anything foolish, I promise. I'll stay in the background, doing what little I can."

"Going back there in the shape you're in is foolish. Why can't you see that?"

"Why can't you see that I have to go? I can't have my friends risk their lives and not be there to help."

"I don't think this is about them. I think this is about you proving something to yourself."

"Like what?" *Here she goes, reading my mind again.* Heat rose in Michael's cheeks, his anger not boiling yet, but getting there.

"Like killing your father doesn't define you. You're good, Michael, but you let that man continue to tell you you're not, that you're evil because you killed him." She closed her eyes and lowered her head, hands on his chest. "You still haven't gotten rid of him. You carry him around like an anvil strapped to your back."

Michael placed his hat on his head, tilted it back. "When the train gets to Saint Louis, stay at Mrs. Fremont's boarding house. I'll meet you there as soon as we're finished."

He limped to the end of the car, knee stinging with each step. Rachel's hands clutched his good arm from behind and turned him.

"I love you, Michael. Don't make me a widow before you make me a wife. I'll never forgive you."

Her lips where on his, full of the promise of their life to come.

The walk to the livery from the train depot took at least three times longer than it should have. As Michael drew closer to his destination, the knee seemed to hurt less. He wasn't sure if he imagined it. He regretted leaving the laudanum in his bag but knew there was no way he wanted his senses dulled or sleepy.

The liveryman brought out a chestnut gelding. Michael examined the animal. *Well, you're not Buddy, but I think you'll get the job done.* He started to mount, couldn't lift his left foot to reach the stirrup. The liveryman, without expression, brought a mounting step over. Even with that, Michael's brain exploded with Fourth of July fireworks as he swung his right leg over the horse. He grasped the saddle horn and swayed, blood leaving his head. He waited, eyes closed, until his head stopped spinning and his stomach settled back into its regular place.

At the edge of town, he kicked the horse into a gallop. After a few strides, he reined it back to a trot when he discovered he couldn't grip with his left leg.

This is going to take longer than I thought.

-->==() ()==<--

Rachel had watched Michael hobble away. *Lord, why did you give me such a stubborn man? Protect him from his foolish pride and from the killer. And protect those he's going to help. They'll really need it now.*

She glared at Caleb's and Jeremiah's replacements. *Big help you were.* They gazed out the other side windows as if Lady Godiva rode out there.

She opened her Bible and stared at pages filled with unintelligible black marks. The view out the window blurred like a landscape painter had swiped a cloth across his work while the paint was still wet.

How can he even ride? An image flashed of Michael lying by the side of the road, thrown from a horse he didn't know and was too weak to control. What if he passed out in the saddle, fell off, and splattered his head on a rock?

How can he shoot left-handed? An image sprang up of Michael reaching into his sling, the pistol getting caught, discharging, and wounding himself still further.

She rubbed her forehead.

Thirty minutes later, the train slowed for the next station. Rachel flexed her fingers, restoring circulation after squeezing them numb. She removed a small box from her luggage and slipped it into her bag, feeling the extra weight as it bumped against the Derringer Caleb had bought for her in Tramlaw.

The conductor entered the car, announcing the upcoming stop.

"Sir, I will be getting off at this stop. Where is the nearest livery stable?"

After receiving directions, she handed him a note wrapped around a coin. "When the train gets to Saint Louis, please have our bags delivered to Mrs. Fremont's boarding house."

Caleb's double looked at her as she tightened her bonnet and made sure her bag was secure on her wrist.

"Mind your own business. You did such a good job of it at the last stop." She resisted the urge to bop him with her bag as she walked by. "Enjoy your trip to Saint Louis."

The liveryman's voice dripped honey as he showed her a horse to rent. "This here is the gentlest animal I have." He stroked the mare's nose. "She'll give you the easiest ride you could ever want. Like your grandma's rocker."

Rachel ran her hand along the animal's flank, studied her legs, grateful for the instruction Geoffrey Barkston and Isaac Walters had given her on horses. Those two knew horses the way Pastor Luke knew the Bible.

"And it'll take her two weeks to get me to Tramlaw. I need something with speed and stamina."

The man looked her up and down, lingering too long on her chest. "I don't know that a sweet, young thing like you can handle a horse like that."

She narrowed her eyes and straightened her shoulders. "You'd be surprised what I can handle. Actually, you probably don't want to know. Show me your horses. All of them."

He led her through the livery to a corral at the back. He hackamored five horses and led them to her. "These are what I have for rental plus that one I showed you."

She selected a raven black mare. He mentioned a price. She smiled, torn between enjoying the negotiating and the urgency to get on the road. "I'm looking to rent, not buy." She did a slow study of the area. "Do you seriously want to lose the only rental you may get for the rest of the day?"

He lowered his price.

She glanced at the sky. "It's getting late, but I think I can get to another livery in town before it gets dark." She offered him half.

He rubbed his chin and nodded.

"Have her saddled and ready in half an hour. I have one more errand to do."

Rachel returned on time, dressed in a dark brown split skirt she purchased from the local dress shop, along with decent riding boots and a tan shirt. She replaced her bonnet with a low-crowned Stetson. No way was she going to ride astride in a dress. After this adventure was over, she hoped to revisit the shop and compare notes with the owner.

The liveryman reached to help her mount, a little too close. She locked her eyes on his. "If you want to keep those hands, back off. Otherwise, they'll be calling you Stumpy."

She mounted with practiced grace to show him and the mare she knew what she was doing. She gathered up the reins and, with a click of her tongue and a squeeze of her knees, turned the animal toward the edge of town. Soon, they were at a canter that would quickly cross the miles to Tramlaw.

Now to find her man and save him from himself.

She prayed she wasn't too late.

CHAPTER 47

Tuesday, July 16, 1878

THE MOON, TWO days past full, helped Caleb and Jeremiah follow Gideon's map to an abandoned farmhouse northwest of town. The barn roof had collapsed, and the house canted to the left where its foundation was undercut by floods.

Caleb handed Jeremiah a container of fruit. "Cold meals for a while."

Jeremiah chewed. "Better than eating hardtack in the pouring rain."

Caleb grimaced at the memory. "That's for sure. When we're done with this fancy meal, let's take a ride, and see if we can find where Dennison and his crew may be hiding."

They headed south and then east around the town, keeping to the woods as much as possible to avoid the moonlight. Three hours later, they reached the road that entered Tramlaw from the north. They stopped in the trees bordering the road.

Caleb stood in his stirrups, head cocked. In the distance, an owl hooted. Jeremiah's horse spooked as a bat flew by. Caleb pitched his voice low. "Miss the sound of a coyote."

"Know what you mean. Everything feels different here."

Caleb held up one hand and drew his pistol. "Thought I heard something."

Jeremiah's saddle creaked as he drew his Colt. "I don't hear any—wait." He paused, pointed north. "One horse coming. Slow."

"That's what I figure." He backed his horse further into the trees, pulling it to a halt in the shadows. Jeremiah followed suit. Tension prickled Caleb's back like a bug under his shirt climbing his spine. He stroked his horse's shoulder to quiet him. And himself. He closed his eyes, concentrated. One horse at a slow walk.

Patience, old man. Let him come to you. Let him pass by.

Jeremiah whispered. "Could be a farmer out late."

"On a week night?"

The lone horse continued to clop along, each step bringing it closer. Caleb's heart sounded like cannons firing a steady, booming cadence. He held his breath to force it to beat slower and quieter.

The clopping louder, no sign they'd been discovered.

The road glowed in the moonlight; its whitish surface contrasting with the dark green leaves and black trunks of the forest.

Caleb stroked his mustache and waited. He felt like a watch spring—ready to fly out if the case was opened. He exhaled, resisted the urge to scratch the itching palm holding his Colt.

The horse came into view, head down, sweat marks glistening in the pale light. The rider slumped over, his head on Caleb's side of the horse's neck. Recognition slowly came.

"It's Michael." He spurred his horse into the road, Jeremiah right behind. Michael's horse was too tired to jump, skitter or run. It stopped when Caleb entered the road, and its head drooped even lower to the ground.

Caleb dismounted and rushed to Michael.

"How is he?" Jeremiah said.

"Can't tell if he's passed out or just asleep. The farmhouse should be only a few miles west of here. Let's take him there and sort this out."

Jeremiah took the horse's reins and led him into the trees. Caleb rode next to Michael, hand hovering to steady him on the rougher terrain.

"Whatever possessed him to come back?" Caleb said.

"Finish what he started."

"He's in no shape to help anybody."

"Not saying it makes sense. Just who he is," Jeremiah said.

"Stubborn."

"Yep. And loyal, too."

They rode in silence until they approached the open ground surrounding the farmhouse. Caleb rode ahead, scanning the area, keeping his mount at a steady walk. He circled the house. When he came back to the front, he waved Jeremiah in.

They settled Michael on the remains of a straw mattress with a bedroll for a pillow. The light was too weak for a detailed examination, but his fever had returned.

"Must've got off at the first stop after we left." Caleb's voice was terse. "Should've told our decoys to make sure he didn't."

"You couldn't've known he'd try something like this. Besides, what could they do? Handcuff him to the seat? They weren't deputies."

Caleb sat crossed-legged next to Michael and applied a wet cloth to his forehead. "Maybe we should have handcuffed him ourselves."

Jeremiah walked to the window. "What is, is what is. This is just going to make it more complicated if we've got to keep an eye on him, too."

Caleb sat, his hands in his lap, staring at the young man. *Why did you have to do a fool thing like this?*

His eyed burned. He wanted to close them and let sleep wash the fatigue and numbness away. "Maybe Gideon or Zechariah can send somebody to stay with him. I'll ride into town in a bit and talk to Gideon."

Jeremiah snorted. "Don't like that. You might be seen."

"I know. I'll be careful."

"If you find someone, bring a rope. I don't want Michael getting loose. He's in no shape to help us or defend himself."

Caleb stretched out, saddle as a pillow. "Let me sleep for a couple of hours, then I'll go."

→⊫⊙ ⊙⊰←

Caleb searched from the glassless window of the house, head in the shadow. No sign anyone was out there. He did the same from the windows on each side. With a nod to Jeremiah, he opened the rear door wide enough to slip through sideways. A quick scamper brought him to the woods where they'd hid their horses. He placed his hand over his animal's muzzle when he heard leaves rustle. He relaxed when a raccoon scampered away.

At the edge of town, he paused, listened. *Must be past midnight.* The town hunkered, silent, settled for the night. In the distance, a cat yowled. Caleb jumped when, a few feet away, a rat darted, scritching along a board on the ground.

Caleb wiped sweat from his forehead and moved toward Gideon's house. As he passed along a fence, a sniff and low growl marked a dog on the alert. Caleb kept moving, the dog quieted, and Caleb took his first full breath in several minutes.

Praying the moonlight wouldn't betray him to any watchers, Caleb slunk to the back door of Gideon's darkened house. He knocked on the door—a light tap, hoping he wouldn't have to raise a ruckus that would alert the neighbors.

The door sprung open at his first knock. "What took you so long? I expected you hours ago."

"Small complication. Michael followed us back."

Gideon cussed. "Can't say I'm surprised. Just wish he'd used his head and let us handle it."

Caleb shrugged. "'S there any way you can get word to Doc MacKenzie? Michael's running a fever."

"Yeah. Wait here. I'll go get him."

While Gideon was gone, Caleb used the dim moonlight filtering through the curtains to pour a cup of cold coffee and munch on a biscuit from a platter left on the table. *Mrs. Larkin's been here.*

Caleb plastered himself flat against the wall at the sound of scratching at the front door. A moment later, Gideon entered. Caleb holstered his pistol as he stepped into the light.

"Good to see you're still alert. Doc will meet you on the North Road, five miles out of town. Didn't want to draw any attention by bringing him here."

"Anybody see you?"

"I'm sure someone did, but I couldn't see them. Assume the worst and plan accordingly."

"Right." Caleb wrapped the remaining biscuits in a napkin.

"Hey," Gideon protested. "Those were gonna be my breakfast."

"I'm sure you can skip one meal in order for me to nurse a sick young man back to health."

Gideon waved his hand in dismissal. "Take 'em, even though you ain't that young or sick."

Caleb grinned. Maybe there'd be a place for him here after this was all settled. It'd be good to work with his oldest friend again.

Doc waited at the side of the road, on horseback instead of in a carriage, his black bag hanging off the saddle horn like a huge bug. Caleb eyed the pistol holstered around Doc's waist.

Doc shrugged and whispered, "Some sicknesses require different techniques to remove them from the body. I can use this as well as a scalpel if I have to."

As Caleb led the way to the farmhouse, the skin along his spine prickled to the base of his skull. Several times, he stopped, listened, heard nothing, and moved on. The prickling nagged.

When they reached the edge of the woods bordering the farm, Caleb reined up. "You go around the back, and Jeremiah will let you in. I'm gonna backtrack aways, make sure we weren't followed."

Caleb made a wide turn, and rode through the woods about a hundred feet parallel to the path he had taken in. He loose-tied his horse to a tree and waited beside the trail. Nothing. *Must've been imagining things.* He stretched and headed back to his horse.

He froze. Listened. What had he heard? A breath? The brush of clothing against a branch? Something soft, almost silent. If there'd been the slightest breeze, the sound would have been lost. He waited. No more sounds. His spine told him something was out there, so he snugged himself against a tree, hiding in its shadow, pistol in hand.

There. Moonlight glinted, winked against something. Winked again. A rifle barrel.

A man came into view, rifle pointed ahead, finger on the trigger.

Caleb held his breath.

The man approached, focused on the path, not turning his head. He passed Caleb.

Caleb let him take three more steps, stepped behind, and pressed the barrel of his pistol into the man's back. The man froze.

"Finger off the trigger," Caleb whispered.

The man obeyed.

"Hold the rifle by the barrel in your right hand and stretch your arms wide."

The man did. Caleb took the rifle, holstered his pistol and centered the Winchester in the middle of the man's back.

"Let's get your horse."

Caleb walked the man to the farmhouse, horses in tow.

"You found a friend," Jeremiah said from his place next to Doc, using his hat to shield the lantern he held from being seen in the windows. Doc bent over Michael.

"He's no friend of ours. What's your name?"

Doc looked up. "That's Billy Ray Andrews. One of Gideon's deputies."

In the weak light, Andrews looked gaunt, thin of face and body. "That's right. Sheriff Parsons sent me out to keep watch, make sure nobody finds you."

Caleb rubbed his chin and sighed. He stepped in front of Andrews, staring into his dark eyes. "Well, that was very thoughtful of the Sheriff, except we agreed no one was to know where we were." He spat at the man's feet. "Now, the town of Tramlaw may pay you, but who do you work for?"

"I...I...I told you, Sheriff Parsons sent me." Andrews' eyes darted around the room.

"I don't have time for this, son." Caleb's fist sank into Andrews' stomach, the deputy's fetid breath washing across Caleb in a putrid cloud. Andrews crumpled to his side on the floor, holding his stomach, knees bent.

"You're a lawman," Andrews moaned through clenched teeth, gasping for air.

"Not anymore. Turned in my badge before I left town. Just a citizen now. Who are you working for?"

Michael coughed, raised himself on one elbow. "I remember you. You're the deputy who I passed on the street just before I got beat up. You took me to the alley." Michael coughed again. "Why'd you do it? Why'd you turn against Gideon?"

Andrews glared at Michael. "Shut up, preacher man."

Caleb grabbed a handful of Andrews' hair and lifted his head. "I used to be a lawman, so I know how to show some restraint." He pointed at Jeremiah. "This man here ain't never been a real lawman, so he don't know nothin' about restraint. Maybe I'll let him question you." He pushed Andrews' head back to the floor, held it there. "One more time. Who're you working for?"

Wide-eyed, Andrews gasped a breath. "Dennison."

Caleb tightened his grip on Andrews' hair. "Who's he working for?"

Water filled Andrews' eyes. "Don't know."

Caleb searched the man's face for the tic, the looking away, the sign that told him the man knew more than he said.

Jeremiah said, "I don't think he knows. Who'd trust a coward like him with important information?"

Andrews' eyes flared. "I'm not a coward. Dennison's the only one I talk to."

"Where can we find him?" Caleb said.

"Don't know. He always finds me."

"Why?" Caleb said. "You seem pretty useless to me. Wonder why Gideon ever hired you."

Andrews coughed, defiance in his eyes. "Useless? Found you, didn't I?"

Caleb hauled him to his feet although the man's hands still held his stomach, and he hunched over. "Yeah, but you let yourself get caught, so that turned out to be useless, too."

Jeremiah walked over and pushed Andrews against the wall, hard. "How were you to let him know you found us?"

Andrews stared at him.

"Well?"

Andrews closed his eyes, shook his head. "I'd rather get beat up by you than killed by him."

Michael coughed again, his voice weak. "What's he using against you, Billy Ray?"

Andrews' eyes widened as he looked at Michael. He opened his mouth, closed it.

"He's using somebody against Billy Ray." Michael took a ragged breath. "Dennison's going to hurt somebody if Billy Ray doesn't help. Am I right?'

Andrews closed his eyes.

"I think you're right," Caleb said. "Tell us who it is, Andrews. We can help you. Protect them."

Andrews nodded at Michael. "Like you helped him and Miss Deborah and Becky Jo? I'd rather take my chances with Dennison. He won't be here forever."

Caleb released Andrews. The man slumped against the wall. "Get some rope, Jeremiah. We'll have to tie him up and keep him here until we get this sorted out."

CHAPTER 48

Wednesday, July 17, 1878

RACHEL SLOWED HER horse to a walk as she approached a crossroads. A signpost told her she was five miles from Tramlaw. She stroked her animal's neck. "Good job, girl. If Sunshine wasn't so jealous, I'd take you home." The horse whinnied and bobbed its head, bridle jangling.

The animal's ears pricked straight up and pivoted right. Rachel held her breath, shoulders tense. A noise to her right. Hoof beats cantering. More than one horse. Who'd be out this time of night? Rachel guided her mare into a stand of trees near the crossroads. From the west, two horses appeared around a bend. The riders seemed at ease and relaxed in the saddles, two men in control of their world.

Rachel held her breath as the riders neared, eyes drawn to the right sleeve of one of the riders. It was pinned to his shoulder.

Dennison. He knows where Becky Jo is.

Her horse shifted its weight and her saddle creaked. She stroked the animal's flank, and it stilled. The men continued to ride, glancing neither left nor right, their own movements blocking any sounds.

Rachel counted to ten, then guided her horse back onto the road. The silhouettes of the riders bobbed a short distance ahead. She urged her mount forward at a matching pace.

If I find where they're keeping Becky Jo, I can tell Gideon.

The urge to draw closer grew. No one would protect Becky Jo if those men decided to molest her, something she wouldn't put past them. She slowed her horse. *Keep your temper, Rachel. Won't be any help if you get yourself caught.*

All she had was the Derringer, which she had yet to fire. She paused, made sure it was loaded, and nudged her animal back to the pace that would keep Dennison in sight, but not too close.

The road curved south and then east. Rachel prayed she'd be able to find her way back, trying to note landmarks. All the trees looked the same in the fading moonlight. No other roads. No houses she could see.

A country road through the woods. A pleasant ride on a sunny day, but now the trees hulked like stoic guardians over the evil ahead.

The men slowed, and Rachel reined her horse. They walked a little ways, seeming to scan the woods to their left. They turned off, vanishing into the trees. Rachel walked her horse to the place where she thought they'd turned off. She looked at the ground. No help. No way she could distinguish one track from another.

She noticed softer ground along the side of the road. Her heart leapt. Maybe she could see where they turned. She started to dismount, decided against it. Better to stay mounted in case she had to run.

She reached the place she was sure they had turned. No hoof prints. She scrunched her eyes and looked again. No sign. She walked down the road, then back, shoulders tense, chest tight, she slapped her hand on her thigh several times. *Come on, eyes. Work. Lord, don't let me get this close and not find her.*

She chewed her lower lip, closed her eyes and sighed. *Relax, girl.*

She froze at a noise from the woods to her right. A fox scampered where she stood. She guided her horse to the spot. There. A mark on the road. She leaned over as far as she could. A hoof print framed by the moonlight, pointing into the woods. Now she saw the narrow trail, barely wide enough for a horse, took an immediate turn once it entered the forest. She doubted she could even find it in daylight.

She scanned the area. Nothing to use as a landmark. She rode to the opposite side of the road and bent a sap-rich branch until it broke enough to dangle.

Breathing shallow and hushed, she entered the path into the woods, reins short and tight. *Lord, help me hear and see before it's too late. Show me what to do to help Becky Jo.*

The trail twisted a maze through the woods. Would she ever be able to find her way back? The path turned around a huge oak tree then ran straight, though she could no longer tell which direction. The tree would be her only landmark. Her heart pounded in her chest, sweat trickled down her back. *What have I gotten myself into?*

Dawn's first light shrouded the world in shades of gray. Rachel followed the path, eyes sweeping the woods in front of her. Did they post lookouts? Where? Has she already been spotted? Was she riding into a trap?

She placed one hand on her chest as if it alone would still the rapid beating of her heart. Mouth dry, canteen empty, she licked her lips. If she were standing, she doubted her knees would support her.

The trees thinned, and she halted. Fifty yards away, a two-story house rose from the morning mist like a dusty, white mushroom. Porches front and rear. Four windows on each floor faced her like a gap-toothed woman. Double doors centered the front of the house, flanked by windows. Some sort of roadway led up to the front door, then curved around the side toward the barn and corral. She couldn't determine where the road came from.

Outhouse behind. One other outbuilding, a small barn, with a corral attached. Two horses in the corral dozed, heads down. A third looked right at her. Her horse pitched its ears forward.

"Shh." She stroked its neck until it calmed. She turned off the path, and sought a circular route around the building, keeping it in sight, keeping herself hidden. The horse in the corral followed her for a while but then seemed to lose interest, and lapped from the watering trough.

She reined her horse to a halt as a buggy clattered up the drive. The woman driver declined the hand of one of the two men who came from the house, and stepped from the carriage with grace and poise. Rachel didn't recognize her but recognized the aura of wealth wrapped around her like precious fur—the air of haughtiness. The man who offered his hand was Dennison. He now held the front door open while the second man led the horse and carriage to the barn, where he loosed the horse in the corral.

Rachel continued a few more feet until the sound of another rider caused her to halt. She slipped behind a tree, and watched a man dismount and wrap his reins around a hitching post. The woman came out and they embraced—a lover's embrace and kiss. Rachel's hands itched to hold a spyglass, and she wished she'd explored Tramlaw more. She suspected she was looking at Christopher Barrett and Emma Winslow, but had no idea why she thought that.

After the couple slipped inside she continued her circuit of the house. *This is foolish. What if I get caught? But I need to know if Becky Jo is here before I ride for Gideon. And what if they've captured Michael and Caleb and Jeremiah?* Her heart beat faster, her stomach rolled from hunger. At the thought of food, nausea bubbled. She closed her eyes, breathed deeply.

Less than ten feet separated the woods from the rear of the barn and corral. Rachel slid from her horse and tied it to one of the trees. She checked her Derringer again, and slid it into the pocket of her skirt. Two shots. And she'd never fired at a person. She shook her head and laughed silently. *I'm either very foolish or very brave. Probably both. I'm counting on you, Lord.*

She crept up the side of the windowless barn and peered around the corner at the rear of the house. The house showed its age. Faded paint. Single door in the left corner, closest to her, three windows on the first floor, four on the second. A sagging-roof covered porch ran the width of the building. Somebody had let the house go. A stand with a pump handle and sink for washing, two backless benches under the windows. No sign of anyone.

Twenty-five yards to the closest part of the house. Looked like five miles. Could she get close without being seen? Her throat constricted. It'd be a challenge for Jeremiah. But she'd learned to creep around the brothels and only got caught once. It was also the last time she did any sneaking.

She pressed her back against the barn and looked back to her horse who watched her and then resumed grazing. So easy to get on and ride to town and let Gideon handle this.

Have to know.

Too risky.

Michael and Becky Jo might be in there.

I might get caught.

Have to know.

She commanded the voices in her head to be quiet. She peered around the corner. Took a deep breath. Ran. Her sprint toward the house felt like wading through thigh deep snow.

She collapsed at the corner of the house, exhaled. Inhaled, filling her burning lungs with air, feeling them pushing against the constrictions binding her chest. A horse in the corral whinnied. The same one that had seen her in the forest looked at her now. *You're too nosy for your own good.*

The back door opened. Rachel slid around to the side of the house, scrunching under the window.

"I'll check." A step on the back porch. "Aw, it's just that horse of yours. Scared of its own shadow." The door closed.

Rachel breathed, hand on her chest, other hand flattened on the siding of the house.

Voices above her. She brought her head just below the window. Indistinguishable murmurs. One might have been the woman's.

She sidled to the next window. She removed her hat and risked a peek. Empty. Crumpled blankets scattered on the floor.

Two more windows on this side.

Dare she risk it?

Have to know.

Her heart felt like it would pound a hole through her chest and escape. She moved forward, peeked into another empty room, not even furniture. Dusty bare wood floors crisscrossed with boot prints. This window and two on the front filled the room with light.

She peered the width of the front of the house. They'd hear her boots on the porch. Dashing around the porch looked too exposed. Crawl?

The front door opened.

A female voice from inside the house. "Don't smoke that stinking thing in here."

Rachel's head swiveled. No way to get back to her horse without being seen. Forest too far away. She forced down the panic that swaddled her head.

There. The underside of the porch wasn't enclosed.

Snakes.

Spiders.

Can't get caught.

Lord, help me.

Rachel dove, scrambling in the moist earth that smelled of decayed animals, tucking her legs out of sight as footsteps above sounded like cannon fire. A cobweb covered her face. She pinched her nose, and whuffed a sneeze, plugging her ears. She strained to listen.

Whoever was above her seemed oblivious to her presence as he muttered about bossy females and struck a match to light whatever it was that got him banished. Rachel soon wished the smoker had been banished to the next county as the stink of a cheap cigar invaded her cramped accommodations. She'd smelled cigars dipped in whiskey. This one reeked of something that had been soaked in snake oil. She gagged and buried a cough in the crook of her elbow.

A spider skittered over her hand. She jumped, and bright circles of light filled her vision as her head encountered a beam supporting the porch. The thump was in time with the man above taking a step.

Two perpendicular green slits appeared under the stairs. They moved toward her. Rachel told herself not to push backwards. Feeling around for a stick or stone while the green slits hypnotized her, she decided touching objects without seeing them first was not a good idea.

The eyes were embedded in the head of a huge white cat that waddled up to her, sniffed her ear, licked her nose, and ambled past her, belly dragging in the dirt.

"Looka the size of that monster," the voice above whispered. A pistol shot reverberated the boards over her head, showering her with, she hoped, only dust. Looking behind her, she saw the cat running away much faster than she thought its size would allow.

A new voice above her. Dennison's growl. "What do you think yer doin'? You want to let everybody know we're here?"

Chagrin filled the other voice. "Sorry. Wasn't thinking. Just having some fun with that stray cat."

"Well, knock it off."

"If you'd let us have some fun with that filly you got tied up, it wouldn't be so boring around here."

"We're almost done. The boss'll be ready in a couple or three days, then we'll get paid and get out of here. You can have all the fun you want with her then."

A set of footsteps went inside.

Becky Jo is here. Doesn't sound like they've hurt her. Yet.

The smoker stepped to the edge of the porch. Through the latticework nailed before her, Rachel saw the butt of the cigar land in the packed dirt of the drive, bounce once and smolder. The man went inside.

Rachel counted to thirty. She needed to scout the other side of the house. Her heart lurched at crawling through this muck. Crawling across the porch ran the risk of noise as well as someone opening the door. Going around the outside of the porch was only a little less exposed. She shook her head. This was the only way to get there unseen. *As long as I don't meet a snake and scream.*

Two minutes—that felt like two hours—later, Rachel emerged like a butterfly escaping its cocoon. She pressed against the side of the house and shook her head. Dirt smeared the front of her outfit, brown and black streaks of who knows what. She flicked off a spider darting up her skirt, and wiped the remains of the cobweb from her face. She'd deal with the remnants in her hair when she had the luxury of a brush and mirror.

Should attract a lot of attention when I ride into town to get Gideon. You should see me now, Michael.

She peeked in the window. What once must have been a library now stood empty, barren bookshelves marching along two of the walls.

The window to the next room was curtained with heavy material, blocking any view she might have. She listened but heard nothing. She raised her hand to tap the glass. No. One of the bad guys might be in there.

The curtain swept aside as if blown by a gale. Rachel gasped, hand to her throat. She wanted to meld into the wall as a man's face stared out the window. He focused straight ahead. If he looked to his left, he'd surely see her. She wrapped the Derringer in the palm of her hand, holding her breath, feeling her eyes widen.

A voice from inside the room. "What are yer lookin' at?"

"Outside. Tired a bein' cooped up here with nothin' to do. Haven't been to town in three days, and Dennison won't let us have fun with her yet."

"I'd rather have fun with the other one."

The man at the window laughed. "Dennison'd kill you before you got one button undone. Then he'll kill you again."

"Let's play cards."

"Why? Already took all your money and your matches. And your boots don't fit me. Whatcha got left to bet with?"

"How about who gets her first?"

"That's only one hand. And I'll win that one, too."

"Well, let's get some grub then."

"Might's well."

He turned from the window, letting the material go. Before it fully drifted back into place, Rachel glanced into the room. The image stayed with her as the curtain blocked her view. Becky Jo on a blanket on the floor, hands and feet bound, mouth gagged.

Did she see me? Does she know help's on the way? Rachel wasn't sure. There might have been a flash of recognition in her eyes. It easily could have been a flash of anger at the men shamelessly discussing their plans for her.

"Hey, what was that?"

"What was what?"

"I thought I saw something out the window."

Rachel ducked, and ran around the back corner of the house. Below boards blocked the porch. Rachel spun in a circle, eyes darting, not focusing. The woods were too far away. Her horse was on the opposite side of the barn. The outhouse. She ran and ducked behind it as the back door opened.

She crouched behind the small building. Gagged. *This one's been here awhile.* She held her breath and listened. Sounds of two sets of boots on the porch, then silence. A twig snapped, tall grass swished.

Rachel peered around the corner to see one man turn alongside the house and disappear from view. She slid to the other side of the outhouse. Another man walked toward the trees, head pivoting, gun in hand. Had she hidden her horse well enough? *Should be all right if he doesn't go to the other side of the corral.*

Her heart sank. He came into view, looking in the other direction. For now. No place to hide. In the outhouse? Just a trap waiting to be sprung. Nowhere to run. What can this Derringer do against a Colt?

Well, Michael, life is certainly an adventure with you.

Rachel froze, eyes glued to the man, to the gun. Dare she breathe? Her heart beat like a hummingbird's wings. Pins and needles tingled in her knees, up her spine. Her hand gripped the Derringer.

"Hey, Joe." The voice came from the back of the house. "Find anything?"

The man turned to his left, away from her. "Nah. Musta been a bird or a deer at the edge of the trees." He disappeared from view.

Rachel slumped against the wall, letting it support her while her knees buckled. She inhaled deeply, ignoring the aroma behind her.

The one named Joe said, "I'll meet you inside. Need to use the outhouse."

Rachel covered her mouth with her hand as her stomach lurched. The door screeched open. She stepped away, knees quaking. From here, the corral was closer than the barn, but that skittish horse already watched her. In a few more steps, the outhouse would no longer provide cover. She hoped Joe's business was loud enough to cover any noise she made—although her stomach recoiled at the thought of his business.

After this, Michael, you will empty and clean all the chamber pots every morning and dig a new outhouse every six months. It's the least you can do.

In two more steps, she'd be visible from the rear of the house. The trees to her left were as close as the corral and would give her better cover more quickly. Becky Jo's room, with its curtained window, was on that side. At least part of the building would be blind to her.

She ran. Now it felt like waist-deep snow. It took several strides before her knees cooperated with her commands. The trees came closer. The outhouse door screeched. Her hand touched the first tree, the second. She ducked behind the third, gasping, lungs burning more than they should have. She realized she'd held her breath the entire sprint.

She peered around the tree. Joe stood to one side of the outhouse, buttoning his trousers, scanning the trees in her direction. He rubbed the back of his neck and stepped toward her.

"Hey, Joe."

Joe stopped and turned toward the house. "What?"

"Grub's ready."

Joe studied the trees, shrugged, and walked toward the house.

Rachel sagged against the trunk and slipped to her knees, the oak bark rough on her palms. She rested her forehead against the tree as her heart pounded and her lungs drew in huge draughts of air. She'd made it. They hadn't seen her. She'd found Becky Jo.

Now to get to Gideon.

CHAPTER 49

Wednesday, July 17, 1878

MICHAEL'S SLEEP-LADEN EYES spied Billy Ray Andrews leaning against the wall, head lolling on his chest. Michael pushed himself into a sitting position, every nerve protesting. Dull aches settled in his joints and head. His face felt warm under his palm. *Can't be sick. Have to help.*

Michael was alone with their prisoner. Doc had prescribed water and rest, and then ridden back to town to alert Gideon about Andrews. Caleb and Jeremiah left a short time later with Michaels's assurance he would be able to guard the deputy until they returned or Gideon rode out.

He sipped from the canteen and gnawed on some jerky. He tried to shake off the memories of cold meals and eating in the saddle with the posse.

But the graves of Vernon's group burned as did the picture of Old Thomas lying spread-eagled in the dirt.

One image hovered at the edge of every waking moment as well as the sleeping ones: Maria slumped against the wall of the cabin, one eye gone, the other staring at him.

Andrews lifted his head. "Thirsty."

Michael braced himself against the wall while he stood. The room blurred as his head spun. He waited until things settled down, including his lurching stomach. His first step was tentative, testing his left knee. It hesitated, then supported his weight.

He held a cup of water to Andrews' lips. The traitor drained it in several gulps. Michael gave him another, checked the knots on the ropes. He tucked his pistol in his waistband, and checked each of the windows. Mist dissipated as the first rays of the sun broke over the treetops. Stillness framed the world. In the distance, a mockingbird called, echoed by another. A rabbit hopped through the grass, and disappeared under a bush near the front door.

Michael inhaled. He imagined Rachel in Mrs. Fremont's boarding house, waking to the aroma of ham and bacon and flapjacks. Soon, he'd be sharing a bed with her, watching her long lashes flutter before opening to reveal her violet eyes. His heart surged at the thought that soon he would be the first thing those eyes saw every morning, and the last they saw at night. His hand caressing her cheek, their lips touching, their union complete.

He smiled at the thought of Rachel's vision. God wanted them married. A life together.

He prayed, struggling. *Lord, what have I done to deserve a gift like Rachel? Surely, there is someone better for her somewhere. Why me?* Silence. No response. Why question God? Somehow, God determined he and Rachel were to be husband and wife. *Maybe I should figure out how to not think about it and relax and enjoy the ride.*

He settled on his bedroll, the wall serving as a backrest.

"Billy Ray, what are Dennison and his boss holding over you? How were they able to turn you against Gideon?"

Andrews' eyes focused on the floor, shoulders slumped. "They promised me five thousand dollars in gold." He muttered his words into his chest.

Michael whistled. "That's a lot of money. But is it enough to turn against the man who took a risk with you, trained you, gave you a chance for a better life?"

A shadow brushed across Andrews' face, a flicker of something beyond the words. "Yeah, it is. A chance to get out of this town, make a name for myself somewhere else."

"Traitor isn't much of a name to be known by. Kind of like being named Judas."

Andrews' eyes narrowed, his nose flared. Through gritted teeth, each word clipped, he said, "Don't throw that religious hog slop at me. Don't mean nothin', never will."

Michael waited. This wasn't the time to give him a lecture in religion. His mouth spoke words he hadn't expected. "It seems like there's more to it than five thousand dollars. Something else to keep you in line."

Andrews shrugged. "T'aint nothin' else."

"What guarantee do you have they they'll pay you the money? They could kill you just as easy when they're done. Why leave you alive? You're a liability to them. So it's got to be more than money they're using as a hold over you."

"How would you know?"

Michael sighed. "I used to run with people like Dennison, and whoever he's reporting to. They only want two things. One is as much money as they can get. So why should they keep their promise to you? Second, they don't want to get caught. So why should they let you live? They're using something else to keep you cooperating with them."

Andrews cast a faraway look out the window. "Ma's sick. Doc MacKenzie thinks a doctor in Philadelphia can help her." He turned to Michael. "Takes a bunch of money for the treatment."

Michael pitched his voice low. "Look, tell us who Dennison's working for. Caleb, Gideon and Jeremiah are smart people. They'll catch them and we'll find some way to help you get the money for Philadelphia."

Andrews sneered. "Leave me alone. I don't need no more of your preacher promises."

Michael shrugged. "Suit yourself." He leaned back, head against the wall, eyes closed to slits, ears alert.

Andrews studied the floor, shoulders hunched, forehead knitted in a scowl. He squirmed. "Can you loosen these ropes some? I can't feel my hands."

"'Fraid not. Only got one good hand. Never was much good at knots."

Andrews cursed him.

Michael smiled. "Help us out, and I'm sure Caleb and Jeremiah will be glad to ease up on the ropes."

Andrews cursed him again. "But Gideon will make sure I go to jail."

"Well, Billy Ray, you did break the law and you violated the trust of a good man, which is even worse. Don't forget, people have been beat up, shot, kidnapped and murdered over this, and you're part of it. There's no way Gideon can look the other way, but if you help us, your cooperation will go a long way. May get your sentence reduced."

Andrews looked away, squirmed and settled into a silence marked by frequent glares at Michael, and long-winded sighs.

Michael snapped awake, head banging into the wall, chagrined he'd dozed off. Andrews stared at him, lips compressed in a tight smile. From the sun's angle on the floor, Michael estimated he'd dozed for about an hour.

He leveraged himself to his feet, feeling stronger than the last time he stood. The nap did some good. His face felt cooler, almost normal. Hunger niggled. He chewed a piece of jerky and surveyed the landscape from the shadow of the window frames. Quiet. No signs of life in front or back. No breeze stirred the grass, and the summer heat draped heavy and moist.

"Got any grub?" Andrews' whine grated on Michael's ears. "Ain't ate noth-in' since yesterday noon."

"All we have is jerky. Not going to light a fire."

"Anything to keep my stomach from eating my backbone."

Michael offered a piece of jerky.

"Untie my hands. Don't make me eat like a baby."

Michael shook his head. "Told you I'm no good with knots one-handed. Just bite a chunk."

He extended his hand closer.

The man smiled. "Well, it's a good thing I can work knots."

Andrews' arms bullwhipped from behind his back. He caught Michael's an-kles and yanked, flipping him. Michael landed on his back, air rushing from his lungs, head bouncing on the floor.

My pistol? There it was on his bedroll. Michael twisted to reach for it, fingers grappling, touching the edge of the handle. Andrews straddled him. "Stupid preacher. Samictonious hypocrite. " Andrews' fist connected with Michael's jaw, shudders of pain lanced into his brain.

Andrews cursed and hit him again. "You and that fool Parsons. I'll show him before this is over. He'll see the business end of my gun if I have my way."

He pushed at Andrews with his left arm, reaching for his jaw. Andrews grabbed his wrist, twisted it away, and dropped his knee hard on Michael's right arm, below the elbow. Shards of pain reeled and blinding white light pierced Michael's brain.

Legs pinned by Andrews astride his hips, left arm twisted away, right arm useless and pressed into his chest by Andrews' knee, Michael turned his head from side to side. Andrews' left fist connected with his cheeks and jaw. He fought against the darkness, seeking some leverage to resist, to push the man off. Another blow to his cheek.

Darkness came. Merciful, pain-free darkness. He sank into it, let it swallow him.

CHAPTER 50

Wednesday, July 17, 1878

RACHEL DARTED FROM tree to tree, vigilant of the house. Gratitude flooded her when she saw her horse, dozing where she'd left it. Sunshine would have stayed awake and kept watch.

She gathered the reins and set her left foot in the stirrup. A horse approached, galloping to the front of the house. *What's going on? Somebody's in a hurry.*

She re-tied her horse and stalked through the woods to where she could see what was happening. Too far to hear voices, but Dennison was easy to recognize. The other man on the porch looked like the one called Joe.

The man on the horse waved his hands and pointed down the road. The sun glinted on his shirt. A badge? *A lawman?* Rachel tried to meld into the tree, keeping one eye on the scene.

He's not acting like he's trying to arrest them. The man called Joe looked in her direction. She held her breath, hoping she blended into the shadows. He turned back to Dennison.

The man on the horse leaned forward as if pleading. Dennison shook his head, drew his pistol, fired. The shot's echo faded as blood spurted from the rider's chest and back, and he sprawled backwards before tumbling to the ground. The horse trotted a few feet away, lowered its head, and grazed.

Rachel's knuckles were in her mouth. She closed her eyes. When she opened them again, the rider still lay in the dirt. Dennison stood over him, kicked the man's foot, and shook his head. She dug her nails into the tree. *Stay put. Don't run.*

Dennison spoke to Joe, and turned toward the house, where the woman and well-dressed man stood at the door. Dennison motioned both of them back inside. Joe draped the rider's body over the saddle and led the horse toward the corral.

She paralleled them, a few steps behind, grateful the horse was between her and Joe. Eyes fixed on the man, ready to duck behind a tree if he turned her way, she didn't see the root that sent her sprawling. The air whooshed from her lungs as she landed, rattling the bush next to her.

She flattened herself on the ground as Joe stopped and looked over the horse's neck. He seemed to stare for hours before resuming his trek to the back of the property.

Rachel raised herself to a crouch and dashed to the next tree. She waited, scanned the ground, then dashed, skipping over another root. The distance to her own horse didn't seem to shrink. The trees spread farther apart, roots rose from the ground like fences and hedges to be hurdled.

She passed the small barn unseen and rested against a tree, gasping, hand on her chest. A door in the small barn opened, and Joe appeared carrying a shovel. He went some distance from the corral and began to dig.

Rachel found her horse, mounted, and followed the path that brought her here.

"Hey, stop."

Joe ran toward her, gun drawn. She kicked her horse. "Now. I need it all." The horse leapt forward. A shot. A branch above and a little ahead of her flew away.

Rachel leaned forward, ducking under branches that slashed at her face and arms.

A second shot. Her left arm erupted, flames of hot pain lanced from her fingers to shoulder and behind her eyes. Light so bright and painful, she couldn't see. She swayed, head swimming, vision blurred. Her body slid to the left. "No." She gripped the saddle horn, tightened her knees along the horse's sides. "Run, horse. Run." The animal found another speed.

She was off the trail, crashing through the forest, the horse weaving around trees, leaping over roots. Rachel leaned as far forward as possible. She lifted her left arm. More blinding light, more fire. She let the arm dangle, aware of the blood running, soaking her sleeve. Aware, too, that she would live. She had to. Michael waited.

The horse leapt a fallen tree and skidded to a halt. They were on the road, a split rail fence bordering the other side. Rachel massaged the space between her eyebrows. Which way? To the right was the main road to Tramlaw. And the most likely way they'd come looking for her. To the left, unknown. But away from those who'd soon be following.

She turned the horse, and urged it into a gallop, leaning over its neck, knees tight.

→►═◉ ◉═◄←

Caleb slumped in his saddle as he and Jeremiah clopped toward their farmhouse hideout. The frustrations of the morning hung in the air. He beat his fist against his leg. "Running out of places to look."

"They've got to be somewhere. Need to be patient and keep at it."

Tugging his hat lower, Caleb said, "I just got this feeling we're running out of time. If we don't find them soon, they're gonna take off, and that won't be good for Becky Jo."

"When we get back to the house, we'll pray with Michael."

Caleb halted as they turned behind the house. "Something's wrong. The deputy's horse is gone."

Jeremiah jumped from his saddle, and ran for the back door—Caleb at his heels, pistol drawn.

Michael lay on the floor, feet and hands tied, sling tied around his mouth. Caleb placed his hand on Michael's chest, relief washing through at the steady beat of his heart and rise and fall of his chest. "He's alive."

"Now Dennison'll know we're back."

"And Becky Jo's life just started a very short wick."

Caleb pushed the thought of the young girl out of his mind. No time for sentiment. Get Michael taken care of, get to Gideon.

Michael stirred as they undid the ropes and removed the gag. Caleb lifted him to a sitting position, and Jeremiah handed him the canteen. Michael gulped, some of the water dribbling down his chin.

"Sorry," he said when he'd drunk his fill. "Fell asleep, and he jumped me." He nodded at a piece of jerky on the floor. "Wanted something to eat and I wouldn't untie him. When I got close enough he flipped me and knocked me out."

"Boy was brighter than I thought," Caleb said. He rubbed the back of his neck. "I *am* too old for this. Shoulda reckoned he'd try something like this and taken him to Gideon."

"Too risky. Somebody might've seen us."

"My fault," Michael said. "Should've made him wait until you all got back."

Jeremiah rubbed his chin. "What is, is what is."

"Can you ride?" Caleb said.

"I don't want to slow you down." Michael shook his head. "Tried to help, made things worse. Why don't you go on without me?"

"Can't leave you here." Caleb gestured at their surroundings. "Andrews probably went right to Dennison. Dennison may not be as generous about letting you live."

"Why don't we wait for them here?" Michael eyes roamed from one to the other.

"Not enough fire power," Caleb answered.

"Too easy to get ourselves surrounded," Jeremiah added. "These walls won't hardly stop a fly, never mind a bullet. Caleb's right—we need to hook up with Gideon."

"And now that they know we're here," Caleb said, "we don't need to hide any more. Can you ride?"

"What about Becky Jo?" Michael said.

Caleb put his hand on Michael's good shoulder. "The quicker we get moving, the quicker we can find her." He braced his arm for Michael to pull himself to a standing position.

Michael's face paled, and Caleb reached to steady him. Michael shook him off. "I'm all right. Let's get going."

Caleb helped Michael mount, hand on his back until he'd gathered his reins. Michael nodded, face gray and pinched with pain.

Caleb tapped Michael's thigh. "You got sand, Michael. I'll give you that."

Michael grimaced. "Too bad I use it for brains."

->==◎ ◎==<-

Rachel knew she pushed her horse too hard. She pulled back on the reins, and let them fall slack, while the horse slowed to a walk. Rachel touched her arm. The dulled pain flared anew, and she gasped for the air that fled her lungs. She examined the wound. Blood seeped rather than flowed, and the bullet had passed through. Her upper arm muscles flinched when she flexed her fingers. The blood flow increased.

The road was quiet in the still, heavy air. Trees bordered the edge, extending branches to form a leafy tunnel. She halted and listened. Cicadas sang in the sultry heat, but no sounds of horse or man behind or in front.

She rounded a curve. To her right, fields planted with corn stretched away, fading in the misty distance. An opening in the fence revealed a dirt track leading to a house. The horse turned in. Rachel agreed. Water would be welcomed, and maybe they could help her get to Gideon.

As she plodded up the road, two children ran up to her. One a girl about ten, the other a teenage boy.

"You're hurt," the girl cried.

"Shush, Millie," the boy said. "Run and tell the Major the lady's hurt. Fetch Pa, too."

Rachel shook her head to clear the muddle. Did he say the Major?

The boy took the reins and walked the horse toward the house shimmering in the sun. Rachel clung to the saddle horn, suddenly weak, as blood drained from her face. She closed her eyes.

Strong arms wrapped around her waist and lifted her from the saddle.

"Gentle with her, Willie. Set her in my rocker in the parlor."

Rachel smiled. It was the Major.

A cool damp cloth bathed her face. The Major's eyes came into focus. "Miss Rachel, what happened? How did you get shot?" The Major ripped Rachel's sleeve away from her shoulder. "Pa, hot water and bandages."

A wheelchair creaked, and Rachel watched a thin, leg-less man maneuver to a fireplace that he fed with fresh wood. Next, he rotated a kettle on a hook over the fire. He wheeled into a back room and soon returned with white linens in his lap.

Rachel put her hand on the Major's arm. "Major, I found Becky Jo. She's alive."

The Major embraced Rachel, arms so tight, the air rushed from her lungs. Rachel cradled the Major against her shoulder, letting the woman's sobs of relief flow. She held and rocked her.

Pa Larkin lurked behind his wife, large, callused hands in his lap, tears flowing into the leathery folds of his face. He lifted his face skyward. "Thank you, Jesus, for protecting our little girl."

The Major's sobs subsided, her arms around Rachel loosened. She wiped her face with her apron. "Where is she?"

"She's in a house on the other side of this road. I don't know how many miles back, maybe ten."

Pa Larkin cocked his head to one side, a frown making his thin face even thinner. "Are you sure, miss."

Rachel nodded, exchanged glances with the Major. "Why?"

He scratched at the stubble on his face. "All that there is Barrett land, part of the Barrett Plantation. Why would outlaws take Becky Jo there?"

The Major clasped Rachel's hands, stared into her eyes. "Are you sure? The Barretts would never get mixed up in something like this. The judge himself offered a reward to whoever found Becky Jo."

The image of the well-dressed man talking to Dennison flashed. What was it about him? "One of the men I saw had one of those small beards." Rachel stroked her chin. "They call it a goatee."

Pa Larkin's eyes widened. "The banker, Christopher Barrett. He wears one of those. Had it since he could grow one."

Rachel stood. "I need to get to Sheriff Parsons."

CHAPTER 51

Wednesday, July 17, 1878

MICHAEL WIPED HIS brow with his sleeve. Gideon's office steamed in the after-noon heat as the bricks turned it into an oven. The faded curtains hung slack at the open windows.

Michael's heart sagged under the burden of watching Gideon receive the news that Billy Ray Andrews was a traitor. Face crumpled, shoulders rounded, Gideon stared at his desk, hands clasped between his legs.

He raised his head and locked eyes with Michael. "And he was one of the ones who beat you up?"

Michael hesitated, wishing he didn't have to answer. "It appears that way. I think he was the one who ordered me behind the bank."

Gideon nodded, eyes heavy. "I'm sorry. Looks like my judgment is slipping."

Caleb spoke from his chair next to Michael's. "Not your fault. Dennison was able to get to him with money."

Jeremiah straightened from leaning against the wall near the window. "We need to figure out what we're going to do next. By now, Dennison knows we're back. Becky Jo isn't any use to him anymore."

Caleb spoke. "From what I remember about Dennison, he'll want to do something public with her. He won't kill her and leave her by the side of the road. He'll want to send a message."

Michael said, "We need new ideas, new places."

The door flew open with a crash, papers flying off Gideon's desk.

"I know where Becky Jo is." Rachel stood in the doorway, breathless.

Her words flew past Michael's ears. He was sure his mouth gaped at the sight of her. Why was she here? Why was she so dirty, clothes smudged and streaked, hair tangled and windblown, glistening with strands of a cobweb? Dirt marked her face like Indian war paint. Then he noticed her arm, bare from the shoulder, bandaged wrapped snug, a red splotch in the center.

"Rach—"

She was in his arms, holding him. "Thank God you're safe."

Her arms were like morning sunshine.

"What are you doing here? Why aren't you—"

"Shush." She clung to Michael and faced Gideon. "Sheriff, Becky Jo is being held at a house on the Barrett Plantation near..." She paused, frowning. "Ivey's Ford Road. That's what the Major said to tell you."

Gideon hitched his gun belt around his waist. A wistful look covered his face and clouded his eyes. "Wish I knew which of my deputies I could trust." He sighed. "It'll have to be the four of us. Are you up to it, Michael?"

At the moment, Michael didn't feel up to anything more than sitting with Rachel and learning what had happened to her. He wanted to take her by her shoulders and shake her. *Why didn't she stay on the train? What was wrong with me? Why did I leave her?* She'd been in danger and hurt. He pulled her closer, held her as tight as he could.

"Michael?" Gideon's voice penetrated the cyclone swirling in his mind.

"I'm up to it. We need to save Becky Jo." He didn't want to leave Rachel.

"Five of us. I'm going, too," Rachel said.

He held Rachel at arm's length. "No, you're not. You're going—"

Her eyes shut his mouth. Her violet eyes, so like velvet, were now hard, determined. "Didn't we have this conversation back in Riverbend? Over lunch, I believe? I'm going. I know where Becky Jo is. I can lead you right to the house. No one else can."

Her eyes softened. She caressed his cheek. "I'm in this, Michael. Don't try to keep me out. Besides, I've got you and these three gentlemen to protect me." She cradled his face in her hands, eyes clear, determined. "I'll take you to the house, and then I'll stay back. I won't get in your way."

Michael knew he was giving into her eyes, her words, her hands. His heart said "NO" in giant letters. He could not, would not, risk her being taken away from him. He wanted to scoop her into his arms, throw her into a cell, lock it, and melt the key in Adam Jones's forge.

He shook his head. "No, I can't let you."

She clasped her hands at her waist. "It's not your decision. I can help."

He swallowed, but the lump in his throat didn't budge. "I don't want to lose you."

"I don't want to lose you either, but we both need to help Gideon do this and clear Ben's name."

Gideon spoke, "Michael, if Rachel can lead us to the house, it'll save us a heap of time."

Shoulders drooped, Michael nodded. "All right." He sighed. "Let's get going."

Chapter 52

Wednesday, July 17, 1878

RACHEL TOLD HER story as they prepared their horses and started out of town. Once on the North Road, Gideon led the way to Ivey's Ford Road, Rachel and Michael trailing at the rear. Michael clenched the reins and felt his teeth grinding. Several times, he tried to speak—stopped when he realized the words would be harsh and bitter.

"You're angry with me," she said.

He didn't see a need to respond.

"Because I disobeyed you?"

He opened his mouth, closed it. *Was that why?* "Because you put yourself in danger. You could have been killed."

"But I wasn't."

"By inches. A little more to the right and that bullet would have been in your back and your heart."

"But it wasn't. It hit my arm. I'd like to think God protected me."

He faced her. His walls and barriers softened and crumbled. "You are so beautiful, even with dirt on your nose and scratches on your cheeks." He smiled. "You are the bravest and most stubborn woman I know."

She laughed. "I'll take both as a compliment."

They rode in silence for a while.

"Michael, you know I'm going to have a hard time taking direct orders from you? Even if they make perfect sense, like you telling me to stay on the train. I have to follow my heart. You know I can't let anyone control me like they did in the past?"

"I know. And you know I'm going to have a hard time not giving orders, at least in the beginning."

"Just at the beginning?"

"I'll do my best to learn quick."

"And I'll do my best to help you."

Gideon turned down Ivey's Ford Road, and Rachel moved up to ride next to him. They slowed to a walk, Jeremiah and Caleb scanning the woods to their left. Michael rode between Rachel and Gideon, ready to jump to her defense if trouble started.

The overarching trees filtered the afternoon sun to muted gold. Dust danced in the silent air. Michael winced at how loud the horses' hooves echoed.

"You all right, Rachel?" Gideon said as Rachel stopped for a second time, examining trees to her front, turning to look at ones they just passed.

"I thought I would have seen my mark before now." She closed her eyes. "Maybe it's ahead a little more."

Michael swiped his sweat-stung eyes with his sleeve and twisted as more sweat trickled down his spine.

Lord, help her.

A couple of miles down the road, Rachel stopped, reached up and touched a branch dangling by a thread of its bark. "This is it."

She pointed across the road. "That's the way in."

Michael saw nothing that resembled a trail.

Gideon rode over to where Rachel pointed. "I see it. Ain't much, but it's a track of some sort." He nudged his horse forward.

"Wait." Rachel rode up next to him. "You'll have to follow me. Otherwise, you'll get lost and make so much noise thrashing around, they'll hear you a mile off."

"No." The word was out of Michael's mouth before it registered in his brain.

Rachel looked at him, a slight smile curving her lips. "It's a maze of little trails and paths in there. I have to lead you. Trust me. I've been here before."

"And got shot."

"That was when I was leaving." Her face turned somber. "I know what I'm riding into. Once I get you close to the house, I will stay out of your way."

Michael felt everyone's eyes on him. *Like I have any control over her.* He nodded.

He slipped his pistol out of his sling and started to follow her.

"Can you shoot left-handed?" Gideon said.

"Sure."

"Let me re-phrase that. Can you hit what you aim at?"

Michael looked at the pistol, shrugged. "Can hit something near it anyway."

Gideon shook his head and motioned him forward.

After a hundred feet, Michael admitted, with great reluctance, that Rachel was correct. If they'd come in without her, they'd be lost in the myriad of trails. He watched her now, leaning forward, eyes on the ground, never wavering.

He admired her slender figure as it tapered to her narrow waist, her arms that held him with such strength. He tried not to look at the way the riding skirt conformed to her lower body as she rode, showing her curves and the slope of her thighs. He would follow her wherever she wanted to go, stubborn independent streak and all.

A gift to treasure and protect. What did Peter say in his epistle? Treat your wife as a weaker vessel? Somehow, he could never picture Rachel seeing herself as a weaker anything. Maybe he could convince her she was the most valuable treasure in his world, one he needed to protect at all costs. She'd insist on being an equal partner in that.

Well, Lord. This should prove to be an interesting marriage. If we can get to the preacher in one piece.

Rachel stopped after they rounded a large oak and pointed down one path separate from the others. "This leads to the house. There's trees that will screen you, but they thin out in some places."

She dismounted, grabbed a stick and sketched out the area they'd be approaching. "House. Corral. Small barn. Outhouse. Stay away from that." She shuddered and marked Becky Jo's room.

She straightened and approached Michael. "And I will wait right here. You just come back to me in one piece." She patted his right hand. "And with nothing else broken."

He slid to the ground and embraced her. When she lifted her face, he kissed her, with a fierceness he hoped conveyed the depth of his love. He didn't want to let go.

"We'd like to get this finished before dark." Caleb's voice clattered them apart. "You'll have plenty of time for that afterwards."

"Sorry," Michael said.

"No, you're not," Jeremiah said.

As Michael remounted, Rachel said, "Would you all have an extra pistol I can borrow?" She pulled the Derringer from her skirt pocket. "This is fine, but a pistol would help me feel safer."

Gideon leaned forward. "Can you shoot a pistol, Ma'am?"

"Had lessons from Geoffrey Barkston back in Riverbend." She gestured at Michael. "Better than he can left-handed. I know I'll hit what I aim at."

"Gideon," Caleb said. "Rachel can do anything she sets her mind to."

Jeremiah reached into his saddlebag. "You can have my spare." He took out a Colt, made sure it was loaded, and handed it to her along with a cartridge belt and holster.

Michael stared, gaping, as Rachel fastened the belt around her hips, adjusting the holster so her fingertips grazed the Colt's handle. She drew it with an easy, practiced grace, checked the cylinder and the front sight, and slid it back into the holster with a solid thump.

"It'll do. Thanks." She laughed when she saw Michael. "I guess that's something else I need to tell you about. I was going to wait until after we're married. Didn't want to scare you off."

Caleb snorted. "Might be too late for that. Somebody want to close Michael's mouth so we can get this over with?"

As they rode away, Michael glanced over his shoulder. Rachel sat on her horse, grinned at him, and winked.

CHAPTER 53

Wednesday, July 17, 1878

MICHAEL INHALED AIR heavy with the aroma of wet soil and decaying leaves, alert for any signs of discovery from the house on his left. He rode last in the stretched-out line of riders. Gideon led, followed by Caleb, then Jeremiah—a space of about ten yards between them. Michael checked behind him. No sign of Rachel. The pressure in his chest eased. She'd be safe at the oak tree.

The house stood silent. Odd not to see a lookout posted. Must be well hidden. Could be at any of those windows. Icy fingers ran up his spine. The trees provided protection but not much. Stealth and surprise were their weapons for now. Both would be gone if they were seen before they reached the barn.

Four horses in the corral wore saddles. The fifth must belong to the buggy parked in front of the barn. A horse trotted up the drive that fronted the house. Michael stopped, waited. The rider dismounted and climbed the steps. *Judge Barrett? He knows about this?*

Michael nudged his horse but held it to the slow walk that Gideon said would attract the least attention. Time dragged in the afternoon air as if weighted by the humidity. The knot between Michael's shoulders tightened into a rock.

After what seemed like hours, they gathered behind the barn in a tight circle, voices kept at whispers.

"All right, here's what we know," Gideon said. "There's Dennison, Christopher Barrett, and two other men."

"Judge Barrett just rode up and went in the house," Michael said.

Gideon cussed. "So he's in on it, too." The sheriff paused. "Don't know that he'd be that good in a fight. Never seen him with a gun. Christopher's a different story. Marksman, experienced hunter. Enjoyed the war too much. So, there's five men, plus a woman I suspect is Emma Winslow. Plus Becky Jo."

He squatted to scratch in the dirt. He outlined the house, drawing an X to mark Becky Jo's room. "I'm thinking they'll divide their forces. Two in front, two in back. The judge is the wild card, but I suspect he'll dive for cover once any shooting starts. If the woman is Emma Winslow, she'll stay out of the way, too. Probably with Becky Jo."

He tapped the stick on the ground as if lost in thought. Michael stifled the rising impatience that wanted to attack now.

Caleb leaned against him. "Easy, son. Let's think this through."

Michael nodded.

Gideon drew an arrow pointing at the back door. "We'll start here. This door and the window next to it. Caleb, you and I will take the door. Jeremiah, I need you to crash this window and, Michael, you be right behind him."

Jeremiah undid his blanket from behind his saddle and scouted the ground. He picked up a large rock. "I'll throw this first and then go in. You follow and shoot high as you."

Michael tucked his pistol in his belt, and shucked off his sling, draping it over his saddle horn. He flexed his right hand. Stiff in the splints, sore, but tolerable. *Must be the excitement.*

Gideon pointed his stick at Caleb. "You'll have to give the door a good kick at the latch and follow right through. I'll be right behind ya. When the rock hits the window, you hit the door."

Caleb nodded.

Gideon gestured at Michael. "Michael, as soon as you're in, head right. Get to the room Becky Jo's in and get her out of there. Bust out a window and take her to the woods behind the barn."

Sweat dripped into Michael's eyes, blurring and burning, as he followed Jeremiah up the side of the barn, Gideon and Caleb ahead of them. At the corner, the sheriff waited, a cougar stalking a steer. Michael pressed against the side of the barn, face to the clear blue sky where feathered strips of clouds drifted. *Have to use violence again. Would it ever end? Maybe this time will be different.*

Heart pounding, Rachel drifted into his mind. Waiting for him, praying for him…

Gideon stirred and ran gimped-legged across the open space between the barn and the house. Caleb hunched himself into a slight crouch, waited, then dashed to Gideon, crouching next to him.

Michael resisted spying over Jeremiah's shoulder as the man prepared to make his run, blanket rolled snug under one arm, rock tight in his hand. He started once, pulled back.

Jeremiah peered around the corner and ran, diving and rolling to halt just in front of the porch. He peeked over the floorboards, ducked back quickly. A shadow crossed the window, rifle cradled. It moved away. Michael signaled Jeremiah the window was clear. He slid up on the porch and rolled to the wall.

Michael leaned forward, ready to run. The shadow reappeared, stayed there. Michael hugged the wall, showing one eye at the corner. He waited. The shadow turned away, then turned back. *Come on.* He wondered if he could get his legs to bend. They seemed like two huge boulders, unable to move.

The shadow moved away. Michael inhaled a deep breath and ran. Each step seemed to take a lifetime: lift the leg, stretch it forward, plant it and then do the same with the other. With each step, pain lanced from his left knee through his thigh and into his hip. The house wavered and seemed to move further away. He urged himself forward, straining to move his muscles faster. Another step. Another. The porch was close. Something moved in the window.

He dove. Misjudged. Slid into the latticework framing the porch, his right arm and shoulder hitting the ground first. Pain seared, his vision gone in a flash of hot light. He bit his lip to stifle the moan. He lay there, gasping for air, fighting the pain.

Two short raps on the porch floor. Jeremiah calling him. Michael peered over the edge.

Jeremiah mouthed, "You all right?"

Michael nodded. He had to finish this. Owed it to Ben and Sam, and Rachel and Becky Jo.

He checked the window. Clear.

He lifted himself to the porch, and rolled next to Jeremiah.

Jeremiah crouched to one side of the window, Michael the other.

Gideon and Caleb took their positions. Gideon nodded. Caleb took one step away from the door. Jeremiah stood, hefted his rock, unrolled his blanket, holding it with his other hand, draping it up his arm.

Jeremiah reared his arm and flung his stone, striking where the four windowpanes met. Caleb kicked at the doorknob. The door flew open, and Jeremiah jumped through the window, blanket as a shield, scattering the rest of the glass before him.

Michael followed, aware Gideon and Caleb came through the door to his left.

They were in the kitchen. Dennison, the two Barretts and Emma Winslow were in the room. Mrs. Winslow's eyes were wide, hand to her throat, clutching her necklace.

Christopher Barrett's eyes narrowed as he struggled to pull his gun from his waistband. Judge Barrett dove under the table.

"Drop your guns," Gideon bellowed.

Dennison stood calm, pistol drawn. He aimed at Jeremiah. *Lord, help me.* Michael fired.

Dennison winced. His gun discharged as he reached for his shoulder. Jeremiah groaned and sank to the floor. *Not again.*

Gideon fired. "Michael, get Becky Jo."

Michael turned to his right. Emma Winslow pushed past him, shoving on his shoulder. Michael staggered as fresh shards of pain flashed into his brain. He found the doorway through the gun smoke. He heard shots behind him as he stumbled into a narrow hall running the length of the house. Plaster showered him as a bullet hit the wall to his left. A door to his right. He turned the knob. Locked.

He raised his right leg to kick. His left knee buckled. *So much for that idea.* He aimed the pistol. "Becky Jo, get away from the door." He fired. Missed three inches to the left, splintering a hole in the door.

He shifted the gun to his right hand, aimed and fired. The doorknob shattered.

Michael reeled as the gun clattered to the floor. He clamped his hand on his right arm to control the pain that left him gasping for air. He picked up his pistol and pushed opened the door.

Becky Jo lay on the floor, eyes wide. He removed the gag.

"Did they hurt you?"

She shook her head. "The one with one arm wouldn't let them."

Bessie, Widow Winslow's maid, huddled in the corner, knees to her chin, eyes wide and darting.

He shoved his pistol in his waistband, and struggled with the knots. His right hand wouldn't cooperate. He turned to Bessie. "Help me."

The woman started to shake her head, then scuttled on her hands and knees to the bed. Her shaking fingers tugged and pulled at the knots, mumbled prayers slipping from her lips.

"Michael, look out." Becky Jo's scream sent him to the floor.

A man in the doorway blocked what little light was in the curtained room. The man fired and a bullet tugged at Michael's sleeve. He heard Becky Jo cry out.

He pulled his pistol from his waistband and fired, right handed. The man clutched his stomach and staggered into the wall across the hall, then slumped to the floor.

Michael froze, staring at the pistol in his hand. *I had to shoot. I had to protect Becky Jo.*

Michael turned back to the girl. Blood ran from her forearm, seeping into the bed covers. He wrapped the wound with her gag.

Bessie lay across the bed, eyes closed. Michael didn't see any blood.

"I think she fainted," Becky Jo said.

A gentle tap on her cheek woke her. "Come on, Bessie. Let's get you out of here," Michael said.

"No, sir," Bessie said, voice quaking. "I got to stay with Miss Emma. Her daddy gave me the job thirty year ago. I can't stop now. She needs me."

He took the woman by the shoulders. "Then you stay right in this room until the shooting's over."

Gunfire echoed in the house. Bessie's lips quivered. "Yes, sir," stuttered from her lips.

He found a knife in the boot of the man he'd shot. He quickly sliced the remaining ropes binding Becky Jo, opened the window and lowered her to the ground.

"Our horses are behind the barn. Run. Wait for us there."

->=◎ ◎=<-

At the sound of gunfire, Rachel urged her horse to the edge of the woods. She stood in the stirrups, straining to see more as the side she faced loomed silent. Reins tight in her fist, she held back on prodding her horse to move closer.

Lord, protect Michael. Keep him safe. End this quickly.

Movement in the corral drew her attention. Someone mounted a horse. A woman, dress flaring out over the horse's back as she rode astride. Not Becky Jo. Who?

The woman rode along the side of the house toward the drive. *She's trying to get away.*

"Yah," Rachel nudged her horse. The mare sprang forward, at a gallop in a few strides.

As she closed the gap, Rachel realized the woman was not a good rider, hands clutching the saddle horn, stirrups flapping empty. The woman chose her mount poorly—it needed a more experienced rider. The animal swayed from side to side as if trying to shake the woman off.

Rachel drew alongside. The woman looked at her, panic-stricken eyes, mouth open wide but with no sounds. Rachel reached for the reins, but the woman pushed and slapped at her, whipping at her with the long end of the reins. One lash caught Rachel along her cheek, just under her eye, stinging like cactus needles. *Try and help somebody ….*

Rachel pushed the woman. As she slid off the saddle, she grasped at Rachel's arm, clamping onto her wrist. Rachel gave a twist, and the woman's hand slipped away. She disappeared from the saddle, and Rachel heard a soft thump and a loud groan.

As Rachel stepped down, the woman attacked her, arms flailing, punches weak. Rachel reached to grasp the woman's wrists, but she threw another punch, catching Rachel's cheek where the reins had lashed.

The woman continued to flail with one arm as Rachel held her other wrist. She kicked at Rachel's shin. Rachel sidestepped and spun the woman, throwing her off balance, allowing Rachel to grab her other wrist.

The woman cursed and spat in Rachel's face, teeth bared, arms twisting to break Rachel's grip.

"Let me go." The woman's face was blotched red, eyes bloodshot, chest heaving against the fabric of her dress.

"Can't do that. I think the sheriff wants to talk with you."

"No." The woman shrieked and lashed out once more with her feet, straining her arms to break Rachel's hold. Rachel tightened her grasp.

"You have no idea who you're dealing with, lady. I've had first-week whores put up better fights than you."

Rachel wrapped her leg behind the woman's and pulled. The woman fell to the ground, breath rushing out. Rachel straddled her. The woman beat at Rachel with her fists until Rachel took out her pistol, cocked it and pointed it at the woman's nose.

"At this range, even a blind man couldn't miss."

"Who are you?" The woman's chest heaved as she tried to gather more air.

"Friend of the sheriff. You'd breathe a mite better if you didn't wear your dresses so tight. I know from experience."

"Get off me." The woman bucked her hips.

Rachel touched the tip of the gun to the woman's nose. "I wouldn't advise that. Gun might go off."

"You wouldn't shoot me."

Rachel fired a shot into the ground over the woman's head.

She pointed the gun back at the woman's nose. "Do you want to risk that?"

"Are you crazy?" The woman's voice rose another octave, which Rachel didn't think possible.

"No. Just angry at people who kill people, beat up people, and kidnap innocent girls who never did them any harm."

"I didn't do any of that."

Rachel laughed. "Tell it to the judge. Oh wait, he's probably in on it too." She stood. "Get up."

When she was on her feet, the woman made another rush at Rachel. Rachel lashed out, her fist connecting with the woman's nose. She fell, spread-eagled, eyes crossed before they closed and she slipped into unconsciousness.

CHAPTER 54

Wednesday, July 17, 1878

MICHAEL WATCHED BECKY Jo reach the cover of the trees. He moved toward the sound of guns still firing, stepping over the man sprawled in the hall. The man gurgled, hands clutching his stomach, eyes glazed.

Calm settled over Michael. Gone was the urge that once rose up when violence started. The urge to strike again and again, to cause pain, to strike at his past by hurting people in his present. He'd shot this man because he had to. It was the only way to protect Becky Jo and Bessie, to protect himself.

In the kitchen, Jeremiah sat on the floor, propped against the wall, left hand pressing a cloth against a bleeding wound in his right shoulder.

In his right hand, his gun wavered in the general direction of Judge Barrett. The man squeezed up against the cook stove, shaking, face pale, eyes wide, unblinking, unable to turn away from Jeremiah's gun.

Jeremiah pointed his chin down the hall. Michael headed that way, ducking as a bullet struck the plaster a few inches in front of him.

Caleb crouched at the entrance to a room on the left of the hall. Gideon stood behind him. Both were shooting into the room and ducking away from return fire.

Gideon nodded at Michael's appearance. "Becky Jo all right?" His voice rasped.

Michael nodded.

Gun smoke drifted in clouds. Michael's eyes itched, and his lungs burned. He coughed, but he still couldn't draw a deep breath.

There was another entrance to the room further down the hall, then the front door. A man entered the hall, and reached for the door. Gideon fired. The man slumped to the floor.

Michael dashed to the other entrance, peered inside. Christopher Barrett was prone on the floor, firing at Caleb and Gideon. Dennison hunched beside the fireplace, reloading.

Gideon called out. "Give it up. We've got you outnumbered and surrounded."

Barrett and Dennison both fired at Caleb and Gideon.

Michael fired. His bullet chipped off stone from the fireplace.

Dennison jumped, startled.

Michael ducked back as Dennison fired at him, the bullet striking the door-frame where Michael's head had been.

The sound of breaking glass lured Michael to peer into the room to see Dennison leap through the side window, a shower of glass trailing behind him.

Using his arms as a shield, Michael dove through the window overlooking the porch. He tumbled, his right shoulder protesting, the pain searing. As he came to his feet, he heard a shot from outside the house.

Rachel. No.

He sprinted to the end of the porch, leaping to the ground, maintaining his balance as his left knee buckled. Gun in his right hand, pain spiking up his arm, he crouched, ready to shoot.

Dennison sat in a lump on the ground, his hand grasping his left thigh as blood seeped.

Several feet away, Rachel crouched beside an unconscious Emma Winslow, her gun pointing at Dennison, wisps of smoke drifting out of the barrel.

"Hi, Michael."

->|=© ©=|<-

The world stilled. Quiet like Michael had never heard settled over the scene. The sun shone, and bird song came back a little at a time.

Gideon's voice came from the porch. "Well, well. Look at what we got here. Good job, Michael."

Crimson heat surged up Michael's neck and face until the roots of his hair tingled. "It wasn't me. It was Rachel."

Gideon seemed to take in Rachel's presence for the first time. "Let me get this straight. You captured Mrs. Winslow?"

Rachel nodded.

"And you shot Dennison?"

Rachel dipped her chin, blushed, and nodded again.

Gideon threw his head back, and guffawed, holding his stomach, laughing until tears flowed. Behind him, Caleb appeared smiling, holding Christopher Barrett by the arm, pistol pressed against the banker's side.

Gideon's laughter tapered off. He wiped his cheeks. "Maybe I need to hire you as a deputy. Miss Stone, I don't think you'll have any problem keeping your future husband here in line."

Rachel stood, holstered her weapon, and pulled Emma Winslow to her feet.

Rachel's eyes pierced Michael to his soul. He'd never felt more vulnerable, more open, more loved.

Her soft voice carried a determination and a promise. "I don't want him in line, Sheriff. I want him beside me."

⤖ ⚫ ⤔

Michael relaxed as late afternoon sun dimpled behind the trees, and a light breeze stirred from the south, drying the sweat on his brow. Rachel snuggled under his left arm, her right arm around his waist. The holstered gun nudging his thigh reminded him what a unique woman she was.

Becky Jo had come out from behind the barn, and now stood on Rachel's left, holding her hand.

Jeremiah sat on the floor of the porch, back to one of the support pillars, face skyward as if drinking the warmth of the sun. Caleb had secured a bandage around Jeremiah's wounded shoulder.

Caleb leaned against another pillar, hand resting on the butt of his Peacemaker. Gideon stood on the porch facing the Barrett brothers, Dennison and Emma Winslow sitting on the backless bench. Bessie hovered near the widow.

Gideon pushed his hat back with the tip of his finger, his gray-streaked hair tumbling from underneath the brim. "Who wants to tell me what's going on here?"

Silence. Christopher Barrett's stony glare and thin lips offered no words. Judge Barrett started to speak, then clamped his mouth shut. Mrs. Winslow, dried blood crusty on her upper lip, twisted her fingers in her dress, head down, eyes closed.

Dennison spoke. "You got to get me to a doctor."

Gideon shook his head. "You ain't dying. Yet. We'll get you to town as soon as I get some answers."

Dennison glowered and rubbed the bandage Caleb had wrapped around his wound.

"Which one of you killed Smythe?" Gideon planted his hands on his hips.

Silence.

"Don't matter to me. You're all going to hang for it." Gideon spat at Christopher Barrett's feet.

"Sheriff," Rachel said. "Dennison—is that his name—the one-armed gent—he's the one who shot your deputy. They buried him out past the corral."

Gideon's head drooped to his chest. "So that's where Billy Ray got to. I was hoping he'd just make a clean getaway."

Dennison laughed. "Dumb fool got too greedy. Came here asking for more money, otherwise he was gonna tell you. Whinin' about his Ma. Had to kill him."

Gideon's Colt was half way out of its holster. He exhaled and let the gun settle back into its leather home. "Billy Ray had his faults, but he didn't deserve that. Anyway, you're gonna hang for it."

"If you can get me to trial."

"Or I could shoot you here and be done with it."

Judge Barrett lifted his head. "You're not that kind of man, Gideon."

Fists clenched, the sheriff. "You'd be surprised what kind of man the likes of you can turn me into."

The judge straightened. "Remember who you're talking to, Parsons."

"I know exactly who I'm talking to. The man who's tried his last case in this county. I may not be able to hang you, but just your being here is enough to get you thrown into state prison for a very long time." Gideon paused. "Or maybe it won't be so long. I'm sure there are some prisoners who'd be happy to make your acquaintance again."

"I was trying to talk my brother into surrendering."

Dennison laughed. Emma's face twisted into a small grin.

Gideon grinned. "Oh. For what?"

Judge Barrett clamped his mouth into a thin line, lips white.

"Christopher." Gideon turned to the trembling banker. "Why did your illustrious brother want you to surrender? For what?"

Christopher cleared his throat. "For cheating people on their mortgages, making them sell to me to avoid foreclosure."

Gideon nodded. "As crooked as that is, I don't think you needed all this fire power—a killer like Dennison here—to protect yourself."

Christopher looked down.

The sheriff rubbed the back of his neck. "Now, I may be just an old country sheriff, but I've learned a few things over the years. Here's what I think happened. Christopher, you fell in love with Emma Winslow, and you wanted to marry her, so you killed her husband."

Gideon stepped in front of Judge Barrett and, with his fingers, lifted the judge's face. "And you sent Ben Carstairs to the gallows so you could protect your brother and his little tart. I don't want to see you hang. I want to see all those prisoners you sentenced welcome you to your new home." Gideon raised his hand as if to backhand the judge's face, then let his arm drop. "You're not worth it."

He stepped back. "But it seems Mrs. Winslow here isn't the monogamous type which should have been obvious to you, Christopher, if you'd thought with your head instead of a certain body part. If she could be unfaithful to her husband, why should she be faithful to you?"

Gideon waited. Christopher kept his head down, wringing his hands between his legs.

"I suspect you found out she was, shall we say, entertaining Mr. Smythe, so you killed him. Or had Dennison do it. Seems like shooting the messenger, but that's what happens when you don't think with your head."

Hands on hips, Gideon stood in front of the four. "Am I right?"

Emma Winslow half stood. "I didn't know he killed my husband or Gordon."

Christopher rose and slapped Emma across the face. "Of course you did. You helped me kill your husband. You set it up so he'd be alone in his office that afternoon."

Tears spilled down Emma's cheeks, her hand covering the red splotch left by Christopher's palm.

Rachel stirred and whispered in Michael's ear. "She's just a higher priced whore."

Michael hugged her close to him, kissed the top of her head.

Jeremiah spoke. "I think you'll find they were going to use the money from the farmers to get away from here and start a new life somewhere else. Philadelphia? New York? Mrs. Winslow looks like a New York kind of woman."

Emma glared at him.

"And," Jeremiah continued, "you'll probably find he's embezzled some of the bank's funds, too. Mrs. Winslow requires a lot of maintenance."

Christopher hung his head.

Caleb straightened from the pillar. "Lot of people died for a whole lot of nothing. I'll hitch up the buggy to carry the wounded, and we can get these people back to town." He stomped off toward the corral.

In a few minutes, Dennison and Jeremiah were in the back of the buggy. Mrs. Winslow, hands tied, sat between Caleb and Bessie in the front. The Barrett brothers, hands tied to their saddle horns, horses tied to the back of the rig, looked lost and forlorn.

Judge Barrett turned to Michael. "None of this would have happened if you hadn't come back and stirred things up."

Michael smiled and looked heavenward. He saluted the sky. "That's for you, Ben, and for you, Sam."

Gideon shifted in his saddle. "Michael, we've got this bunch under control. Will you and Miss Rachel take Becky Jo home?"

Jeremiah waved him over to the buggy. "Are you planning anymore adventures like this?"

"Don't think so. Why?"

"Riding with you is hard on my health."

--><==◯ ◯==<--

They rode three across, Michael on the left, Rachel in the middle, Becky Jo on the right on Jeremiah's horse. Every glance found Rachel meeting his gaze, smiling. Beyond her, Becky Jo focused forward, face pale.

Michael enjoyed the cool shade of the overhanging trees as dusk settled over the land. Crickets chirped from the nearby woods and night birds began their serenades. As long as Rachel was by his side, his world spun in perfection. She was his sun.

They turned into the Larkin farm, and Becky Jo kicked her horse into a trot. "Mama, I'm home. Pa."

The Major burst from the house and down the porch stairs. The two embraced as twelve other children gathered around, screaming. The joy at having Becky Jo home rang in the air, drowning out birds, insects, cattle lowing.

Rachel took Michael's right hand and squeezed. He wondered if her touch had the power to heal. It sure made him feel better.

Two men appeared on the porch. Mr. Larkin in his chair, lean, face weathered into brown leather, creased with wrinkles of work, hands thick and knotted. The younger one was tall as Michael, heavier, body straining his shirt. The older one nudged the younger, who stepped into the yard and approached the crowd gathered around Becky Jo. The children quieted, and the Major stepped back, holding Becky Jo's hands. "Someone's been waitin' for you, darlin'."

Becky Jo turned, saw the younger man drawing near.

"Edward." She ran to him, buried her face against his neck.

For the first time he could ever remember, Michael heard Becky Jo shed tears. Rachel squeezed his hand. A tear on her cheek.

"Hold me," her voice hoarse, choked.

He pulled her into his arms, holding her as she shuddered against him.

He caressed her tangled hair. She pulled back, locked her eyes with his. He was pulled into that place he would always go in those eyes. Their lips met.

CHAPTER 55

Thursday, August 1, 1878

THE LIVE OAK shading the Carstairs' family cemetery stirred in the afternoon breeze drifting down the valley. Michael's heart weighed heavy as Ben's casket was lowered into the ground.

Sadness joined with a sense of completeness—he had accomplished what he set out to do so many months ago. Ben was back with his family. The feeling was bittersweet as Ben was buried next to the mother he knew only through a worn Celtic cross, a cross now entwined in his father's hands, the symbol of their reconciliation.

In three months, he'd met Rachel, reconciled Ben with his father, and cleared Ben's name. An adventure in more ways than he ever imagined.

He'd faced and defeated the lie that was the old Michael, the monster who fed on the lust of violence and inflicting pain. The lie that said the monster was the real him, that he couldn't be controlled. He turned that lie to the truth of protecting people, defending them.

Rachel's hand tightened on his arm. He covered her hand with his, smiling at the woman who would be his wife in two days.

If it wasn't for Ben, we never would have met.

Joshua Carstairs picked up one of the shovels from the pile of dirt next to the grave. Michael took the other, ignoring the splint. Together, they filled the hole in a steady, quiet rhythm. Lupe Carstairs stood next to Rachel, the two holding hands, tears coursing down Lupe's cheeks.

Her accent thickened by emotion, she said, "So sad, none of the family ever knew him as he really was."

Joshua rested on his shovel. "We only knew the Ben our Pa wanted us to see, the Ben he hated." He looked at Michael. "Until that changed on the day the old man died."

Michael held a shovel of dirt at waist height. "I don't think Ben ever knew who he really was, either. Just what everybody told him." He dropped the dirt into the hole.

A short time later, the grave filled, Lupe made the sign of the cross and looked at Michael, dark, almond-shaped eyes, penetrating. He coughed, clasped his hands at his waist and bowed his head. His mind went blank. What to pray?

"Lord, we thank you for revealing the truth so Ben's name could be cleared. We believe he is in heaven getting to know his mother and his father. We thank you that you will strengthen Joshua and Lupe as they go forward."

Lupe touched her stomach. "And that you bless us with many bebés to keep the Carstairs name alive." She paused and placed her hands on Rachel's stomach. "And that you bless Rachel and Michael with many bebés, too."

Rachel smiled and embraced her friend, eyes meeting Michael's over Lupe's shoulder. She winked at him.

Later, sitting at the table in the dining room, Michael slid an envelope across to Joshua. "This is what's left of the money you gave me to bring Ben home."

Joshua pushed it back. "Keep it. Think of it as an advance on your salary."

"Salary?"

Joshua's blue eyes held a hint of amusement. "I want you to work for me."

"On the ranch?" Confusion reigned in Michael's mind. He had no ranching skills. What could Joshua possibly want to hire him to do?

Joshua chuckled. "No. In town. I want you to help run the businesses I don't know anything about. The bank. The land. I want you to take Pa's journal and make amends like he said to Caleb."

"Why me?"

"Caleb tells me you're a good man. And, I think having someone from outside the town would make it seem fair to everyone."

Michael shifted in his chair. It seemed like an answer to prayer. They'd stay in Riverbend. And Rachel could keep her shop. But what about Zechariah and

Deborah and Gideon and his friends in Tramlaw? *Is this what I really want? Is this what you want for me, Lord?*

Rachel and Lupe came in carrying platters of steak and potatoes, vegetables, and sourdough biscuits. He studied the woman who would be his wife. This was her home, the first one she'd had since she was a child.

Her dream was here.

Rachel's Hope in more ways than one.

Peace settled over him. This was his home now. He and Rachel together, side by side.

He shook hands with Joshua. "When do you want me to start?"

"Monday. We'll meet at the bank first thing."

CHAPTER 56

Saturday, August 3, 1878

THE DAY DRAGGED like a mule that wouldn't pull.

And it sped like a train on a downhill run.

Michael couldn't tell which he preferred.

Speeding meant Rachel would be his sooner, but it dragged when he thought of what that meant. Commitment, caring for someone else, someone who was very capable of caring for herself, someone who wanted a partner, not a lord and master.

The river provided a place of solace, a place of peace, to be alone with his thoughts, to pray. He rested against a tree, head back, eyes closed, relishing the breeze and the gurgle of the river, the plops of fish broaching the surface, the cardinals singing as they flitted among the branches.

There were only two marriages he could draw on, Zechariah and Deborah, and Luke and Martha. Both men of the cloth, both wives supportive and understanding of their husbands.

Two similar men. Luke and Zechariah dedicated to the Lord and to serving their congregations. Two unalike women. Deborah so mild, almost meek, in her marriage and her church. A strength of caring and love supported her determination to be the best pastor's wife she could be. Martha, sharp-tongued, bold and devoted to her husband.

And then there was Rachel. Totally unlike either Martha or Deborah. A fighter, a victor over rape and abuse and the degradation of prostitution. Independent.

Lord, I'm glad you gave Rachel a vision of our marriage. I don't think it'd be happening otherwise.

Rachel twirled before the mirror in her room, her dress flaring out from the bottom. "The hem's long on the left side. I need to shorten it."

"Rachel, stop it." Annabelle O'Brien's face took on her scolding schoolteacher look. "You've been fussing and primping on this dress for three days. It's perfect."

Rachel studied her reflection. The yellow dress with dark blue trim did what she hoped it would. The colors brought out the violet of her eyes and the different shades of her brown hair.

"Besides," Martha said, "It looks like it was painted on. Don't want to give certain people in this town reason to talk."

Rachel smoothed her hands over her flat stomach. *Wonder how soon that will swell with a baby? I'm not ready to have a baby. I don't know how to be a mother.*

"Uh-oh," Martha said. "She's got that look in her eye."

"Which one?" Annabelle said.

"The one that says, 'What have I gotten myself into? I'm not ready to get married.'"

"I don't remember that look," Annabelle said. "I don't think I ever had it. Did you?"

"Right up until my father said, 'I now pronounce you man and wife.' Last thing I wanted to be was a preacher's wife. Saw what my mother put up with."

Rachel chewed her lower lip, massaged her queasy stomach. "How about now?"

Martha's gaze wandered out the window, her face calm, thoughtful. "Wouldn't give it up for the world." Her voice was soft, full of love and wonder.

Rachel's heart pounded. Warmth crept up her neck and into her face. "That's what I want to say when I've been married as long as you."

Martha eyes held hers in a long searching look. "You will, Rachel, you will."

� ❂⇇

Michael faced Rachel, her hair falling loosely to her shoulders, shimmers of light reflecting off it. Lips full, moist, so kissable. Her deep violet eyes looked into his. Eyes that loved him. Eyes of the woman he loved, who would soon be his wife.

The church and the congregation disappeared. Pastor Luke faded into a blur.

They were overlooking a valley, broad, a silver-blue river meandering through it. Fields of tall grass and wildflowers blended into forests of green. The aroma of rich, sweet flowers wafted into his nostrils. The mountains stood like white-capped sentinels, protecting the valley, protecting them. Rachel stood with him, her wedding dress glowing, her eyes sparkling with sunlight.

A voice resonated in the depths of his heart. "A man shall leave his father and his mother, and shall cleave unto his wife, and they shall be one flesh. What God has joined together, let no man put asunder. This is the woman I have chosen to be your wife."

The church was back. Luke was there. "I now pronounce you man and wife."

Their kiss made everything else disappear again.

CPSIA information can be obtained
at www.ICGtesting.com
Printed in the USA
LVOW08s1636310117
522741LV00005B/1120/P